THE NIGHT PEOPLE

SAM AND JADE'S ALIEN ADVENTURES: BOOK 1

C. S. HAND

Copyright © 2023 by C. S. Hand

All Rights Reserved

No part of this book may be reproduced in any form or by any electronic or mechanical means, including information storage and retrieval systems, without written permission from the author, except for the use of brief quotations in a book review.

This is a work of fiction. Names, characters, places, and incidents either are the product of the author's imagination or are used fictitiously. Any resemblance to actual persons, living or dead, organizations, events, or locales, is entirely coincidental.

Content Editors: Bethany Bryan, Kristen Susienka
Copy Editor/Proofreader: Michael Jarnebro (Vigilant Proofreader)
Beta Reader: Lena Vorobets
Cover Design by: Rafael Andres
Interior Design by: Nola Li Barr

Printed in the United States of America

ISBN 979-8-9851177-0-7 (ebook)
ISBN 979-8-9851177-1-4 (paperback)

For more information, email ecowritercarol@gmail.com

Content Warning: There are possible triggers involving child (teen) physical abuse.

To my son Rowan—by far the best part of me.
Do what you love; never give up.

CONTENTS

PART ONE

1. Meeting — 3
2. 3:03 — 10
3. Avoiding — 14
4. Ambush — 18
5. Discovery — 25
6. Partners — 32

PART TWO

7. Entrance — 43
8. Missing Time — 47
9. Sam Retreats — 54
10. Jade Advances — 58
11. Fact-Finding Mission — 65
12. Jade's Revelation — 70
13. Underground — 75
14. Major Jepson — 85
15. Aftermath — 94
16. Confessions — 102
17. Abduction — 110

PART THREE

18. Alienation — 117
19. Alien Boy — 122
20. Two Worlds — 127
21. The Scientific Method — 132
22. Ravi — 138
23. Testing — 143
24. Bugged — 147
25. Betrayed — 153
26. Alone Again — 159
27. Jepson Causes Trouble — 166
28. Mr. Macklin Gets Personal — 172
29. Sam Deliberates — 178
30. In the DUMBs — 184
31. Morgan — 194
32. We Are Together — 205

33. Convergence	213
34. Morgan's House	222
35. DUMBs Within DUMBs	229
36. Area 51	236
37. Facing the Music	244
38. Practicing Trust	250
39. More Confessions	256

PART FOUR

40. Extraordinary Evidence	265
41. Worst Fears	275
42. Breakout	284
43. Consequences	291
44. Sam Endures	297
45. Accepting Safety	304
46. Letting Go	313
47. What the Visitors Want	319
48. A New Dad	325
Thank You	335
Acknowledgments	337
Excerpt	339

PART ONE

A real friend is one who walks in when the rest of the world walks out.
--Walter Winchell, journalist

CHAPTER 1
MEETING

HIS BODY WAS TINGLING—SHARP prickles all over, like being wrapped in a cocoon of needles. As he came to, Sam realized he was lying on the ground. There were no needles. He was covered in the dust of the chat piles. It made his nose and throat tickle, and he sneezed. He sat up. He was surrounded by tiny flickering lights, which dissipated quickly. The tingling was disappearing more slowly. His ears were buzzing; he was dizzy and shaky. *Oh no*, he thought. *Please don't let them be back, not after three whole years.*

This morning, he'd felt a compulsion to visit the chat piles, as he had off and on since spring, when Mr. Macklin talked about them in ninth-grade earth science. There were dozens of them here, stretching out of sight along both sides of a dirt track off the main county road. They weren't hard to get to, but they were so off-putting that people driving by just ignored them. He must be crazy, Sam thought; no one with any sense came here. It wasn't just the dirt and ugliness—the mounds had an oppressive vibe. Plus, all his life he'd heard the dust was dangerous. Sometimes he tied a bandana over his mouth and nose to keep it out, but it was annoying, and he doubted it helped much anyway.

Since Mr. Macklin's lessons, Sam had come here several times. It was more than just interest. He felt like the chat piles were calling him. Trying to chat with him, he thought wryly. He felt a brief pang, for a moment wishing he had a friend who would appreciate his stupid pun. But that would never happen. Anyway, what kind of idiot feels "called" by filthy piles of old mine waste? Yet, here he was.

Sam explored new chat piles on every visit. Today's choice appeared unremarkable. The composition of rocks didn't change. There were a few scraggly, dusty weeds near the center of the track. He shook his head—what did he expect to find? Then, rounding a corner, he felt, more than saw, a brief flash of light. It drew his eyes to a flat area on the side of the chat pile. What was a flat surface doing there? And what was that light? He ran his eyes carefully over the flat area. Only when he glanced away did he glimpse the light again, out of the corner of his eye. It was dim, subdued by the midday sun. It seemed to trace the outline of a large door, which disappeared when he looked directly at it. Puzzled, he scrambled over boulders to the flat area, and placed his palm in the middle of it. Then, he woke up on the ground.

As he sat there, recovering and trying to figure out what had happened, someone ordered, *Go! It's not time yet.* The voice was inside his head. It was quiet, but very clear, and it was not his voice. The last time—the only time—he remembered hearing a voice in his head, he was five years old and the Night People were in his room. *No, no, please no!*

Sam leapt up, quivering with panic. Tingling, blinking lights, dizziness, even blacking out were nothing compared to a voice in your head. He stumbled around the chat pile to his bike, wheeled it around, and streaked off toward the county road. Now, he was pedaling furiously down the main highway toward town. Damn! He needed faster transportation than this stupid bicycle. Not for the first time, he cursed his youth and poverty. He'd taken driver's ed and had his restricted license, but it was useless—he had nothing to drive. Although—why was he running? If the Night People were back, they could get to him anywhere.

Sam was pedaling so fast and was so freaked out, he didn't realize he had entered town and was racing down the sidewalk on Clayton Street. He almost crashed into the U-Haul before he saw it. He slammed on his brakes and swerved—right toward a petite girl with a long, messy braid who had just come from the back of the truck carrying a packing box. He swerved again, this time ending up in a heap on the lawn with his legs tangled in his bike and a painful scrape on his arm. He opened his eyes to see a pair of long, tan legs. Looking up, he met concerned greenish eyes. He winced from embarrassment as much as from pain. This day just got better and better.

"Are you okay?" the girl asked.

Sam felt like an idiot. Not to mention he was filthy, covered in gray dust from the chat piles. Great! What a way to make a first impression on the new girl. Now there'd be another one laughing at the weirdo loser.

"Uh, yeah, I'm fine. Sorry."

The girl set the packing box down and reached out a hand to help him up. "I'm impressed. Going that fast, you should have crashed right into me. Hey, your arm is bleeding. You'd better come in and let my mom fix it. She's a doctor."

"Oh no," Sam said in alarm. "I don't need a doctor. I'm fine."

The girl laughed. "She's not just a doctor. She's my mom. Don't worry; she doesn't bite. And she'll be thrilled I've made a friend before we've even moved in. I've been pretty mad about moving here, so she feels guilty. Come on—you'll be doing me a favor."

"Um . . . okay."

She talked fast, and he couldn't think of a way to refuse without being rude, so he followed her into the house, feeling a little dazed. She'd called him a friend! Well, she was new. That would change when she started meeting other people—in fact, it had to change. Sam couldn't afford to have friends, especially if the Night People were back. But her easy acceptance felt good. And he had no idea why, but she seemed familiar. Those eyes—they weren't green exactly, more like hazel, with green flecks like tiny gems. They were memorable, even exotic, and he could swear he'd seen them before. But that was impossible.

To distract himself, he glanced around the house. They had entered a large living room, empty except for several boxes stacked near the picture window on the right. The furniture must be in a different truck. To the left was a large, curved staircase with shiny wooden rails. Straight ahead, a wide doorway led into the kitchen. Sam supposed this was typical of rich-people houses in Cassidy. The girl's mother was a doctor, so by Sam's standards, they were rich. He hoped she never saw the dump he lived in.

"Hey, Mom!" the girl called. "I've brought you a patient."

"What?" A tall, pretty woman hurried in, her honey-blond hair piled up in a careless bun. "What happened?"

"This is—oh, gosh, I don't even know your name. Mom, he almost ran me down on his bike, but he crashed instead. He's got amazing reflexes."

She turned to Sam. "My name's Jade, by the way. What's yours?"

"Sam. Sorry about that. I wasn't paying attention and I didn't expect the U-Haul."

"Well, Sam, I'm Jade's mom, Melody Mathieson. Let's clean up that arm so it doesn't get infected, shall we?" She headed for the kitchen, and Sam followed.

"Uh, thanks. Sorry I'm so dirty."

"Not to worry," she said, smiling. "Trust me, I've seen worse."

Sam didn't really want to tell them anything, but he hadn't counted on Jade. While her mom washed Sam's arm, found gauze and disinfectant, and expertly bandaged his scrape, Jade pumped him for information.

"Where have you been to get so covered with dust?" she asked.

"Um, I was exploring the chat piles west of town," Sam explained.

Jade looked blank. "Chat piles? What are they?"

"They're like, uh, big mountains of mine waste. They're left over from the lead and zinc mines that used to be there."

"So, why were you exploring them? If it's just waste, what is there to see?"

Sam shrugged. "Nothing, I guess. I was just curious. I learned about them in earth science last spring."

"So, you didn't know about them before? Are you new here too?"

Sam felt a little silly, but he answered honestly. "Well, no, I've lived here all my life. I knew about the chat piles—everybody does. But people just kind of ignore them because they're so gross. I did too. But after we studied them, I just wanted to—check them out."

Jade nodded, although she still looked puzzled. She continued questioning him, and he knew she was wondering why he had been riding so fast. He did his best to downplay his trip and avoided mentioning any of the weird stuff. Jade looked ready to ask more, but after a quick glance at her mother, she changed the subject. She chattered away about their move from Kansas City and her mom's new job as head of the emergency room at the county hospital. Jade had just turned fifteen, and she was thrilled to find that Sam was the same age and they would be starting sophomore year together.

Sam thought he must be dreaming. He felt comfortable with both Jade and her mom, and that never happened. Dr. Mathieson was gentle as she bandaged his wound. She reminded him of his abuela, his dad's mom, who had returned to Mexico when he was five. He still missed her. His own mom was never so gentle and kind. And Sam still felt he already knew Jade, but he'd never been to Kansas City. His parents never went anywhere.

As they talked, Sam felt something warm rubbing against his leg. He looked down. A little calico cat was gazing up at him expectantly. He reached down and scratched her ears, and she purred loudly.

Jade was amazed. "Sadie likes you!" she exclaimed. "She's usually really shy. Well, that settles it. I already thought you were a good guy, but if Sadie likes you, you definitely pass."

Jade's mom looked amused but agreed. "Sadie's never wrong about people," she said.

Sam continued to pet the little cat, feeling pleased. "Animals usually like me for some reason." *Unlike people*.

He was grateful for Sadie's calming presence. He wasn't concentrating too well. He couldn't get the door, the hum, the tingling, and the general strangeness of that place out of his mind. And the voice—much as he tried to ignore it, that voice kept floating through his consciousness, pushing all his internal panic buttons. *Not time for what?* Plus, he had checked his phone as he followed Jade into the house. It was at least an hour later than it should have been. Had he really been knocked out for an hour? He didn't feel bad—just tired and a little shaky. Even the tingling was gone. He closed his eyes briefly. The missing time made it official—the Night People were back.

Sam escaped as soon as he could, saying he had to get

home. He was getting nervous. As they talked, he'd noticed Jade sneaking sidelong glances at him. What was she thinking—did she find him familiar, too? No, that was silly. There was no way they could know each other.

At the door, Jade said, "Let me get my phone. We should exchange numbers."

But Sam shook his head. "Sorry, I have to go."

"Come visit tomorrow," called Jade as he rode away on his battered bike.

Sam didn't answer—just gave her a wave. As much as he liked her, it was best not to make friends. Safer for him and for her.

CHAPTER 2
3:03

SAM AWOKE SUDDENLY, drenched in sweat, trembling, heart pounding. The room was pitch-black. He tried to roll sideways, but he couldn't move. He couldn't even lift an arm. A dream—it was a dream, right? But he knew it wasn't. The overwhelming fear was all too familiar. So was the faint musty, spicy odor. The Night People were back. Three years and four months after they had last tormented him, they had returned. Just when he had finally begun to relax and hope they were gone for good.

That last time, he'd been not quite twelve, and in the sixth grade. He hadn't remembered the NP experience; his main clue was his first-ever nosebleed during the night. The next day, he'd dozed off in study hall and relived the entire episode. He fell out of his seat, screaming in fear, feeling the probe up his nostril, the crunching sound, the pain in his sinuses. And woke up to a shocked teacher and laughing classmates, watching his meltdown.

Now, he was lying flat in bed, arms at his sides. Panic coursed through his body in waves. The worst part was being helpless, unable to move—knowing that even if he figured out what to do, he wouldn't be able to do it. *Stop! Control the fear. You're not a little kid anymore!* Sam closed his eyes and took deep breaths, trying to calm himself. Then he slowly, deliberately lifted his right arm. He could move again! He turned on his side and looked blearily at the clock on his bedside table: 3:03 a.m. They were definitely back.

It always happened in the deep of night. He knew they came earlier, but he always awoke around this time, just after they left or, sometimes, as they were leaving. Not always at 3:03, but usually within five or ten minutes of that time. He knew their schedule; he'd begun recording their visits in his Coward's Notebook when he was seven. He guessed he'd better dig out the notebook and start making new entries, although it's not like he ever really remembered anything. Sam figured they knew this was the safest time. He was asleep and vulnerable, and even if he woke up, he would be groggy and think he was dreaming. He always awoke panicked like this: disoriented, paralyzed, trying to piece together what had happened. It was the deep, gut-wrenching panic that convinced him it was real. That, and the smells.

He had taken a shower and gone to bed about eleven, exhausted from the trip to the chat piles and then meeting Jade and her mother. And when he arrived home, there had been a brief but stressful encounter with his own mother. Her Walmart shifts seldom left her time to cook a real dinner, but today they had. He had picked this day to be late, and she was angry. As her anger and bitterness washed over him, Sam mused that she was the exact opposite of Jade's mom.

"Where have you been?" she had demanded. "You knew I was cooking tonight. Did you stay out late just to spite me?"

Actually, he hadn't known she was cooking. She never told him her schedule unless he asked, and he hadn't asked. But contradicting her would lead to a fight, and he certainly couldn't tell her why he was late. He was irritated, but he tried to sound conciliatory.

"No, of course not. I'm sorry. I was hiking, and I went farther than I intended."

"Well, you've missed supper. You'll just have to eat it cold."

"That's fine, Mom."

She had stomped out of the kitchen, and he ate his cold lasagna. He could microwave it, but why bother? Why was his mother always angry with him? He wasn't a model son, but he tried his best not to antagonize her. She had begun to change after his first encounter with the Night People, when he was five. She still took care of him, but she was seldom loving. She did her best to avoid touching him, backing away if he got too close. Sam felt like some kind of exotic pet—one his mom feared but was forced to keep. He knew her fear was related to the Night People, but what did she know and why wouldn't she tell him? She must have some feelings for him; she still tried to protect him from his dad's abuse. At least his dad wasn't here tonight—he was probably at the bar, drinking his supper. Had he eaten the lasagna first?

As he lay awake, his heart thumping, he tried to remember exactly what had happened after he went to bed. But the memories were sketchy and vague. Small, shadowy figures surrounded his bed, milling around, moving rapidly so he couldn't fix on any of them. He'd groaned and said, "Oh, please, do we have to do this tonight?" And then huge black eyes stared into his, and he wasn't afraid anymore. Those eyes had a way of suppressing his fear and making him do what they wanted. He didn't want to do what they asked; he just couldn't resist.

Fuzzier memories followed. Floating. Bluish light. Something metallic. Weird smells—mold, something sulfurous that made him gag, a hint of a strange spice. A human face—broad, Black, comforting, smiling down at him. At one point, he seemed to be holding hands with a girl.

That last part was definitely crazy. He certainly didn't know any girls who would hold hands with him.

Having heard nothing but silence from them since his sixth-grade meltdown, he had hoped the Night People had lost interest in him. But in late April, just after his birthday, his dreams became more intense. He awoke terrified for no reason or exhausted or with sore muscles or sore spots on his neck or nose. Once, he found three small red dots on the inside of his wrist, shaped like a triangle. They didn't hurt, and they went away after a day or two, but where had they come from?

Around the same time the intense dreams started, Mr. Macklin had talked about the chat piles, and Sam started feeling compelled to visit them. Was there a connection between the visits of the Night People and the dead, dusty chat piles? The timing certainly seemed suspicious. So did today's and tonight's experiences. But how could they possibly be connected? Then he remembered the electric tingling, the missing time, and most of all, the voice in his head. Suddenly, he had a connection.

CHAPTER 3
AVOIDING

SAM STAYED busy for the next few days, mowing lawns and doing odd jobs. He hoped work, plus music, would keep him from dwelling too much on the two topics roiling around in his mind—Jade and the Night People. Work was necessary—he had to rack up some cash for school clothes and supplies. His mom had told him he was on his own for that stuff now. His dad kept getting fired from construction jobs for drinking or ditching work, so money was tight. Sam had to work if he wanted anything. He had bought his first phone—the cheapest smartphone he could find. He had no friends, but he had customers, and, with the Night People back, he had to keep track of time. Best of all, he could finally have good music anytime.

Last year, the junior high music teacher had taken his class to see a concert by the Southeast Kansas Symphony Orchestra. The music was a revelation. He immediately took his new phone to the library, where he could download music from the internet. He started combing YouTube and Spotify—starting with classical music like the orchestra had played, then quickly adding pop and rock songs. One day, searching randomly, he heard Radiohead singing "Creep." He was blown away. *Wow. That's me. Why didn't I know about this?* Now he was obsessed, ferreting out old groups, searching for more treasures.

All summer, headphones on, he had listened and sung along as he mowed lawns. But now, the Night People disturbed his listening. He had never really remembered anything, but they haunted his dreams. There were electrical sensations—static or sparks or flickering lights. The world seemed to stretch out and become porous when they were around. Like you could just slide through to another time or place. Even in bed, he felt detached from Earth. He dreamed about strange round rooms. Metal examining tables, medical-like instruments, poking and prodding. But when he woke up, everything was normal. Three years and four months since he had last seen them, but he still remembered the feelings—the spookiness, terror, eerie sensations, disconnected details. Everything about them made him cringe.

The word "alien" kept creeping into his thoughts. Aliens were part of society, but they were jokes. The big-eyed, big-headed little creatures were everywhere—keychains, T-shirts, plastic toys. He'd even read a couple of books about them, including an old one, *Communion*, that had a scary, realistic picture of his Night People on the cover. It had taken him a while to get up the courage to read that book and it freaked him out. It was way too close to his own experiences.

Still, he wasn't ready to call the Night People aliens. Even the *Communion* guy didn't call them aliens—he called them "visitors," and admitted he didn't know who, or what, they were. Sam found that comforting. Deep down, he felt like, if he called them aliens, he was admitting he really was crazy. So, he decided they were just . . . Night People.

Sam knew the Night People had visited him over the years, but their visits had been . . . subtle. He never saw them clearly, and mostly remembered strange, disturbing, even terrifying dreams. There were clues that these "dreams" were related to the NP. Weird smells, static and sparks. His sixth-grade meltdown. Often, there was missing time during the day. And always, a constant, pervading fear that left him nervous and jumpy. But this was different. When he was five, the voice in his head was just soothing. Now, it was giving him orders. Expecting something from him.

This time, he had to be better prepared. He had to stop being such a coward. He had to figure out who they were and what they wanted with him. Since he was five, his greatest fear had been that some adult would find out about the Night People, decide he was crazy, and have him carted off to the nearest mental hospital. His Aunt Lucy had been locked up. He was terrified the same thing would happen to him. People would say insanity ran in the family.

And now, in addition to the NP, Jade kept sabotaging his thoughts. She had been so friendly, and he had never had a real friend. But they couldn't be friends. Keeping busy gave him an excuse not to visit her again. It had been surprisingly hard to stay away. He had considered going back the next day and offering to help them empty the truck or move things. It would be neighborly. And he really liked Jade's mom. Seeing her would be almost like seeing his abuela again. But he stopped himself, that day and the next and the next. A corner of his mind wondered what Jade would make of the Night People. But the larger part—the rational part—warned him that she could never know.

Even though he'd only talked to her that one time, Sam had seldom felt as connected to another human being as he had to Jade. Certainly not his parents. His abuela, maybe. And Grandpa Joe—his mom's dad. But both of them had disappeared from his life when Sam was very young. Around the time the Night People had come.

And now, here was Jade, with her curiosity and her

friendly smile, inserting herself into his life. She was so nice, so pretty. Her long, messy braid made him smile. It was practical, and it showed she wasn't overly preoccupied with her looks, like so many girls at school seemed to be. And those questioning, green-flecked eyes—he could see them every time he closed his own eyes. He wondered if the green was why she was named Jade. But the flecks in her eyes were brighter than jade. More like emerald. Still, pretty eyes were no excuse for getting friendly.

Plus, he knew the urge to see Jade again was more than his need for a friend. He was attracted to her. Really attracted. Adolescence was a pain. It was inconvenient. And scary. He needed to be in control, and his irrational, confused feelings for Jade could instantly strip away all that control. Even at a distance, she was affecting him—in the last few days, he had stopped obsessing over old pop groups like Radiohead and The Police and Coldplay. Instead, he played Ed Sheeran's "Perfect" over and over, embarrassed that he pictured Jade every time he heard it, but unable to stop.

He shook his head, trying to banish thoughts of her. *You're a loner, remember?* He never spoke unless spoken to, never sought people out, did school assignments alone unless the teacher required a partner. He never socialized with anyone and was all-business with his customers. He always hiked alone. He didn't like it, honestly—he daydreamed about having someone to talk to, to confide in. But he knew there was no one out there who would understand.

Being alone saved a lot of explanations.

CHAPTER 4
AMBUSH

FINALLY, Sam's work was caught up, and the chat piles were calling him again. He grabbed a water bottle and notepad and set off on his bicycle. Taking the long way around and bypassing Jade's house would add another mile each way to the trip. Surely, he could just race past without being seen. It was unlikely she would be outside. He didn't want to answer a bunch of questions—or worse, end up having to take her with him. . . . He should have known better. When he reached her street, Sam could see her from a distance, standing on her lawn, right by the sidewalk. There was no way to avoid her; he had to stop. How did she know he was coming?

"Hi," Jade said. "So, you finally decided to come visit me?"

Sam opened his mouth and closed it again. Anything he said would sound bad. He lowered his eyes and said nothing.

"I'll take that as a no," she said after a moment. Her disappointment was obvious. "Well, you're here, so why don't you come in anyway and have some lemonade? Mom started work today, and I'm kind of rattling around in this place."

"Thanks," Sam said. Like last time, there was no polite way to say no.

Jade and her mom had made a home. Their furniture had arrived. The living room had a comfortable-looking couch, a recliner, a couple of chairs. And a piano! A big roundish one, like the orchestra had. A grand piano. Wow—she liked music! How could they not be friends? *Stop!*

In the kitchen, a table and chairs had replaced the boxes. Half-a-dozen pots of herbs were growing on the windowsill, and several jars of loose tea sat on the counter. Jade noticed his glance.

"Mom's into herbal teas," she explained, rolling her eyes. "She makes her own. She's kind of a fanatic about it."

She motioned him to a chair. She got out glasses and took her time pouring lemonade. She opened a tin of homemade cookies, put some on a plate, and set it on the table. Finally, she sat down and sipped her lemonade, staring at him. He kept his eyes on the table.

"So, why didn't you come back?" she asked finally. She sounded hurt. "I enjoyed talking to you last time. I thought . . ."

"I'm sorry," Sam said. "I've had a lot of work this week, and . . ." His voice trailed off. *Damned hormones*, he thought. With her mother gone, he felt uncomfortable around her. He'd spent most of the week thinking about her. And he really wanted to touch her. *No!* She watched him for another long moment and then apparently decided to give him a break.

"Okay, you're forgiven," she said. She smiled at him, although she still looked uncertain. "But I hope you're willing to hang out with me sometimes. You're the first person I've met here. And you'll probably think this is crazy, but you seem familiar, like we already know each other."

Sam tried not to react, but he knew his eyes widened.

"Don't panic," she said quickly. "I know we don't."

"No," Sam said. "I mean . . . well, I felt the same way. I'm not good with people, but I felt comfortable with you right away. And your mom. That never happens to me." *Idiot! Why did you admit that?* he thought. She sapped the self-control right out of him.

"So . . . does that mean you're okay with hanging out sometimes?" She sounded relieved.

"I guess," he said. She was asking to be his friend. What could he say? *I don't want to hang out? I don't have friends?*

He paused. "I have a question."

"Sure." Jade sounded surprised but pleased.

"Why were you standing by the sidewalk today? It's like you knew I was coming."

Jade hesitated. She looked slightly embarrassed. "I'm not really sure. I've been kind of watching for you every day, hoping you would come. But this morning, I had this feeling. I just knew. I can't really explain it."

Sam digested that thought. Someone who could anticipate his thoughts and actions—that was scary. No one had ever understood him or wanted to. Even kids who tolerated him considered him a freak. And Nick and his crowd still occasionally—more than three years after Sam's sixth-grade meltdown—delighted in calling him "alien boy." Sam hadn't done anything weird at school since that awful day. He had even dared hope that in high school he might be considered normal. But now, the Night People were back.

As they sat at the kitchen table drinking lemonade, Sam almost forgot he had been heading to the chat piles. Jade plied him with questions about himself. She seemed genuinely interested, which amazed him.

"How do you spend your time?" she asked. "Besides exploring chat piles?"

Sam hesitated. He never talked about himself; he wasn't sure what to say. Finally, he shrugged. "I don't do much, I guess. I hike in the woods. Read. Work."

"What kinds of things do you read?"

"Anything. I just like to read."

"But what do you like *best*? Fiction? Nonfiction? Favorite authors? Kinds of books? I like fantasy a lot," she added. "Harry Potter, *Lord of the Rings*, anything supernatural or fantastic. I just discovered the Harley Merlin series. I loved *The Hunger Games*. And I like regular, realistic books about teens and their problems. Like anything by Laurie Halse Anderson or John Green."

She reeled off her list of likes rapidly, then stopped and looked at Sam. He realized he was staring at her.

"Okay," Jade said. "I told you some of my favorites. Your turn."

"Um . . . I like everything you just listed," he admitted. He was astounded.

She raised her eyebrows. "Why is it so hard to tell me what you like best?"

He shook his head. "Sorry. I guess . . . science fiction and fantasy. And nonfiction—mostly science, nature, technology, outer space. That kind of thing. And I . . ." He hesitated. *Why am I telling her this?*

"What?" He had piqued Jade's interest. No going back now.

"Two years ago, I found this book, *The Riverside Shakespeare*. It has everything he ever wrote, and I decided to read it all. I checked it out all summer, but the language was —hard, and I didn't get very far. At the end of the summer, the librarians gave it to me. They said they were buying a new copy. I've read most of it now. It's getting easier."

Jade laughed and shook her head. "And I was worried

about whether you liked reading. I'm going to love knowing you!"

Sam changed the subject—talking about himself was embarrassing.

"So, you play the piano?" he asked.

Jade's sharp intake of breath startled him. Her eyes had filled with tears.

"I—I'm sorry," he said quickly. "You have a grand piano. I just assumed . . ."

She shook her head, breathing rapidly and trying to pull herself together.

"No, it's fine," she said after a moment. "I just wasn't expecting . . . It was my dad's. It's just a baby grand," she added. "Smaller. Mom and I both play a little, but he was really good. Not professional; he just played for fun. For us, for parties sometimes."

Sam stared at her, feeling very uncomfortable. All past tense. He wanted to know, but he couldn't bring himself to ask the obvious question.

Jade had regained her composure. "He was killed two years ago last spring," she said flatly. "Drunk driver."

"Oh, god," Sam said quietly. "I'm so sorry, Jade."

"Me, too. I thought I was finally . . . mostly over it, and then we moved. The move brought it all back."

"Leaving the place you lived with him," Sam said, closing his eyes. "I'm so sorry I said anything."

He understood, kind of. His abuela used to take him to El Pueblo Mexico, across town. There was a playground where kids spoke Spanish, a grocery store, a church, and a little café where they played Mexican music. He'd loved it. His abuela hadn't died, but she was gone. He hadn't been back since she left.

"Don't be," Jade said. "I need to deal with it. Funny thing is, *he's* the one who could have helped me deal with it. He was a shrink." She gave a shaky laugh.

Her hands were bunched into fists. Sam had fantasized about their first touch. Something romantic. But she needed comfort. He placed his hand over hers. She looked up, smiling through her tears.

"Thanks," she said.

After a moment, she stood up and refilled their lemonade glasses. She turned the conversation to Sam's last visit to the chat piles. He tried hard not to say too much, but she kept pressuring him about why he'd been riding so fast.

"You looked like you were being chased by wolves!" she insisted. "Nobody rides that fast and doesn't pay attention unless they're really afraid of something. So, what was it?"

Finally, he sighed and gave in. "I found this door-like thing on the side of a chat pile."

"Door-like thing? Was it a door, or wasn't it?"

"That's what's so weird," he admitted. "When I looked straight at it, it just looked like a flat side, concrete maybe. But when I looked out of the corner of my eye, it was like I could see the outline of a door. Stupid, I know."

Jade stared at him, frowning. *What's she thinking?*

"So, what did you do?"

He shrugged. "I walked up and put my hand on it. Next thing I knew, I was waking up on the ground. I felt woozy, and my whole body was tingling, and lights were flickering all around. It freaked me out, so I got on my bike and got out of there fast. Dumb, right?"

"Stop saying you're dumb or stupid," Jade chided him. "You're not. Anyone would have freaked out. So, what do you think was going on?"

He shook his head but tried to be matter-of-fact. "No idea. I was really scared, but there has to be an explanation. I just don't know what it is."

Sam left out the voice in his head. She would think he

was a nutcase for sure. And she would find out about the Night People. That couldn't happen.

"That's where you were headed today, wasn't it?" Jade asked. "You were going back to the chat piles to try to figure it out."

What could he say? He had to admit that, too.

CHAPTER 5
DISCOVERY

SO HERE THEY WERE, riding their bikes to the chat piles. Jade wouldn't take no for an answer, even when Sam stressed how filthy the chat piles were, how long the bike ride was. He hadn't wanted to bring her. He never explored with anyone else. No one else knew about his visits to the chat piles, or for that matter, his hikes in the woods at home. None of their business, and no one had ever been interested, except Nick the jerk, who just wanted to torture him—who knew why?

Anyway, Sam preferred exploring alone—he could do what he wanted without anyone making fun of him. Besides, it was safer. Weird things happened to him; that was just part of his life, and there was less to explain if he was alone when they happened.

But Jade was a new kind of problem. She really wanted to come with him, and he had no idea how to tell her no. Honestly, he didn't want to. He liked her, *really* liked her, and it was nice—if strange—to have someone who liked him, too. He steered his bike automatically, wondering what to do. Or if, at this point, there was anything he could do. Letting her into his life, making her his friend—that was the exact opposite of what he should be doing. Of what he had promised himself he would do. No friends meant less chance of anyone finding out about the Night People, less chance of further humiliation, less chance of being branded a nutcase and getting locked up. Had he just blown all his careful planning by being too gutless to say no?

When they rounded the last curve and came upon the desolate landscape of chat piles, Jade gasped. She stared at them with disbelieving eyes.

"Why did they just leave all this stuff here?" she demanded. "Why didn't they clean it up or put it back in the ground? Aren't there laws about cleaning up messes like this?"

Jade's reaction brought Sam out of his musings. Her voice was sharp; she sounded horrified and outraged. Her passion surprised him and made him defensive.

"I don't know. It's not *my* fault!" he protested.

Jade looked startled. "I'm not blaming *you*," she said. "Why would you think that?"

"Sorry." Sam shook his head, embarrassed. Her sharp tone had reminded him of his mother, who was always angry at him.

Jade was watching him uncertainly. "No, I'm sorry," she said. "I get carried away about environmental things sometimes. It's like people don't even see what they're destroying. Makes me crazy—and a total nerd, I guess," she added with a wry smile. "Anyway, I didn't mean to snap at you. Of course, it's not your fault."

"You're right, though," Sam said. "It does seem like this should have been cleaned up. I don't know why it wasn't."

The chat piles had been here since long before Sam was born, but he hadn't thought much about them until recently. They were ugly, but, like most people, he just took them for granted and stayed away from them. Or had, until earth science class. Mr. Macklin had shown them photographs and played a video of members of the Osage Tribe talking about the effects of mining on their community. That had struck a chord—Sam's Grandpa Joe was Osage. He probably knew some of the people in that video.

So, Sam had started coming out here. At first, he just wanted to see the chat piles up close to see if they really were as awful as Mr. Macklin said. And maybe imagine what it was like when the mines were open. What his grandpa's friends had experienced. But, with every visit, he became more obsessed—like there was something about them that he needed to figure out. Like they had something to say to him. *Chatting with the chat piles,* he thought again, and glanced quickly at Jade. Maybe he should share his stupid pun with her. No, definitely not.

Looking at the giant waste mountains through Jade's eyes, he saw why she was upset. He remembered Mr. Macklin talking about the EPA, but he couldn't remember if they had done a serious cleanup. It didn't look like it. Frankly, he had zoned out of the discussion by then, already planning his first visit. He thought Mr. Macklin had talked about avoiding dangers, but Sam never bothered much about physical safety. He could take care of himself.

Finally, Jade remembered they had come to see Sam's door. Still on his bike, he led the way along the chat piles. At the fourth mound, he looked back at Jade and gestured to the right. They left their bikes and hiked around the pile, scrambling over and around boulders. He found the door easily, following his footsteps from last time. It didn't look like much, just a flat side. But he gestured toward it and watched Jade's reaction.

"That's it?" she said. "I guess I'd expect a door into a mountain to be more impressive—like the magic one in *Lord of the Rings*, remember? Are you sure this is even a door? Maybe the rock is just flattened from the mining."

"But they didn't mine here," Sam reminded her. "They mined underground. Then they dumped the waste up here. This should just be a pile of rocks and dirt. It shouldn't have a door or even a flat area. That's why I noticed it."

She nodded. "Yeah, who would build a door in a rock pile? It doesn't make sense. And even if there was something inside, there's no road to get here, so what's the point?"

Sam thought there might have been a road, or at least a track, that was now strewn with fallen boulders, but he didn't comment.

Jade walked along the flattened area, not touching, just trying to see its extent. Sam followed. The flat area was wider than he remembered. He paced it off, careful not to touch it. It was maybe thirty feet wide—more than five times his height. It had looked smaller because several gigantic boulders stood in front of it, hiding both ends. Smaller rocks were scattered between them. The door area was dusty, definitely unused. It was dull gray and looked like one piece. He thought it was concrete, but it was hard to be sure. It almost seemed camouflaged. Looking at it now, Sam was having second thoughts. Why had he been so sure it was a door? He turned sideways and observed the area out of the corner of his eye, but saw no lights.

Jade suddenly called out from where she had squeezed behind the largest boulder on the left. Sam squeezed in beside her and looked up where she was pointing. A rusty, broken door frame extended fifteen or twenty feet above the ground. Dusty strings of old cobwebs hung inside it. They looked at each other and crawled out from behind the boulder.

"Well, you were right," Jade admitted. "It's definitely a door. Or was. But it hasn't been used for years, and I don't see any way to get in. It looks like it's been covered over with concrete or something."

Sam sighed. "I know. Looking at it now, I'm not sure why I ever thought it was a door."

"By the way, how do you feel?" Jade asked. "Any tingling or other symptoms?"

"No, but I haven't touched the door, or whatever it is," Sam said. "Last time, things only happened when I touched it."

"It doesn't look dangerous," Jade mused. "And like you said, no electric lines. I'm going to try. You can rescue me if I get zapped."

Sam was nervous, but he didn't object. He watched as she walked calmly up to the middle of the flat area and placed her hand on its surface. Nothing happened. Sam wasn't sure whether to be relieved or disappointed. He wanted confirmation that he wasn't crazy, and if Jade had felt something too . . . He stopped. What kind of person was he? Was he hoping Jade would get hurt just so he could reassure himself?

"Well," Jade said, "I didn't feel a thing. You want to try again? Maybe it's just you."

"Or maybe I'm just crazy," Sam mumbled.

She gave him a speculative look. "Well, something happened to you last week, or you wouldn't have been so terrified." Then, she grinned at him. "You don't *look* like the crazy type. But who knows?"

Sam thought she was teasing, but he wasn't sure. He gave her a wry smile. "You don't know me very well yet. Maybe I'm crazier than I look."

Jade's grin was challenging. "Well, how about we figure out what happened to you? Then, I can decide for myself."

"You don't have to get involved in this."

"But I want to. It'll be an adventure. Go on, try touching it again. If anything happens, I can rescue *you*."

Sam sighed in resignation. He walked to the door and placed his palm on it. Nothing. Just a dusty old door face—or rock face, or concrete face—with two new handprints on it. He looked at Jade and shook his head.

"Well, whatever it is, it's turned off today," Jade said. She looked around. "How many of these chat piles are there, anyway?"

Sam shook his head. "I don't know. I've only seen the outer row. I had no idea there were so many until recently."

It wasn't until someone turned onto the side road that they saw the extent of the piles. He had started exploring here in late spring and hadn't made much progress. He had ridden a mile or so toward the west along the side road—more of a dirt track, really—and counted ten huge chat piles stretching into the distance. They were long, probably two or three times wider than they were high. He didn't know how tall they were, but once he'd seen heavy equipment partway up the side of a distant pile, scooping gravel into a dump truck. The giant vehicles looked like tiny Matchbox cars perched on the side of the chat pile. He knew there were more rows of mountains behind the ones he could see—and he had only hiked in the outer row.

Mr. Macklin had compared the area to a Martian landscape—dust and rocks with no visible life. The comparison was spot-on, except the dust was grayish-white, not red.

"If we ride all the way around them, maybe we'll see something that will give us a clue about what happened to you," Jade suggested.

"Mm, I doubt that," Sam said. "It might be faster to climb up and look from the top. If there's anything to see."

They retrieved their water bottles and the lunch Jade had packed and hid their bikes behind a large boulder. Sitting in the shade of the boulder, they ate sandwiches before starting the long hike upward. It wasn't an easy hike. The bigger rocks—the ones that gave them a foothold—were rough and sharp, but much of the terrain was loose gravel and dirt, and they kept slipping backward. Itchy, irritating dust filled the air. Before long, they were covered in it. Mixed with sweat, it gave their skin a sickly, grayish tinge. *Like the NP*, Sam thought. Plus, it got in their nostrils and made them sneeze.

Finally, Sam grabbed Jade's arm, panting slightly, and motioned her to stop. He took off his backpack and dug around inside, sighing in relief as he pulled out two crumpled bandanas. He had no idea why there were two, but for once something was going his way. He passed the cleanest-looking one to Jade and tied the other around his nose and mouth. It wasn't ideal, but it kept out the worst of the dust.

It took more than an hour to reach the top. When they dragged themselves up onto the broad plateau and looked around, they were shocked into silence. Chat piles extended for a couple of miles in all directions. Sam couldn't believe this incredible wasteland had existed so near where he had lived all his life without his knowing how huge it was.

But its size wasn't the most amazing part. The area was not a solid forest of chat piles. Near the center was an oval ring, with at least three rows of chat piles around its perimeter. The innermost ring formed an almost solid gray mass, with little space between the mounds. The oval was a bare, flattened plain—perhaps an area that had been mined and filled long ago. Enclosing the plain was a rectangular fence, probably twelve feet tall, topped with coiled razor wire. Inside the fence, near the northwest end, was a small collection of official-looking buildings and warehouses. At the short ends of the rectangle were two huge electrical transformer poles and, at the end with the buildings, a cell tower.

Jade stared at the cell tower and the complex of buildings. They looked new—not at all unused or abandoned.

"And I was worried about moving here because I thought this place would be boring," she said.

CHAPTER 6
PARTNERS

SAM AND JADE were quiet as they hiked back down the chat mountain. Going down was easier—they slid part of the way—but Sam's legs were aching when they reached the bottom. Sweat was running down their faces. They rested in the shade of the boulder, ate apples, and shared the last of their water. Finally, Jade said, "We need to find out what's going on over there. It's got to be connected to your blackout."

"Maybe," Sam said. "But not today. It's pretty far away. It would add at least two miles to our trip, and I'm already exhausted."

"Me, too," agreed Jade. "Plus, we have to get home before my mom gets off work. I told her I would stay close to home today." She looked guilty and quickly changed the subject.

"What do you think that place is?"

"Not a clue," Sam responded, shaking his head. "Mr. Macklin—my teacher—said the mining company left in the 1970s. So, it's probably not them."

Jade nodded, looking thoughtful. "That didn't look like it had to do with mining," she said. "More like the government, don't you think?"

Sam nodded. "Or someone who's keeping a secret. I'll bet all those signs are Keep Out signs."

"Whatever they're doing, they seem to need a lot of power."

Sam nodded again. "That big metal box behind the concrete building? I think it's a generator, like the one at the hospital that keeps lights and respirators and things running when the power goes off."

"What do we do next?" Jade asked. "Do you know anyone we can ask about that place?"

"Not really," Sam responded. "Besides . . ." He paused. "Jade, can we please keep all this between us? I know you don't know anyone yet, but when you do . . . I'd rather not share it with other people."

"Okay." Jade was puzzled. "I can keep a secret. But why?"

They were still leaning against the boulder. Sam sat up and crossed his legs, facing Jade. This was not the most comfortable place to talk, but he needed to settle this before they went home—limit the damage, if he could. He took a deep breath, gathering his courage. *She can't be your friend*, he reminded himself. *She can't find out about the Night People!* But she was here, she had seen the things he had seen, and he had to tell her something. He was convinced that the chat piles and all the weirdness, even this hidden installation, were somehow connected to the Night People. Was this what he had felt compelled to find? Whatever was going on, he had to protect Jade from it, and above all make sure no one else found out. Images of mental hospitals slithered through his brain. But he also had to explain himself somehow. *Stay close to the truth.*

"I usually do things on my own," Sam said. "You're the first person I've ever brought on a hike. Other people—well, they don't really understand the things I'm into. They think I'm . . ."

"Weird? Strange? Nerdy?" Jade suggested.

He gave her a sidelong glance. "Yeah, something like that."

Jade laughed, but she seemed nervous, too. "To tell you the truth, I'm relieved! I was a nerd at my last school, but at least there were several of us, so we could hang together. I was worried, with this being such a small school, that there wouldn't be anyone for me to hang with."

She had startled him, again. "You were a nerd? But you're so . . . pretty."

"Well . . . thanks." Her face reddened under the dust, and she brushed a loose strand of hair out of her eyes.

"But not all nerds have thick glasses or wear suspenders and bow ties, you know. You don't! And you're awfully pretty yourself," she added. She gave him a quick, shy peek. "Handsome, I mean." She was blushing, obviously embarrassed by what she had just said, and changed the subject.

"Anyway, I did wear glasses until a few months ago—braces, too. I decided, if I had to move, I might as well do kind of a makeover. I thought if I looked different, people might start with a better impression of me."

Handsome? She must be joking. I'm just another Brown kid. Sam decided to ignore that comment. "Well, it worked," he said. "I figured you were a cheerleader. I thought you'd probably hang out with the popular crowd, not someone like me." He was counting on that.

"Really?" She looked hurt. "You thought I would drop you so I could fit in with cheerleaders? That's kind of insulting."

Sam cringed. Obviously, his enforced solitude hadn't helped him develop tact.

"I'm sorry," he said quickly. "I didn't mean to insult you."

"What did you mean?"

Sam wasn't used to having to explain himself, mainly

because he never had real conversations. But he had to fix things.

"It's just . . . you seem like the popular type—you know, pretty, outgoing, friendly. And I'm not. So, if you hadn't met me first, well, maybe we would never have got together. You would have been surrounded by other people, and you wouldn't have noticed me."

"Trust me, I would have noticed you."

Sam was startled again. Was she making fun of him? Why would she notice him? He was too embarrassed to ask. Finally, he just shrugged and replied, "Like I said, I'm not popular. People don't hang out with me."

Jade shook her head. "Well, then people don't know what they're missing. I'd love to hang out with you. If you . . . don't mind, of course." She glanced at him sideways. She seemed uncertain, like she was afraid he might say no.

Sam hesitated. This conversation was not going the way he expected. The way it should go. He knew he *should* say no. It was dangerous to get too friendly. And he was having those . . . feelings again. But whatever she thought of him now, that would change once school started and she saw what things were like. So maybe it was okay to enjoy it now. Still, he should be honest.

"But we're really different," he said. "I can't even talk to people I know, much less strangers." He might as well confess it all. "In fact, you're the only person I've ever talked to this much."

"Well, I'm flattered." Jade smiled. She seemed relieved. Sam felt relieved and not relieved at the same time. Was that even possible?

"Like I said, I don't know why, but I feel like I've always known you," she continued. "Besides, people can't be strangers when they've discovered a secret—whatever—

together. What *is* that place, anyway? And how are we going to find out about it if we can't ask anyone?"

Sam sighed with relief. She had changed the subject. This was becoming a long conversation, but one he was enjoying, despite the heat and uncomfortable surroundings. He felt good just being with Jade. Still, he had to make sure she kept the installation secret.

What might people be hiding from the world behind rows of chat piles and a twelve-foot razor-wire fence? they wondered. And who was hiding it? They kept circling back to the government, probably the military. But they had no idea what might be going on there. The southeast corner of Kansas wasn't quite the middle of nowhere, but it was close. Any reasonably large city was several hours away. Because the chat piles were so nasty and uninviting, there was practically no traffic in the area. And they completely hid the fence and buildings.

"You know, it's kind of genius, really," Sam said. "These chat piles are so awful, people just stay away from them. No one comes here for fun—except weirdos like me, of course. Something could stay hidden for years . . . and I guess it has," he added with a short laugh.

"Where's the nearest town?" asked Jade. "Cassidy, right?"

"It is now. There was an old mining town right in the shadow of these piles. But it's abandoned now. The government shut it down because of the danger."

"What danger?"

"The dust is toxic. Lead, mostly. It makes kids sick. Well, adults, too, I guess. There's a lot of asthma and lung cancer and stuff in the area. The water is polluted, too. Filled with acid. And of course, mine collapse. There've been a bunch of cave-ins farther south in Oklahoma."

Sam was kind of amazed at how much he remembered

from earth science class. But Jade was gazing at him with an odd expression on her face.

"Nice," she said. "Thanks for the warning. At least you finally thought of the bandanas, but we've been breathing this dust all afternoon."

Sam felt another surge of guilt. What an idiot he was! "I'm sorry," he said. "I'm just not used to thinking of other people—like I said, I spend most of my time alone. You don't have to come here again."

"What about you, dummy? You shouldn't be breathing it, either! And, of course we'll come again. We'll just be better prepared. My mom's a doctor, remember? I'll sneak some hospital masks."

It had never occurred to Sam to worry about breathing the dust. It was just annoying. But, if he was going to explore with Jade, he obviously had to be more thoughtful. Her health mattered, even if his didn't.

They returned to the question of what was going on at the hidden complex. Military research, maybe, or building some small part for a plane, or some kind of small weapon. Or biological or chemical weapons. That kind of research probably wouldn't take much space. It was a scary thought.

Sam realized the sun had moved so far west they were no longer sitting in the shade. It was getting late! He hated to end his time with Jade, but he said, "We'd better get back. We don't want your mom to get home first and be worried."

"You're right," Jade said. "But we have to come back and get close to that fence, so we can read the signs and figure out what's going on in there!"

"Okay, Jade, but you've *got* to keep this to yourself. Please, promise me!" Sam begged.

"Okay, I promise," she said, giving him a curious look. "I really don't understand why, but it'll be fun having a secret adventure."

"Thank you," Sam said with relief. "I think the first thing," he continued, "is to find the road that leads to those buildings. There has to be a road—people aren't going to hike to work there every day."

"And I'll bet most of the action happens at night," Jade added.

Sam nodded. "Even if there are lights at night, no one will see them from the road. They're completely hidden in there."

"So," Jade concluded, "we have to make at least two trips—one in the daytime to find the road, and another at night to see the activity."

———

When Sam got home, his mother started yelling as soon as he walked in the door.

"Where have you been? Sneaking off with some girl to do who knows what and you only a sophomore! You get her pregnant and you're out of this house, do you hear me?"

Sam was horrified. He knew his face had turned crimson. "Mom!" he gasped. "What are you talking about? How can you think I would—d-do that?"

He hadn't told his mother about Jade. Why would he? He hadn't meant to get friendly with her, and besides, he made it a point *not* to share things with his mother. He'd learned that lesson when he was five. After asking a few questions, he figured out that someone had seen them heading off together on their bicycles and mentioned it to his mom at work. *Damn small town. Everyone thinks your life is their business.*

Sighing, he explained who Jade was and how he had met her and her mom. "We weren't sneaking anywhere," he said. "I was just showing her places in town."

He tried to sound innocent, and he didn't mention the chat piles. He always stopped at the park bathroom and cleaned up as much as he could before he came home. His mother didn't know about his visits, and he meant to keep it that way. But why would she assume he would get a girl pregnant? Jade was the only girl he'd ever really talked to, and he didn't even have the guts to touch her. He didn't ask his mother why she assumed the worst about him, but he wondered. Other than telling her about the Night People—once, way back when he was five—he had tried hard never to arouse her suspicions about anything.

Of course, there had been things he couldn't hide. Missing time. His pajamas covered with dirt and leaves. Blood on his pillow. His meltdown in sixth grade. He knew she suspected those things were related to the NP, but what exactly did she know? And what did the NP have to do with getting girls pregnant? He sighed. It was probably simple enough—having dealings with the NP made him untrustworthy, period.

Eventually, his mother stopped yelling and left for the kitchen with a final warning. He shook his head wearily. One more thing to keep secret. At least, she hadn't made him promise to stop seeing Jade. With a start, he realized he had accepted Jade as his friend and partner. In a week. After only two meetings. Had he just made the biggest mistake of his life? Sam turned away, just as his father came in the front door. Great! He pursed his lips and headed up the stairs.

"Yeah, you better make yourself scarce, you little weirdo." His dad's voice was contemptuous but not threatening, for once. Not drunk, Sam thought. That's a first.

"And here I was hoping for some quality father-son time," Sam said over his shoulder. He didn't bother to hide his sarcasm. Nothing like a loving family, he thought. At least, his mother wouldn't tell his father about his "sneaking off" with Jade. She wasn't that heartless.

PART TWO

There are always new things to find out if you go looking for them.
--David Attenborough, natural historian and broadcaster

CHAPTER 7
ENTRANCE

TWO DAYS LATER, Sam and Jade made their daytime visit to the chat piles. They biked two more miles west along the dirt road, and there, finally, was a service road off to the right. It was just a track between two rows of chat piles, even narrower than the dirt road. No one would think of turning there; it looked like it only led to more chat piles. But it had faint tire tracks, and when they followed it north, it ended, curving to enter a wide gate in the chain-link fence. And there were the buildings. They hid their bikes quietly and carefully. They hadn't seen or heard anything, but they knew they were snooping.

They crept down the road toward the gate. Like the fence, it was twelve feet high and topped with razor wire; it was obvious they weren't likely to sneak through it. The signs made clear what would happen if they tried. The top one said Authorized Personnel Only; the one below said Violators Will Be Prosecuted. Jade nodded toward the right and Sam followed as she angled toward the fence and began to walk quietly along it, past the buildings. They stayed close together and well back from the fence. It was strange, Sam thought, how easily they had slipped into this partnership.

They seemed to know what to do without talking. The fence had more signs. They said things like Keep Out and Absolutely No Trespassing. There was another Violators Will Be Prosecuted, for good measure. None indicated who owned the area or what happened there, but whoever they were, they obviously didn't welcome visitors.

The buildings weren't unusual or mysterious, though none of them had windows. Sam counted five fairly small warehouses, although he couldn't guess what they might be storing. He could see part of the generator peeking out from behind the sturdiest building, a single-story cement structure about half the size of the warehouses. The building didn't look big enough to hide many secrets.

Jade nudged him. "Look for signs or logos," she said quietly. "We need to figure out who owns this place."

"I've been looking," Sam replied just as quietly. "There's nothing. They really don't want anyone to know what's going on here."

"Let's see if the fence is electrified," she suggested. "Do we have any tool with a plastic handle?"

Sam thought there would be a hum if it was electrified, but he took off his backpack and rummaged through it. He removed a folding trowel with a thick rubber handle. "How about this?"

Jade nodded. She unfolded the trowel, held it by the handle, and scraped its metal edge along the metal of the fence. No sparks.

"Well, it's not hot." She handed him the trowel, hesitated a moment, and then touched the fence with a finger. "Nothing," she said. "I think we're safe."

Sam touched it, too, partly to verify Jade's assessment and partly to prove himself. He remembered biking away from the abandoned door at top speed, as though demons were after him; the memory still made him squirm with embarrassment. The fence was hot from the sun but not electrified. They continued walking along it, past the buildings, but there was nothing else of interest. Sam was beginning to feel uneasy. He couldn't pinpoint a reason, but something didn't feel right. He was ready to get out of there.

"We should go back," he said finally. "There's nothing more this way. We need to concentrate on the buildings."

"I agree," Jade said. "I'm just not sure what to do next." They turned back and had almost reached the gate when it happened. A charge like a lightning bolt went through Sam. His body tingled all over, his ears buzzed, and bright lights flickered around him.

And here he was, lying flat on the ground again. He groaned and tried to sit up. Jade was beside him, pulling herself upright and looking dazed. Sam tried to focus, but the flickering lights made everything blurry. He squinted at Jade's face and then reached up and touched his own. He looked around. They had been wearing face masks Jade had stolen from her mom. Their masks were missing.

"Is this what happened to you before?" Jade asked. She was gasping and shaking.

"Yeah, but this was stronger," Sam said. He didn't mention that there was no voice in his head this time. But there was a brief image—a memory? A tall, broad, Black man wearing army camouflage. Looking friendly. Looking familiar. Sam shook his head in confusion.

"It feels like electricity," Jade said, shaking her head in a daze. "But the fence isn't on."

"And even if it was, we weren't touching it," Sam added.

"Oh, this is intense." Jade rubbed her hands and flexed them several times, then shook her head from side to side.

Sam struggled to his feet. "C'mon. Let's get out of here." He grabbed Jade's arm and pulled her up. He tried to pull her toward the road, but she stopped him.

"Wait. We need to figure out what happened. Do you see anyone over there or anything moving?"

Sam felt shaky, but he stood his ground and surveyed the area around the buildings. Everything shimmered in the sunlight, or maybe he was still seeing the flickering lights. But nothing seemed changed and there was no movement. Apparently, Jade didn't see anything either. As she turned to leave, she reached for his hand and he grasped hers. A shiver ran through him—he was holding Jade's hand! But he quickly shook off the thrill. She wasn't flirting. She was scared, and so was he, and the contact gave them both courage. They walked quickly away from the fence and up the road toward their bikes, not speaking. They were still shaky as they mounted the bikes and headed home. The farther they got from the secret complex, the more their strength and energy seemed to return.

CHAPTER 8
MISSING TIME

"WHERE HAVE YOU TWO BEEN? Your note said you'd be home by three. And what's happened to you? You're filthy." Dr. Mathieson sounded more worried than angry.

They had planned to clean up and discuss their experience before Jade's mother got home. But it was after five and she was already here. Sam's heart sank. *Not again!*

"Sorry, Mom, I guess time got away from us. We didn't realize it was so late," Jade said. Sam didn't say anything.

"You've been out at those chat piles, haven't you?"

"We're *fine*, Mom, really. We can take care of ourselves."

Jade sounded annoyed. Sam wished she wouldn't act like that. He could tell Dr. Mathieson was just worried about their safety. Jade didn't know how lucky she was to have a mother who cared.

Dr. Mathieson looked from Jade to Sam and back again. Sam tried for his innocent look—no need to seek out trouble. She sighed. "I'm getting the feeling there's more to this than you're telling me. I won't push for now, but you need to be careful. Those chat piles worry me." She was silent for a moment. "Wait here."

She left the room and returned with a box of surgical

masks, which she thrust at Jade. Sam assumed it was the same box Jade had stolen today's masks from.

"If you go out there again, I want you both to wear these masks. They aren't perfect, but at least you won't breathe in so much dust."

"Thanks, Mom. Don't worry, we'll be careful."

Sam felt conflicted. He hadn't wanted a partner, but he was already depending on Jade. The return of the NP had unnerved him, and Jade helped with that—she didn't know about them, but somehow, she made him feel calmer. Besides, he just liked being with her. But the missing time was a wake-up call—she wasn't safe from the weirdness surrounding him. He had no idea what to do.

Dr. Mathieson invited Sam to stay for dinner. But first, she made them wash the dust off each other with the garden hose.

"I'm not having all that mine dust in the shower and washer," she said. "With the hose, you can leave most of it outside."

When they were clean, she gave Sam a T-shirt and shorts that had belonged to Jade's father. They were too big, but they were dry and clean. It was hard not to feel close to Jade and her mom, they were so friendly and normal. But he had to break off his developing partnership with Jade. It wasn't safe for either of them.

During dinner, Jade's mom brought up their trip to the chat piles again. She was obviously not thrilled about their visit.

"You know, you two could go to the swimming pool, or the park, or the library," she said. "Or a movie. Wouldn't any of those be more fun than making that long, hot bike ride and ending up exhausted and filthy? Are those chat piles really that exciting?"

Jade frowned. "They're just different, Mom. Something new. It's an adventure."

"Or, Sam, you could introduce Jade to some of your friends. You could take a couple more people when you go. It would be . . . safer."

Sam stared at her, speechless for a moment. *What friends?* "I—I—uh, don't really hike with anyone else. Jade . . . is the only person who's ever wanted to go with me."

Jade's mom gave him a piercing look. He did his best not to look away, although he knew he was blushing. Finally, she relaxed slightly, her lips twitching. Apparently, whatever she saw in his face reassured her. "Okay. For now, I'll let you go. But if I see the slightest problem—of any kind—don't expect a free pass. Either of you. Understand?"

"*Okay*, Mom," Jade said. She sounded annoyed. Again.

"Yes, ma'am," Sam said. She raised an eyebrow at him, and her lips twitched again. Finally, she changed the subject.

After dinner, they went to Jade's room. Sam was not used to having parents keep track of his comings and goings—unless the neighbors clued them in. He found Jade's mom intimidating. Jade seemed to find her actions normal, if annoying.

"We'll have to be careful," she said. "She'll come to check on us." She left the door open so they could hear. She even opened a website about chat piles. Then, she looked up at Sam.

"We need to talk," she said. "What's going on? What happened to us? And how?"

Sam shook his head. He had no idea what to say.

"Someone obviously wants to keep us from finding out what's going on out there," Jade said. "But this was so creepy. There was no one around, so we must have been knocked out by electricity. But how could that happen? And if someone wants us to stay away, why not just tell us? Why do all that?"

"I don't know," Sam said.

He didn't know anything—except he was convinced the NP were involved. There had been no voice in his head this time, but there was that guy . . . The secret complex both pulled them and pushed them away. There seemed to be no way they could get inside. But someone (the Night People?) was luring them and wanted them there. Why else were they both so obsessed? Why else had they lost the time? And which side was the army guy on?

Sam wanted to share his suspicions with Jade. But he couldn't. She was nice, but she was a stranger. He could not get close to people. Anyone who knew about the Night People could expose him. They would say he was crazy because he "believed in aliens," and he would end up like his Aunt Lucy. The thought tormented him. Sam didn't *know* that aliens, or NP, had been involved in his aunt's commitment, but his mother's weird attitude made him suspicious. He dragged his thoughts back to the present.

"We've got to go back at night," Jade was saying. "That's the only way we'll find out anything."

"I guess," Sam said.

The thought of visiting that place at night gave him chills, but Jade was right. The only problem was, he needed to go by himself. He had to talk her out of this. But how? Jade didn't seem to notice his lack of enthusiasm. She was talking at her usual top speed, making plans for later in the week when her mom would be working the night shift. Sam didn't worry about his own parents. He was used to sneaking out. They had no idea what he did with his time outside school and didn't care as long as they weren't inconvenienced—or worse, embarrassed.

He shivered, thinking what could happen if he embarrassed his dad. Over the years, he had become careful to avoid causing talk, and he had become expert at avoiding his father. It had been a few years since anything bad had happened. But, now that his mother was clued into his friendship with Jade, he would have to be extra careful. No matter how innocent he was, she would assume the worst. She was wrong about the reason, but right that he shouldn't be doing things with Jade. Maybe he could scare Jade out of going. *Worth a try.*

"There's something we should talk about," Sam said. Jade looked up questioningly.

"The time thing," he said. "You know how we got back two hours later than we'd planned?"

"Yeah," Jade said. "That was strange. We need to be a lot more careful. If we start being late all the time, my mom will crack down, and I'll never get out."

"That's not what I meant," Sam said. "I don't think we lost track of time. I think we lost the time. I think there were two hours when something happened that we can't remember."

Jade stared at him, wide-eyed. "What makes you think that?"

"Well, think about it. When we woke up after we got zapped, we were groggy and disoriented—and weak. Right?"

"Well, yeah. But being hit by an electrical charge would make us feel that way, wouldn't it?"

Sam took a deep breath. "Maybe," he said. "But I don't think so, because it's happened to me before. The day I found the door—the day we met—I realized when I got to your house that it was more than an hour later than it should have been. And that wasn't the first time. It happened to me a lot when I was little. My mom used to get really mad—she thought I was doing it on purpose."

Jade's eyes widened. "But—that's not possible. How

could we lose time? Maybe we just had a really bad shock. We were knocked unconscious."

"Maybe. But could we really be shocked and unconscious for two hours and then just get up and walk away? You'd think we'd end up in the hospital, not riding our bikes home."

"But what else could it be?"

"I've had years to think about this, and no one to talk to," Sam said. He grinned crookedly. "So, I've considered a few possibilities. The only one that makes sense to me is hypnosis."

"Hypnosis. You mean like . . . mind control?"

"Kind of," Sam said. "I read this book about hypnosis. It's like being put into a different state. You're still conscious, but you're a lot more suggestible."

"So, you think we lost two hours because someone hypnotized us and suggested we forget them? Who? We didn't see anyone. And why would anyone do that?"

"We didn't see any way to get zapped by electricity, either. There was no lightning. We weren't touching the fence or anything else. We were just walking. In rubber-soled sneakers."

They stared at each other for a long moment. "We should give this up, before we get hurt," Sam said. "What if we aren't so lucky next time? This shock was stronger than the ones before. What if they keep getting stronger? What if we don't wake up, or can't get back home?"

"And . . ." Sam paused. Should he say this? Yes. It wasn't strictly true, but he needed to scare her. "Sometimes people use hypnosis to—control you. Make you do things you don't want to do."

"You think, while we were knocked out, someone made us do things? What things? And why?"

"In two hours, they could do a lot, and we'd never know.

But whatever it is, we need to stay away from that place—so they can't make us do anything."

"But don't you want to find out what's happening to us?"

"Well, yeah, but not if we're going to get hurt or killed. Whoever they are, they're a lot smarter than we are. They can do whatever they want."

"How do you know that? You just figured out what's happening or at least came up with a good hypothesis."

Reluctantly, Sam smiled at the word "hypothesis." Jade was definitely a nerd—a science nerd, at that.

"We can figure this out together," she insisted. "We have to go back. You're not on your own anymore, you know. We're partners now."

Sam's shoulders slumped in defeat. He should have known he couldn't scare her out of going back. Nothing scared her.

Jade stared at him. "Sam? You're not going to flake out on me, are you? We're going to do this, right?"

"Yeah, sure. I've gotta go." He left quickly, without looking at her.

CHAPTER 9
SAM RETREATS

SAM FELL into bed soon after he got home. Spending time with Jade was exhausting. She considered them partners and was excited about investigating the chat piles. He wanted her as a partner. And a friend. More than a friend—he shut off those daydreams quickly. *That* would never happen . . . . Anyway, the missing time changed everything. It meant she was officially sucked into the strangeness in his life. He could neither justify making her part of it nor figure out how to discourage her. Obviously fear tactics didn't work. *I have to find a way!* Maybe an idea would come in his sleep. But as he was falling asleep, the day's events floated uneasily through his mind, and deeper currents from past memories surged up to replace them.

The following morning, drifting up from an uneasy sleep, Sam realized he had been reliving an NP event from when he was seven and still adjusting to having them in his life. He had awakened in the woods, shivering with cold but not afraid. He knew the Night People had taken him, but he hadn't seen them and he couldn't remember much—just bits and pieces, like the crackly, electrical feeling that always accompanied them. He remembered walking back home in the dark and meeting his mother in the kitchen. She was harsh and angry, as usual, but also relieved, he thought. He told her he had just woken up in the woods and didn't remember anything. He didn't mention the Night People. She knew they were taking Sam, but they both pretended it wasn't happening. Always. She explained his night forays into the woods as dreaming or sleepwalking. That made him sad. But even at seven, he was determined to handle the Night People by himself. Sooner or later, he would figure out who they were and what they wanted. He just had to get bigger and less afraid. And remember better.

The emotions his dream triggered in him were clearer than they had been in years. The terror he felt, the resolve to learn about them. After that age-seven experience, he had started his Coward's Notebook. He wrote down what happened, plus his thoughts and feelings about the NP, since he couldn't talk to anyone about them. As he got older, he thought more deeply about who they could be and what they wanted with him, and as he learned more about science, his entries became more scientific. He still considered himself a coward—although he thought the NP would terrify anyone. But this year, he resolved to finally learn who they were. And to finally begin to stand up to them.

Still, he could not involve Jade. The NP were his problem, not hers. It was unfair, even dangerous, to make her part of this—whatever this was. Because, despite years of writing in his notebook, he was still guessing. He had no idea who the NP were or what they wanted. And deep down, he still wondered if maybe he was just imagining them. Maybe he really was crazy. Maybe, like his father said, he belonged in a mental hospital—only his dad used more colorful terms, like loony bin or nuthouse. Every time his dad said something like that, Sam thought of his Aunt Lucy and shivered. He couldn't imagine anything worse than being considered crazy.

And sent to a mental hospital, even for a short time. He *had* to keep his connection with the NP secret—from everyone!

He wasn't sure how to get Jade out of the situation, but he knew he had made a big mistake involving her, and he had to fix it. He could say he had changed his mind and was no longer interested, but she wouldn't buy that. He could say he had to work more and no longer had time to solve the mystery. That wouldn't go down well, either, but she couldn't really object to it. If he refused to investigate, surely, she would give up. And he did have plenty of work to do, so he wouldn't be lying, exactly.

———

During the next week, Sam ignored Jade completely. He mowed lawns, weeded gardens, and cleaned and organized a really filthy garage. He made a bunch of money and bought a couple of new T-shirts for school. He psyched himself up for a future with a lot of boring work and study and very little mystery-solving. Better for everyone, he thought.

Jade texted every day, but he didn't return her texts. She called and left messages. He didn't respond. She said it was really important—she had learned something new and they needed to talk. Sam was curious, and he knew he should talk to her. At first, he promised himself he would later, after he figured out how to make her give up on the secret complex. Then, he decided it was probably best to make a clean break. Maybe, if he just ignored her, she would get the hint and stop trying.

Thursday night—the night Jade had planned they would visit the secret complex—Sam did not show up at her house. His guilt was so intense, it was almost paralyzing. He knew he was being a coward. He at least owed her an explanation. But he had to protect her from himself and from the NP. He told himself she would get over it. She couldn't possibly care that much about him—after all, they barely knew each other. She had friends back in Kansas City (she'd said they kept in touch through Snapchat), and she would have more when she got acquainted here. His feelings about her—that was another matter. He didn't have tons of friends. He just had Jade, and he was unprepared for the feeling of emptiness her absence left. He even missed those embarrassing fluttery feelings. But he would get over it. He had survived without friends all his life. Friends were for other people, those who weren't dealing with the NP.

Sam was depressed and dripping with sweat as he made his way home Friday afternoon, pushing the old lawn mower, his headphones surrounding him with old, sad songs by Coldplay. He had quit earlier than usual. He had decided he would figure out the secret complex and the NP's connection to it on his own. It would take longer, and he would miss Jade's help and their blooming friendship, but she would be safer. This time, he would take a different street and turn onto the highway after he was past her house, so she couldn't waylay him like she had last time. He closed his eyes wearily. He *had* to stop being such a coward and talk to her. But he was afraid he couldn't convince her to quit and he would just give in again.

His eyes were downcast as he turned into the driveway. He had almost reached the doorstep when he looked up and saw Jade sitting there, chin in hand, waiting for him.

CHAPTER 10
JADE ADVANCES

SAM STOOD THERE, staring mutely at Jade. He pulled his headphones off. He knew his face was red, but he was so hot and sweaty, he hoped the added heat wasn't noticeable. Despite his guilt, he felt a surge of joy at seeing her. But what must she think of him?

Jade stared back at him. She looked angry. "Well," she said, "are you going to invite me in?"

"How did you find me?" He had been careful not to give her his address. He was embarrassed to live in this crumbling old neighborhood filled with ramshackle houses, unkempt lawns, and decaying cars. It felt like even the town was embarrassed, tacking the neighborhood onto its very edge, as though reluctant to admit it was part of the zip code. But the neighborhood was the least of his worries. There was his mother to contend with. And, heaven forbid, his father. Thankfully, neither was home, for the moment, anyway.

"I followed you home last time," Jade said. "Since you obviously weren't planning to tell me where you lived. Good thing I did, or I might never have seen you again."

Sam closed his eyes. Of course, she would find out. It wasn't that hard, and she never quit. "Okay, come on in," he said. He tried to sound courteous but wasn't sure he succeeded.

Jade followed him into the dingy kitchen. It was embarrassing, too. The kitchen in her house was so bright and new—this one was a reject from the last century. The countertops had stains that wouldn't wash out, and their edges were crumbling. The linoleum was cracked and peeling. But here she was; he couldn't change that. He gestured toward the kitchen table, and she sat down. "I'm afraid there's no lemonade," he said. "You'll have to settle for water."

He poured two glasses of water and set one in front of her.

"Is that why you think I'm here?" she asked. "For lemonade?"

"Why are you here?"

"Seriously?" She was definitely angry. "You disappear for a week, you refuse to answer my calls and texts, and you bail on our night trip to the secret complex. You didn't think I'd find any of that strange or want to know what's going on? You might have been sick or hurt. How would I know? And how would I find out, since you never told me where you live?"

Sam hung his head. "I guess I didn't think it would matter that much. I thought you'd just move on."

"You want me to move on? Our partnership—friendship—means nothing to you?" Jade's voice broke slightly.

"No, no, that's not what I meant. I just . . ." He stopped. He had no idea what to say next.

"You just what? I thought we were getting along. Maybe even becoming friends. If you're going to throw that away, I think you at least owe me an explanation."

Sam checked the time. His mother could be home from work any minute. His dad—well, he was learning to stand up to his dad, but he didn't want Jade there if it came to that.

"Look, I promise I'll try to explain. But please, could we do it somewhere else? Can you give me a few minutes to clean up and change and we'll go to the park and talk?"

She looked surprised but agreed. Five minutes later, Sam returned. He led the way on his bike, and they settled at the picnic table farthest from the street.

Jade looked around. "You must really be embarrassed to be seen with me," she commented. "Getting me out of your house so quickly and then coming here where no one will see us."

Sam groaned, his head in his hands. "No, you've got it all wrong."

"Then explain it to me."

"Look, when we got zapped that day and lost all that time, I realized how much danger I was putting you in. I just thought it would be safer to keep you out of it."

"You mean, because I'm a girl, you decided I was a delicate flower that needed to be protected?"

"No, no, it's nothing like that!"

"Then explain it to me. Because I really don't understand."

Sam closed his eyes and took a deep breath. He had to get this right. "Okay, all my life weird things have happened to me. Missing time, nightmares, waking up in the woods, other . . . things. Stuff just happens and gets me in trouble or makes me do things people make fun of. I don't know why this stuff happens, but I know I'm better off without friends, so no one else can get hurt or tangled up in whatever is happening to me. . ."

He stopped and raised his eyes briefly to Jade's face. She was listening intently; her brow was furrowed, but she seemed less angry. Relieved, he continued. "Before, it didn't matter so much because no one wanted to be friends with me. They were happy just making fun of the weirdo. But you're different. I don't want you to get hurt or mixed up with my weird life."

He stopped. He wasn't used to talking so much. It was all true, just not the whole truth. He hoped it would be enough.

Jade was silent for a long moment. Had he blown it again? Finally, she responded.

"Wow. That's the longest speech I've ever heard you make. Thank you for explaining. But you're missing a few things. First, I should have some say in whether I get mixed up in your weird life. You shouldn't just cut me off without asking. Second, like I said before, people are idiots if they don't want to hang with you. I'm not an idiot. I like hanging with you. And third, we have a mystery to solve. I'm sure you can solve it alone—and I don't think for a minute you've given up on it—but things are always easier when people work together. And more fun."

She watched him, looking nervous. He looked down, but she stayed quiet, and eventually he had to meet her eyes. Those eyes got him every time. He knew he should say no. But she was so logical and so sincere, and he really wanted her in his life. He couldn't help himself. Maybe it could work, even though her chance of finding out about the Night People was becoming greater every day. Still . . . maybe she wouldn't think he was crazy.

"You really want to do things with me? And you're not worried about what might happen?"

"I really do. And no, I'm not worried. You said things happen to you all the time, and you're fine. But someone is messing with our lives. We need to find out who and what they're doing to us and why. I have as much stake in this as you do."

"I . . . okay. You're right." He looked across at her, shamefaced. "I'm sorry I disappeared like that. It was stupid. But I didn't know how to explain, and I was afraid you'd talk me out of dropping you as a partner. And you did."

"Well, I'm relieved to hear it." She was blushing, but she met his eyes resolutely. "Please, promise me you'll never disappear like that again? Friends don't disappear on each other. And you can talk to me about anything. I won't ever laugh or make fun of you."

He nodded. "I promise."

"Now," she said. "Let's get down to business. After you left, I Googled 'missing time.' You'll never believe what I found."

Jade told him about professors at Harvard and other universities who had studied people with missing-time experiences, and who stressed that these people were not crazy. She said there were lots of books by and about people who thought they had been abducted by aliens, and some people —though obviously not all—took them seriously. He let her talk without interrupting. He wasn't sure what to say. She seemed serious, and she was straying dangerously close to Night People territory—not that he had ever admitted to himself that NPs might be aliens. Aliens were fodder for jokes, and people who believed in them were crazy. Just ask the kids who had tormented him all these years. He thought everyone felt that way, and sometimes he felt like every adult wore a white coat and was just waiting to drag him away.

"Well, what do you think?" Jade asked finally.

"I'm not sure," he said. "I guess I'm a little surprised you're taking this kind of thing seriously. You seem so practical and scientific, and I thought people just made jokes about aliens. I figured you would, too."

"Well, my dad always said humans aren't as smart as we think we are. He said it's arrogant to assume we know everything, and he told me to keep an open mind and always look for evidence, instead of just dismissing things. Even things other people consider crazy."

"Did he include aliens in his list of things not to dismiss?" Sam asked, smiling slightly.

She returned the smile. "I don't think the subject ever came up."

Sam sighed with relief. Jade was . . . okay . . . with the idea of aliens. And she had just talked about her father without getting tearful.

He tried for a lighter tone. "So, just so I understand what you're saying: You think when we passed out for two hours, aliens did that to us?"

"Oh, I know it sounds crazy. And of course, there must be plenty of other explanations. There were websites that talked about causes like being drunk or having multiple personalities or amnesia or even being possessed. But we weren't drunk, and I don't think either of us has serious mental problems, do you?"

"Not you, but I wonder about myself sometimes."

"Well, you seem pretty sane to me. Just prone to self-doubt," Jade said, smiling slightly. "And I'm not saying we should assume aliens are doing this. I just think we should add them to the list of possibilities. Could we follow my dad's suggestion and not dismiss them? Consider all the possibilities and look for evidence?"

"Um, okay, I guess. It's not like we have any other ideas. But how do you look for evidence of aliens?"

"I'm not sure, but I figure reading's always a good start. Find out what other people know or think. I made a list of authors who've written books about their own abductions, or studied other people who've been abducted, or think they have."

"Okay, I'm game."

Sam hated to admit it, but Jade's idea gave him a slight

thrill. The *Communion* book had freaked him out, but maybe he would handle the fear better if he read the books with Jade. Plus, reading about people who took the idea seriously appealed to him, even though he, personally, was afraid to accept it as real. After all, if there really were aliens on Earth, everyone would know about them, he thought. How could governments even keep a secret that big? Did they know about the Night People?

"And," Jade said, giving him a fierce look, "we are going to the secret complex at night. Both of us. You're not ditching me again, understand?"

"Yes, ma'am!" Sam responded, grinning slightly and saluting. Deep down, he was still worried, but it felt so good, so right, to be back with Jade.

CHAPTER 11
FACT-FINDING MISSION

IT WAS several days before Sam had a break from work and Jade's mother had another night shift, so Jade could sneak out without getting caught. They spent some of the time researching in the library and online. Sam was jittery with excitement. Now that he and Jade were partners again, he was eager to check out the secret complex. More than eager—obsessed.

That night, when they reached the track to the locked gate, Sam was anxious, and Jade was uncharacteristically quiet. He wondered if she was as scared as he was. He was desperately trying to hold it together—looking like a coward in front of her wasn't an option. Even though she was nervous around him sometimes, she always seemed so cool and unruffled in situations like this. The trip had been pitch-black and slow, the night sounds muffled and the moon smothered in dense clouds. Their bike lights barely showed the way. The lack of traffic made biking safer, but it increased Sam's anxiety level. The woods at night didn't frighten him, but on the highway, in the open, in the dark, they were fair game for anyone, including the Night People. They missed the turnoff leading to the complex and had to backtrack.

Now, they were riding slowly, ready to douse their lights if anyone appeared. At the last chat pile before the gate, they hid their bikes and turned on their headlamps. They tiptoed toward the gate.

As they approached, they heard noise from behind the fence for the first time—a chugging sound, like a muffled engine. The generator! They shared a quick glance—half triumph because they were right, someone was using the place, and half fear, because they could be caught at any minute. Rounding the final curve, they saw faint outlines of the fence and buildings. The sound became louder. They turned off their headlamps. Downlights on the tops of the cell tower and transformer cast pale gleaming circles on the ground below. The buildings themselves had no lights. Of course—no windows. Surveying the dark hulks of the surrounding chat piles, Sam wondered if people could see the lights of the cell tower and transformer from outside. The tower had to be slightly taller than the chat piles, or signals would be blocked. Still, he'd bet the lights were almost invisible except to people flying over. The place was definitely meant to be secret.

"What time is it?" he whispered to Jade.

She checked her phone. "Eleven forty-five," she whispered back.

They crept closer to the gate, straining to see. After a whispered consultation, they switched on their headlamps again and swept the lights slowly around the buildings. Nothing. "Wonder where they park?" Sam commented softly. As if on cue, an engine sound behind them caused them to leap to the side. They doused their lights, scrambled to a small hollow at the base of the nearest chat pile, and hunkered down. They could still see the gate and buildings, but (they hoped) they wouldn't be noticed if they kept quiet and no one was expecting company. A medium-sized truck pulled up, its lights off. Sam heard a crunch of gravel; a dark figure jumped from the passenger side and approached the gate. The chain fell away with an echoing clang, and the gate creaked inward.

The truck moved slowly inside and stopped just past the door of the cement building. The driver got out and entered a key code—Sam could barely see lights on a keypad—and the door opened, spilling a narrow carpet of muted light onto the ground. Two more people emerged from the truck and were joined by two from inside the building. The door was wide open now, and they were moving cartons from the truck into the building. A lot of cartons. The truck must be full. It was military, Sam decided. It had that look. Boxy, dark, utilitarian. There was too little light to see the color or a logo.

So, the place was being used, maybe by lots of people. These guys were just delivering stuff. Which meant something significant must be happening inside. But what? And where were they fitting it all? The place didn't look that big. Maybe he had it all wrong and this whole place was just a storage area. But his gut told him otherwise.

Sam realized Jade was inching forward, trying to see better. He touched her arm and shook his head. "Be still," he hissed. "They'll see us!"

"We should try to get through the gate while it's open," she whispered.

He shook his head. "No. There's nowhere to hide. We'd get caught for sure."

She sighed but gave in. Getting caught wouldn't solve anything. They watched and waited. After a while, everyone except the driver entered the building, and the door closed. The driver moved the truck outside the gate, replaced the chain and lock, and drove away alone, his lights still off. The chug of the generator continued. Sam and Jade sat for a couple of minutes, then crept slowly toward the gate. Jade was bent on cracking the secret of their missing time experience. Sam wanted that, but even more, he wanted the key to the NP. He was convinced they were part of the same secret. Maybe he would meet the ones who spoke in his head. Or the big army guy who kept turning up in his NP experiences.

But how could they get inside the gate? Jade checked the lock and turned it over to show Sam. It was a large padlock. They would need a key or bolt cutters. They had neither. Or they could climb over—possible, Sam supposed, but not easy. The razor wire looked deadly.

"We could go around the whole perimeter and check for breaks or loose spots," Jade suggested.

"Maybe," he agreed. "But I'll bet the fence is patrolled and repaired. And we'd have to do it in the daytime to see everything."

The only other method that occurred to him was waiting for the next truck and hitching a ride, hanging on underneath. Not a fun thought. And there wouldn't be another truck tonight.

They turned away. They wouldn't get in tonight, but they wouldn't give up. Sam wanted to know what was in there, and Jade was obviously not the quitting type. Now, she inclined her head toward the road, and Sam nodded. Time to leave. They had taken only a few steps when a light shone behind them, and a male voice shouted, "Hey!" They sprinted for their bicycles without looking back and rode pell-mell toward the road.

When they reached the main road, they paused for a moment to listen, but there was no sound behind them. Sam looked at Jade. "I can't believe we didn't get caught," he said.

She looked worried. "Oh, I'm sure we got caught. He didn't chase us because there were no cars. But I'll bet they have cameras. We should have thought of that."

"We didn't see any cameras when we came before."

"We didn't look. What do you bet he goes back in and starts checking camera footage until he finds our daytime visit?" She shook her head. "We were idiots."

Idiots or not, there was nothing they could do about it now. They headed down the highway, riding as fast as possible. As they traveled farther from the secret complex, Sam's terror level ramped up. *They're out here!* he thought. He heard Jade gasp beside him. He followed her gaze and saw a massive yellow-pink glow rising to the left. A gigantic, dark, mushroom-shaped object emerged from its center, moving slowly and soundlessly until it rested over Sam and Jade. Bathed in its pinkish glow, they stared dumbly up at the broad metallic underside, unable to speak or move. *Do not fear*, Sam thought—or heard.

He didn't remember the ride back to Cassidy. They arrived home around four a.m., instead of two thirty as planned. Exhausted, they simply said goodnight and went to their respective homes. Sam slept deeply; if he dreamed, he didn't remember.

CHAPTER 12
JADE'S REVELATION

JADE HAD SUDDENLY REALIZED that whoever ran the secret complex must be using the old mines, too. That was why the aboveground buildings were so small—most of the action was underground! She called Sam the next morning, excited to share her revelation. Sam was annoyed he hadn't thought of it. He also felt unsettled and vaguely disturbed, as though there was something important he should remember. Something about the Night People. But it was gone.

There had to be miles of abandoned mines, probably all interconnected, Jade said. And the abandoned doorway—had that once led into the complex? If they could get it open again (which, granted, seemed impossible), or find another smaller back door in the area, perhaps they could sneak in from behind. Jade was less sure about her other idea—that during their missing time episode, they had been spirited into the underground facility. She had no idea how to prove it, but she hoped getting inside might trigger their memories.

They were sitting at their usual table in the park. Jade was being strange—Sam knew there was something on her mind besides the back door and the underground complex. She had been slightly distant since they had renewed their partnership. More so today. Like she wasn't quite sure of him or maybe hadn't quite forgiven him for deserting her. Sam wouldn't blame her—he had been kind of a jerk. He considered telling her about his unsettled feeling, but he couldn't put it into words. And making things right with her was more important.

Maybe he should apologize again. Talking about personal things was new for him—and hard. But this was Jade. He asked hesitantly, "Are you okay? Is something bothering you?"

She looked a bit startled. After a pause, she said, "I dreamed about my dad last night."

"Oh." Sam wasn't sure how to respond. Finally, he asked, "Is that good or bad?"

She shook her head, refusing to meet his eyes. That was unusual.

"You don't have to tell me if you don't want to," he said. "You just seemed . . . I don't know, upset. I was afraid . . . you were still mad at me."

She looked up at him. "No, I'm not mad." She blushed. "This is kind of embarrassing."

"You don't have to tell me."

"No, I should. I dreamed about both of you. I saw him, and he changed into you. It's like you became the same person. I think . . . I was realizing how much you're like him."

Sam's eyes opened wide. He knew he was blushing. "Like your *dad*?"

Jade gave a small laugh. "That's not a bad thing, you know. You're crazy smart, like he was. You have the same rational way of looking at things. You even love good music."

Sam had confessed his newfound love of classical music and Jade told him she played the cello but had stopped taking lessons since her dad died. Playing reminded her too much of him—he had often accompanied her when she played solos. She showed him her cello, hidden in her bedroom closet. Then, she showed him YouTube videos of the 2CELLOS, playing both classical and pop songs. Which he had loved.

But this confession left Sam speechless. Finally, he said, "Well . . . thanks." He reminded her of her dad? Not quite the impression he was hoping to make.

Jade smiled slightly. After a pause, she said, "Anyway, Daddy would tell me to get smart about this secret complex thing. He taught me to think things through, and do research, and figure out the best approach. I got so carried away, I stopped thinking. I never rush in headlong the way I've done with this."

"This is kind of different." Sam commented. "Before, you were all gung-ho about visiting the place."

"I know. But we're seriously thinking of trying to break into a secret area that's plastered with Keep Out signs. If we get caught, we'll be in real trouble. And, if we do get in, what do we do? We have no idea what's in there or who. We don't know anything about what mines are like—at least I don't. We aren't prepared to go in there."

Sam hesitated. Finally, he asked, "What would your dad do?"

A look of sadness passed over Jade's face. Then, she straightened her shoulders and put on her practical face before answering matter-of-factly.

"He would probably research the mines, see what they're like inside. Then use that information to look for a way in."

"Then let's do the research," Sam said. "But we can't do it together—I'll have to go to the library. No computer." He sighed. "I really have to get one. Maybe I can find a used tablet or something."

Jade nodded. "The sooner the better. You'll need one for

school anyway. You have some money from working this summer, right?"

"Some. Not enough for a laptop, though."

"We'll find you something used online. For now, let's just use mine."

Several hours later, they had a much better idea of what the old lead and zinc mines looked like. Mainly dirty and nasty, Sam thought. Definitely not exciting or romantic. The only interesting thing they found was a map showing the extent of the original mines. They were huge, encompassing parts of Kansas, Oklahoma, and Missouri. Nothing that really helped them.

―――

The next day, they took off as soon as Jade's mother left for work. They went to the doorway, rather than the secret complex. Deep down, they knew there was no way of getting in, but they gave it one last try. They examined the doorway along both sides and the bottom. They checked around the rest of the chat pile, looking for another door, a crack, any opening. Nothing. No suggestion of anything inside. It was just a giant rocky chat pile, with one strangely flat side. Now, their backpacks lay open, tools discarded on the ground. Sam looked up; Jade was leaning against a nearby boulder, her face mask on the ground beside her. He sighed.

"This is a waste of time," he said.

"You're right," Jade agreed. "I don't know what I was thinking."

"Not your fault. We knew it was a long shot. And it was the only idea we had."

Sam leaned back against the boulder next to Jade. He pulled off his face mask and dropped it. He was feeling light-headed. Inside his mind, a picture startled him—two military men confronting each other: the large, friendly Black guy he had seen before, and another smaller one—angry, mean, red-faced. Sam shivered. Suddenly, his body began to tingle. He heard a clear, quiet voice inside his head. *Now, it is time.* He couldn't move. He heard Jade calling his name, and knew she was frightened, but he couldn't respond. She grasped his arm, shaking him. He felt her hand begin to tingle, too. And then, blackness.

CHAPTER 13
UNDERGROUND

AWARENESS RETURNED SLOWLY. Sam and Jade sat up, shaking their heads. Sam's fingers tingled; every hair on his body stood on end. Jade was rubbing her arms. The light around them was dim, like twilight. It wasn't obvious where they were or where the light was coming from. It was cool, and there was no sun. Jade's eyes swept the area, moving up and up and up. She gasped as she took in the vast space above and around them. Sam followed her gaze.

"Oh, crap," he breathed.

"Where are we? Are we in the mine?" whispered Jade. Sam nodded.

"I think we made it inside the complex," he said faintly.

"But how? We never got the door open!" Jade's voice was urgent, scared. In a tiny corner of his mind—the only part not buzzing with panic—Sam realized it was the first time he had seen her truly afraid. Even when they woke up outside the secret complex, she hadn't seemed that scared, just mostly curious about what had happened. He grasped her hand and looked around slowly. The dim light was emanating from both the left and right. There were huge tunnels at both ends of the space.

"We didn't do this. We couldn't have." Sam had no idea where they were, but he knew they hadn't come here by themselves. The voice had brought them—the Night People. *Now, it is time*, the voice had said. Time for what, exactly? Then he remembered the two men. Had one of them brought them here? If so, which one—the mean one or the friendly one?

Thoughts of the NP, and their mysterious helpers, galvanized him into action. "Let's move," he urged. "We're right out in the open."

They stood up quickly but hesitated again. There were few places to hide. The space was gigantic and empty, except for several huge floor-to-ceiling pillars. The walls curved upward into a dome at least a hundred feet high. So, they were far below ground. They were near one end of the huge space. Behind them, where they had awakened, there was no obvious wall, just loose rocks. A floor-to-ceiling, mountain-sized pile of debris. Like an indoor chat pile. Ahead, there was just the gigantic open domed area and the two tunnels.

In the dim light, the cavern sides and ceiling appeared to be dull, hollowed-out rock, grayish-white, with red streaks. Rust, he thought. Iron oxide. He was remembering last year's lessons on the mines and chat piles. He took a deep breath. *Good. Think of facts, practical things. Control the panic.* The walls had straight vertical gouges at equal distances, reaching up and over the dome. *Machines did this. Huge machines.* The floor space was maybe five times as wide as the ceiling height. Straight ahead was a wall, and in front of it, two tracks running across the cavern and through both tunnels. They were odd, not like typical train tracks. Newer, wider, flatter. Shiny. The tunnels were maybe thirty or forty feet high and almost as wide. At least the space continued on in both directions. And the tracks meant there was a way out.

"Let's take a look," he suggested.

Still clasping hands, they moved quietly toward the left-hand tunnel. It seemed safest to stay near a wall, or at least a pillar, in case someone showed up. They peered down the tunnel, but there wasn't much to see. Inside, it was grayish-white, like rock, but smoother and shinier than the open cavern space—more like ceramic or glass. *Melted rock?* The light was diffuse and seemed to come from somewhere inside the tunnel walls or ceiling.

Suddenly Jade pulled on his hand. "Listen," she said.

The space had been quiet. Now, a rumbling sound echoed through the tunnel, a vibration that shook everything and spread through their bodies. The rumble became louder. It was accompanied by a whooshing sound and, at one point, a short shriek that made them wince. The sound engulfed them, like standing too close to a jet engine. They backed up and covered their ears. A blinding light appeared far down the tunnel. Almost instantly, a short, bright-red and silver train car roared through the opening past them and disappeared through the tunnel at the far end. As the train passed, its rushing wind knocked them backward off their feet. The noise and vibration were gone as quickly as they had appeared.

As they picked themselves up, Jade said, "I could swear that train wasn't touching the track."

"Yeah, it wasn't," Sam said.

"But that's impossible!"

"After this, you still believe in impossible?"

Jade's laugh was shaky. "Good point," she said.

The train had been a brief distraction, but the central problems remained. Where were they? How did they get here? How would they get out? How would they explain being here if they got caught? Someone, somewhere, had to be running the train—or trains. And presumably someone was riding on them. Sam and Jade stared at each other. No need for discussion—their situation was obvious. Sam was terrified, but they couldn't pass up this opportunity.

He said, "Well, we're finally down here. Maybe we can find out what's going on. Plus, we have to figure out how to get out."

Jade was breathing deeply, probably trying to curb her panic. Finally, she nodded.

"We need to find out where the people are. Maybe there's an underground city. Or at least a train station."

"Yeah," Sam agreed. But he still hesitated. Jade might be getting it together, but he wasn't sure he was. He kept thinking of the Night People. The NP had brought them here, he knew. But why? Did they *want* him and Jade to get caught by evil humans (the mean guy he had seen, maybe)? He shook his head. Didn't matter. They were here. He started forward.

"Wait," Jade said. "If we meet someone, we should have the same story about how we got here. We can't just tell the truth."

"Why not?" Sam responded. He paused. "I've spent my life having to get out of sticky situations," he said. "I've found it's best to be as honest as possible but say as little as possible—and if you're backed into a corner, pretend you don't know or can't remember."

Jade gave him a sidelong glance. "Wow. We'll discuss your lying skills later. Right now, I bow to your superior abilities." She actually bowed her head, giving him a slight grin. "What should we say?"

"The truth—we have no idea how we got here. We were exploring the chat piles, stopped to rest, and woke up here."

"Nobody will buy that," Jade objected.

"First, it's true, and second, they can't argue with it. If they know an ordinary way we could get in, they'll check and find out we didn't. If this place is secret, every way in will be monitored. If they do know how we got here, they won't admit it because it'll be top secret. Plus, the fact that we got in at all means they're not really in control. So, what can they do?"

"I hope you're right. How did you figure all this out?"

Sam shrugged. "It just seems . . . reasonable."

Jade shook her head. "You really are incredibly smart, you know," she said. "Logical, like my dad."

Briefly, delight overcame Sam's fear. She had compared him to her dad—again! It was still weird, but he knew it was an incredible compliment. He gave her a small smile.

"We have to follow the train," he said.

This part of the mine was abandoned, but the train meant other parts were not. Sam wasn't sure of directions down here, but if they assumed the area where they woke up was just under the chat pile, the train must have been heading toward the secret complex, at least the underground part of it. It should be maybe a mile away. They followed the track and entered the far end of the tunnel. There was plenty of space to walk beside the tracks, and the muted light made things bright enough to see.

They settled into a quick walk, almost a jog. Neither wanted to be caught in the tunnel when another train came by. The tunnel sloped downward, not steeply, but enough to speed up their travel. As they jogged, they talked quietly. They agreed they must have been brought here for a reason, maybe to figure out what this place was. Maybe when they learned what they were supposed to learn, whoever had brought them here would return them to the surface. Or maybe they would find a way out as they explored. Sam was careful not to mention the voice. Or the two men. He didn't *think* he was crazy, but . . .

The light finally brightened and the tunnel opened out on either side of the tracks. Sam and Jade stopped just inside the tunnel to stare. A subway station would be narrow and enclosed, with tracks and passenger walkways. This was a city—an underground city with a train track running through it. On either side, as far as they could see, were streets, buildings, people walking. But they weren't really buildings. Each side of a street was one huge, curvy, rocky sculpture. The rock was shiny, like the inside of the tunnels. You could tell individual buildings by differences in their size and shape, and Sam knew that inside, there must be steel and other technological materials. But outside, the effect was organic and natural. Like giant caves. He hadn't doubted that the train system was human made, but these strange buildings gave him pause. Were they entirely human or were they partly alien-inspired?

There were no vehicles other than occasional bicycles. The streets were narrow, and the nearest one had an iridescent strip, wide enough for five or six people, running down the middle. The strip was moving.

"It's an automatic walkway, like in airports!" Jade whispered. "Like an escalator, only horizontal. They must use this instead of cars or buses. Cool!"

The city seemed compact and efficient. Very quiet, without vehicles. Along the tracks were occasional stone pillars, made of the same shiny substance—melted and cooled rock, Sam was sure. The whole city had a peculiar, almost alien vibe to it, Sam decided, as though the NP's . . . essence had touched it.

Their eyes were drawn upward to a brightly lit dome, crisscrossed with intricate supporting bars forming rectangles, triangles, and starbursts. It was maybe two-thirds as high as the abandoned mine area—and much more impressive. From this vantage point, the city looked larger than Cassidy. Many of its buildings were taller—not skyscrapers, but multistoried, maybe five or six stories. It looked so clean, and futuristic, and . . . His imagination failed him. It didn't look like anything he had ever seen, even online.

"Not like New York subways," Jade murmured beside him. She looked a bit dazed.

"No," Sam agreed, gazing around wide-eyed. "More like a future city. Or an alien one. Wonder if anyone up top knows about this."

Venturing cautiously from the tunnel, they walked quickly and quietly toward the nearest buildings on their right. They stayed close to the buildings, trying to avoid being noticed. Like any city, it had restaurants and shops. These had regular windows. Other buildings were completely enclosed or had darkened windows—one-way glass, maybe? That would figure if this was a secret base. Sam's eyes gravitated to a vertical, glassed-in structure at the far end. He saw movement inside and realized it was an elevator. He touched Jade's arm and pointed. As they watched, the car inside moved down past their line of sight. There was more to this place than they could see! He wondered how deep the elevator went—and what was down there.

Of the few people visible, many wore military uniforms or fatigues. Sam could see army, navy, air force. They must be cooperating. He supposed they did that; although on the surface, he was pretty sure military bases were for single branches. Others wore civilian clothes. What were they doing in a secret military base? Who would be in a secret base? Secret agents? Not Night People, it seemed. Or at least, if they lived here, they were hidden.

The train was gone; it apparently hadn't stopped here.

It was ironic. They had worked so hard to figure out how to get in here. And now, here they were, dropped in by some agency Sam couldn't identify, and his main thought was, how were they going to get out? He was pretty sure they would get into trouble before that happened, but they were stuck for the moment. Might as well make the most of it and learn what they could. He wondered about the NP, though. Why drop them here if they weren't going to show up?

"Well," he said quietly, glancing at Jade, "we need to look around. But how do we keep from getting caught?"

She shook her head. "We'll have a hard time hiding. Wish we could find some uniforms or something, but that's not likely. Maybe just try to act normal—like we belong here? Stay in the shadows? And walk, don't run?"

"Worth a try," Sam agreed. "I'd like to know where those trains go."

Jade pointed to a lit sign on an attached building several hundred yards ahead. It had a picture of a train car with a bullet-shaped nose, red with a silver top, like the one they had just seen. They headed toward the train station, walking as casually as they could.

Acting like they belonged wasn't easy given their barely controlled fear, their obvious youth, and their grubby shorts and T-shirts. They stayed close to the buildings. Fortunately, the street was almost deserted. They reached the train station and peered in, ready to duck down or run if anyone was inside. There was no one. Sam nudged Jade and pointed to a large U.S. map over the counter, titled Maglev Routes. It had an amazing number of stops on it. They saw a jagged line across the middle of the country, with several short side stops. A red star showed their location, and a short southward jag emanating from it suggested where the last train had come from—Tulsa, maybe?

"Maglev," Sam said under his breath. "That explains why it wasn't touching the tracks. I had no idea the U.S. was using maglev."

"Okay, genius, remind me what maglev means?" asked Jade.

"Short for 'magnetic levitation.' They run on magnets—

one set keeps the train above the track and another set pushes it forward. It's efficient—no friction, no carbon pollution."

"And you know this because . . .?"

Sam shrugged. "I read a lot, remember? I know a lot of weird stuff. They're noisier than I expected, though."

He stared at the map for a moment. "Jade, d'you have your phone handy?"

"Yes."

"Can you take a photo of that map without anyone noticing?"

Jade brought her phone out of her pocket and pointed it through the glass. While Sam shielded her with his body, she took several quick snaps of the map.

"Looks like over a hundred stops, some of them really big," she said. "The next one west looks like Hutchinson, maybe? A couple in Colorado, a bunch in the Southwest, and in California. They're not all in big cities."

Sam was stealing glances at the map, in between scrutinizing their surroundings. "They go all across the country, both directions from here."

"Yeah. There's one in western Missouri, not far from Kansas City. But not in it, either."

"Whiteman Air Force Base, maybe," Sam mused. "I'll bet these stops are all military bases. A whole underground military nobody knows about. What do they *do* down here?"

Jade shook her head. "Let's look around. Maybe we can figure it out."

They moved past the station and looked into other windows. Jade kept her phone out, discreetly photographing the city—the buildings, the dome, the walkway. They would be caught, Sam thought, but maybe they could get some clues first. At least, getting caught would get them back to the surface. Unless they were thrown into a dungeon down here and forgotten. He quickly suppressed that thought. They walked down the sidewalk, sticking close to the shops. They looked for names of businesses or any indication of what was going on inside. There was little to see. Apparently, people down here didn't need signs—they knew where to go and what to do. Several doors were marked Authorized Personnel Only. One had a radiation sign—the only logo they recognized.

"This is frustrating!" Jade said. "Presumably whoever put us down here expected us to figure out what this place was and what's going on. But how are we supposed to find out anything? Should we just walk in someplace and ask?"

"Let's head for that elevator," Sam suggested. "If we can get on it and go down, maybe we'll get some idea of what they do."

Jade nodded in agreement, and they continued walking toward the elevator, trying not to attract attention. A small insignia on a window caught their eyes. As they leaned closer to examine it, they heard a shout from the direction of the elevator. A young man in fatigues was running toward them.

"I know you two. You were snooping around the gates the other night. What the hell are you doing down here? How did you get in here?"

They were caught.

CHAPTER 14
MAJOR JEPSON

PANIC, already simmering just below the surface, instantly boiled over. Without hesitation, Sam and Jade turned and ran back down the street. They passed the train station and the storefronts and raced into the tunnel, running full speed back in the direction they had come. This time, the tunnel sloped upward, slowing their progress. They heard shouts and running footsteps behind them, but they did not look back. Sam had no clue what they would do when they reached the abandoned mine, but right now, they just ran.

They were more than halfway back, and their pursuers were gaining on them, when a massive shudder ran through the tunnel. They were thrown to the ground, and the shaking continued for a long minute before gradually dying away. The air was thick with dust, but nothing larger was falling. The tunnel appeared intact.

"Was that an earthquake?" Jade asked incredulously. She was covered in dust and gasping for breath, and her eyes looked wild and stunned. Sam had no doubt he looked the same.

"Must have been," he gasped. "I knew we were starting to have quakes around here, but I never felt one before."

"Since when does Kansas have earthquakes?"

"Since the oil companies started fracking," Sam replied.

"What's fracking?"

"Later. We'd better keep moving. That guy won't stop, and I think he has buddies."

They picked themselves up and ran on, finally reaching the abandoned mine. The earthquake damage was worse there. Nothing had caved in—the quake hadn't been that strong—but the air was filled with dust, and rocks and gravel were strewn everywhere. The space also seemed lighter than before. At the top of the rock pile at the far end, a few tiny rays of sunlight penetrated. The rocks had shifted, opening up cracks to the outside. The openings were small, but surely, they could shift enough rocks to make a crawl space. They were at least a hundred feet below the surface, and it would be a steep climb, but they could get out. They flew across the open space and leapt onto the pile. Sharp rocks cut into their hands and knees, but they kept going. They were about halfway up when they heard shouts behind them.

"Stop right there. Get back down here. There's nowhere you can go."

Sam risked a glance back. The same young soldier was standing below them, a scowl on his face and a gun in his hand. The gun was pointed directly at Sam. Another soldier stood beside him, his gun pointed at Jade. Sam looked up at Jade poised motionless a few steps above him. Her shoulders were slumped in defeat, and he could see the terror in her eyes.

"Okay, fine," Sam said. His voice was shaking. "Don't shoot. We'll come down."

Even though he was trembling as he slowly climbed down, Sam tried to put on a brave face to keep Jade from freaking out any more than she already was. At least, getting caught gave them a way out of the underground. But what would happen *before* they got out? His insides were curdled with fear, and he thought he might faint. But he couldn't. He had to suck it up and stay strong—for Jade and for himself.

As Sam and Jade touched down on the mine floor, the soldiers stepped forward. The first one—Jimenez, his name patch said—kept his weapon trained on them. Within thirty seconds, his buddy—Nelson—had handcuffed them both. Sam sneaked a glance at Jade; she was quiet and trembling. She was usually so brave, but this was far outside her experience. He wanted to squeeze her hand in reassurance, but his hands—and hers—were cuffed behind their backs. He settled for winking at her and mouthing "it's okay." It wasn't, of course, and she knew it, but what else could he say?

"Move," ordered Jimenez. The soldiers' weapons remained drawn as they hustled Sam and Jade before them, back toward the tunnel and the underground city. Jimenez went first, grasping Sam's arm; Nelson followed, grasping Jade's.

Sam took a deep breath, hoping to quell the tremor in his voice. "Where are you taking us?" he asked. It worked—he sounded much braver than he felt.

"Shut up!" snapped Jimenez. Okay, then. No talking.

He had to hold it together. He kept taking deep breaths, one after the other. It helped control his terror with the NP; maybe it would help here, too. He had no problem staying upright—Jimenez was grasping his arm and forcing him along. Jade was hidden by Nelson, but he could hear her uneven breathing. She was more rattled than he was. And both soldiers seemed really jumpy, constantly glancing sideways at Sam. Why were *they* nervous? He and Jade were the ones in trouble.

As they left the tunnel and entered the underground city, they slowed down. Maybe they didn't want to attract attention? A little late for that. Two grim-faced soldiers, guns drawn, marching a pair of grubby, handcuffed teenagers through this bright, pristine street? Yeah, they stood out. People were watching, with expressions ranging from mild interest to shock. Sam had imagined lots of bad things happening to him but being marched down a public street in handcuffs was not one of them. How humiliated could you be and still survive? And Jade's silence was starting to worry him. Normally, she would be screaming that they needed to see a lawyer or at least get a phone call. For now, all he could do for her was be an example of courage. He pursed his lips tightly, stood up straight, held his head high, and stared straight ahead as he walked.

At the end of the street, the soldiers marched them into the glass elevator. Jimenez pressed a button, and they traveled down many floors. Between floors, rough walls of rock surrounded the elevator's glass sides; light open spaces strobed by as they passed each floor, but the speed was too great for Sam to tell what was going on. The elevator stopped in a bright area dotted with cubicles where people worked busily; only a few looked up as they left the elevator. Their captors led them away from the work area and down a darker corridor with thick steel doors on either side. Jimenez unlocked a door and gestured for Sam to go ahead of him. Jade started to move forward, too, but Nelson held her back, giving her a sardonic grin.

"Not so fast, sweetheart. You don't think we're stupid enough to leave the two of you together so you can get your stories straight? You get your own cell."

"Cell?" screamed Jade. "You can't arrest us. We haven't done anything. We have rights! We need to make a phone call. We need a lawyer!"

Sam sighed in relief. Jade was back.

Then, he jumped as the door slammed behind him. The lock turned. Jade was gone; he was totally alone. He drew a shaky breath and looked around. This was not a cell; it was an interrogation room. Everything was dark gray. A steel table in the middle had four heavy steel chairs, two on each side. The table and chairs were bolted to the floor; the chairs had chains that looked like they were used to fasten prisoners in place. There were cameras in all four corners and a large opaque window on one side. He'd seen enough TV cop shows to assume someone was watching him. The idea both frightened and infuriated him. How could he convince his captors that he and Jade hadn't intended to come here?

Sam felt the same helplessness he felt with the Night People. Jade was getting it together, finally, but he was still worried about her. She was smart and self-sufficient, but she had never been in a situation like this. Of course, neither had he. How could he help her when he couldn't even help himself? Briefly succumbing to despair, he rested his head on his folded arms. He was exhausted from the day's events, but fear surged through his body, making him hyperalert. Adrenaline, he thought—fight or flight. Something else he had learned from Mr. Macklin, this time in eighth-grade life science. Too bad Macklin hadn't taught him how to use those feelings.

At least, with his face hidden, he could think without anyone monitoring his expressions. Maybe they would think he was crying or asleep—either might give him an advantage. But the only plan he could come up with was telling the truth, as he and Jade had discussed. Jade knew nothing about the Night People, so she could give nothing away. And he certainly wouldn't. He might be just a kid, but he would stand up to his questioners. He was done being a coward.

Sam had no idea how long he sat there, head on his arms, but he must have dozed off. A sound at the door jolted him awake. He looked up and gasped. The man who entered was older, with close-cropped graying hair and a red face. It was the mean, angry man from his vision. He wore a military uniform with a gold leaf-like insignia; he was an officer, but Sam wasn't sure what rank. Military ranks—one of the many things he hadn't yet studied. He'd had no idea the information might be useful. A nameplate on the officer's left pocket said Jepson. His small, menacing eyes were fixed on Sam.

"How did you get into this facility?" Jepson demanded. His glare and his harsh voice instantly drained Sam of all courage. He shook with fear and stuttered as he tried to answer.

"I—I don't know," was all he could manage.

"Don't lie to me," Jepson snapped. "How did you get in here?"

Forcing himself to take slow, deep breaths, Sam felt his body begin to relax. If not exactly calm, he could at least make himself less terrified. Like he did with the Night People. And the simple act of not backing down gave him strength.

Just before Jepson began to shout at him again, Sam said, "I don't know how we got in. We were exploring the chat piles. We got really tired, so we leaned against a boulder and fell asleep. When we woke up, we were here."

Of course, Jepson didn't believe him—he barely believed himself. The interrogation that followed was grueling. For more than an hour, Jepson fired questions at Sam. How did they get in? Why were they snooping? What had they learned? Who were they working with? *Working with?* Why would Jepson think they were working with someone? He asked the same questions over and over, in slightly different ways, trying to trip Sam up. Between questions, he alternated outraged shouting with soft, menacing threats. Sam's fear was acute—fear of Jepson, of being separated from Jade, of being imprisoned with no one knowing their whereabouts. But every time the fear welled up, he forced himself to quash it. He could handle the Night People; surely, he could handle this bully.

Sam might be only fifteen, but he considered himself grown-up. He took care of himself. Throughout Jepson's interrogation, he firmly told himself he didn't need a rescuer. He didn't need an adult to show up and make Jepson stop. Even if his parents knew where he was, neither would come for him. And if they did, he wouldn't be safe. His father would call him worthless and say he got here through his own stupidity. And then beat him for embarrassing them. He had been twelve the last time that happened, but today's events would definitely trigger his fury and abuse. His mother wouldn't hit him, but she would blame him—she would say he must have done something wrong to end up here.

Jade's mother was different—if they were even an hour or two late returning home, she would harass the police and everyone else until she found her daughter. And Jade would tell them about Sam. But would it help? No one knew about the underground base. No one knew about Jepson.

After Sam denied, yet again, that he had deliberately trespassed in the underground base, Jepson roared, "You're lying! I know you're working with them!"

Suddenly, it became clear. Jepson had seen the videos of Sam and Jade outside the secret complex. He knew what had happened during their two hours of missing time. Had he seen them disappear? Had he seen the Night People? He must think Sam knew what had happened. Or he wanted Sam to admit that he and Jade were working with the Night People. Well, if he wanted that, he'd be waiting a long time. Still, it was odd—Jepson's eyes were filled with fear, like his mother's when she was thinking about the Night People. Why were they so afraid? Jepson's questions made it seem like the NP were evil. They were scary, no question, but they didn't seem to hurt people. Jepson, on the other hand . . . Jepson was military, so Sam should trust him, he supposed. But he didn't. There was something really off about the man.

Exhausted, Sam rested his head on his arms again. Jepson moved behind him and grabbed a fistful of his hair, pulling his head upright and looking into his eyes.

"Answer me!" he shouted.

Sam was fed up. "Enough!" he shouted. "I don't know how we got here. I'm not working with anybody, and I haven't done anything. Neither has Jade. Let us go."

With a disgusted snort, Jepson let go of Sam's hair and walked around the table, head down, frowning.

"Where's Jade?" Sam asked. "You can't just keep us here. We need to go home, or we need a lawyer. We haven't done anything."

"Haven't done anything? You are in violation of United States Code Section 1382 of Title 18. You are trespassing on a military base—a secret one at that. The only question is whether you came here with the specific intent to do harm."

"We *didn't*," Sam insisted. "We didn't even intend to come here, so how could we intend to do harm?"

"Well, you'd better hope your little partner in crime is telling the same tale you are."

Finally, Jepson heaved a gigantic sigh and left Sam alone in the gray room, slamming the door. Sam slumped with relief. It occurred to him that neither Jimenez nor Jepson had put the chains on him. What did that mean? Maybe Jepson assumed he was no threat because he was just a kid. A fair assumption, he reflected. He not only hadn't posed a threat; he had barely held his act together. Eventually, Jepson returned, looking angry but resigned.

"Well, it's your lucky day. Since we can't prove you came here with intent, we can't hold you. But understand—from this moment on, you are banned from this facility. If you ever show up here again, even on the outside, you will be in violation of the law, and I will put you in prison. Is that clear?"

"Yes, sir. Very clear. Where's Jade? Can we go now? Please?"

"Oh, yes, we're going now. Time to inform your parents what you've been up to."

CHAPTER 15
AFTERMATH

JEPSON HERDED Sam out the door, back into the elevator, past the underground city, and all the way up to the ground-level entrance. It was the concrete building they had seen from the outside. The elevator was at the back. In front, an entryway led into several offices and a large room filled with screens—probably the security area that had caught them on video. Several soldiers were monitoring the screens, no doubt looking for trespassers.

Sam cringed at the thought of Jepson telling his parents what had happened. *Oh, please, let my father not be home*. He was briefly distracted from his fear when Jimenez appeared from a side office, pushing Jade in front of him. She looked tired, stressed, and slightly tearstained, but breathed a sigh of relief when she saw Sam. He sighed, too, only then realizing he had been holding his breath.

"Are you okay?" he asked. Jade nodded.

"You?" she asked. He nodded, too.

Jepson frowned at both of them, his eyes narrowed. "You two will say nothing to anyone, ever, about being inside this facility. As far as you're concerned, there *is* no underground facility. Understood?"

"Yes, sir." Neither of them argued; they wanted out of there.

The trip to Jade's house was short; with Jepson in the car, they had no chance to talk. Jade's mother came running out of the house when she saw the car, and sagged with relief as Jade and Sam got out. Her eyes widened at the sight of the army officer accompanying them.

"Mrs. Mathieson?" Jepson asked.

"*Doctor* Mathieson," Jade's mother corrected him, drawing herself up as tall as possible. Her voice was crisp. Sam relaxed slightly—it appeared she too had taken an instant dislike to Jepson and would not be intimidated.

Jepson nodded. "Major Benjamin Jepson," he introduced himself. "We need to talk about your daughter's activities."

Jade's mom looked Sam and Jade over quickly but carefully. "Are you two okay?" she asked. They both nodded.

"All right, come in," she told Jepson.

Jepson's description of the afternoon's events was accurate, up to a point. But he glossed over both the location of the military base and the fact that Sam and Jade had been inside it. Jepson did not paint them as criminals, as Sam had expected. He did make it clear they had trespassed and would be in big trouble if it happened again. Unfortunately, Sam knew Jepson's sudden reasonableness would not impress his father. Being delivered home by an army officer was enough to doom him. If his mother was home, and if Sam was lucky, she might stop the beating before it got too bad.

"But they're not in trouble now?" Dr. Mathieson asked. "There will be no repercussions from what they've done?"

"Not if they stay away from the base from now on," Jepson said.

"They *will* stay away." She eyed both teens sternly as she spoke.

Jepson raised his eyebrows. "You're in charge of the boy, too?"

"Sam's not my son. But he and my daughter always explore together, and if she doesn't go, he won't either. Right, Sam?" Her look pinned him to his chair.

"Yes, ma'am," he said. He knew Dr. Mathieson would have plenty to say to both him and Jade later, but for now, she was protecting him from Jepson, and he was grateful.

"Hmph," grunted Jepson. He didn't look convinced. "Well, I still have to deliver him home and tell his parents what he's done. Let's go, kid."

"Bye," Sam said to both of them, trying his best to project nonchalance rather than dread. The last thing he wanted was for Jade and her mother to know about his home life. But Dr. Mathieson was giving him one of those keen looks that seemed to see inside him, and Jade's eyes followed him with worry.

Neither he nor Jepson said anything on the drive to his house. When they arrived, Sam slumped further in his seat. Things were as bad as they could be. His father was home. His mother was not.

———

Sam fought back this time, but his dad was far too big and strong. Although he had grown several inches in the past year, Sam was still only five-nine. He was growing up tall and thin like Grandpa Joe, his mom's dad. His dad was six-three and built like a refrigerator. Still, Sam was quick and strong, and he didn't run away. He got in several hard kicks, including one in the butt that made his dad roar with rage. But his dad punched him all over and didn't quit until Sam managed to grab his nose and twist it savagely. When his dad screamed and let loose, Sam escaped.

Afterward, he frantically considered how to hide his misery from Jade and her mom. He was in pain and would need at least three or four days to recover. Not that there were any visible marks—even drunk, his dad was careful about that. But it was hard to walk or sit or even breathe normally and impossible to run or ride his bike. In the past, he had either holed up in his room or deep in the woods. But this time, he had a friend and she had an inquisitive mother, and high school enrollment was tomorrow. If they noticed anything, they would force the story out of him.

Sam wondered yet again why his dad hated him so much. During junior high, he had tried to piece the story together: things his mother accidentally let slip, bits overheard at school, snippets from old yearbooks and photos. His dad had been a football star—good-looking, popular, set to go places after graduation. His mom was really pretty and always on the honor roll. Neither of them was in the yearbook their senior year—the year he was born. It was no mystery what had happened and why they both resented him. But damn it, it wasn't *his* fault. He was younger now than they had been, and he knew about birth control. Why hadn't they? And they'd had other choices—adoption, even abortion. Still, his dad's hatred seemed extreme. Sam was convinced it had to do with the NP, although he had no real evidence. He sighed. Nothing he could do, except avoid his father and recover.

Sam went alone to enroll; he didn't need—or want—a parent. Jade and her mom were already there, and Jade's mom insisted on helping him. He gave in, easing himself onto a chair and moving as little as possible. They didn't seem to notice. He ended up having English, Spanish, and biology with Jade. That might make school more bearable. Jade knew Sam loved music and listened all the time, and she begged him to join mixed chorus with her. Her mom was making her take it. She wanted Jade to get back into music to help her deal with her continuing grief. Sam had always avoided such activities—too much socializing—but they got credit for chorus, and it was only two days a week. Finally, Sam agreed. He liked singing, and Jade needed his support. If his singing was really bad, the choral director could always kick him out.

Jade's mom took Sam to lunch and back to their house afterward. Sam knew she wanted to quiz him, and probably lecture him, on the irresponsible behavior that had led him and Jade to be nearly arrested by the military. Before lunch, Jade whispered to him that she was grounded for two weeks. Her mother had been unsatisfied with her explanation of the day's events. Jade had stuck to Jepson's account—they had seen only the outside of the base and the interrogation rooms. She had taken his warning seriously, leaving out the underground city and maglev trains. Besides, there was no way to explain how they got into the base. She was furious with her mother, and she hated being grounded, but Sam pointed out that house arrest was better than jail. And they agreed—the less their parents knew, the better.

Jade asked if he was grounded, and he shook his head.

"You didn't get in trouble?" She looked astonished.

He hesitated. Finally, he said, "Yeah, I got in trouble." But he looked away and didn't elaborate. Jade looked concerned but didn't push him.

Dr. Mathieson was nicer than Sam expected. She didn't blame him any more than she blamed Jade, and she seemed relieved when their stories coincided. But she was annoyed when he refused to give the location of the base, citing Jepson's warning. And she made both of them promise—again—to stay away from the military base and the chat piles. Sam was not happy and wasn't sure he could keep his promise, but he agreed.

Sam and Jade thought the military would leave them alone after they promised to stay away from the underground base, but Sam began to see a black SUV every time he left his house. It had no logo or insignia, and the windows were tinted, so he couldn't see who was inside. When he worked or went into town, the SUV followed. When he went to Jade's house, it parked nearby. When he left for home, it stayed close. It was a constant, silent, menacing presence. Jade had a similar shadow. They discussed alerting the police, but they knew it was Jepson or his lackey—and whatever Jepson told the police could get them into more trouble.

By three days before school started, Sam and Jade were both thoroughly spooked. They were still burning to know what was happening in the secret complex and why they had been dropped into it. But Jepson had banned them from returning, and Sam knew only the Night People could get them in. If that happened, they would be arrested. They had no control. Finally, they met at the park picnic table to discuss their next move. Within minutes, Major Jepson showed up and sat down.

Jade's bravado was back. "Why are you following us?" she demanded. "We haven't been near that place."

Jepson looked them over, smirking. "Been checking up on you two. You," he said, nodding at Jade, "you're a smart girl, just moved here from some hotshot Kansas City school. This grungy little country school's gonna be a comedown for you, huh?"

Jade's mouth opened in shock.

"What do you want with us? We're not bothering you or your military base. Leave us alone!" Sam sounded more assertive than he felt.

"And you!" Jepson turned to Sam. "A whole long list of

craziness in your records, isn't there? Better watch out. If this one finds out all the secrets you're keeping, maybe she won't be so keen to go exploring with you."

Sam felt his throat close up. What did this guy know about him?

"Please, leave us alone!" begged Jade. "We're doing what you asked."

Jepson stood up. "Just remember—I've got my eye on both of you. You won't make a move I don't know about. Got it?"

After Jepson left, Jade drew a shaky breath. "Sam," she said, "I've got to tell my mom about this. She's been a pain lately, and I won't tell her what happened at the base, but she needs to know he's harassing us."

Sam felt shaky, too. He didn't want Jade giving her mom any more information, but he couldn't stop her. And Jepson was definitely fishy. He was obviously a bully. He was so polite to their parents, yet so threatening to Sam and Jade. They might be safer if a parent knew that. He wondered exactly what Jepson's army job was. He had a uniform and access to the base, but there was something off about whatever he was doing. For one thing, he just acted creepy. For another, he seemed to be working alone. There were plenty of soldiers underground, but he was the only officer they had seen. Sam would feel safer if someone besides Jepson knew what was happening to them. Maybe he was being paranoid again, but he was afraid Jepson was conducting some kind of rogue operation on his own.

Sam shared his thoughts with Jade, and she agreed. She would tell her mom their suspicions and that Jepson had accessed their school records. Fortunately, she couldn't mention the Night People—she didn't know about them.

When Sam arrived home, neither parent was there, and his room had been completely trashed—books, papers, tablet, clothes, everything was tossed around the room. What were they looking for? He had nothing worth stealing except his used tablet, newly acquired with Jade's help, and it was still here. Wait! His Coward's Notebook! Quickly, he checked the compartment under his desk; the journal was safe. As were his Shakespeare and nature books. He heaved a sigh of relief. Jepson, he thought. Except Jepson had been with him and Jade. His lackey, Jimenez, then. His cell phone rang, and he dug it out of his pocket.

Jade's voice sounded hysterical. "Sam, my room—"

"Mine too," he said. "It must have been Jimenez."

"We are in so much trouble," Jade said.

"Check to see if he took anything," Sam said. "Meet me at the park at eight tomorrow. We have to figure something out."

CHAPTER 16
CONFESSIONS

NEITHER SAM nor Jade found anything missing from their rooms. Jimenez could have downloaded their hard drives onto a flash drive and walked away with a copy of their lives in his pocket. Although, why didn't he just access them from a military computer? Why trash their rooms? Intimidation, they decided. But why not threaten them with the videos of them outside the underground base? Perhaps they really did disappear and Jepson couldn't explain that.

So far, Sam had evaded Jade's questions about his secrets. He suggested Jepson probably just meant his previous visits to the chat piles. After all, how could he know anything about Sam's life? But she wasn't convinced. He had to tell her about the NP, and the knowledge left him almost numb with panic. He knew what happened when other people found out; Nick had made sure of that, way back in third grade. And if an adult found out, he was still convinced he would end up in a mental ward. But for her own safety, Jade had to know.

Now, Sam was in her bedroom, with a chair pulled up beside her desk. Her half-dozen new books on alien abductions were scattered across her bed. She was bent over her laptop, taking notes, flipping between her document and a website on underground military bases. She was focused on finding out what was going on inside the secret bases and how they had ended up inside one. But, sitting so close to Jade, Sam closed his eyes and his thoughts drifted away from underground bases, angry army officers, and strange Night People. Jade's hair was slightly damp and hanging loose. It smelled clean and citrusy, and he wanted to run his fingers through it.

No! He had to focus. Things were getting dangerous. It was no longer just missing time. They were being threatened by the military—well, one member of the military—for trespassing inside the base, even though they had no control over their actions. Sam couldn't see any way forward. He got up and paced the room, chewing on his fingernails.

On top of the major's threats, the NP had come again last night. Again, he couldn't remember much, except that his glimpses of the Night People were getting longer. Hands, mostly—long, thin, four-fingered hands. Huge black eyes, staring into his. Some kind of medical thing, like a probe, flitting in and out of his vision. And always smells. Musty. Spicy. Sulfurous. He knew they were near from the smells alone. And from the electricity—tingling, or sparks, or static. He remembered glimpses of the NP and humans in military uniforms working together, including the huge Black guy with the kind smile. He *really* wanted to meet that guy and find out what he knew. And what he was doing with the NP.

Why were the NP back? What did they want with him and Jade? The chat piles, the underground base, the NP . . . how were they connected? And who should they be afraid of —the NP, the military, or both? He continued to pace, searching for answers.

Jade kept glancing over at him. Finally, she said, "Maybe we can steal a gun and some ammunition and threaten

Jepson into telling us what they're doing. What do you think?"

"Yeah, maybe," Sam answered, still pacing.

Jade threw up her hands. "What is *wrong* with you?" she snapped. "I thought you wanted to figure out what's happening to us. You haven't heard a word I've said. And, you're biting your nails again."

Sam snatched his hand away from his mouth. Jade hated it when he chewed his fingernails. "Sorry, I'm just tired."

"You're not just tired. You're completely out of it. You're not just worried about Jepson and his threats, are you? There's something else. Like the weird things that happen to you, and what they have to do with all this. Right?"

He shook his head. "I don't know."

Jade's voice was exasperated. "Yes, you do. You just don't want to tell me. Sam, I need to know your secret. We're in this together. Besides, you know I'll get it out of you eventually!"

He couldn't help laughing. She was right. He couldn't keep anything from her. All his determination to go it alone evaporated around her. And he had promised they would be partners. It would take both of them to keep the major off their backs. And to figure out the mystery of the underground bases, especially since they had no sure way to get in —and were forbidden, anyway. Plus, Jade trusted him. No one ever had before. Maybe he should trust her, too.

"Well?" she said impatiently. She was watching him.

"Okay. You win. You need to know what's going on with me. I'm sorry I haven't told you everything." *And I won't now*, he promised himself. *Just what I have to*.

"But, if I tell you, you have to promise not to tell anyone else—not even your mother."

Jade rolled her eyes at him, but she promised. "Not even my mother."

Half an hour later, Sam was sitting on the floor, leaning back against Jade's bed, his head down. Sadie had crept in as he talked and snuggled into his lap. He stroked her, comforted by her warmth and soft purr. He felt drained and hoarse. He had never talked so much to anyone. Ever. He was both relieved and panicked now that Jade knew about the Night People. He had told her more than he intended, although not quite everything. She had twirled her chair around to face him and listened intently, asking brief questions only if he seemed ready to stop talking. Now, she took a deep breath.

"Wow!" she said. "You've been carrying all this around by yourself since you were five?" She seemed more upset by that than by the story itself. She also didn't seem angry that he had kept the NP from her. He was relieved.

He shrugged. "Who would I tell? My dad thought I was nuts. Still does. My mom was terrified I would say something in public and embarrass her. So, I couldn't really tell any other adults, could I? And you know what kids do to anyone who's different. I get enough grief when they just suspect things. I don't need more."

Jade remained silent. That never happened. He must have really shocked her.

Finally, he looked up. "So, do you believe me?"

"Of course, I believe you!" She paused. "To be honest, at first, I might not have. But after everything that's happened . . .. This is why you're so secretive about everything, isn't it? Like not wanting to tell anyone about the secret complex?"

"Yeah," he admitted. "I'm used to hiding the real me. And I've taken a big chance telling you. If you tell anyone at all, I'll end up in a mental hospital."

"Oh, that's crazy!" He gave her a look. "Sorry, poor choice of words. But seriously, even if people think you're weird, they're not going to lock you up! At least not in a mental hospital," she added, glancing toward the window. They couldn't see the black SUV, but they knew the major was out there somewhere, watching them.

"You don't know this place. Around here, being too different gets you locked up really fast. It happened to my aunt. I think something happened with my mom, too, but no one tells me anything, and I can't ask."

"Your aunt went to a mental hospital? Why?"

"I don't know. It was before I was born. Something happened when she was in high school, and they sent her to the state mental hospital. I think they released her, but she never came back here. My mom won't talk about her, but people at school call her Loony Lucy."

He hadn't told her about his own meltdown near the end of sixth grade, how it started with the NP, and the resulting fallout—the humiliation, the revival of the "alien boy" label, the mandatory trips to the counselor's office, the fear that the counselor could decide at any minute that he was crazy and should follow his aunt into the mysterious depths of the state mental health system. He also didn't mention that his aunt's name had come up during this time and kids had taunted him with Loony Lucy.

"Well, your secret's safe with me," Jade said.

Let's hope.

"And thank you for telling me. I'm glad we can trust each other." She paused. "I do have one question, though. Do you think all this is what the major meant when he said I don't know everything about you?"

Sam closed his eyes. "I don't know. Yesterday, I would have said no, he's just bluffing. How could he know about this? But last night, I had another dream or experience or whatever. And this time, there were humans with the NP—soldiers. I even kind of recognized one of them. Not him. But if they're working together, that could explain how they know things about me."

"Yes, but it's like the NP want us to get into the underground base, and the military want to keep us out."

"It does sound like they don't play well together, doesn't it? I wonder who's in charge."

They were both silent for a while. Then Jade said, a bit hesitantly, "You know, I haven't had any experiences as strange as yours. But I do have a lot of weird dreams. I call them Harry Potter dreams. They seem kind of like what happens to you."

There was a long pause. Apparently, Jade was as worried as he was about sharing. Who knew? Finally, he said, "Well, are you going to tell me? I told you my deepest secrets." *Most of them, anyway.*

She gave him a serious look. "Same deal, okay? You won't tell anyone?"

He nodded. "I promise." *She still doesn't get it. Who would I tell?*

Jade never saw people—Night People or otherwise—in her dreams, so at first, Sam didn't think they resembled his experiences. But as he listened, he began to change his mind. Even though she didn't see faces, there were obviously people involved. She described "wands" that pointed at her and touched her forehead, nose, or ears. Sam remembered the dream during his sixth-grade meltdown—the long probe with a bulb on the end being shoved far up his nostril and then pulled out without the bulb. He remembered his nosebleed the night before the meltdown, the first he'd ever had. He hadn't told Jade about the bulb or the nosebleed—even for him, the implications were too scary. And really, how different was a wand from a medical probe? It was all in the interpretation.

But it wasn't just wands and touching. Jade described

strange smells, which she related to potions in the Harry Potter books, although she never saw the potions. And she saw owls. Barn owls came and sat in her window or hovered outside and looked in. They came into her room at night and watched her from a corner—but when she came fully awake, they faded away. He felt a chill, remembering his experience when he saw the NP for the first time, and how they faded away as he awoke. His fear grew deeper as he listened. Finally, Jade stopped talking and stared at him. Sam stared back. He didn't trust himself to speak.

"I'm starting to feel pretty creeped out," Jade said. "I wasn't sure my dreams were related to what happened to you, but now . . ."

"They sound pretty related. Do they feel like dreams, or are they different?"

"Well, I always assumed they were dreams. What else would they be? But now that you've told me what happens to you, I don't know. They're really vivid, for one thing. With most dreams, I wake up and know I've been dreaming; I just can't remember much. But with these—some of the images are so clear, I can't forget them. And the same images keep coming back. Especially the wands. And the owls."

"I haven't told you, but I see a lot of owls, too. Not in my room or at my window. Out in the woods. The weird thing is, I see them in the daytime. I've always thought I was just lucky. Now I wonder if it's luck. And if they're really owls."

They sat quietly. Sam was comparing his experiences with Jade's. He knew she was doing the same. He was pretty sure they were coming to similar conclusions. The NP were visiting them both. They were having the same types of experiences. That meant the NP were probably taking them to the same place, maybe at the same times, although there was no way to compare dates. That could explain why, when they first met, they felt they already knew each other. And it meant they were probably intended to meet in "real life." That the NP wanted them together. That the NP were controlling them.

"Okay," Sam said finally. "There's one more thing. I wasn't going to tell you. I didn't want you to think I was totally insane. But you know everything else."

Jade gave him a searching look. "There's more?" she asked.

"Yeah." Sam took a deep breath. "I hear voices sometimes."

He told her about the day they met, when the voice told him, *Go! It's not time yet,* and the day they were taken into the underground base, when the same voice said, *Now, it is time.*

"You didn't think I needed to know that?" Jade demanded, her voice rising.

He couldn't meet her eyes. "I hoped everything would make sense without having to admit it. It's hard enough that *I* think I'm crazy, without having you think so, too."

She sighed. "Sam. You're not crazy. I've never thought so, and I still don't. Weird things happen to you, including the NP. In fact, I'd guess all the weird things happen *because* of the NP. Including the voices. Right?"

"I think so. I didn't put them all together until recently. But it makes sense. And for some reason, they want us both to know about the underground bases."

"But why? What are we supposed to do?"

"I have no idea."

CHAPTER 17
ABDUCTION

THEY CAME LONG AFTER MIDNIGHT. Sam was sunk deep in sleep and did not stir as they spirited him from his bed, through the closed window, and into the night. He awoke lying on his back, on what felt like a metal table. He was cold. The space around him felt thick and murky. It had an unnatural, unpleasant odor—mold mixed with something spicy and irritating. It was terrifying. And familiar. He opened his eyes and gasped. Huge, black, almond-shaped eyes were inches away, peering directly into his. The Night People! He tried to sit up but could not.

Be calm, the eyes said. *You are safe.* He was breathing heavily. His body trembled as fear surged through him. There was a cool touch on his forehead and then one on each temple. His breathing slowed and became steady. His body felt relaxed, but nothing would move, not even his head. He could see nothing except huge eyes.

Where am I? What are you doing to me?

The eyes reassured him. *You are safe. No harm will come.*

After a moment, nothing seemed to matter much. Whatever they were doing, it was okay. At some point, he became aware that Jade had appeared on a table beside him. They had floated her in, he thought. He vaguely remembered her lying flat in the air. Could that be right? Maybe—they could do plenty of things humans couldn't. There were a lot of them. They were all so similar and so busy. There were no colors here; everything was in shades of gray, like a moonlit night. He wanted to see clearly, but his vision was blurry and dim, like viewing things through fog. But that was okay, he guessed; he wasn't supposed to remember anything while he was here. This life was secret and separate from his waking life. The NP said so.

Over the next hour, things happened to him on the metal table—Sam had no idea what. He felt nothing. Then, the black eyes were looming over him again, staring into his. His senses subsided from vague to sleepy. He awoke in a round room, his mind still confused. He was not comfortable, but he was upright and able to control his body. After a few moments, the NP brought Jade to sit beside him. Again, he thought she had floated in. She looked groggy, but she reached out her hand and he grasped it. Other people surrounded them. Night People—and bigger ones. Military people? He couldn't tell; everything was blurry. He struggled to pay attention—he knew what they were showing him was vital and frightening. He had brief glimpses, brief thoughts: Earth, life, environment, danger, panic, destruction. Whatever it meant, he needed to understand it. He breathed deeply and focused with all his might.

The next morning, Sam lay in bed, feeling achy, fatigued, and extremely unsettled. He knew something important had happened the night before, but he could not bring it into focus. As usual, his mind felt blurry and he was grasping for any strong, clear memory that he could drag into the light of day. There were many glimpses of events and activities, but precise memories mostly remained just out of reach. His feelings, in contrast, were overwhelming. Mainly, he felt dread—something awful was about to happen, a catastrophe. He reached for his phone. He had to talk to Jade. Whatever it was, they had to stop it.

Half an hour later, they sat at the picnic table, trying to piece together their memories. It felt like a breakthrough that they could both remember the abduction and seeing each other there. They both remembered being together in a round gray room. And they both felt dread—and purpose. Vague, imprecise purpose centered on some unknown environmental catastrophe. And extreme dread related to the environmental catastrophe—whatever it was.

"We need to get specific," Sam said. "Can you remember anything at all—anything you saw or heard?"

Jade chewed on her lower lip, thinking hard. "Only one thing. I have this—impression—of Earth hanging in space, and we're watching it, seeing everything at once."

"You saw Earth from space? Was it . . . okay? Normal-looking?"

"Normal-looking? I guess. It was—beautiful. Blues and greens and whites and browns. So alive and, I don't know, peaceful."

"I remember glimpses of Earth, too," Sam said. "Sometimes it was like you describe, but I had lots of glimpses where it wasn't just hanging there. It was rotating—fast. And things were happening—storms and wars and catastrophes. It was like watching everything bad that ever happens all at once, speeded up."

"Well, that would explain why you're worried about environmental catastrophes. But why am I worried? I didn't see the bad stuff."

"Did you see anything else?" Sam asked.

Jade shook her head. "Not that I can remember. Maybe more will come to me." She paused. "I keep wondering how they did that. Did they actually take us into space?"

"No," Sam said. He felt pretty sure about that. "We were in a room. They just projected something in front of us."

"Like a hologram?"

"Maybe. Does it matter? I think we need to concentrate on what they wanted us to see and why. And if it's so important, why won't they let us remember it? It's so frustrating!"

Jade sighed. "And what do they expect us to do? I feel like we're supposed to do something, fix things somehow."

"Yeah," agreed Sam. "Let's get back as many memories as we can. Let's start from the beginning and write down what happened to each of us. As we keep thinking, maybe we'll have more memories, and we can keep adding to the puzzle. Maybe it'll start to make sense."

But remembering was easier said than done. They both remembered going to bed and waking in a new place. Sam had vague recollections of being in similar places, but Jade did not. There were no clues to tell them where the medical-like tables, or the round room, might be. Eventually, Sam remembered one more thing.

"There were people watching," he said. "A bunch of Night People were in kind of a semicircle in front of us. And behind them, there were bigger people. Humans, I think."

"Were they military?" Jade asked. "I kind of remember that, too. Not clearly, just an impression of greens and browns. I remember thinking, 'That's camouflage, like army people wear.'"

Try as they might, that was all they could remember. And they had no idea what to do with the information. But it was a start.

PART THREE

Courage is resistance to fear, mastery of fear – not absence of fear.
--Mark Twain, author

CHAPTER 18
ALIENATION

SAM PLOWED through the jostling crowd between classes, head down. All day, the hallway had echoed with shouts and squeals of friends reconnecting after a summer apart. Sam wasn't reconnecting; apart from Jade, there was no one he considered a friend or wanted to see. He felt the way he always felt on the first day of school: stressed, panicked, depressed. Like he was navigating a foreign country, a dangerous foreign country—Yemen, maybe, or Syria. He felt like an alien—a human alien—about to be caught and imprisoned.

Besides these typical back-to-school feelings, his mind was still roiling as he replayed scenes from the past few days —the underground mine and military base, Major Jepson's interrogation, his father's abuse, sharing his NP experiences with Jade and learning about her Harry Potter dreams. And, he kept reliving, over and over, what little they had remembered of the NP abduction night before last.

"Sam, there you are."

Jade appeared in front of him, smiling, flushed, excited. This was the third time he had seen her today—they had already had English and Spanish together. She'd been happy all day, like nothing life-changing had happened, like they had nothing to dread. Obviously, she liked school a lot better than he did. And she bounced back from a crisis better or at least compartmentalized better. As always, he calmed down when he saw her. He was starting to depend on that feeling. That scared him almost as much as the weirdness.

"Hi," he said. "How're you doing?"

"Apparently, better than you are—you look even more stressed than you did this morning."

He shrugged self-consciously. "I told you, I don't like school much."

"We have to fix that," she said. "You're so smart, you should love school. But right now, you'd better lead me to biology. Otherwise, I'll wander the halls and be late again. I was almost tardy to psychology."

When Sam saw Mr. Macklin standing outside the biology lab, he grinned slightly, making a bet with himself that after school Jade would gush about how handsome their biology teacher was. And she'd be right. He was tall, well over six feet. He had a deep tan, and his already blond hair had lighter streaks—he had obviously spent his summer in the sun. He was always neat and well-dressed and always had perfect posture. Today he looked even starchier than usual. Sam looked down at his own T-shirt and jeans, which were clean but certainly not new. He guessed he must be the only person, student or teacher, who hadn't bothered to dress up for the first day of classes. He didn't see the point—it wasn't a celebration.

But he had been happy to discover that Mr. Macklin had transferred to teach at the high school. Of all his past teachers, Macklin was the only one who had ever cared what Sam thought about anything. He was a decent guy, for a teacher. Macklin smiled and raised his eyebrows as they walked up.

"Hey, Sam! You're looking really tall—you've become a

young man. And we have a new girl. Who's this?" He looked at Sam, eyebrows raised.

"Um, this is Jade Mathieson," he mumbled, his eyes on the floor.

Jade gave him an amused look. She shook hands with Mr. Macklin and explained about her mother's new job and their move from Kansas City. Then she asked, gesturing toward Sam, "Is he always this shy at school?"

"He's a pretty quiet guy," Mr. Macklin said. "But I'm guessing he's not that shy with you, right?" His blue eyes twinkled as he smiled at Sam.

Sam blushed. He had no idea what to say, and he couldn't believe Jade was talking so easily with a teacher, especially one she'd just met.

"He's fine with me," Jade said, grinning at Sam. "And he's really smart, so if we have lab partners this year, and if we have a choice, I'd like him to be my partner."

Mr. Macklin laughed. "I think that sounds like a great idea," he said. "You might be just what Sam needs to bring him out of his shell. Now, get in there. You two are first, so you get your choice of seats."

Sam was in a daze for most of the class. He was processing the idea that Mr. Macklin wanted to bring him out of his shell, when he spent most of his time at school trying not to be noticed. And Jade—what was it about her that made everyone sit up and take notice, even teachers? She was no nerd—nerds don't have that effect on people. She had certainly fixed herself up for the first day. Her bright, flowery top brought out the green in her eyes. Her usual messy braid was gone; she'd pulled her light brown hair back so it fell in a long shining tail down her back. *Cheerleader*, he thought again.

He paid little attention to what Mr. Macklin was saying, stuffing lab assignments and schedules into his backpack without looking at them. Mostly, he thought about how he didn't really belong here but had to go through the motions, at least for a while. The thought was new and surprising. Sam had never liked school; he just assumed it was where he had to be. Where would he be if he wasn't in school? He was startled when the bell rang.

He breathed a sigh of relief. The first day was finally over. As he and Jade walked down the hallway together, Jade chattered about biology class and the huge semester project Macklin had just assigned them. Sam guessed he should have listened in class; he didn't remember anything about a project. Apparently, they were going to learn to do scientific research. They got to choose their own project, with Macklin's approval, and it would count for a third of their semester grade. Yes, he'd better pay more attention from now on.

A heavy weight slammed hard into his shoulder, throwing him against the wall. Jade jumped aside to avoid being knocked to the floor. Nick. Who else?

"Hey, Costas! Who's the hot chick?"

"Shut up, Nick."

"Looks like you had yourself some fun this summer. Too busy playin' with her to play in the woods, were you?"

"Shut *up*!"

"O-o-oh. Little Sammy's got a girlfriend! Does she know all about you, Sammy? Does she know you're a nutcase? Does she know you talk to little green aliens?"

"Stuff it, you jerk. Stay away from her. And stay away from me!" Sam shoved Nick as hard as he could. Nick barely moved—he was built like a tank—but he was caught off guard and let Sam pass. The smirks and laughter of the watching students washed over Sam. He cursed inwardly. But this year, he promised himself, he was *not* putting up with Nick's crap.

Jade regarded Nick scornfully. "I hope you don't think being a thug and a bully makes you impressive. Because it just makes you look stupid."

Nick leered at her. "O-o-oh. Sammy's got himself a feisty one!"

Jade tossed her head and stalked away from him. "Let's go, Sam. We have better things to do than waste time with idiots."

Sam walked with her, shaking his head.

"He won't stop," he said as they left the school. "He'll keep bugging me—and now you. He's been doing it since I started school."

"He's a total jerk! You can't let people like that get away with anything. You have to stand up to them."

"I know, and I do. I will. But he never gives up, and we'll have to watch out for him. He keeps trying to find out what I'm doing. He used to follow me in the woods all the time, but so far, he doesn't know about the chat piles. At least I don't think he does."

"Why does he pick on you?"

"No idea. But he's the one who outed me to the whole school about the Night People. Back when I was nine. Since then, school's been kind of a nightmare."

"Tell me," Jade said.

"Let's go to the park," Sam suggested. They rode their bikes to the park and settled at their picnic table.

CHAPTER 19
ALIEN BOY

SAM STARED off into the dappled sunlight under the trees. It was beautiful, just like the day Nick discovered his secret and began his downfall at school. He relaxed, letting his mind reach back to that morning six years ago and the woods near his home.

"Nick had been stalking me for weeks," Sam said, "ever since I got new binoculars for my birthday. He was in the store when my mom bought them for me. She said something about bird-watching, and of course he picked up on that."

"That day, I was in the woods, pretending to be an exobiologist on a new planet," he continued. "I was watching baby rabbits eating flowers and staying really still so I wouldn't scare them."

Jade smiled as she listened to Sam's story.

"Nick showed up carrying his air rifle and grinning. He started making fun of me, calling me 'bird boy,' and generally being a jerk. He must have hiked a couple of miles to find me."

"Why did he pick on you?" Jade asked.

Sam shook his head. "No idea. He's done it since I was in

first grade. I was scared of him and he knew it. And I was always weird. At first, I didn't know enough to keep my mouth shut about the Night People, and I said some crazy things."

"And you just let him get away with harassing you?"

Sam flushed. "Yeah, at first. He's like my dad—huge and scary. I didn't know what to do, so I just ran away. But that day, I got really mad. He was taunting me. He called me a girl and said a real man would shoot all this stuff instead of just looking at it."

Jade rolled her eyes. "A girl. The ultimate insult."

"I was nine," Sam said defensively.

"Anyway, then he shot his air rifle up into a tree. He didn't hit anything, but I heard a loud squawk and wings fluttering, so he came close."

Now Jade looked outraged. "I hope you did something then," she said.

"I did, finally. I stood my ground and said something like, 'You think shooting that stupid gun makes you a man? You're not a man; you're just a dumb boy and a big bully!' Nick was so surprised that at first, he just stared. Then, he lunged for me. I stuck out my foot and he tripped and fell flat."

Sam grinned slightly and shrugged, embarrassed. "Then, my courage gave out and I ran."

"Probably smart," Jade said, "since he's so much bigger. And you did stand up to him." She paused. "So, then you just went home?"

"No, then I saw the Night People—in the daytime."

Jade's eyes widened. "What happened?"

"I wanted to get away, so I went crashing through the woods toward home. But as I calmed down, I felt sort of— compelled—to go in another direction that I hadn't explored. After a while, I started to tingle all over. The woods got bright and blurry. And there were tiny sparkling lights all around."

Jade watched him but said nothing. He smiled.

"I remember it felt like I was walking through fog into a fireworks display."

"That definitely sounds like the Night People," Jade said. "Like at the chat piles."

Sam nodded. "Then, I saw this huge pair of eyes. They were pulling me toward them, and I remember thinking, 'It must be an owl.' But then, thoughts started traveling from the owl directly into my mind. Really fast, but I still understood them. The thoughts were about nature—about the woods, and growing stronger and cherishing life, not death. Not giving in to people who thought killing was fun or okay. Things I understood but had never been able to say."

"And you still remember all this." Jade sounded amazed.

"Yeah." Sam nodded. "It's one of the few NP experiences I remember clearly. The owl made me feel really peaceful and sleepy. And as I fell asleep, I saw it clearly. It was a Night Person."

He sighed. "And then Nick came charging through the woods. He taunted me about running off and asked what I was doing. I was sleepy and not thinking straight. I said I was talking to the alien—no, the Night Person—no, the owl. And of course, the only word he got from that was 'alien'."

"And that was it," Sam concluded. "The next day, he spread the story all around school: 'Sam sneaks around in the woods and talks to imaginary little men from outer space.' From that day on, I was 'alien boy.' It's never entirely gone away, and whenever I do anything the least bit strange—which happens a lot with me—it comes back even stronger."

Before the experience in the woods, Sam had always been quiet and other kids pretty much left him alone, which was fine with him. He had his reading and nature study projects.

He had never belonged in his own home or at school, so he lost himself in fictional worlds. And he roamed the woods, observing life, learning how things lived, trying to identify everything. Trees, plants, birds, insects, mammals—whatever was out there, he tried to give it a name. If he could name it, it became his friend. The elementary school media lady accidentally helped him with this. He'd found a set of nature identification guides, and she let him check them out as often as he wanted, because no one else ever did. When they became hopelessly frayed from overuse, she let him keep them. And now, he had a whole lot of plant and animal friends.

"So," Sam said, "that day in the woods and what Nick did afterward just proved I was right—in the real world, I could never trust anyone, never have friends."

From that day on, Sam told her, he retreated even more into the woods and into books. He spoke only when spoken to, thought carefully before he said anything, and then said as little as possible. He learned to hide his feelings. It was Sam against the world, and he didn't see how that was ever likely to change.

"Until you came," he said, looking sideways at Jade.

Jade was quiet after Sam finished his story.

"So, Nick's always been a jerk," she said finally. "But now, you won't have to face him alone. Or anyone else. That's the good thing about having friends. Someone always has your back."

Sam smiled at her. "Thanks," he said. "I just hope you know what you're getting into."

"He's a teenager, and an immature one at that," she responded. "How hard can it be? I'm more worried about our other problems. Have you remembered anything else?"

Jade seemed oblivious to the fact that she and Sam were also teenagers. But she was right, he thought. Nick might be older, but he was definitely less mature. And remembering the abduction was more important.

"I think," Sam responded, "that the Earth hologram, or whatever, was speeding up when all the bad things were happening. Like there were more and more hurricanes and forest fires and floods and droughts and wars, and they were happening faster and faster."

"But what does it mean? Why did they make us watch it?"

Sam shook his head. "No idea."

Jade paused, thinking. "How have you been feeling since then? Emotionally, I mean. I'm pretty sure we were both terrified while it was happening. But do you still feel different from before?"

Sam didn't even have to think about it. "Yeah. I still feel the dread, like something really bad is about to happen. At first, I thought it was school—I always dread school—but this is different. It's huge. I think it's related to the catastrophe. And I feel like I need to do something about it."

Jade nodded. "I agree," she said. "They want us to be worried. Either about the environment in general or some catastrophe in particular."

"But why? It's not like we can do anything about problems that big. And what does it have to do with the underground bases? They're showing us all this stuff, but none of it fits together or makes any sense."

"I don't know. But we're making progress. They're letting us remember, even if it's going slowly. Maybe if we just keep at it, we'll eventually figure it out."

Sam sighed. "Maybe. I guess there's not much else we can do right now."

But, as they gathered their things and prepared to go home, he felt relieved to be sharing this weirdness with Jade instead of confronting it on his own.

CHAPTER 20
TWO WORLDS

SAM AND JADE were so focused on the NP and the military that school became a minor irritation—a mosquito annoying them when they needed to focus on the giant angry bear, or bears, rushing toward them. Plus, going to school now felt like entering another world, in some ways more alien than the NP.

Their classwork was far too easy. Jade was bored after a week—her previous school had been much more challenging. Sam enjoyed classes slightly more than before because three of them, plus chorus, were with Jade. Spanish was fun. His abuela had talked and sung to him in Spanish, and although she'd left when he was five, the words all sounded familiar and friendly and easy.

Every day after school, unless he had work, Sam escaped to Jade's house, where they blew through their homework and then continued their research. Sam could access the internet now, with his tablet and the wireless at Jade's house. For the first time, he could download music without being on a public network. It was heaven. Sometimes, they went to their picnic table. By mutual agreement, discussions of UFOs, aliens, or alien abductions were totally off-limits at school and iffy at Jade's house. In the park, they could talk in private.

If school had just been classwork, things would have been easy. But socially, Jade was struggling. Almost immediately, she started to lose the excitement and glow of that first day. She became quiet and looked stressed. While she insisted nothing was wrong, Sam knew better, and had strong suspicions about the reason.

During the first week, he saw her talking with Whitney and Jessica, and looking upset. He could imagine that conversation. Most kids either ignored Sam or treated him with casual contempt. They weren't hostile. But those two were toxic—rich, arrogant, entitled. Whitney's dad owned Cassidy's major bank and Jessica's was a doctor, a dermatologist, he thought. They bullied everyone, even their own friends. Through the years, they had harassed Sam almost as much as Nick and his friends had. Sam was poor, from the wrong side of the tracks. His clothes came from Walmart or the Salvation Army, and he was weird—he talked to aliens. So, he had no doubt Whitney and Jessica were giving Jade an earful. They were telling her—threatening her, probably—that hanging around him would make her an outcast, just as he was.

Later, he asked her, "Were Whitney and Jessica warning you to stay away from me?"

Jade gave him a quick look and flushed slightly. "Um—"

"I know what they're like. Jade, it's okay if you want to back off from me."

It killed him to say it. What would his life be like if she dropped him? But it wasn't fair to make her stay.

She looked insulted. "Sam, I told you I wouldn't drop you, no matter what people said."

"I know, but maybe you didn't realize how bad it could get. I just want you to know I would understand."

"Stop!" she said. "I wouldn't do that. Ever."

When he looked into her eyes, he knew she meant it. He saw anger and hurt, but for the first time in his life, he also saw friendship.

Every day after that, Jade seemed more stressed. But she wouldn't talk to Sam. On the second Friday, he was waiting outside the door when she reached the biology lab. She was trembling and clutching her backpack tightly, but she gave him a wan smile.

"Are you okay?" he asked.

"I'm fine," she said. "Let's go in."

She pushed past him and dropped her backpack under the lab table. Mr. Macklin frowned and gave her a searching look.

"Everything all right, Jade?" he asked.

"Everything's fine," she assured him. She gave him a slightly more confident smile than she had given Sam and seemed to relax a little.

Mr. Macklin had approved Sam and Jade's proposal to do their semester project on the likelihood of extraterrestrial life. He had told the class they could choose anything biology-related, and they could do any combination of lab, field, or library research. Sam and Jade had worried about proposing this project—it wasn't directly about aliens visiting Earth, but it was close. They hoped it would be safe, since it was "real science" and could not be dismissed as fantasy or mental illness. Mr. Macklin, of course, assumed they would do only library research, but he also wanted them to design a realistic lab or field study. They exchanged glances as they read his note, thinking they might do some secret field research. Either way, the project wouldn't be boring or irrelevant, and no one needed to know their ulterior motives.

As they walked down the hall together after biology, they heard hysterical laughter and saw people looking at their phones. They were greeted with a chorus of taunts. "Hey, alien boy, you got yourself an alien girlfriend!" "Love the green skin!" "You from Mars, alien girl?" "Let's see your Mars face!"

Some guy shoved his phone in their faces. The picture had been photoshopped, badly. It showed Sam and Jade looking into each other's eyes. It was obviously their faces, but they had huge heads and eyes and their skin was a sickly shade of green. A pair of aliens.

Rage suddenly overcame Sam. This was Rodney, one of Nick's bully friends. If he could handle aliens, surely, he could handle this moron! He grabbed the phone from Rodney's hand. Rodney tried to grab it back, but Sam was quicker. He punched in a number and hit Send. He returned the phone, smirked at Rodney, and said, "Have a nice weekend!"

As they left, Jade asked, "What did you do?"

Sam grinned. "*I* didn't do anything. But Rodney just sent that picture to the principal."

Jade collapsed in a fit of giggles. "Oh, Sam, that was genius!" Then she stopped. "Wait, how did you know Mr. Burke's number?"

Sam shrugged. "It was just the school office number. I remembered it from the enrollment papers. But Mr. Burke will get it."

They escaped from school and made their way to their picnic table. Sam noticed the black SUV creeping along behind them, but he did not point it out. Jade was better since her giggling fit, but she was still stressed. When they were settled, she finally recounted her face-off with Whitney and Jessica and the subsequent week of teasing and harassment. She was trying to be matter-of-fact, but Sam heard the catch in her voice. His guilt was overwhelming.

"I knew I should never have involved you in my life. Now you'll be an outcast, just like me. I'm so sorry."

She shrugged. "It would have happened sooner or later, when they got to know me. Once a nerd, always a nerd."

He reached across the picnic table and touched her hand. She looked up gratefully. Jade was naturally outgoing, and she always put on a brave face. But that's all it was, he thought. Under the surface, she was almost as insecure as he was. And he knew how much she missed her dad—he had been her confidant and had built up her self-confidence.

"But we'll fight back, okay?" he said. "We won't let them get us down."

"Right! We have each other's backs. I felt awful when they ganged up on me. But you and Mr. Macklin were both worried about me, and I felt better. And what you did to Rodney was epic! That's how we'll get through it. Helping each other—and fighting back."

Sam shook his head. Smiling at her, he quoted from their latest English assignment:

> "She was a vixen when she went to school,
> And though she be but little, she is fierce."

Jade frowned at him, puzzled.

"From *A Midsummer Night's Dream*," he explained. "It's how I'm going to think of you from now on."

Her eyes widened, and she gave him a tremulous smile.

He knew she couldn't just brush off the harassment that easily. He couldn't either. But she *was* fierce, and he promised himself he would always have her back. If he could handle the Night People, he could handle a few stupid bullies.

CHAPTER 21
THE SCIENTIFIC METHOD

SAM AND JADE WERE—FOR now—too intimidated by their military shadows to visit the chat piles or the secret complex. Outside of school, they reviewed their dreams. The memories returned in bits and pieces, often at night. They awoke each day feeling slightly more certain of what had happened. It was as though the abduction had been too much for them to handle all at once, so they were reliving it a little at a time, piecing their memories together, slowly building a jigsaw puzzle that evoked both of their experiences.

The abduction books were strange and fascinating. In them, abductions resulted in missing time and events similar to their own experiences. People were taken to other locations, presumably spacecraft or other NP living spaces. Living spaces—that thought brought Sam up short. He felt his blood curdle as he considered the implications of these creatures living on Earth, unnoticed, among humans. Surely that wasn't happening . . . It was odd. He had been aware of the Night People for most of his life but had never wondered where they lived. In the underground bases, maybe?

But he was also experiencing an overwhelming sense of relief. He had been resigned to a life of solitude and secrecy.

Reading the abduction books had opened his eyes—there were other people like him. *Communion* was old, written almost twenty years before he was even born, so he had kind of assumed encounters with the NP were rare. If they were even real. He wasn't sure how to process the idea that thousands of people knew about them. Jade didn't seem that surprised, but he thought she was relieved, too.

Jade didn't remember most of her past experiences and had never felt the same fear that Sam did. But lately, he'd remembered several past NP encounters where they were together. No wonder she'd seemed familiar when they met. Then, there was the flood of information they had received during the Earth scenario. They both knew they had learned something valuable and assumed it still existed in their brains somewhere, but neither could access it. It was maddening. Still, he now knew the NP were real and others knew about them.

Of course, skeptics and debunkers dominated the abduction literature, explaining with authority and careful condescension why "believers" were so deluded. The latest explanation was cell phones. Everybody had one, they said. So, if aliens were really visiting us, by now we should have tons of high-quality videos. No videos, hence no aliens. Obviously, no one using that argument had ever met an NP, Sam thought. They had never felt the loss of will and complete paralysis that the NP engendered. They hadn't experienced their speed, their night visits, their ability to fade in and out of view, the terror they caused. . . .. He shook his head. Experience was the only teacher. And most skeptics would never encounter them.

After the Earth scenario, Sam and Jade also began Googling environmental problems and ordering books. If the NP wanted them to feel dread, they figured they should understand exactly what they were dreading. Maybe they could even uncover the NP's agenda. They started with chat piles and earthquakes, then added other issues: climate change, pollution, pandemics, animal extinctions. Before long, Sam feared he had made a mistake turning Jade's attention in this direction. The more she knew, the more outraged she became.

"Why are you so upset over this?" he asked finally.

"Aren't you?" she countered.

"Well, yes, but you seem much—angrier about it."

Jade sighed. "I come from a family of ecowarriors. Mom is a real fanatic. You'll see when you know her better. Her dad —my grandpa—died from cancer. They think it was caused by the pesticides he used on his farm."

"Oh." He paused, nodding. "That makes sense. But what's upsetting you right now?"

"I just can't believe people *do* things like this!" she said. She was reading a fracking website. After their experience in Cassidy Base, Sam had explained to her how oil companies used fracking to get oil out of the ground. And how the pressure of chemicals they pumped into the bedrock sometimes caused earthquakes.

"What are they *thinking*, pumping nasty chemicals underground like that? Don't they know that stuff gets into the groundwater and poisons people? Don't they know it causes earthquakes?"

"I doubt if they care," Sam responded. "Most likely they just want to get the oil out and make money. Besides, most of them deny that fracking causes earthquakes."

"Of course, they do," she said furiously. "They're horrible people!"

Jade continued her search, her anger unabated. Finally, she threw up her hands.

"I'm Googled out," she said. "This stuff is too depressing. I can't remember it all, and right now, I don't see how it all fits together. What does the fact that humans are destroying Earth have to do with aliens? Why would they care?"

"Maybe they want to live here," Sam suggested. "Or maybe they already do."

Jade stared at him. "I wish you hadn't said that," she said. "I'm trying to be cool with all this, but I'm already freaked out by the thought that aliens exist and are messing with us. I'm not ready to deal with them living here."

Usually, Sam felt sort of inferior around Jade—despite her insecurities, she seemed so cosmopolitan, so calm and collected, so . . . brave. Just the opposite of how he usually felt. But she had been really stressed lately. And he'd been dealing with the NP all his life, although he'd tried to avoid thinking of them as aliens. And he'd dealt with things she probably hadn't. It was mean, but he couldn't resist. Maybe he could make her feel less uptight. He looked her in the eye.

"Don't you think you're being politically incorrect?" He made his voice very stern, like Mr. Macklin when a student was causing trouble. "Just because they're from somewhere else doesn't mean you're better than they are. I was born here, but I'm Brown, so a lot of people think I'm an alien. It's not a nice feeling."

Jade turned fiery red and covered her mouth with both hands.

"Oh, Sam, I didn't mean . . ."

He burst out laughing. "Chill out! I'm just messing with you. I know you're not prejudiced."

"That was really mean, you know," Jade said, but she laughed, too. And she did seem to relax a little.

"Sorry, not sorry," he said, grinning at her. "I just think you should lighten up. But it did occur to me that it might be easier to accept the NP if we consider them immigrants. Think of them as coming from another country, instead of another planet."

"I guess." Jade didn't seem convinced. "But people from another country are still . . . people."

Sam felt a little giddy. He was on a roll.

"Or maybe they're not from another planet. Maybe there's a multiverse, and they're from another Earth. Or they're from another dimension on this Earth and they just cross over. Or they're really humans from the future. And they might not be immigrants, just tourists, looking us over."

"You're not helping."

Jade was just beginning to face the enormity of the NP problem and how much they didn't know. But Sam was psyched. He was finally beginning to see some explanation for his experiences during all these years. He also realized they might never know exactly who, or what, the NP were or where they came from. Not unless the NP chose to tell them.

"Anyway," Sam continued, "I have another idea. We're both kind of science geeks, right? So, why not set this whole thing up as a scientific study? Use the scientific method, collect data, follow the evidence. Like your dad suggested. Those books talk about how scientists ignore UFOs and abductions—pretend they don't exist. Or make fun of people like us who experience them. But what if we treat them like a regular science project?"

It was something active they could do—better than waiting around to be arrested by the major or his military police.

"That sounds promising," Jade said finally. "What would we do?"

"Why not do it like the project we're doing for Macklin? The same procedure, same kinds of research, same types of data."

A good scientist would start with a literature review—a summary of what was already known. Using the internet was essential, but since Jepson had started watching them, Jade had been paranoid about being tracked. What if the military were watching their online activities? Sam thought it was probably too late to worry about that. But he kept quiet; no need to increase Jade's stress.

"There's one thing we might do," he suggested hesitantly.

"What's that?"

"Well, there's this guy at school, Ravi Roy. He's a junior. He's a geek, like us, only he's into computers. He could probably show us how to tell if someone is tracking our internet use. Of course, we'd have to make up a reason."

Jade put her head in her hands. "This is getting to be too much. Those bullies at school are stressing me out. And the NP and the abduction are really scaring me. We're not safe in our own homes, or even our own minds. They're making us dread something, and we don't even know what we dread. And the military is breathing down our necks because of things the NP are making us do. And we can't even try to find out why it's all happening because we'll be arrested if we explore. And we have to lie to everyone. I hate lying."

Sam smiled a bit grimly. "I know. I hate to say 'I told you so,' but . . ."

"I know, I asked for it. This is all just so new. I promise I'll get it together. Okay, let's talk to your computer geek."

Then, they would organize their own experiences. They decided on two journals each: one on past experiences and one on current events—anything strange or unexplainable, including dreams. They would date all experiences as precisely as possible. Sam didn't mention his Coward's Notebook, which he'd started at age seven, but it would help. For now, they would put everything in writing—actual writing, not computer files, not until they were sure their computers were safe. And they would hide the journals well.

CHAPTER 22
RAVI

ON MONDAY, Principal Burke called Sam into his office. Rodney had blamed him for the alien photo. Sam told the truth—he had sent the photo from Rodney's phone because he was tired of being harassed. Mr. Burke was not angry; he grinned at Sam and complimented his ingenuity. Later, he gave a scathing anti-bullying lecture over the intercom. But unfortunately, only Rodney got detention.

That afternoon, Sam approached Ravi Roy and asked him about detecting computer surveillance programs. He explained that his friend Jade wrote science fiction stories and was developing a character who thought the government was spying on him. She wanted to describe how he tested his computer to figure out if he was right. She wanted to make it realistic but wasn't sure about methods she had seen online. Could Ravi give her some pointers?

Ravi looked interested but slightly suspicious. "Why doesn't she ask me herself?"

Sam shrugged. "I know who you are and that you're good with computers, so I said I'd ask you. Could you help her?"

"Sure, there are lots of things you can do. I can go through some of them, but it has to be in person. Bring her by the computer lab after school, and I'll give her some tips."

"Thanks, I appreciate it," Sam said, giving Ravi a rare smile. "We'll be there."

Ravi was in the computer lab when Sam and Jade arrived. Sam introduced Jade, and Ravi nodded curtly.

"Okay," he said. "Let's get to it. Set up your computer and we'll see what you've got."

"Oh." Jade looked surprised and a little uncertain. She shot a glance at Sam, who shrugged. "This isn't about *my* computer. I just wanted to know for—"

"For a story you're writing. I know. But the easiest way to explain this stuff is to actually show you how to do it. And there's nothing wrong with upgrading the security on your own machine, right?"

"I guess not." She turned on her laptop.

Sam pulled out his tablet. "Guess I might as well learn, too," he said. "Better safe than sorry."

Ravi smiled. "Right."

They spent the next hour going through a series of security features, including checking for viruses and programs they couldn't identify. No viruses—their virus protection software was working. But Jade's computer had a program Ravi didn't recognize. Apparently, it was using much more CPU and memory than he would expect an innocent program to use. He shook his head in confusion when he couldn't locate the program online.

"What does that mean?" Jade asked.

"I'm not sure—I've never had that happen before," Ravi admitted. He gave her a speculative look. "Any reason someone would want to track your computer use? I mean other than obvious ones, like Google and Amazon?"

Jade looked horrified. "I—no, of course not!" she stammered.

He smiled. "Don't panic. I was just trying to think of reasons a program name would be hidden, and that's all I can think of. It's probably just some shady business checking out your buying habits. Do you save your files to the cloud?"

"No," Jade said.

"Well, let's do that first. It's easy, and it will keep everything safe unless someone is *really* trying to mess with you."

Ravi walked them both through the process.

"Now," he said, "let's save everything again on this flash drive."

He held up the drive and then quickly inserted it and saved Jade's files. Finally, he wrote down the name of the rogue program from Jade's computer and handed her the slip of paper.

"Now I'm going to delete this program," he continued. "If nothing changes when you use your computer, you're fine. But if you have trouble accessing something or doing basic tasks, that probably means I've deleted some vital Windows system file. We can either try to reinstall it, or if that doesn't work, we can do a system reset. Does that sound okay?"

"I—I guess. I've never done a system reset before."

"I won't delete it unless you're okay with it. Even with the reset, we can ask it to save all your files. And they're backed up on the cloud and the flash drive. But if you get stuck later, you can always give me a call and I'll fix things." He pulled out a card and gave it to her, looking a bit sheepish. "I even have business cards, not that there's much use for them around here."

Jade took the card, eyeing it and then Ravi. The card was inscribed *Ravi Roy, IT Consultant*, with a phone number and an email address. It looked very professional.

"Can we afford you?"

He responded with his first real smile—almost a grin. "If I

like someone, or it's an interesting job, I do it for free. Don't worry. This one's free."

Jade returned his smile. Sam wondered which reason was making it free, but he didn't ask. Neither did Jade. "Okay, go ahead," she said. "You seem like you know what you're doing."

"I do," he assured her. He sat down at her laptop and after about five minutes of concentrated work, he said, "Okay, I think it's gone now."

Ravi shut down the laptop and let it sit for a couple of minutes. No one spoke. Then, he rebooted it. The reboot happened with no problems, and he checked to make sure the offending program had vanished.

"Well, I think you're fine," he said. "I don't know what that program did, but since it was there, you should check your program list periodically to make sure nothing sketchy shows up. Especially something that uses a lot of CPU or storage space, like this one did."

"Thanks," Jade said. "I was just looking for information. I didn't expect you to find something wrong with my computer. But I appreciate it."

"No problem," Ravi said. "And, there are a few other things you can check, or things you can do to protect yourself—or the character in your story." He spent another fifteen minutes lecturing them on computer and cell phone security. He started with deleting cookies and continued on to more high-powered methods. Both Sam and Jade were seriously spooked by the time he finished.

"Sorry, I'm not trying to scare you," Ravi said, finally noticing the shocked looks on both faces. "It's just—most people don't realize how much their lives are monitored when they're online. Pretty much everyone collects data on us, and usually we're totally unaware of it. Better to know and take steps to limit the theft, wouldn't you say?"

"Yeah," Sam said fervently. "Definitely better."

They thanked Ravi and promised to come to him if they had more questions. Sam kind of liked Ravi, although he was a bit curt and all-business. And he was grateful for the help, unsettling though it was. But Sam had no plans to keep consulting him. The guy was already suspicious. Sam realized their excuse about Jade writing a story had been pretty thin. He was sure Ravi didn't buy it. He shared his unease with Jade. She nodded.

"Yeah, he didn't," Jade agreed. "He was curious about why we were asking. But I don't think we need to worry about him. He seemed nice—more interested in doing his computer thing than getting us in trouble."

"And he won't get us in trouble if we never confide in him again," Sam insisted. "Okay?"

Jade frowned. "Sam," she said. "We didn't confide in him *this* time. We just asked him how to keep a computer secure. But we could tell him some things without giving away our NP secret. We could tell him about visiting the chat piles and getting caught by the military—not about getting inside," she added hastily when she saw the horrified look on Sam's face.

"You promised you would keep my secret!" Sam said. "You promised."

"And I *am* keeping it, and I will. But don't you think you're a bit too paranoid about confiding in people? Like I said, we wouldn't have to mention the NP. But if the military keeps following us, we might need help. Maybe even adult help. Ravi didn't say so, but it had to be the military that put that program on my computer."

Sam shook his head stubbornly. "Even if it was, we can't tell anyone. If anyone finds out that I talk to the NP, I'll end up in a mental ward. Like Lucy. You know I will."

Jade sighed. "I disagree. But I'll keep your secret."

CHAPTER 23
TESTING

THE NP STAYED quiet during the first weeks of school. The military, not so much. The black SUV was following them. There had been an unexplained program on Jade's computer. And on Friday of the third week, Major Jepson reappeared. He stayed off school grounds, but he stood in front of the diner across the street, so both Sam and Jade saw him as they arrived. He wore army fatigues and said nothing, just raised his eyebrows and sneered. They did not see him again that day, but if he wanted to rekindle their fears, mission accomplished.

At Jade's house that evening, they continued their alien research, suppressing their unease about Jepson. Sam thoroughly enjoyed the process. He liked doing research, but mostly, he loved being this close to Jade. The scent of her hair was distracting him again, and he sat closer than was strictly necessary, brushing against her whenever he could. She didn't move away, which gave him hope.

But she didn't encourage him, either. She kept him focused. And she noticed something that seemed to contradict the skeptics.

"You know," she said, "all these people who make fun of

abductees? They say abductees are influenced by the culture—they just copy what other people say or copy books or movies or TV. But *we* didn't. We were already having the experiences. We only found out about abductions when we went looking for answers."

Sam agreed. "I sure wasn't discussing this stuff when I was a little kid, and my parents would *never* talk about it. They're too afraid of looking crazy. And I just kept hoping I wasn't crazy. I never wanted it to be aliens." He thought about his tormenters, like Nick and Rodney, and shuddered. *No way.*

"And there's something else," Jade continued. "The skeptics, or debunkers—none of them seem to do any research before they write about it. They list all the reasons why it can't be aliens, but they don't give any evidence. They just say the 'so-called abductees' are suffering from some brain problem or night paralysis or something. They've obviously never experienced it. But it's like they've never read anyone else's experiences, either. They just make up explanations. Isn't that odd?"

Sam frowned. "It sounds like a cover-up," he said after a moment. "They don't care what's actually happening or what people are going through; they just want to protect their own beliefs. It's the same with UFO sightings. People always explain away UFOs as weather balloons or funny clouds or something, even when they're obviously not. Even if hundreds or thousands of people see them, the military just blows them off, like they never happened. The media either ignores them or treats them like jokes. They laugh and call people who see them crazy. I suppose after a while, a lot of them think they are."

Sam had thought *he* was crazy. He still did, sometimes.

He had relaxed in his usual position on the floor, leaning back against Jade's bed. Sadie was curled up in his lap. She had adopted Sam and always stayed close when he visited. Jade smiled as Sam stroked the purring little cat.

"I should be jealous, you know," she said. "She used to curl up in *my* lap."

"She's sweet," Sam said, closing his eyes. "She relaxes me."

Suddenly, Sadie gave a cry Sam had never heard from any animal before. With every hair standing on end, she leapt off Sam's lap and bolted out the door. Sam jumped up, grabbing his leg where she had dug in her claws as she fled. Her cry had shot a bolt of terror through his heart.

Jade jumped up, too. "What happened? What scared her?"

Sam shook his head. "No idea."

Sadie—sweet, calm Sadie—had completely lost it. Her tortured cry wrenched Sam back to the first time he had encountered the Night People. In his childish terror, his cries must have sounded much like that. Before he could share this insight with Jade, electric tingling enveloped his body. *They're here!* Suddenly, he was catapulted away and the world went black. He awoke crumpled on the ground, surrounded by rumbling, shuddering sound, buffeted by showers of dust and pebbles. *Another earthquake?* He opened his eyes, trying to orient himself, but he was still in blackness. He scrambled onto his hands and knees, trying to stand, but the shaking was too intense. Where was he? In Cassidy Base?

Where was Jade? He reached out a hand, and encountered a body lying very still. *Oh, no!* He called Jade's name, but there was no response. Frantically, his hands explored the body. Bare legs, denim shorts, sleeveless top, thick braid with tendrils escaping. Jade. Not moving, not responding. He ran his hands over the delicate, heart-shaped contours of her face. He felt a gash on her forehead; blood had seeped down her face in thick, sticky rivulets. Sam could see nothing. He had no idea what to do; Jade was unconscious, and he could not help her.

Think! He couldn't carry her and couldn't see where to go anyway. They were totally alone. At least the shaking was finally subsiding. He breathed deeply, ignoring the dust, forcing himself to calm down. Suddenly, he realized he *did* know what to do—Jade herself had taught him. Her mother was an ER doctor, so Jade had learned basic first aid at an early age. A-B-C, he remembered—airway, breathing, circulation—check those first. He bent down and tilted Jade's head back, lifting her chin slightly, and listened to her breathing. He placed his hand near her mouth and felt her breath on his fingers. It seemed normal, not labored, so airway and breathing were probably okay. Circulation. He checked her head wound. The bleeding had stopped. Then pulse. He reached for her left wrist; her pulse seemed strong and steady. He sighed in relief. She had been hit on the head and knocked out, but perhaps the injury wasn't serious.

What else could he do? Recovery position? No, better not move her. She might have a spinal injury. The air was clearing slightly as the earthquake dissipated and the dust settled. He bent over Jade and kept calling her name; surely, she should be waking up by now.

A pulse of electricity surged through Sam. *Oh, no!* They couldn't take him away now. But he was no longer in control. As the darkness took him, he realized he was being watched. A small crowd of Night People gathered in a group—*above him? You can't do this*, he raged. *I have to save Jade.* Among the watchers were two faces he recognized—his own personal NP and the large man with the kind face that he had seen several times before. The man gave him a slight smile: sympathetic, Sam thought. And then the world disappeared.

CHAPTER 24
BUGGED

THE NEXT MORNING, Sam bolted upright, torn from sleep by a terrifying nightmare—Jade was injured, unconscious, and he had to save her. But every time he had tried to get close, reaching out to help her, he was snatched away. He had to make sure she was okay! Just as he reached for his phone, it rang. He grabbed it and breathed a sigh of relief when he heard Jade's voice.

She sounded breathy, almost hysterical. She had to see him immediately. It was urgent but she couldn't explain over the phone. Sam tried to get more information but she was adamant. They had to talk in person—at the picnic table, not at her house. Sam was confused, but he didn't argue. He had to see her anyway to make sure she was okay. His dream was too real to be just a dream. He thought back to the night before and realized he couldn't remember how the evening had ended. He and Jade had been doing research, and then . . . what?

Sam dressed quickly and rode to the park. They reached the entrance at the same time. Jade leapt off her bike and showed him a small, cylindrical structure with wires on one end. He studied the object with a frown.

"What is this?" he asked.

"I think it's a bug!" she said, whispering. "I found it inside my lamp this morning."

"Inside your lamp?"

Her eyes went wide. "Oh, Sam, there was an NP in my room last night. She told me to look in the lamp."

He frowned. "She?"

Jade nodded. "I just got a female vibe from her. I don't really know why."

"Must have been the one I see. I get a female vibe too. Let's go sit and talk about this."

Sam's mind was working furiously as they walked toward the picnic table, pushing their bikes. He was desperate to find out if his dream had been real, but that would have to wait. Her forehead showed no injury, so maybe it was just a dream. And, if the military were planting bugs on them, and the NP were warning them about it, the gravity of the situation had reached a whole new level. The NP still terrified him, but the military could cause them serious problems in the real world. And if they had planted a bug in Jade's bedroom—he stopped short and gripped Jade's arm. She looked at him in surprise.

"Don't talk again until I say something to you, okay?"

"Okay. Why?"

He shook his head. When they reached the picnic table, he dropped his backpack on the ground and began methodically running his hands over the top of the table. Jade watched him, understanding and horror dawning in her eyes. He slid his fingers carefully along the spaces between the planks. Then, he crawled under the table and did the same. And there it was, tucked invisibly between the two middle planks at the far end of the table, where they always sat to talk. He worked it loose and held it between two fingers as he backed out and stood up. It looked identical to the one Jade had found. Jade covered her mouth, stifling a gasp. Sam locked eyes with her and put a finger over his lips.

He whispered, "Piece of paper."

Jade opened her backpack and ripped a piece from a notebook. Sam placed the bug in the middle of the paper and motioned Jade to do the same with hers. He folded the paper over and over until the bugs were buried in many layers. He took the folded paper and jogged to a tree a hundred feet away. He placed the paper and its contents on the ground, carefully securing it with small rocks. Then, he jogged back to Jade. They sat at their picnic table, wondering if they could call it theirs anymore.

"Well, this is disturbing," Sam said quietly. "Tell me exactly what happened."

Jade recounted her tale. She had been restless, feeling surrounded by shadowy forms. She had felt cold fingers touching her.

"They kept saying, 'You must see. You must find.' Like they do with you, using telepathy."

He nodded. "They told you to look in the lamp?"

"One of them kind of floated over to the lamp and kept pointing to it and saying 'find.' Then I fell asleep, but this morning when I woke up, I just . . . looked until I found it."

Sam said, "Jimenez must have planted them the day Jepson interrogated us. The day they trashed everything."

"That means they know all about our NP and Harry Potter experiences," Jade said. "Our research project—and exactly how we're doing it. The books and websites we're reading. Everything we've talked about. And we were talking in these places to be safe. We're idiots!"

Sam shook his head. "We were pretty slow figuring out what they were doing. But we're not idiots."

"What do you mean?"

"Until recently, I thought I was crazy," Sam said. "But

since you came, and we started reading all this stuff, I finally realized I'm not. The NP really exist and are—different—from us. And the military are really interested in us. They don't think we're idiots—they think we're dangerous. So, they're dangerous to us."

Jade shook her head. "How can we be dangerous? We don't have control over anything! Stuff is happening *to* us."

"We don't have control, but we know a lot, and that scares them."

"Well, whatever they think, we still have to figure out what to do. I'm so scared I can't think straight."

"Me, too," Sam admitted. They sat quietly.

Finally, Sam said, "Jade, did anything else happen to you last night?"

Jade looked confused. "What do you mean, 'anything else'?"

"How did your evening end? When did I go home?"

Her brow creased. After a moment, she said, "I don't remember. When did you go?"

"I can't remember either. I remember Sadie freaking out and running. And then I had either a nightmare or an NP experience."

He told her what he could remember about the earthquake, the darkness, finding her knocked out, trying to help her. She didn't remember any of it. And her forehead was uninjured.

"You must have had a dream," she said. She was more worried about the bugs.

If so, it was a very realistic dream, Sam thought. And they moved him. He woke up at home in bed, with no memory of getting there.

"Sam, what about cameras? Do you think they're watching us, too?"

Sam closed his eyes and rested his forehead on one hand.

"Who knows? I think there are detectors for finding bugs and cameras—wonder how much they cost."

"I'll Google them. Are you checking your tablet for strange programs?"

"Yeah, nothing so far. You?"

"Just the one Ravi found. It hasn't come back and I haven't seen anything new."

They debated what to do with the bugs. Because they had moved both, whoever planted them knew they'd been found. So, they decided it was okay to destroy them. No need to make it easy. If the military wanted to listen, they could keep replacing the bugs or find some other way. Sam retrieved the bugs and used a rock to smash one of them. He gave the rock to Jade, and she smashed the other. They dumped the remains in the nearest trash can. It was very satisfying.

When they parted ways, Jade seemed less agitated. She returned home to research anti-surveillance methods and promised to get back to him.

Bugging—just one more thing to worry about. The worries were piling up. Sam needed to focus. He doubted a couple of teenagers could stop government agencies intent on tracking them, but they could make it harder. And they needed to deal with the whole mess: Night People, secret military bases, avoiding arrest, underground earthquakes, and now—Jade being injured. Jade was probably right; it was just a dream. But it felt so real—especially the NP and the friendly army man. Who *was* that guy? And why did he just watch—why didn't he *help*? Sam was almost sure they had been observing him to see his reaction. Another test. *Why?*

Sam's personal goal was keeping the NP secret from all the adults who might decide he was crazy. Maybe he was just paranoid—Jade certainly thought so. But they had committed his Aunt Lucy, at least for a while. He had never met Lucy, but he'd been thinking about her a lot lately—her and his mom. His mom was always so squirrely at any suggestion of the NP in Sam's life. Not just that first night, when he was five, but other times—waking up in the woods, missing time events. Had his mother and her sister experienced their own encounters with the NP and been less lucky than he was or less able to cope? Were the NP the reason Aunt Lucy became Loony Lucy? Some of the books talked about several generations of the same family being involved. It would be just his luck to be part of one.

Clearly, his relationship with the NP was the key to everything, including his problems with the military. The NP had started it. They had set him, and now Jade, on this path. They initiated everything. They kept appearing. They took him, did things to him, and never told him what they were doing or why. Usually, they didn't even let him remember. At least sometimes, they took him and Jade together. And now, they were pointing him directly toward the underground base. Why? It was time the NP started giving him some answers. He needed to communicate with them—and remember their previous communications. He was convinced they had been teaching him for years. But what good was learning if he couldn't remember any of it? That had to change—somehow.

CHAPTER 25
BETRAYED

ON MONDAY, biology class seemed to drag on forever. Sam had no idea why, but Jade was either angry at him or really upset. She wasn't even trying to concentrate, which was very unlike her. At first, she kept her gaze fixed on Mr. Macklin's shoes; later, she did her share of the lab work but said nothing to Sam and refused to look at him. When he spoke to her, she gave one-word responses. At the end of class, as they cleaned up their lab space, Mr. Macklin stopped by.

"I'd like you both to stay after class for a few minutes. I have a couple of questions."

Jade looked at him fearfully; he met her eyes, unsmiling. "Just a few minutes," he said firmly. Sam looked from Jade to Mr. Macklin and back again.

"What's going on?"

"In here, please," Macklin said after the last student had left. He gestured to his office at the front of the lab, waited for them to precede him, and shut the door. Jade was nearly in tears; Sam was just confused. Macklin waved them to chairs. For a moment, he just stared at them.

"There's no way to ease into this, so I'll just say it: I know you two are in trouble. I don't know precisely what the trouble is, but you, Jade, have an army major intimidating you, and it appears that the army—or someone—is bugging you."

Sam was stunned. Jepson wasn't subtle, but how could Macklin know about the bugs? Only Jade knew. Sam felt fear, followed by anger that rapidly built into a roaring fire of rage.

"Since you two are always together, I assume that you, Sam, are in the same trouble. Now, which one of you is going to tell me what's going on?"

Sam glared at Jade. "You talked to him! After promising me a million times! I knew I should never have trusted you!"

"I didn't tell him anything important!" Jade cried. "I swear I didn't!"

"You promised to keep my secret. You lied!"

Jade buried her face in her hands. Sam stood and confronted her, hands on his hips.

"What did you tell him?"

"Just about Jepson. I thought . . . maybe he could help. We need help, Sam."

"Enough, Sam!" Mr. Macklin said sharply. "Jade has told me almost nothing because of her promise to you. She certainly didn't give away any secrets. And Sam—there's nothing wrong with asking for help."

Until today, Sam had been so shy he could barely talk to Mr. Macklin. But now, he glared at his teacher. "She promised me. And she talked."

"I'm not stupid, Sam. I can deduce some things without being told. I confronted the major outside, and I saw a printout that fell out of Jade's backpack. I'm assuming it was meant for you. He hasn't seen it yet, Jade?"

She shook her head, staring at the floor. She looked miserable.

"Show him," Mr. Macklin ordered. Trembling, Jade pulled

out a description of an anti-surveillance device and passed it to Sam without looking at him.

Sam looked at the ad, his lips pursed. He remained silent.

"Neither of you has anything to say?" Mr. Macklin looked from Sam to Jade.

Neither spoke. Jade continued to stare at the floor; Sam glared defiantly at Mr. Macklin, then looked away.

"Well, neither of you is denying it. That tells me I'm right about what little I know. I can't imagine how a couple of high school sophomores managed to get on the wrong side of the military, but I have to tell you, it's a dangerous place to be. Where did you even cross paths with an army officer?"

Sam sagged with relief at Macklin's question. She hadn't told him everything. But she had talked. Mr. Macklin eyed him speculatively.

"The major said something about you learning to keep your nose where it belongs," Macklin continued, turning back to Jade. "Were the two of you exploring and found something you shouldn't have?"

Sam drew in a sharp breath. Had she told him about the chat piles? *Please, no.* He didn't respond. Neither did Jade. Macklin shook his head in frustration.

"I'm guessing whatever you saw was classified. Otherwise, they would just warn you to back off. And the major was very evasive, which makes me think this involves more than the army. If it's classified, that might mean an intelligence agency. Which makes things worse."

Macklin looked from Jade to Sam and back again. Still, neither said anything. They didn't make eye contact with him, or with each other.

Macklin sighed. "All right," he said. "I can't force you to talk. Until today, I thought you were just stressed because of the harassment here at school. But now—I'm worried about both of you. I wish you would trust me. I was in the army; I might be able to help."

"Are we done?" asked Sam. His voice was cold.

Macklin looked at Sam, his eyes troubled. "We're done—for now," he said. "But I have to inform your parents—both of your parents."

They stared at him in horror.

Sam grabbed his backpack, swung it over his shoulder, and strode from the room.

"Sam, wait!" cried Jade, taking several steps after him. He ignored her and kept walking.

Outside, he flung himself onto his bike and peeled out of the parking lot. Usually, right after school, he and Jade biked to the picnic table, where they talked over their day, discussing how to deal with the latest harassment. They shared anything new from their reading or websites or NP dreams or insights or ideas of what to do next. Their conversations had been the highlight of Sam's day. Today, he had thought they would talk about how to counter the military surveillance. Jade apparently had the same idea, which would explain the printout.

But that was over. He could never trust her again. She had talked to Macklin, after all her promises. She said she hadn't told him anything important, but still, he should never have told her about the Night People. What a fool he had been. He had known for years that you can't trust anybody. Two people can't keep a secret. One will tell, every time.

At home, Sam tossed his backpack onto his bed and looked around restlessly. He wasn't used to being home this early. He needed to move. He grabbed his binoculars and headed into the woods behind the house. It had been weeks since he'd hiked here. He had been going to the chat piles or spending time with Jade. Now, the trees were turning yellow, and falling leaves were starting to cover his old paths. He'd forgotten how peaceful it was. Maybe a hike would work off some of his fury. He strode toward the center of the woods.

He couldn't remember ever being this angry. Nick and the other bullies—they were just ignorant. They made his life miserable, but they didn't really matter. His parents—his father hated him and beat him whenever he got drunk and Sam got careless. Sam had avoided him until Jepson threw them together. He shuddered to think what would happen if Macklin contacted him. And his mother—she was alternately caring and neglectful, concerned about him and worried he would embarrass her. Mostly she just let him go his own way. It was best to fend for himself and avoid antagonizing either of them. But Jade—he knew his fury with her was greater because he had let himself care about her. He had believed her promises, even thought she might become more than a friend . . . *Stupid, stupid, stupid!*

He slowed down. The woods around him were starting to feel wavery. Or he was. The air around him had a slight shimmer. Everything looked misty, out of focus. Suddenly, it seemed so quiet—no bird sounds, no crickets or cicadas. It was so peaceful, he almost felt like taking a nap. Well, why not? He had nowhere to be.

What was that up ahead? It looked like a large owl, but it was still daylight. And it was on the ground. Its eyes were huge and very black. He had to go closer; it was beckoning him. Entranced, he walked toward it, following as it moved away. They reached a clearing, and the owl turned to him. Oh, it was beautiful. . . .. The black eyes locked onto his. His mind opened like a flower. His entire life was opening, without boundaries. He was a seamless part of the universe, and the black eyes were drinking him in. He was disappearing into the eyes. It was all good, he thought dreamily; they would take, but they would also give.

Sam awoke lying on his back, staring up into a hickory

tree. A leaf with yellowing leaflets loosened and fluttered down onto him. He lay there quietly, waiting for his eyes—and his mind—to come back into focus. *What a weird place to take a nap. Why did I do that?* And then he realized, *I didn't. It was the NP.* It had been several years since his last NP experience in the woods. Or had it been years? They made him do whatever they wanted, and he only remembered things if they wanted him to.

The owl had been an NP. It had opened his mind and dumped in a huge amount of information. And it had looked at all of his information. Thoughts, memories, emotions. He wasn't sure how he felt about that. He hated it when humans —like Mr. Macklin—tried to get inside his head, but this was different, somehow. It seemed necessary, part of the plan. *What plan?* It made no sense for the NP to give him information and not let him remember it. And for some reason, he felt guilty. Why? As he lay under the tree, he heard the voice in his head. The NP, repeating over and over: *You are together. You are together. You are together.*

CHAPTER 26
ALONE AGAIN

SAM WAS AGAIN DREADING SCHOOL. This year had not been fun—the boredom of sitting through classes, the constant ridicule and bullying, the guilt of knowing he had drawn Jade into his world. But Jade had made it bearable. Seeing her every day—practicing Spanish, singing in chorus, learning Shakespeare together, being biology partners—had made him happier at school than he had ever been. Now that was gone. He was alone again. His own fault—he should never have trusted her.

The next day, Sam managed to avoid Jade most of the day; he arrived late to English and slipped into the back row to avoid sitting beside her. Mrs. Metzger noted his empty seat and gave him a puzzled frown when she located him in the back. Fortunately, she didn't comment. He did the same in Spanish. But he couldn't avoid her in biology. He arrived early, hoping to persuade Mr. Macklin to let him switch partners, or even better, work alone. But Macklin wouldn't budge.

"Sam, I never expected you to be cruel—you're doing the same thing to Jade that other kids have done to you. She talked to me, but she certainly didn't tell me any secrets. She's your friend, and you're treating her very badly."

"So, you won't let me switch partners. How about if I work alone at another table?"

"No. You need a partner. You need to learn to work with people. Even people you're angry with or don't like."

Sam glared at him.

"This is not like you, Sam. I hope you'll rethink the way you're behaving. And that you'll consider telling me about the trouble you're in."

Sam gave a loud sigh and sat at the far end of the lab table. He pointedly placed his backpack in the middle of the bench so he and Jade would be separated. When Jade arrived, she got the message at once. Her lips trembled, but she made no comment. The class crawled by. Mr. Macklin gave them lab instructions and got them started. Then he moved around the room, helping each group and giving them time to ask questions about their term projects. Both Jade and Sam shook their heads when he stopped by their table. He hesitated and then moved on.

Ordinarily, they collaborated on lab work, but this time, Sam worked alone, his eyes fixed on his tablet. Frowning, he studied a magnified onion root tip, counting and recording the number of cells in each phase of mitosis. Jade kept glancing toward him but remained silent. Mr. Macklin stopped by again, placing a microscope and two slides in front of her. He looked sympathetic, but his message was clear—give Sam space. She complied. Several students were watching them. Rumors of their rift would soon be all over school.

After class, Sam grabbed his backpack and left the room hurriedly, still ignoring Jade.

At home, he sat in his room. Macklin's criticism had stung. He didn't see why it was unreasonable to expect a friend to keep a promise or to drop the friend if they broke that promise. He shoved to the back of his mind all the things he and Jade had done together, all his faults she had overlooked. What a good friend she had been. And the NP's recurring dictum: *You are together*. None of it mattered. If she told someone too much, it could literally ruin his life. She had opened the door to an adult finding out about the NP and Sam's being outed as crazy and carted off to the state mental hospital, like Aunt Lucy.

His mind lingered, yet again, on Lucy. Her name kept coming up at school, usually when he did something people considered crazy. But his mother never mentioned her. The only time he'd mentioned Lucy, she had gone ballistic—like when he was five and first mentioned the NP. The topic was clearly off limits. But why? The more he thought about it, the more certain he was that Lucy had seen the NP too. And if his mother hadn't seen them, she at least knew Lucy had. No one ever mentioned *how* Lucy was crazy. Maybe kids his age didn't know. But, if she had seen them, and—like him—accidentally did something weird at school, teachers would know, and this made his situation even more precarious.

Angrily, he gnawed on his fingernails. A couple of them were bleeding. With Jade's constant reminders, he had grown them out to a normal length, but two days without her, and they were chewed down to the quick again. He got that Jade hadn't been through what he had, so she didn't really understand the stakes. But she did know how much secrecy meant to him. Yet, she had talked.

He closed his eyes and tried to focus. Jade was gone from his life, but the problems remained. The NP still plagued him, and the military (and if Macklin was right, some secret spy agency) was still following him. No one could know about this. But Macklin was telling their parents. If he talked to Sam's mother, things would get unpleasant, but he could cope. He just had to figure out what to say before she cornered him.

If his father found out, Sam figured his life was probably over. The last time, when Major Jepson brought him home, had been bad enough. This time, his father would likely beat him to death. He had toyed with the idea of running away a few times, but since Jade arrived, he had pushed those thoughts away. Even before, he'd hated the idea—it reeked of cowardice. But now . . . maybe he could look for Grandpa Joe.

He had been five, maybe six, when Grandpa Joe had left—shortly after his abuela. Both his parents hated the stories his grandpa told him about his Osage ancestors. After Sam's NP experience, his dad had somehow connected the NP with the Osage stories. Sam had already ruined his life by being born, his dad said, and now, this "damned Indian" was filling his head with crazy, creepy rubbish. His dad and grandpa had a horrific row. His mom had screamed at Grandpa Joe, too. So, he had gone back to Oklahoma—he'd never even written a letter as far as Sam knew. But he had liked Sam once. Maybe he would again. Lucy was his daughter, so surely, he knew what had happened to her. Maybe Sam could find both of them through the Osage Nation.

At least, since he and Jade were no longer together, the military would have a harder time tracking him. But he still had to get them off his back. He was still monitoring his tablet for spyware and they could still track him through the library computers. His biggest worry was the underground base. It was secret and he'd been inside—he was afraid the military would never let that go. But the NP controlled whether he went inside the base.

After his experience in the woods yesterday, he realized the NP had been with him all along. He had spent hours in those woods and had several experiences that seemed strange, even mystical. He'd just thought he was really attuned to the woods and their life. But was there more to it? He didn't remember seeing the NP—except yesterday—but that didn't mean they weren't there. All those owls. Waking up groggy, after naps he hadn't meant to take. Getting home hours later than planned. How naïve he had been! Of course, they'd been with him in the woods. But doing what? What did they want with him? He had to figure it out—and soon.

Deep in thought, he was startled when his phone beeped. He knew what he would see. He hesitated, then read Jade's text:

> *Pls let's talk. I really didn't tell M*
> *any secrets. Pls let me explain.*

It wasn't her first text. She had sent several last night and he had deleted them all. He deleted this one too. Even if she hadn't told Macklin any secrets, she had talked to him, after she specifically promised not to. *Never trust anyone.* He tossed the phone onto his bed and went back to his thoughts.

He had pondered the NP and their mysterious purposes since the encounter when he was five. The encounters seemed to stop when he turned twelve. He'd dared to hope that, whatever they'd wanted, they were finished with him. But these new recollections of experiences in the woods suggested they had never left. They had just backed off—buried the experiences more deeply so he wouldn't remember them. Maybe they didn't want to traumatize him. Maybe they wanted to make sure he didn't tell anyone. But now he had to dig those memories out. He needed to remember; he needed to *know*. But how? *Maybe I should just talk to them and tell them what I need.* He wasn't sure it would work, but when they'd used telepathy, he had understood them. Presumably, it worked the other way.

His phone beeped again. Jade. She just wouldn't quit. This text said,

> *At least let me explain.*
> *You owe me a talk.*

She had gone from pleading to angry. Well, that made two of them. He stabbed at the screen, deleting the text, and threw the phone again. It bounced off the wall and onto the floor. He had to get out of the house.

But even the quiet woods didn't calm him. He strode along the paths, fueled by anger, oblivious to everything around him. It was absurd, considering the situation, but he missed Jade like crazy. Before her, he had always been alone, so he had nothing to compare his loneliness to. It was just . . . life. Now, he knew what it was like to have a real friend, and there was a gigantic echoing cavern in his life where she had been.

Maybe he should try to contact the NP. He threw himself under a tree, closed his eyes, and took several deep breaths, trying to calm himself. He called out to them in his mind. Maybe the owl NP would come back. *Please tell me what you want from me.* He repeated it over and over. Nothing happened. Just as he gave up and started to leave, he heard an answer: *You are together.*

———

The next couple of weeks were agony. Sam ignored Jade completely—or tried to. He sat separately from her in English and Spanish. He had gone from loving chorus to hating it. Mostly, it was the guilt—he had promised to support Jade as she adjusted to having music back in her life. But now, when he even looked at her, his whole body tensed with anger. In biology lab, he spoke tersely, saying only what was necessary. He debated what to do about their research project for Macklin. Maybe nothing yet. Sooner or later, he guessed he'd have to talk to Jade, even forgive her. But not until he figured out how to control his anger.

As for their personal research project—he couldn't deal with that. He thought of their excitement as they delved into alien abductions and UFO sightings, analyzed what the stories might mean, finished each other's sentences. He thought of sitting close to Jade, touching her hand. His whole body ached and tears burned his eyes. *Don't think about it.* Now, when he was in the woods, and every night in bed, he called in his mind to the NP, asking what they wanted from him, how he could stay safe from the military. The voice said the same thing over and over: *You are together.*

CHAPTER 27
JEPSON CAUSES TROUBLE

ONE DAY DURING FIFTH PERIOD, an intercom announcement directed both Sam and Jade to report to the principal's office. There was murmuring and laughter in Sam's geometry class; someone said softly, "Ooh, aliens in trouble." Sam was stoic; he followed the rules, but people suspected him anyway. If there was a fight near him, they blamed him first. If something went missing, they searched his locker. He was never guilty, but no one trusted him. He was Brown and from the wrong side of the tracks. So, he was suspect, as long as he lived in Cassidy.

He had no idea what had happened today. Since their blowup two weeks ago, he had not spoken to Jade except when necessary. His anger still lurked like a living thing coiled in his belly. He did his best to control it, but sometimes . . . When they met in the hall, Jade asked timidly, "Do you know what this is about?"

"No," Sam snapped, and he sped up to avoid walking with her.

Principal Burke; Ms. Mott, the guidance counselor; and Mr. Macklin met them. Mr. Macklin looked tense but gave each of them a small smile as they entered. Sam sat as far from Jade as possible and refused to look at her. Principal Burke studied them both. They stared back. Jade looked fearful. Sam was barely controlling his anger.

"Relax," the principal said, "neither of you is in trouble. I called you in today because we have some concerns about your safety."

Both Sam and Jade looked up, surprised, but neither commented.

Principal Burke continued, "Mr. Macklin informed me some time ago about an unmarked SUV lurking around school, carrying an army officer, a Major Jepson. It's still showing up near here and around town. When Mr. Macklin confronted the major, he admitted following you, Jade. Were you aware of this?"

He was looking directly at Jade. She lowered her head and whispered, "Yes."

The principal nodded. "The major is not breaking rules—he's never on school property—but he's not subtle. He wants you to know he's following you, and he doesn't care if other people see him. He says he's on 'army business' and he's left alone. He's obviously trying to intimidate you. He also mentioned you, Sam, and suggested that the two of you are 'working together.' You are both students here, and it's our job to protect you, but we can't do that unless we know what's going on. Would either of you care to fill us in?"

Sam tensed and felt Jade tense beside him. Both kept their eyes on the floor and neither responded to Principal Burke. Sam was well aware of Jepson's intimidation; an SUV followed him, too. He had no idea what Jepson's game was. He and Jade hadn't visited the chat piles for weeks, and if Jepson was any kind of spy, he must know they weren't together anymore.

"Jade," the principal continued, "I've contacted your mother and made her aware of the situation. Mr. Macklin has also talked to her. Sam, I've contacted your mother and left a message. When she responds, we'll set up a meeting that includes both parents."

Sam's fists clenched, but he did not respond. He did not want his mother involved—but he breathed an inward sigh of relief. At least the principal hadn't called his father.

"In the meantime, I'd really like to get an idea of the situation. What we need to protect you from." Principal Burke paused.

Sam and Jade remained silent.

The principal sighed. "The major made two accusations. One seemed plausible, but the other was pretty bizarre. The more reasonable one was that the two of you were caught trespassing in a secret facility." He stopped and looked at both teens. "Is this true? Jade?"

Sam felt Jade glance at him, but he stared straight ahead, unmoving.

"We didn't trespass," she said. "We didn't do anything deliberately. We were just exploring—"

"Speak for yourself," Sam cut in savagely. "Leave me out of it." He looked at the principal. "Whatever she says, it has nothing to do with me. I speak for myself."

"Sam!" Mr. Macklin said sharply. "Jade is trying to be honest, and you are being extremely rude."

The glare Sam directed at Mr. Macklin telegraphed boiling rage. Mr. Macklin sat back, looking shocked as he met Sam's eyes. Ms. Mott looked from one to the other, a satisfied smirk on her face.

"Okay," said Principal Burke. He, too, seemed shocked by the force of Sam's anger. "Let's dial it back, shall we? We're just trying to find out what happened and get both sides of the story. Or all sides. Jade, will you continue, please? You can speak only for yourself if that would be more satisfactory to everyone." He glanced in Sam's direction.

Jade stared straight at the principal as she spoke. Her hands were clenched, but she was calm and articulate. "I was exploring and found some buildings. They were army buildings, but I didn't know that. I was looking around, trying to figure out what I'd found. But there were cameras. I guess that's how Major Jepson found me. He's been hanging around, kind of stalking me, for several weeks. I—I was afraid to tell anyone. He told me to stay out of things that didn't concern me. Then, he started coming around school, so I would see him when I arrived. That's all. I didn't trespass—I found the buildings by accident."

Mr. Burke regarded her for a moment. "Okay. So, where are these buildings you found?"

Jade shook her head. She looked fearful again. "I'm sorry, I can't tell you. You should ask Major Jepson. He was very clear that I couldn't talk about that."

He nodded. Then he turned to Sam. "Okay, Sam. Is there anything you would like to add to Jade's story? Or change?"

Sam had been clenching his fists as Jade talked, trying to control his anger. He was embarrassed. Jade had concisely summarized what had happened, without giving away any of their more incriminating activities. He didn't want to, but he had to accept her story. Finally, looking at his feet, he said, "No."

"So, you're saying that her account is true, and you accept it as a correct account of what happened to get you both on Major Jepson's radar?"

Again, Sam hesitated, and again, he had no choice. "Yes," he said.

"Okay," the principal said. "Technically, it's not the school's business if you trespassed, but the major is making it our business by harassing you in our presence. His actions seem . . . unusual. Mr. Macklin is an army veteran, and he is looking into Major Jepson. He can help you if you need help. So, please, tell one of us if you do. Understand?"

Both Sam and Jade nodded.

"Now, the major's second accusation is pretty off-the-wall. He's accused you both of being part of some secret group dealing with aliens in the military. He says you're spreading rumors." He smiled wryly. "Actually, his accusations make me wonder more about him than about you two. But he is an army officer, and he is harassing you. So . . ." Principal Burke shrugged and stared at both teens.

Sam's head snapped up when he heard the word "aliens." A surge of terror cut through his simmering fury. Beside him, he heard Jade's indrawn breath. He sneaked a glance at Macklin, who looked horrified.

Macklin protested, "Principal Burke, you can't seriously think these two—"

The principal held up a hand. "Let's let them answer, shall we? Sam, do you know what this is about?"

Sam shook his head. "No, sir," he said.

"Jade?"

Jade, too, shook her head, more vehemently. "No, sir," she said.

Macklin intervened again. "Principal Burke, do you think the issue might be Major Jepson's? Frankly, that sounds a little unhinged. Maybe he has a psychological problem? Something his superiors are unaware of?"

"The major was very angry," Mr. Burke said, "and my impression was that he wanted revenge. For what, I have no idea. But there seem to be some anger management concerns in this room, as well. So, perhaps the issue isn't *all* Major Jepson's."

Mr. Macklin sighed. "In fairness, Mr. Burke, I think the anger in this room is a personal matter that needs to be worked out between Sam and Jade."

Both kids were staring at the floor. Neither responded. The two men shared a slight smile, and the principal nodded. "Agreed," he said.

Ms. Mott had been silent, listening throughout the questioning, but now she spoke.

"I think there are some issues that need to be addressed here, Mr. Burke," she said. "This accusation of spreading stories about aliens in the military, for instance. Don't you think we should get to the bottom of that?"

Mr. Macklin intervened. "Principal Burke, you know both of these kids have been taunted and bullied about this alien nonsense—Sam for several years, Jade since she arrived this year. It's ridiculous, and neither of them did anything to deserve it, but Jepson could easily have tapped into the rumors in this school and used them for his own ends, whatever those are. I don't see how pursuing it will accomplish anything."

"Well, the anger issues certainly need pursuing," insisted Mott. "We can't have angry students running loose around the school. Who knows what they might do? They need to learn to control their anger."

Oh no, thought Sam, *she thinks I'm going to be a school shooter*. He kept his eyes firmly on the floor. *I've got to learn to control myself*.

Principal Burke considered Mott's suggestion. Finally, he said, "I don't think a little counseling would hurt. Why don't you see them both, separately, twice a week for now?"

If Ms. Mott resented the principal dictating the details of her counseling appointments, she hid it well. In fact, she was smirking, and Sam thought she looked quite pleased with herself. It sent a chill down his spine.

The principal gave both kids a stern look. "Tell us if you need help. We'll meet after we've talked to Jepson again and when your parents are available."

CHAPTER 28
MR. MACKLIN GETS PERSONAL

THAT AFTERNOON IN BIOLOGY, Jade caught Mr. Macklin's eye. He gave her a reassuring smile and said, "Later." Sam ignored them both, remaining intent on his lab work and cleaning up his lab space early. Mr. Macklin touched his shoulder.

"Don't try to cut out early," he said. "I want to see you both after class." Sam scowled at him, but Mr. Macklin gazed at him and said very quietly, "Don't test me, Sam." Sam subsided, angry but resigned. He always gave in to Mr. Macklin's gentle discipline. Everyone did. He had no idea what made that stern look and quiet voice so effective. After the other students left, Mr. Macklin waved them both into his office and shut the door.

He smiled at Sam. "You can relax, Sam. I'm not going to lecture you or get involved in your problems with Jade—tempted though I am. I just want to give you both a warning."

"About Counselor Mott," Jade said.

Mr. Macklin nodded. "You got stuck doing sessions with her, and I want to ask you both to tread carefully. I know I'm breaking the teacher code by speaking ill of another faculty member, but I'm worried she doesn't have your best interests at heart. I can't prove it, but I think she has ulterior motives."

"She makes me nervous," Jade said, "but I'm not sure why. Why is she involved in this, anyway?"

"She heard Principal Burke and me talking about Major Jepson and inserted herself."

"Does she know Major Jepson?"

Sam looked up, suddenly alert. Mr. Macklin looked surprised. "I don't know," he said. "Why do you ask?"

Jade shook her head. "It's probably nothing. She just gives me the same vibe Jepson does—a bad one."

"You should listen to that vibe and act accordingly. You'll be okay—just be careful. And remember, you can *always* talk to me."

Jade nodded. "Thanks."

"Okay, Jade, you can go. Sam, I'd like you to stay for just a moment. Not long, I promise," he added with a smile.

"Sit," he said, waving Sam to a chair. Sam sat, with ill grace.

"First," Mr. Macklin said, "I want to apologize for calling you out in front of other people earlier. But you need to learn to control your anger. I'm proud of you for how much you've grown this year—you're so much more open and less shy. And you can thank Jade for a lot of that, you know."

He stared straight into Sam's eyes, and Sam hung his head. It killed him to admit it, but Macklin was right.

"But if you're going to express emotions, anger isn't the best choice. Uncontrolled anger can get you in a lot of trouble. You saw Ms. Mott's reaction."

Sam kept his head down, but he could feel Mr. Macklin's scrutiny. "You and I are really a lot alike, you know," Macklin said. "I've spent most of my life learning to control my anger. Or control myself in general."

Despite himself, Sam looked up at this admission.

"You? You're never angry. Mean sometimes but not angry."

Macklin's grin was amused, and his blue eyes twinkled at Sam. "Mean? You're referring to the fact that I don't put up with your crap? Like today?"

Sam blushed and hung his head again.

"Well, you're right about that. But I am angry a lot. You don't often see it because I've learned techniques to control it. And I practice them constantly. I've developed a lot of self-discipline over the years, but it's not easy. I can teach you some techniques, if you want."

Sam looked up, fear in his eyes.

"Relax, Sam. That was an offer, not an order. And the offer is open, any time you want it. Do you understand?"

Mr. Macklin suddenly seemed less like a teacher and more like a regular human being. Kind of how he imagined a good father might act. Sam wasn't sure how to respond. Finally, he just nodded.

"Good," said Mr. Macklin. He paused. "Sam, I know you're a very private person, but I have to ask. Is everything okay at home? How much trouble will you be in if your parents find out about the—trespassing? Will you be safe?"

Sam was shocked. *How does he know?* He looked up and then quickly away. There was no way he could talk about this. Finally, he said, "I'm . . . everything's fine."

"Sam, you need to be safe. If you're not, you need to tell someone. You need to tell me."

"I . . . there's nothing to tell. I'm fine."

Sam was breathing heavily and squirming in his seat. His words did not match his body's response. And Mr. Macklin knew it.

"I know you don't like sharing things, Sam." Mr. Macklin's voice was very gentle. "But when I look at you, I see a lot that worries me. Not just anger, but stress and sadness and pain. And fear—a lot of fear. That's what worries me most. Please let me help you, Sam."

Sam's tension mounted as Mr. Macklin talked. How could he know all of that just by looking? At the very least, it meant Sam was doing an awful job of hiding himself from people. He remained silent.

Mr. Macklin sighed. "Okay. But please, come to me if you're in trouble. I'm a good listener if you ever want to talk about anything—home or school."

His smile was a little embarrassed. "You'll probably find this hard to believe, considering how I've messed up your life and Jade's, but Ms. Mott isn't the only psychologist in this school. I'm one, too."

At this, Sam did look up. He was surprised—and interested.

"I thought you were a biologist."

"I am. But while I was in the army, I started taking online psychology courses. After I started teaching here, I finished my master's degree. So, technically, I'm qualified to help you with your problems." He smiled wryly. "But, since I can't get either you or Jade to talk to me, I guess I'm not very good at it."

For the first time, Sam smiled—a tiny smile, but a real one.

"I'll bet you're pretty good at it." He looked Mr. Macklin in the eyes—another first—and this time his look was imploring, not angry. "Please, can I go now?"

Mr. Macklin smiled. "Go," he said. "But remember, be careful with Ms. Mott . . . Oh, one more thing."

Sam paused.

"Jade said Ms. Mott gave her the same vibe as Jepson. What vibe does she give you?"

Sam hesitated. "I agree with Jade," he said. "I feel the same way."

Mr. Macklin nodded. "I think I'll find out if those two know each other," he said. "Thanks, Sam. Go."

Sam left, feeling Mr. Macklin's worried eyes on him.

It was Sunday evening, several days after the meeting with the principal and his talk with Mr. Macklin. Sam was reading about alien abductions and listening to music—he had done a search for sad pop songs and downloaded a bunch; these days, anything upbeat grated on his nerves. His phone bleeped, making him jump. It was a text from Jade:

> *Sam, I need to see you. Mom and Mr. M just ambushed me. They've been doing research. I have information but will only talk in person. Let me know.*

Sam groaned. He was trying so hard to resign himself to living without her. When he was around her, he felt blazing anger—like that day in Mr. Burke's office. But, deep down, he knew the anger was helping him bury the pain. And now this text, while he listened to Calum Scott's soulful voice pleading in his ears, "You are the reason." Sam's eyes filled with tears. He had to stop listening to these songs.

Jade hadn't texted him for at least ten days, so he assumed she had finally given up. He had seen her once with those two poisonous girls, Whitney and Jessica, but she had left them quickly. He had seen her talking to Ravi several times. They appeared very friendly. He had vacillated between being glad she was doing okay, jealous that she was talking to Ravi, and terrified that she would talk more and give up something really important this time. When she saw Sam, she walked by without acknowledging him. It was good Jade was moving on, but . . .

He read her text several times. What if Macklin and her mom had learned something major? He had to talk to her, but could she really just tell him and leave? He doubted it—Jade was all about discussing things. And he wanted to. He missed her. His anger had finally cooled, leaving him mostly just sad and miserable. He knew he should forgive her, and he knew he should apologize too. She had broken her promise, but he had been really mean to her. Finally, he answered her text.

Ok. Tomorrow after school. Park table.

Her response was almost instantaneous.

c u then - thx j

Sam slept badly that night. He wasn't sure if the NP had given up on him, or if he just couldn't remember their visits. His life would be so much simpler and less frightening if they just disappeared, but if they did, he would have no one. *You're pathetic*, he thought. He was so lonely, he was actually looking to NP, or aliens, or whatever they were, for friendship. He tossed and turned for what seemed like hours, before falling into an uneasy sleep where he heard three words repeated over and over: *You are together. You are together. You are together.*

CHAPTER 29
SAM DELIBERATES

SAM WANDERED, zombie-like, through the next day's classes. He couldn't concentrate, but school this year was kind of a joke, anyway. He understood everything without listening or reading, and the homework—which he was still doing religiously, even without Jade to goad him—took almost no time at all. Why bother paying attention?

When he walked into biology, Jade was already there. He still placed his backpack on the bench between them, but this time he gave her a brief look and a nod. He did not smile. She returned the nod. They made it through class as usual, doing what was necessary but not talking. He noticed Mr. Macklin watching them both more closely than usual, once giving Jade a slight smile. Lately, they seemed much friendlier than he was comfortable with. It was clear he sided with Jade and was disappointed in Sam. After class, Sam gave her another brief look; said, "See you there"; and left quickly. He both craved and dreaded this meeting. He wanted so much to talk to Jade, to have things back to normal. But he didn't know how to make that happen.

When Jade arrived, Sam was sitting at the picnic table, his back straight and unyielding. He promised himself he would be strong. Jade parked her bike, dropped her backpack beside it, and kept her back turned for a moment. He wondered if she was finding this meeting as hard as he was. Finally, she turned and sat down opposite him. He wanted to be nice, but it wasn't happening.

"Well?" he asked curtly. "What do they know?"

She didn't answer immediately. She looked him over and finally said, "You look stressed. You're biting your fingernails again."

Sam hid his hands in his lap, cursing under his breath. He'd forgotten about his fingernails. He said nothing, just stared at her.

"I miss you, Sam."

Sam closed his eyes. He missed her too, but he was not admitting it. "What do you have to tell me? Or did you just say that to trick me into coming here?"

"I didn't trick you. There's something you should know. But I also have something to say, and you're going to listen. You won't get the information until you do. I'm tired of you refusing to talk to me."

He sighed explosively, looking down. "So, talk. But make it quick. I have things to do."

"Do you, though? You don't have friends. You're not doing sports. And it's just a guess, but I'm betting you already know everything we're supposedly learning in school and can finish your homework in about five minutes, every night."

Sam jerked his head up. "What do you mean?"

"It's true, isn't it? You feel about ten times smarter than you did last year. School is ten times easier than it's ever been. And it was already easy for you."

Well, that had grabbed Sam's attention.

"The same thing is happening to me," she continued. "You don't want to talk to me, and I respect that, although it would be great to discuss whatever's going on. But I do want to tell you what happened that day—the day you ran out on me."

"Fine, tell me. But it won't make a difference."

"That's up to you. I just want you to have all the facts. And you don't."

Sam could tell that day was burned into Jade's memory, and now she relived it for him. She told him about sleeping badly, dreaming about bugs and Night People. She described seeing the major before school, being hassled by Nick's bullies and by Whitney and Jessica, being shoved against the wall before lunch by a group of kids who called her "alien girl" and told her to go back where she came from.

She explained how Mr. Macklin had rescued her and followed her outside, where he had seen and confronted Jepson, and how he had taken her to his office and questioned her.

"I talked to him, Sam, and I'm so sorry I broke my promise. But I didn't tell him any secrets. I was just—scared and overwhelmed, and he's so nice. He wants to help us, Sam."

"Exactly what did you tell him?"

"I told him we'd been visiting the chat piles. And I told him about Jepson catching us and how mean and scary he acted. His threats. But I swear, I didn't mention the Night People."

"Good," he said with relief. "How about the bugs? And the underground base?"

"My backpack came open and that printout fell out, and he grabbed it before I could. I'm sorry. But I didn't tell him we'd found bugs. Or got inside the base."

She stopped talking and watched Sam.

Sam had just wanted to get through the meeting and leave, but Jade's story sucked him in. He could feel her honesty, and he believed her. She had been swept along that day by a series of unpleasant events caused by nasty people. Any one event would have been painful. Together, they would be nearly overwhelming. He'd had many such days during his own school career, and he sent a silent "thank you" to Mr. Macklin for rescuing her and for being kind. But he knew his anger had added many days of unnecessary pain to her life and his. His guilt was suddenly a heavy weight on his heart.

Sam looked up. Jade was still watching him, looking hurt and sad. That was worse than anger. He had to make this right.

He closed his eyes. "Jade . . . I'm so sorry. So ashamed. I should have realized I could trust you. I should never have overreacted like that, but . . . I'm just not used to trusting people."

She sighed with relief. "I know. It's okay, I forgive you. I just wish—why can't you talk to me, Sam, instead of running away mad?"

"I'm not used to talking, either. I promise I'll try harder from now on. Jade, why aren't you furious with me? You should be. I deserve it."

She gave him a twisted smile. "Yeah, you do. You were a real jerk. And I was angry. But I did talk when I said I wouldn't, so you had reason to be mad at me. You just stayed mad way too long."

He looked at her, shaking his head, embarrassed. "Would it be okay if we just . . . moved on now? Maybe talk about what your mom and Macklin said?"

"Yeah, we should," she said. "Macklin called someone he knew from the army and found out there's a secret base near here. He and Mom drove out to the chat piles on Saturday and found it." She smiled slightly. "It took them a long time. He said we were good detectives."

"What else do they know?"

"Apparently nothing. Just what I told him—that we were

snooping around outside the base, we were caught, and the major warned us to stay away."

"What about the anti-surveillance thing?"

"They think I got paranoid after Jepson caught us, and figured the military might bug us, but Mr. Macklin told me not to worry. He said, since we only saw the outside of the base, we didn't know what they were doing, so they had no reason to bug us."

Sam smiled. "How did you take that?" he asked.

"It was all I could do not to blurt out what we *really* know. But I didn't!" she assured him.

He nodded. "It's infuriating when they talk down to you, like you're a dumb kid."

Jade nodded. Then she said, giving him a sidelong look, "Oh, and Mr. Macklin said it made him suspicious that we both got a bad vibe from Mott."

Sam nodded, flushing. "Yeah. He asked me what I thought of her, and I said I agreed with you."

"Anyway, he checked. She was in the army too."

He frowned. "I'll bet they're working together."

Jade nodded but remained quiet. Sitting here with her felt peaceful and right; Sam didn't want it to end. He stood up.

"Well, I have to go."

She nodded. "Are we okay now?"

"I am if you are." He gave her a brief smile and then a long look, for some reason feeling a need to memorize every detail of her face. Then he left.

———

As he biked toward home, Sam basked in the first feelings of relief and happiness he'd had since that awful day in Mr. Macklin's office. And for the first time, he admitted his own guilt. Jade was right—he had been a jerk. Yes, she had talked when she'd promised not to, but Jade was used to confiding in adults. He should have realized that. And he should have realized that she wouldn't reveal secrets she had promised to keep. Why had he been so quick to blame her? Why had he thrown away their precious friendship? He knew it all boiled down to fear. Fear of the NP, his parents, everyone at school—adults and kids. Fear of his NP experiences being discovered. Fear that ignorant, judgmental adults would decide he was crazy. He needed to get past the fear. But how? Maybe Jade could help with that. Maybe she already was.

Back home, the woods were the only remedy for his restlessness. He walked through the trees, listening to the rustling leaves, absorbing the transmutations from summer into fall—spider webs, fading flowers, squirrels busily gathering acorns and hickory nuts. This peaceful, natural place reminded him that not everything is about humans and their problems, that other creatures live their lives, Earth revolves and seasons turn, and one day his worries and fears, his shame and guilt, would be far behind him. Life would go on, and he would survive. With Jade as his friend again. He smiled. Life was looking better.

Deep in the woods, Sam began to feel sleepy. He sat under a tree on a bed of fallen leaves, leaned back against the broad trunk, and closed his eyes, breathing in the clean earthy scents. What would he and Jade do now? The military hadn't given up—the SUV was still lurking. The NP could still grab them at any time. They needed a plan. Maybe they could discuss everything tomorrow after school. As he drifted toward sleep, a sudden hush fell over the woods. Shadowy shapes appeared around him. Tiny lights danced around him and he felt electricity prickling on his skin. The sparkling lights surrounded him, and the woods faded away.

CHAPTER 30
IN THE DUMBS

SAM AWOKE ENGULFED IN RUSHING, clattering sound. He felt like he was inside a drink bottle being shaken vigorously. It wasn't painful, just disorienting. The noise was loud but muffled. It was coming from outside the—bottle. *Okay, concentrate!* He was in a compartment with four well-padded seats, two pairs facing each other. The floor was carpeted. The upholstery was rich, thick black velvet; the metal sides were silver with a red stripe. Curved, darkly tinted windows extended up and over him along both sides. A pod car—a luxurious, futuristic one.

He sat up, trying to orient himself. Oh, this was too bizarre. The Night People were messing with him again. He picked a seat and fastened the seatbelt. The shaking was much less intense, but he could still feel the speed. Was this what flying felt like?

He must be on the maglev system, somewhere in the underground. There was nothing visible outside the windows, so he must be in a tunnel, like the one under the chat piles. It appeared the NP didn't bother with exact placement or comfort on underground trips. They just dropped you in the approximate place. Had they dropped him into a fast-moving train? Their aim must be very good. He wondered what happened if they missed, then decided he'd rather not know. More likely, they had dropped him into a parked pod, and he woke up after it took off. But why was he here?

This was not the same type of car he and Jade had seen. That one had been bigger, like a regular train car. But they had the same red-and-silver color scheme. Were they the same all across the country? And was it planned, or accidental, that he was the only passenger? He was relieved to be alone because he had no idea how the undergrounders would react to him. But stuck inside the pod, he had no idea where he was or where he was going. He looked around. Maybe this futuristic vehicle could tell him.

Between the two rows of seats was a narrow desktop with two screens set into its surface and a row of buttons below each. He pressed the left button. The screen nearest him rose vertically and moved forward. *Okay.* He pressed the next button; the screen lit up and gave him a menu. He studied it, and pressed Maglev-DUMB System and then Real Time. *Yes!* A U.S. map appeared, with a tiny red dot zipping steadily toward the west along one strand of a web of jagged lines— the maglev tunnel system, he assumed.

He played with the screen, zooming in on the map until the red dot magnified and he could read the names of sites along the lines. Maybe those were DUMBs, whatever they were? His pod appeared to be traveling northwest between Hutchinson, Kansas, and Colorado Springs—closer to Hutchinson, but moving fast. So, he had probably been traveling only a short time, and had entered the system fairly close to home. But what was in Colorado Springs?

He remembered his and Jade's conversation from weeks

ago. Why did the military want to keep them out of the underground bases, while the NP wanted them inside? He had no answers, but he had a few ideas. Maybe most of the military didn't know about the NP or believe they existed. Or maybe they did know and were keeping the public ignorant and misinformed. But he would bet that, somewhere in this maze of underground cities, there was a place where at least some NP lived and maybe worked with military people or people in some secret agency—people with an extremely high security clearance. He wondered if "his" NP were among them. If they were, he had no idea how to find them. Or what would happen if he did.

Sam felt an intense stab of loneliness. He wanted to discuss all of this with Jade. Why had the NP brought him here without her? He had been so angry with her and so miserable at giving her up, and then, just as they patched things up, the NP had dropped him here—alone. Why couldn't they have brought them both? Had she tried to call or text him? That would have been a waste of time—his phone was back in his room. He wondered if cell phones even worked down here. Would Jade figure out what had happened to him, or would she assume he was mad at her again? He cringed at that thought. He hoped she was okay and wouldn't have second thoughts about forgiving him when—if—he made it back home.

When the pod stopped in Colorado Springs, Sam was alert. The doors on either side opened, rising up in the air like wings. He got out warily and looked around. Several tracks converged here, and other pods were opening behind him. Security on the surface probably prevented unauthorized people from getting into the underground or using the maglev system. If he acted like he belonged, maybe everyone would assume he did.

But, if the NP wanted him to accomplish something, they

would have to guide him. Before he was taken, he had tried communicating with them—asking them for help. All they said, over and over, was *you are together*. But that was communication. Why not try that here? He needed help. He couldn't exactly walk up to a stranger and ask, "Do you know where the aliens hang out down here?"

Start with the basics. In his head, Sam conjured up an image of the NP. They all looked the same, but each individual had a different feel—a different essence or vibe. He zeroed in on the feel of his NP, the one who "felt" female and looked into his eyes and calmed him. He called out to her in his mind: *Please, show me where to go. Show me what to do.* He heard no answer, but his panic lessened slightly. The phrase *let go* floated through his mind. *Let go of what?* Well, since he was here, he might as well explore life in the underground.

He turned left and walked along the maglev track. On the other side of the broad sidewalk, the city began. Its architecture was similar to Cassidy Base. The shells of the buildings were rounded, grotto-like, made of shiny melted rock like the tunnels. Their grayish-white color gave the whole city a light, bright feel. Windows revealed typical city shops: cafés, a bank, a medical clinic, an electronics store. Televisions attached to several buildings were aimed down to be easily viewed by passersby. They were playing regular aboveground channels—he saw CNN, NBC, and Fox as he walked. He considered how they got TV reception so deep underground, and gave it up. He didn't know enough about physics or electronics. Maybe Mr. Macklin—no, that would never happen.

The maglev track divided here; one part continued ahead, the other veered left toward Cheyenne Mountain, whatever that was. The name sounded familiar, but he couldn't remember why. It was frustrating, knowing a little, but not enough.

On the business side of the track, a street led out of the

maglev station, into the underground city. That looked more promising. Sam memorized several landmarks and street signs so he could find his way back. Then, he stepped into the city. Except for the architecture and narrow streets—and the quiet—it was much like any big city, he supposed, although he lacked experience with cities. Cassidy was small even by town standards. He had grown up with woods near his house, the large green park in the center of town, yards filled with flowers and shrubs, overflowing summer vegetable gardens. There was none of that here. Everything was clean, shiny rock. Inside the buildings, everything appeared to be clean, shiny metal. But he didn't see any wood or plastic.

This city was technological, almost outer space in its design. Certainly, nature didn't exist here. He wasn't sure what was above except tons of rock and dirt. And Colorado Springs above that? A few buildings went up and up, forming giant cave-like skyscrapers. Metal girders glinted high above, inside a dome that seemed to go on forever. But a whitish mist floated around and through them, making it impossible to see details.

There were many more people than in the small Cassidy Base. Most were walking. Again, there were no vehicles, just glittery moving sidewalks. Everyone seemed focused; they moved with purpose. Something he should keep in mind, he thought; otherwise, he would stand out. That was already a slight problem. Most people ignored him, but he got some stares, probably due to his youth. Not for the first time, he wished he looked more like a man and less like a skinny kid. At least this time, he was wearing school clothes. He didn't look like a soldier or an office worker, but he was clean and neat, not covered in dust from the chat piles.

Sam closed his eyes and called in his mind to the NP. *Please help me. Show me where to go.* Finally, studying the maze of narrow streets, he noticed and followed an even narrower corridor heading away from the city. Inside the corridor, many horizontal branches led off in both directions. This was promising. Whatever went on here, it wasn't everyday city business. He would probably get hopelessly lost exploring this maze. Oh well, he was already lost.

He walked down the main corridor and turned into a side corridor on the right. Along its length were evenly spaced, inset doors. No nameplates or signs, no doorknobs, just a tiny round window in each at about eye level. He stood on tiptoe at one of the doors to see in, but nothing was visible. It must be a retinal scanner. A highly effective security device —he would only get in if his scan was recognized. Suddenly, he heard a click from the scanner and a warning buzzer from inside. The sound was muted, so the door was probably thick and shielded. But the buzzer meant he was in trouble. He turned and ran toward the main corridor, just as the door opened.

"Hey!" yelled a voice behind him. Sam risked a quick look back. It was a tall guy in a military uniform, with a gun—a serious gun that looked automatic. Scarier than the ones Jimenez and Nelson had pointed at them in Cassidy Base.

"Hey, come back here, kid! I'm not going to shoot you."

Well, that's a relief. Still, Sam had no intention of giving himself up. He kept running. And the cop kept chasing him. He was almost at the end of the main corridor, ready to disappear into the city, when he was caught. Sam was a fast runner, but he couldn't compete with the cop's longer legs. He cringed as the guy caught him by his T-shirt and braced him against the corridor wall. His eyes were level with the guy's name patch, which read Ross. Damn, the guy was tall! He wore fatigues, and the patch on his left pocket said U.S. Air Force.

"Settle down. What's your hurry? And what the hell are you doing in these corridors? You know they're off limits."

"Sorry," Sam said. "I was just curious."

"Curious? You're old enough to know what's down here, and you know the retinal scanner goes off if it's triggered by someone not in the system. You had to know you'd get caught. Are you *trying* to get in trouble?"

"No, sir."

"What's your name?"

Sam thought quickly. "Uh, David. David Gutierrez."

"Where are you supposed to be, David? Do your parents know you're running around down here?"

"I just got back from visiting my dad on the surface. My mom's at work. She doesn't know I'm back. I . . . I thought I'd explore for a while."

The cop rolled his eyes. "Explore. Look, kid. I'm not going to turn you in this time, but I am going to check you out, and if I ever see you down here again, you'll go straight to the commander. Understood?"

"Yes, sir. Thank you, sir."

Ross grabbed Sam's shoulder and guided him along the corridor until they reached the main city. There, he let go and gave him a push.

"Get out of here. Go home where you belong."

Sam didn't hang around until the guy checked out David Gutierrez and found out he didn't exist. It was time to get out of Dodge. He raced back through the city streets, forgetting about blending in, just looking for the maglev track. He almost tripped when a flattened round thing like a giant Roomba zipped across his path—a street cleaner? At the maglev track, he dived into the first open pod. Thankfully, it closed behind him. He wasn't sure where to go, but out of state seemed like a good idea. He brought up the computer map of the maglev system, and by trial and error, programmed in Dugway Proving Grounds in Tooele, Utah. The pod took off. This time he would be prepared. He returned to the main menu and found a list of Maglev stops. He zeroed in on Dugway and began to read the site description.

Sam desperately wanted the information, but for some reason, he kept losing track and nodding off. Then, he noticed the computer clock: 1:40 a.m. He slumped in his chair. Of course, he hadn't thought of time. The city was brightly lit, and there was no sky to orient him to the time of day. He had been running so hard and fast since he arrived, he hadn't stopped to process his exhaustion. And now that he had stopped, he realized he was not only dead tired but extremely hungry and thirsty, and he really needed a bathroom.

First things first. He scanned the pod compartment again and breathed a sigh of relief when he saw the enclosed cubicle in the corner. The bathroom was tiny and cramped but functional. There was even a faucet. After washing his hands, he bent down and drank from it. He immediately felt better. That left food and sleep. The pod seemed the obvious place to sleep, but how could he keep it closed until he woke up? Captured while sleeping—how humiliating. Back to the computer menu—and there it was. Basic commands for use of the pod. And most were voice commands. He blessed the designers. If only they had provided a snack machine.

Wait—maybe they had. Separate but attached to the bathroom cubicle was a smaller compartment. At the bottom was a slanted opening. On top were pictures of half-a-dozen unfamiliar items that *might* be food, and a circle marked Pay. *Might as well try*, Sam thought. He touched a picture, then the Pay button. A melodious female voice responded: "Sorry, you are not in our system." *Well, that's going to be a problem.* Belatedly, he remembered the retinal scanner and hoped the underground police weren't waiting for him at Dugway.

The pod had taken Sam late Monday afternoon. That had been several days ago, and since then, he had been traveling, stopping at various stations and exploring. The design of all the underground cities was the same, including the narrow branching corridors like those in Colorado Springs. He was sure these corridors must hide secret research. Based on computer descriptions, he now had a vague idea of the types of research going on at different sites. On the surface, for example, Dugway Proving Ground tested things like military hardware, weapons systems, and aircraft. Below, he was pretty sure the research related to chemical weapons—some combination of design, testing, detection, and countermeasures. But what did any of this have to do with him?

It was odd—whenever he found something that might get him closer to answers, he managed to alert someone to his presence and ended up fleeing back to a maglev pod and on to another destination. He didn't make the mistake of triggering the optical scanners again, but he got caught anyway. Mostly, he supposed, he looked like a kid, so he ended up in places where kids weren't supposed to be and people challenged him. His instinct was to run, so every time, he ended up in a new pod, headed for a new city. Almost like he was being herded. He was becoming convinced the NP were guiding him. He hadn't seen or heard them. But, in every new city, that tingly, panicky, otherworldly feeling he associated with them grew stronger. Sometimes he even thought he could smell them. He'd been traveling west. Did they live out here?

The last stop had freaked him out. As he had started back through the city, toward the maglev track, someone had yelled, "Costas! Stop right there!" He knew that angry voice: Major Jepson. Fortunately, he had a head start. He hurtled through the maglev station and into the pod at the very front. He gave voice commands to lock the doors and programmed the pod for Los Alamos National Laboratory in Santa Fe, New Mexico—the first destination he saw on the map. It was close, and he supposed Jepson might follow him, but for the moment, he was safe.

CHAPTER 31
MORGAN

AT LOS ALAMOS, Sam exited the pod, still tense after his near encounter with Major Jepson. He glanced at the pods opening behind him, afraid Jepson had hopped one and followed. That was unlikely; he didn't know Sam's destination. But the guy was devious, and he might have a way to find out.

Sam had been underground for nearly four days, and he still had no idea why. The NP had apparently deserted him. He was extremely hungry and tired. Lack of food was becoming a serious problem. He was sure those small compartments in the pods were snack machines, but he had no way to get the food out. He wasn't in the system, he had no money, and this underground city didn't even seem to generate garbage to pick through. What did they do with it?

Despite his innate honesty, Sam finally tried stealing. His first attempt was two days ago. He tagged along after a family entering a convenience-type store. Watching out for cameras and mirrors, he discretely pocketed a single granola bar. Not his favorite food but easy to grab. No one caught him, but he still ran. He felt relieved, if guilty, as he ate it—again, safely inside a pod—and put the empty wrapper in his pocket. He did the same thing the next day. He wanted to go for larger items, or more of them, but the thought of getting caught stealing was so horrifying, he couldn't bring himself to do it.

This morning, his stomach clenched with hunger, he tried again—this time, a grocery store with an outdoor fruit stand. He waited until there was no one nearby and snagged a banana and an apple, stuffing both under his shirt. He walked away rapidly, but not before the store clerk, sticking her head out the door at the wrong time, called out, "Hey kid, come back here!" His flight instinct took over, and he raced back to the maglev station and the nearest empty pod. He was pretty sure the clerk wouldn't follow—she was alone in the store—but he headed for the next town, just in case. Safely underway, he devoured the fruits. He was left holding a banana peel and an apple core, with no idea how to dispose of them. Finally, he flushed them down the pod's toilet. He felt better, but he would have killed for a burger or a couple of burritos.

Sam now had some grasp of the vastness of this network of underground bases. They were far more impressive than he and Jade had imagined from the wall maps at Cassidy. Each stop had a huge, self-sufficient underground city. The United States had an entire civilization living deep underground, while people on the surface remained oblivious. How was this paid for? Where did the people come from? How did they keep it secret?

Standing outside the pod, Sam stayed quiet, concentrating on controlling his breathing and fighting back his panic about Jepson. He felt like he had been running the whole time he'd been down here. And he was afraid he'd have to run again. Although if he didn't get some food soon, he wouldn't have the energy to run. He felt faint with hunger.

"So, what would happen if you just stopped running?" asked a deep voice to his right.

Sam whirled around. A huge, muscular Black man in army camouflage was leaning against the wall about ten feet away, watching him. Sam felt an immediate flash of recognition—it was the man from his NP experiences! The man had a broad, kind face, and at the moment he looked amused. Sam considered running again, but the man's words stopped him. Was he reading Sam's mind? He looked trustworthy, but what was he doing here? And what *would* happen if Sam stopped running?

"I—don't know," he admitted.

"Maybe it's time to find out."

"I know you," said Sam. "I've seen you before. You're with them . . . in my dreams, visions, whatever."

"You remember! That's excellent, Sam."

He knows my name. But that didn't mean he could be trusted. Sam tensed again. He still needed to be able to run at any hint of danger.

The man still looked amused. "I'm not going to hurt you. I'm offering to be your guide down here. You look like you could use one."

"Why would you do that?" Sam asked.

The man shrugged. "Maybe I'm just a nice guy. Or maybe there are things you'd like to know that I can tell you. Or maybe you'd just like a hot meal?"

Sam was wary, but he had seen this guy with the NP—several times. He always seemed friendly, even comforting. An ally. Plus, Sam couldn't resist the offer of food, and the man knew it. Finally, he said, "Okay."

"Good," the man said. "Name's Morgan Grant. Call me Morgan."

Morgan led him from the train station through a series of narrow, winding streets. Los Alamos looked similar to the other underground cities—steel buildings inside shiny, organically-shaped rocky shells. A lot of people, most in military uniforms. Still no cars; most people were walking, a few bicycling, and the narrow main streets had shimmery automatic walkways. The shivery, slightly exotic feeling that reminded Sam of the Night People was more pronounced here. Sam was nearly running to keep up with Morgan. After about ten minutes, they stopped before a doorway emanating the unmistakable smell of Mexican food. Sam's stomach growled.

"Mexican okay?" Morgan asked. "There's a lot of weird food down here, but I thought you might prefer something familiar this time."

Sam nodded. "Mexican's great. Thanks."

Inside, the restaurant seemed normal. A few people were seated at one end. Morgan ordered lunch specials for both of them. "And, Claudio, don't be stingy—we're both starving," he said, grinning at the guy behind the counter.

"Yeah, yeah." Claudio rolled his eyes and grinned back at Morgan as he piled tacos, refried beans, and rice onto two plates. "You're always starving. Can't fill you up." His slight Mexican accent made Sam feel comfortable, as he had years ago with his abuela.

Claudio plopped the overflowing plates onto the counter. He grabbed two large glasses and filled them with iced tea. As he worked, he glanced at Sam. "Who's your friend? Looks young to be down here."

"This is Sam," Morgan said. "And Claudio, you know if he's down here he's supposed to be here. You think he broke into this place?"

The cook shook his head. "Course not. Nobody could break in here—we're two miles down. He just looks . . . young."

Morgan shrugged. "He is. The smart ones start young."

Sam listened, bemused. Morgan talked as if he knew Sam, as if he belonged here. And apparently Claudio didn't know about the Night People. So, this place wasn't *all* about them.

They picked up their plates, and Morgan led the way to a

corner booth on the empty side of the restaurant. Claudio followed with their drinks. "Do us a favor, will you, Claudio? Don't seat anyone near here for a while. We need to talk."

"Sure. Enjoy."

Morgan looked at Sam. "Eat," he said. "You look hungry. I'll talk, catch you up on a few things."

But first, Morgan asked how long Sam had been underground, and he was shocked when Sam said four days.

"They told me you'd been on your own for a while," he said, "but I had no idea it was *that* long. No wonder you're hungry."

Morgan's brow was furrowed in what Sam thought was anger.

"I'm sorry," he said. "If I'd known, I'd have found you a lot sooner. Your parents must be panicked." He frowned. "And, unfortunately, I can't fix that. There's a blackout. We can't contact the surface right now."

Sam shrugged. "Don't worry. My parents probably haven't even noticed I'm gone. And they won't care anyway." Sam realized he didn't mind if Morgan knew about his parents. The man exuded—something—that made Sam trust him.

Morgan looked shocked again. He studied Sam with narrowed eyes. "Are you sure about that?" he asked finally.

Sam nodded. "I'm sure," he said. "It's not a big deal. I'd really like to know about this place, though."

Morgan took a deep breath, obviously deciding to postpone his own questions. Sam took in Morgan's information almost as eagerly as he did the food. They were not two miles deep, as Claudio had said, more like a mile and a half. This underground city was about three cubic miles in size and was connected to other cities by cross-country maglev trains and tunnels.

"These places are called DUMBs, by the way," Morgan said. "Didn't know if you'd heard that term."

Sam shook his head. "I saw it on the maps in the pods, but I didn't understand it. What does it mean?"

"It's an acronym," Morgan said. "Short for 'deep underground military bases.' I'm sure you know by now, there are a lot of them around the country. Last count was one hundred thirty-two, I think."

"What are they for? And why are they secret?" asked Sam.

"They have lots of uses. They store weapons, other dangerous things. A lot of research goes on down here, most of it so top secret it never gets to the surface. And by the way, the internet stuff about conspiracy theories and taking over the world—you can ignore all that."

"Okay, but who pays for all this? Where do these people come from? And how does all this stay secret? People up top don't know about this place, do they?"

"Whoa!" Morgan held up his hands, laughing. "Things are top secret for a reason, you know."

"Well, somebody brought me here. Shouldn't I know this stuff?"

"Yeah, but there's a lot I don't know. We all have top-secret clearance, but it's compartmentalized. We only know what we need to. Ask your questions. I'll tell you what I can."

"Where do all the people come from?"

Morgan pursed his lips. "Different places. Some are regular military, all ranks, all services. They work down here, but their jobs are classified, so they don't discuss them with their families. Their families assume they work on the surface. Some are civilians with special skills—same deal. They're sworn to secrecy, and usually come temporarily, for special projects. Some belong to intelligence services—CIA-type groups, what you'd call 'secret agents.' They never tell *anyone* what they do or where they go. And some people have just disappeared from the surface and live down here.

"Not as surprising as it sounds," he added, smiling at Sam's astonished face. "Thousands of people go missing every year—they just vanish. Some of them are recruited and are here by choice. Some have been here for a couple of generations now, since the 1940s, when the DUMBs were first built, raising families."

Sam blew out a breath. This was hard to believe, but the DUMBs exist, so . . . "Okay, who pays for all this?"

"Good question. Wish I knew." Morgan smiled wryly. "The government has a huge black budget that pays for secret projects. But this setup is worth way more than that. So, there's a huge influx of cash from somewhere. I have no idea where."

Sam sighed. "Okay. Who are the NP, and what do they want with me?"

"The NP?"

"Sorry—that's what I call them. You know how I got here, right? The little people that take me and drop me in different places, whether I want to go or not?"

Morgan grinned at this description. "Yeah, I know them. Why NP?"

"Short for Night People because when I was little, I thought they only came at night. I know better now, but I'm used to calling them that."

"I see. So, you think they brought you here?"

"Didn't they?"

Morgan sighed. "Yes. They just didn't bother telling us humans. That's why you've been on your own for four days."

"So, this place—the DUMBs—it's basically a nest of Night People? With their human helpers? Or slaves or whatever?"

"It's not a 'nest.' And we're not slaves. We work together. It's just—even after all these years, we don't communicate that well. They're—different. Hard to understand."

Sam closed his eyes. "No kidding. So, they live down here, right? I can feel them."

"Yes, many of them do. Researchers, mainly. They live and travel through the DUMBs, just like people, but they're concentrated in the Southwest—like here. But you won't see their homes. Or them, usually. They keep their lives secret from us."

"And you're okay with that?"

"Not really," Morgan said. "But we don't have much choice. They're a lot smarter than we are. We just interact—professionally."

"What do you do—professionally? Experiment on people? Like me?" Sam didn't really want to hear the answer to that question. But he had to know.

Morgan looked uncomfortable. "Well . . . I guess that would be accurate. Although, I don't want you to think they have any evil intent. Or that we do."

"So, what *is* their intent? Your intent?"

"It's . . . complicated. We're trying to—save ourselves. And them. I can't explain it in a few words. It'll make more sense if it unfolds gradually."

Sam asked the question that had been tormenting him for four days. "Why am *I* here?"

"Not sure. I have an idea, but let's leave that for later, shall we?"

Morgan eyed Sam's empty plate. "Time for dessert. Ever had Mexican brownies?"

Sam shook his head. His dad was Mexican, but his mom was the cook. And she didn't do Mexican, or anything different, really.

"Time you tried them!" Morgan said, grinning. "I'll get a bagful from Claudio. We'll take them along."

As they left the restaurant, Morgan handed Sam a brownie and watched his delighted expression as he took a bite. "Claudio's specialty," Morgan said. Cinnamon and chili powder."

They walked back toward the maglev station, Morgan swinging the bag of brownies. *He's like a big kid,* Sam thought. He liked the guy, but he still wanted to know what Morgan was doing with the NP—and with him. Morgan had been much more forthcoming than he had expected, but now, Sam's mind was crammed with new, unsettling information. And they were going on a field trip—amazingly—to Area 51, the top-secret base and the location of so many supposed UFO sightings! At least, the underground part. Despite his fear and uncertainty, Sam was thrilled. He asked if the rumors were true, and Morgan replied that some were, some weren't.

They entered a pod and Morgan programmed the computer for Area 51. He told Sam the trip would take less than twenty minutes. The train traveled at Mach 2.5—nearly two thousand miles an hour! Sam felt a surge of excitement and then, almost immediately, a searing pang of loss. He sighed. Morgan looked at him closely.

"Okay," he said. "It's your turn to talk. Why the sigh and the long face? I thought you were excited."

"I was. I am. Thank you very much for rescuing me and helping me understand all this. And for the food," he added. "I'm just missing my partner. We're supposed to have adventures like this together."

"So why aren't you together?"

Sam looked up. "Because the NP brought me here alone. They didn't bring her."

"Why do you think they only brought you and not Jade?"

"You know Jade, too? Jeez, don't we have any privacy at all?"

"People as important as you and Jade—not much. It's

hard to accept, but I hope you'll come to realize it's for a good cause."

"Important? We're in high school." His fear was starting to spike again. Maybe Morgan wasn't as nice as he seemed. What if he was some kind of pervert? Or if he and the NP had evil plans for them? He wasn't creepy, or a bully, like Major Jepson. But still, he knew way too much about them.

Again, Morgan seemed to read his thoughts. "I'm on your side, Sam. You trusted me when we met, and nothing has changed. Now, tell me why you think your NP didn't bring you and Jade here together."

"I don't know," Sam said. "I really miss her," he admitted, looking up. His emotions were raw and close to the surface, and he clenched his fists to control himself. He would not cry in front of this macho army man! But after four days on his own, he felt totally lost. And he still had no idea why he was here. "I'm starting to feel like I'll be down here forever, and I'll never see her again."

Morgan exhaled, stretched out his legs, and stared thoughtfully at his army boots. "I'm not sure what your NP are up to—we just call them Visitors, by the way, capital V—but I've learned to trust them. I think they might have separated you so you'll realize how much you need each other. Especially you. You're the one who dumped Jade and left her hanging for weeks."

Sam reddened. "I can't believe you know that. You guys have cameras on us, don't you?"

"No. I know very little about your personal life. I actually got that from the Visitors. I can read their thoughts sometimes—when they're really strong. And they've been pretty ticked off at you lately."

"But why do they care?"

Morgan shrugged. "You and Jade were doing so well together, and suddenly, it all just fell apart. The Visitors don't realize how strong human emotions can be. Our emotions upset their plans for us, and they get—confused—about what to do."

"They have plans for us?"

"Of course. Did you think they were studying you just for the fun of it?"

"I don't remember most of what they do. And none of it makes any sense."

"You and Jade were figuring it out. You were making progress, until you got mad at her, and quit."

Sam hung his head. "I was an idiot and a jerk. Believe me, I know. I tried to make it right with her just before they dropped me down here. But now they don't seem to want to take me home. They've never kept me overnight before. What if they keep me here forever?"

Morgan laughed. "Nothing lasts forever. I'm sure you'll see your girlfriend again soon."

"I hope you're right. But she's not my girlfriend; we're just friends," Sam said.

Morgan raised his eyebrows. "Really?"

Sam looked down at his hands, blushing in confusion. Morgan grinned. They were silent for the rest of the trip.

CHAPTER 32
WE ARE TOGETHER

AS THE POD began to decelerate, the air suddenly crackled, and Sam's hair stood on end. He felt the eerie stretching of time, or space, that heralded the NP. And he realized he did not want to go home, not yet. Were they really going to beam him away, just as he was getting some answers?

Before he could panic, Jade materialized in the seat next to him, looking dizzy and half-asleep. She gave him a bleary stare and said, "Sam?" After a brief, startled moment, he leapt up, pulled her to her feet, and engulfed her in a crushing hug. He could feel tears falling, and he knew Morgan was watching, but he didn't care. He buried his face in Jade's hair and lost himself in its sweet scent. He felt weak with relief and joy.

"Oh, Jade," he whispered. "I thought I'd lost you!"

He held her tightly in his arms, feeling her relax against him. He had never hugged her before, and he observed, as if from a distance, how perfectly they fit together. After a moment, Jade pulled back slightly, still locked in his arms, and looked up into his face. "They brought me to you," she said. There was wonder in her voice. "I asked them to bring me, and they did."

They continued to cling to each other. Finally, Morgan said, "Well, kids, I know you want this moment to last forever, but we need to get out of this pod."

They both jumped. Jade looked from Morgan to Sam and back again.

"Who are you?" she asked. He smiled and motioned them out of the now-open pod door.

Outside the pod, Sam introduced Jade and Morgan and explained about the field trip. He was lost in her eyes and kept finding reasons to touch her. He knew he was acting like more than a friend, but he didn't care—Jade was here; nothing else mattered.

Smiling, Morgan said, "You two need time to catch up. I know a place you'll like."

He led them into the city, taking a circuitous route. Eventually they came to a wider street dominated by a gigantic freestanding glass building filled with light and green plants. It formed an irregular pyramid, with rooms, gables, even open decks jutting out in unexpected places near its pointed top. Sam and Jade looked up in awe. It was a living skyscraper.

"What is it?" Jade asked Morgan.

"Kind of a refuge; keeps us undergrounders from feeling like moles and badgers," he said with a grin. "The upper floors are hydroponic farms; they grow the city's fresh produce. The bottom floor is a botanical garden. It's always open so people can go in and relax, and be in nature for a while."

"So, we can go in?" asked Sam. This was what he had missed most in this underground world—everything was sterile and technological; there was nothing natural. He appreciated technology, but he needed nature.

"That's why we're here," Morgan assured him and led them inside. The vast garden was probably ten stories high, with pebbled pathways winding among full-grown trees, vines snaking through branches, and exotic flowers poking gaudy heads out here and there. It was a tropical paradise. It smelled clean, earthy, and sweet and had a hushed feeling, like Sam's woods at home. And there were animals! Bright-colored birds flitted through the trees, calling and shrieking. Bees buzzed and butterflies darted among the flowers; Sam saw an iridescent blue-and-green lizard zip up a tree trunk and disappear. Both he and Jade jumped at a sudden loud screech. They looked up, searching the treetops. Sam caught a brief glimpse of a small brown body with a long tail as it leapt to a nearby tree.

"Is that a *monkey*?" he asked.

Morgan grinned. "Yeah, there's a small troop of macaques in here. They can be holy terrors, but I like them. They're fun."

He led them to a stone bench nearly enclosed by hanging vines. Some exotic flower was blooming nearby; it wasn't visible but its sweet scent filled the air.

"You two get reacquainted. I'm going to take a walk; I'll be back in a while."

He pulled a squashed bag of brownies from inside his jacket and handed them to Sam. "Here, introduce her to these. The way to a woman's heart . . .," he added, winking.

He turned and disappeared up the path.

They sat on the bench. Sam opened the bag, took out two brownies and handed one to Jade. He watched, smiling, as she bit into it. "Oh!" she said. Her eyes widened in question as she looked at him.

He grinned. "Mexican brownies—cinnamon and chili powder." Although they were new to him, too, he felt pride in introducing her to a tiny piece of his culture. They finished their brownies, staring into each other's eyes. Why hadn't he realized? He didn't just like her, he loved her.

Finally, Jade said softly, "You are together."

He looked at her in shock. "What did you say?"

"It's what the NP kept saying to me. For four days, I kept asking them to please, please bring you home, and that's all they would say. Finally, I changed what I was asking. I thought, 'Take me to Sam. We are together.' And they brought me to you, right away."

He shook his head in amazement. "They've been saying that to me for weeks. It's all they've said, since I . . ." He stopped and looked down at his hands.

Jade watched his face. Finally, she said, "They want us to be together, Sam. It's okay. We both could have handled things better, but it's over now."

He looked up at her, his eyes filled with tears. "I still feel bad. I'm so sorry I doubted you. I was such a jerk. You didn't deserve any of that."

"You were kind of a jerk," she said, smiling. "But I understand better now. Since you've been gone, I've learned so much more about what your life has been like. Knowing the NP took you, and trying to figure out how to find you, with the adults just wanting to call the police and hospitals and put out alerts for runaways."

"People were looking for me?" he asked, astonished.

"Of course, people were looking for you! They still are. You disappeared. You've been gone for four days."

He shrugged. "I didn't figure anyone would notice, or care, except . . . maybe . . . you."

She looked into his eyes. "Sam, I understand why you might feel unloved. I've talked to both of your parents. But my mom and Mr. Macklin have been frantic since you disappeared."

"Your mom was worried about me? And Mr. Macklin? Why would he care? I'm just a student."

Okay, maybe Mr. Macklin took an interest in him sometimes. Sam remembered the special books, starting in seventh grade. And lately, his concern about Sam's anger, his home life, and his and Jade's relationship. Maybe Sam even daydreamed, sometimes, about having him as a dad. But that didn't mean . . .

"He took charge of finding you—immediately. Sam, he was nearly in tears when we were talking about what to do. I've never seen an adult more emotional, except my mom when my dad was killed."

Sam could not speak. He couldn't believe any adult cared that much about him. He had always tried to avoid getting close to adults. It seemed safer for so many reasons. The thought of Dr. Mathieson and Mr. Macklin looking for him was hard to believe, but it gave him a small, happy glow. And Jade's closeness was more comforting than anything he could remember. They sat quietly, just being together. After a moment, Jade took Sam's hand and laced their fingers together.

Suddenly, she began to cry. "Oh, Sam, I've been so scared. I couldn't figure out where you'd gone. First, I was afraid you had run away. Then, when I realized it must be the NP, I kept thinking, 'I need Sam. He would know what to do.'"

"But I didn't know, either. I was afraid I'd be stuck down here forever, and I'd never see you again." He paused. "Morgan thinks the NP separated us so we would understand how much we need each other."

"Well, it worked!" she said, with a watery laugh. "But why did they bring you here? Do you know?"

He shook his head. "No idea. They just dropped me here and . . . left me."

She sat up and dried her eyes. "Well, there must be some reason. To learn about the underground, maybe?"

"Maybe. But I think there's more. I think Morgan knows some of it."

Her gaze was thoughtful. "You're learning to trust. You trust Morgan, don't you?"

"Yeah, I think so."

"Why?"

"Well, partly because I recognize him—he's the guy from my NP visions. Remember when we first met and felt like we knew each other? It's like that, only more—definite."

Jade nodded, her eyes wide.

"Morgan seems like a good guy. He's on our side."

She nodded again. "I don't recognize him, but I like him. He seems nice and caring and friendly. I'm glad there's someone down here to help us. It would be so scary on our own."

"You have no idea!" Sam's voice was fervent.

"What do you mean?"

"I only met him a few hours before you came. I've been on my own down here until today."

She looked shocked, but he waved away her questions. "It's a long story. I'll fill you in when there's more time."

Morgan appeared from a side pathway. He was frowning at his phone but put it away when he saw them.

"You two doing okay?" he asked. He gave them a searching look.

"We're fine," Jade said. "Thanks for giving us some time."

Morgan nodded. "I've been thinking," he said. "It's been a long day, and I think we should put off our field trip until tomorrow morning. I don't know about you, Jade, but this young man has had only one meal in the last four days. So, I'm guessing he's probably hungry again?" He looked at Sam, who grinned and gave a self-conscious nod.

"So, I suggest we go eat, and I'll tell you some things about your NP. Give you a better understanding before our field trip. And then I'll take you home with me, and you can get a good night's sleep."

"You live here?" Sam asked. He hadn't thought about where Morgan lived.

"Most of the time," Morgan said. "I work in the DUMBs, but I spend time on the surface, too. My wife's a geneticist at one of the labs here. You'll meet her tonight."

Jade looked confused. Sam quickly explained about DUMBs and the one hundred thirty-two underground cities. He reminded her of the maps in Cassidy Base. Morgan listened. He looked approving.

"My son's not home now," Morgan said, "so his room is free. And we have a comfortable couch."

"You have a son?" Sam said.

Morgan nodded. "Nathan—Nate. He's eighteen. He's on the surface, in college. About to start graduate school."

"Graduate school? At eighteen?" asked Jade. "So, he's a genius?"

Morgan smiled. "He's about the same as you two. I expect you'll do the same."

They both stared at him in disbelief. He cocked his head and raised an eyebrow. "How are you doing in school? Any problems this year?"

They looked at each other and then at him. "Actually, school's incredibly easy for both of us," Jade said. "What does that mean, exactly?"

"I'm guessing it means that, if you wanted to, you could finish high school this year and head straight for college. But what do I know?"

"What *do* you know?" demanded Sam. "Is there some reason we're suddenly smarter than we were? Have the NP been messing with our minds?"

Morgan shrugged. "Don't you like being smarter? Most people would be happy."

Sam was perfectly happy to be smart. It was the invasion of his mind that bothered him. He wanted to be smart on his own, not because some alien was playing with his brain or his DNA. What had they done to him? To Jade? To Nate and how many others? And why? He looked at Morgan and shook his head. He felt overwhelmed.

Morgan seemed to understand. "It's a lot to take in. Let's go eat, and I'll tell you what I know."

CHAPTER 33
CONVERGENCE

IT WAS A TYPICAL UNDERGROUND RESTAURANT, Morgan said. It had no kitchen or cooks or servers. Above the counter were photos of food items (or so Sam assumed) and names, with a digital button under each. Sam stared at the photos and buttons.

"I've seen these before—in the pods."

Morgan nodded. "Yes. But the pod ones are snack machines—very limited choices."

As in the pods, the names and photos were not helpful. Sam and Jade looked at Morgan, who grinned.

"I'll choose for you. Trust me, you'll like it."

He retrieved three trays, and randomly, it seemed, punched buttons until they all contained a selection of foods. A couple were cylindrical and looked crunchy. Others were softer, with different shapes and textures. There were no utensils or wrappers. Then, Morgan pressed the Pay button and laid his index finger on a small, clear plate. After a moment, a musical chime sounded, and an electronic voice said, "Thank you. Enjoy your meal."

The flavors were unusual but tasty. Sam bit into a crunchy

cylindrical thing, similar to a cookie but with a light, meat-like filling.

"This is really good—what is it?" he asked Morgan.

"It's called a gryllie. Glad you like it."

They tried bites of several foods and liked them all. Morgan watched them, looking amused. Finally, Sam asked, "So, what is this stuff?"

"Well, these"—Morgan pointed to several foods— "are made on-site, using inorganic ingredients. If the molecular structure is stored, the computer can make it. People here call them 'replicators,' like on Star Trek. They're like 3D printers for food," he said. "Others are made from a base of insects or bacteria or algae. The first thing you tried, the gryllie—that's from crickets. Everything provides complete nutrition. And tastes good."

They both stared at him in shock. He grinned and shrugged. "You asked."

Sam closed his eyes. "Okay." He had asked. And it was good, and he was hungry, so he kept eating. So did Jade, after a short hesitation.

The day had been stressful, and they were finally relaxing. But suddenly, Sam sat up straight and looked at Jade in horror."Jade, I just realized—you're here! You've disappeared, too. Your mom must be going crazy!"

Morgan looked up, interested.

Jade's face was the embodiment of guilt.

"I'm sure she is. By now, she's called Mr. Macklin and told him the whole story, and they've probably called the police." She shivered. "They're going to be so mad at me."

"What whole story?" asked Sam. Had she finally told her mother about the NP?

She pulled herself together and gave him a look. Startled, he realized it was just like Mr. Macklin's no-nonsense look. When had she started doing that?

"No, Sam, I didn't tell them about the NP. Although it's been hard not to, with you disappearing. They kept doing all the wrong things to find you—like police and internet. But I knew the NP had taken you, and I knew they wouldn't believe me if I tried to explain it."

She looked tearful. Sam reached out and touched her hand.

"I was so worried. I couldn't figure out why you hadn't come back. So, I came up with a plan . . . They're going to be so mad," she said again.

"But," she added, "when we do get back, we have to tell them what's going on. They deserve to know. Not to mention, they'll demand an explanation for where we've been."

"Jade, you know they won't believe us."

"My mom will, I think. She knows how honest I am. And we can explain everything that's been happening. Mr. Macklin—probably not. He's totally scientific, and he just dismisses all this alien stuff as nonsense. But, Sam, he really cares about you, and that won't change, even if he doesn't believe us."

"He'll think I'm crazy and try to send me to a shrink. Or a mental hospital." He didn't worry about Jade—her mom would protect her. And he didn't bother to comment on "he really cares about you." Whatever Jade thought, that was ridiculous.

She shook her head, frustrated. "No, he won't! And I told them about your Aunt Lucy," she added.

Sam made a choking sound, and she fixed him with another Mr. Macklin-type glare. "Don't even start. They had to know. You were missing, remember? That's one of the times he almost cried, by the way, when I told him you were afraid people would think you were crazy, like her, and try to . . . send you away."

Morgan had been following their conversation. Now, he interrupted. "Jade? How did you get here?"

"I—asked the NP to bring me."

"And they just . . . did?"

She nodded.

He stared at her in wonder. "What did you tell your mom—before?"

"Nothing, really. I asked her if she thought I was sane and rational. She couldn't figure out why I was asking, but she said yes. Then, I got her to admit that Sam was, too. Then, I told her something unusual might happen soon—something she would have trouble believing. And if it happened, to please remember that Sam and I are both sane and rational."

Morgan laughed. "That was a masterful stroke, Jade. Did you leave a note?"

Jade nodded. "I just told her I'd gone to look for Sam. I didn't want her to worry that I'd been kidnapped by some random criminal—they never said it out loud, but that's what they were thinking about Sam." She sighed. "She'll still be worried and furious, though."

"Yes, but she'll know you planned it, plus you've primed her to understand about the Visitors." He shook his head. "I still can't believe they just did what you asked."

Jade looked at Sam. "She asked if what was happening had anything to do with Major Jepson."

Morgan's eyes widened. "You know Jepson?"

"Yes," Jade said. "He's been hassling us since the NP dumped us in Cassidy Base." She gave him a probing look. "You know him, too."

"Unfortunately," Morgan said. "I'll tell you later."

"What did you tell your mom about Jepson?" asked Sam.

"That she should consider him a piece of evidence—that the fact that he's so obsessed with finding out what we know means what you and I are into is real, not imaginary."

Morgan grinned, shaking his head. "Perfect. But we have some decisions to make about secrecy, with you two appearing down here. You're right, Jade, when you get back, you'll have to tell them something—preferably the truth. I'll discuss it with my CO and we'll talk about it later. I'm guessing you can convince your mom, Jade. Maybe not your hidebound scientist—a teacher, right? I assume *he* thinks you're both sane and rational?"

"Let's hope," Sam said.

"This teacher, or scientist—his name's Macklin?"

Sam nodded.

"You know his first name?"

"Greg," said Jade. "Why?"

Morgan shrugged. "The name's familiar. You know how old he is?"

Sam shook his head.

Jade said, "My mom's thirty-eight, and they look about the same age. He might be a year or two older. You know him, too, don't you?"

Morgan shook his head. "No. I heard of a guy named Macklin in the army, some time back. But I didn't know him. Thought it might be the same guy, but probably not."

Sam watched him. He wasn't saying everything he knew. "Mr. Macklin was in the army," he said. "He used his army contacts to help us with Major Jepson."

"Good for him. Glad you have a protector up above."

Morgan stopped talking and seemed deep in thought. After a moment, he looked up.

"If Macklin is protecting you two, make sure he knows Jepson is dangerous, maybe even . . . unhinged, okay?"

Sam was startled. He glanced at Jade, who looked equally spooked. "He knows," Sam told Morgan. "He's even used the word 'unhinged.'"

Morgan nodded. "Good. Tell him to be careful and vigilant. I'm sure he knows that, but tell him anyway. Never hurts to have someone corroborate your gut instincts."

"What do you know about Jepson?" Jade asked. "We should know, too."

"Yes, you should." He hesitated and sighed. "He's one reason we're on digital lockdown and I can't contact your parents."

They looked at him, alarmed. He shook his head. "Don't worry, you're safe with me."

"He knows I'm here," said Sam. "He saw me at the maglev stop before I met you."

Morgan's head snapped up. "You're sure he saw you?"

"Yes. He yelled out my name, and I ran. That's why I was so freaked out when I met you. I was afraid he'd followed me."

Morgan pulled out his phone and typed a quick text. Sam started to speak, but Morgan held up his hand, stopping him. He watched his phone until he received a reply.

"Okay, my CO knows the situation. But we should leave now, get off the streets. We'll go to my place."

Before they left the restaurant, Morgan pulled three button-sized electronic devices from a pocket and pressed each, causing them to glow. He attached one to his collar and instructed Sam and Jade to do the same.

"What are these?" asked Jade.

"Monitoring devices," Morgan said. "We can be tracked, even if we get separated."

Sam and Jade looked alarmed again, and he smiled. "Don't worry; that's not likely. It's just a precaution."

But Morgan was now tense and alert in a way he had not been before. His eyes scanned the streets around them and—to Sam's surprise—even the higher levels of surrounding buildings. The buildings' sculptured appearance made it hard to imagine they contained windows that could hide spies, even snipers. When Sam was alone, streets in the DUMBs had been scary mainly because they were unfamiliar. With Morgan, he had relaxed and enjoyed exploring his new environment. Now, he was acutely aware that they were trapped underground and that every person they passed, not to mention every person hidden above, was a potential threat.

"What do you think he'll do?" Jade asked. She sounded breathless.

"Not he, they," said Morgan grimly. "He was one of us, or so we thought. But he has radical anti-Visitor beliefs. He considers them evil and thinks they should be eradicated. So, he started an anti-alien group. The military ordered him to disband it, but he didn't. He was demoted from colonel to major. Two drops in rank. It's rarely done, and he's not happy about it. He stays in the background, but his group's activities are becoming more open and more violent. So, we're taking no chances."

"Do you know about Mott?" Sam asked.

"Mott? Who's that?" Morgan asked. Sam explained about the school counselor and her possible connection to Jepson.

"Okay, we're definitely having a talk when we get home."

Morgan hurried them along the main street, then turned, taking a twisting route that left both Sam and Jade disoriented. They followed quietly—Morgan was in no mood for conversation.

As they walked, an insistent whining noise, like an angry bee, began to impinge on Sam's senses. But there were no bees in the DUMBs—well, not outside the botanical garden, anyway. He swung his head around, trying to locate the sound. The whining grew louder and angrier. Suddenly, Morgan threw an arm around both teens, forcing them to the ground. A flattened, hummingbird-sized object zipped over their heads, but Morgan's large body shielded them both.

Sam heard a sharp ping. Morgan grunted, and a tremor ran through him.

"Are you okay?" Sam asked. "What happened?"

"A drone," replied Morgan, gasping a little. "Shot me in the shoulder. Stay still. Someone will come for us."

And within minutes, they did. The monitoring devices clearly worked. A man and a woman, both young, both in army fatigues, helped them up and quickly checked them over. The drone had disappeared.

The young woman's dark hair was sleeked back into a bun. She wore a worried frown. "Are you kids sure you're okay?" she demanded.

"I'm fine," Jade assured her.

"Me, too," Sam said.

The man was arguing with Morgan. "Colonel, you have to go to the hospital."

Colonel?

"It's not serious—it's just a flesh wound." Morgan sounded impatient. "I've got to get these kids home."

"They'll come with us. General's orders. That's not a flesh wound; it's a puncture—a shot. And we don't know what was in it. So—hospital."

Morgan sighed but gave in. Fortunately, the hospital was close. They took an automatic walkway, with the two soldiers guarding them. Morgan began to feel faint, and the male soldier radioed ahead, requesting a wheelchair. At the ER entrance, Morgan sank into it. Tests showed the shot had contained a potent sedative but no poison. Morgan was given a drug to counteract the sedative and returned to normal fairly quickly. The soldiers decided the attack was probably meant to sideline Morgan, allowing Sam and Jade to be kidnapped. No one seemed to doubt that Jepson's group was behind the attack. Or that Sam and Jade were its targets.

"But why would they kidnap us?" asked Jade.

Morgan shrugged. "The Visitors are very interested in you two, and Jepson and company will do anything to hinder the Visitors."

Back to the same question, thought Sam: *What do the Visitors want with us?*

They were on their way to Morgan's home, traveling on another moving walkway. Morgan called them autowalks. It was faster than walking and gave them a chance to rest. Their escorts—the same two young soldiers—were hanging back, allowing Morgan and the kids to talk privately.

"You're going to catch these guys, right?" Sam asked Morgan.

Morgan sighed. "We're trying, but it's been tricky. Jepson is a sneaky one. His MOS is intelligence analyst, and he's always two or three steps ahead of us."

"MOS?"

"Sorry—Military Occupational Specialty. His job—what he's trained to do for the military. Don't ask me how someone with his messed-up psychology got accepted into Intelligence, or even the army, but here we are." He sounded depressed, which made Sam feel guilty. He felt like he had put Morgan in danger—not to mention Jade's mom and Mr. Macklin. And Jade herself.

He had to learn how to protect himself—and others, Sam thought. Something else to ask Morgan.

CHAPTER 34
MORGAN'S HOUSE

MORGAN TURNED the subject from Jepson. As they traveled, he asked, "Were you two aware the Visitors brought you together?"

Sam nodded. "We figured."

"Can't say I'm surprised. How did you figure it out?"

"I met Jade the day she moved to Cassidy," Sam said. "We both felt like we already knew each other. We found the secret base together a week later. When we started comparing our experiences, we realized how closely they matched. And then, we were abducted together—three times that we know of."

"And there's my mother," Jade added.

"Your mother?"

"Moving to Cassidy seemed like a weird decision. We both had friends in Kansas City. She had a good job; I liked my school. And all of a sudden, she decides to move us to this little grungy, know-nothing town in the middle of nowhere—sorry, Sam."

She flushed as she glanced at him, realizing she had just insulted his hometown.

He grinned and shrugged. "Sounds like a spot-on description to me."

"Anyway," Jade continued, "I was really mad. I was more or less resigned by the time we moved, but I wasn't happy. Then I met Sam, and everything changed. I was so glad we had moved, or I would never have known him."

"Oh, you probably would have—the Visitors would have found another way. But this obviously worked well. Your mom might be more connected to the Visitors than you're aware of. I don't know that for sure," he added as Jade looked at him in surprise. "But that's a big change for someone who's perfectly content."

"And there's one more thing," said Sam. "'You are together.'"

He looked at Jade, and she nodded.

"What does that mean?" asked Morgan. He turned, scrutinizing the two of them.

"You know when I was mad at Jade and just left her?" Sam was embarrassed talking about it, but Morgan, to his credit, did not make a flippant comment; he just nodded. "Well, all that time, I was trying to communicate with the NP, the Visitors, I mean. You know, with telepathy. I figured the only way I could stay safe from the military was by getting the Visitors to help. Especially since I wasn't with Jade anymore. But the only thing they said to me during that whole time was 'you are together.' They said it over and over."

"And the same night they took Sam, we had just made up," Jade continued. "And the next day Sam was just gone. I figured the Visitors had taken him, and I begged them every day to please bring him home. But they didn't. They just kept repeating, over and over, 'you are together.' So, when I let them know I understood that, they brought me here."

Morgan put an arm around each of them and nearly crushed them with his hug.

"I don't know you kids that well yet, but I am *so* proud of you already! I think the Visitors have outdone themselves putting you together. Outsmarted themselves, even."

Sam and Jade looked at each other, confused.

"What are you talking about?" asked Sam. "What did we do?"

"Do you know how many thousands of people the Visitors try out? They abduct them, test them, analyze them, teach them. They're looking for people with the right characteristics, who can help with their agenda, who can understand and learn and adapt. They try to make sure no one remembers anything, but of course memories bleed through and people wake up before they're supposed to. Almost always, people are terrified into helplessness. They can't think or react, they just freeze. And later on, a lot of them have psychological problems.

"But you two—you haven't just made great strides in overcoming that paralyzing fear. You think and analyze, you go to great lengths to remember, and—God help us—even figure out what they want and give it to them! You actually communicate with them! Do you realize how rare that is?"

Sam and Jade shared another glance. Sam still wondered what the big deal was. He shrugged. "We were just doing what we always do—identifying a problem and trying to solve it."

Morgan smiled at them. "Never mind. Just keep doing what you're doing. And here we are."

Morgan's apartment was high in one of the large buildings along the same avenue as the botanical garden. It was spacious and light and spare, with hanging plants and a lot of books. It was homelike and fit Sam's impressions of Morgan, except there was no hint of the Visitors. Of course, there wasn't at his house either. Morgan introduced them to his wife, Sarah. She was a contrast to Morgan—a petite woman with flawless dark skin and a cascade of black, curly hair. She was neatly dressed in blue lab scrubs. But like Morgan, she had a bright smile and an easy laugh, and she immediately made them feel at home.

They spent half an hour getting acquainted with Sarah. Then, Morgan made them tell him everything they knew about Jepson and shared his own information. Jepson was clearly dangerous, and—Morgan thought—becoming more mentally unstable. Sam vowed to be much more careful from now on.

Morgan found some of Nate's clothes for Sam, and Sarah gave Jade a nightgown and a change of clothes for the morning. Sam finally began to unwind a bit and enjoyed a long, hot shower—his first in four days. The underground showers were unique. Morgan called them "space-age"—water was collected from the drain, purified, then recycled, making it both water- and energy-efficient.

Afterward, in Nate's bedroom, Sam sat cross-legged on the bed, wearing a pair of Nate's pajamas and watching Jade. She wore a short, sleeveless nightgown covered in bright tropical flowers, and was rubbing her long, damp hair with a towel. They looked clean, calm, and happy. Sam looked up to see Morgan standing in the doorway, smiling at them.

"Hey," he said. "You two doing okay?"

"Fine, thanks. Is this where we're going to sleep?" asked Sam.

Morgan nodded. "Well, one of you. The other can sleep on the couch in the living room."

Sam glanced at Jade. He really wanted to stay with her, but that obviously wasn't going to happen. "I'll sleep on the couch," he volunteered.

"Okay. I'll set you up when you've said good night. Sleep

well, Jade; we have a big day tomorrow." He smiled at them and left.

They looked at each other. Sam was so thankful they were together again, but he was afraid Jade might disappear at any moment. He remembered earlier, hugging her and holding her hand. He longed to touch her again, but here, alone like this, it was . . . harder.

"You haven't told me what happened to you the last four days," Jade said.

He hesitated, then said, "What if we wait until they go to bed, and I'll come back and we can talk?"

Her smile was shy but inviting. "I'll be waiting."

An hour later, when the apartment was quiet, Sam crept back to Nate's bedroom. Jade had left the bedside lamp on.

"Come sit by me," she said quietly, pushing the covers back and patting the bed. It'll be easier. We can whisper."

"What if Morgan comes back?"

"He won't—they're asleep."

Sam sat close to Jade and quietly described his underground adventures. As he talked, she slowly inched her fingers into his. He squeezed her hand, his breath hitching slightly, but he continued talking, pretending nothing had changed. A bit later, he fell silent and they just held hands. When Sam stole a sidelong glance at Jade, her eyes were closed and she was breathing evenly. He was exhausted. He knew he should return to the couch, but it was so peaceful here, close to Jade, with her hand warm in his. He would stay for just a few minutes.

Much later, Sam was startled awake. Morgan was kneeling beside him, touching his arm. Sam's eyes widened fearfully when he realized where he was. Morgan smiled and put a finger to his lips. He removed Sam's hand from Jade's, led him back to the couch, and pulled a blanket over him. Moments later, Sam was asleep again.

The next morning, Sam vaguely remembered seeing Morgan during the night but couldn't remember why. He and Jade took turns in the bathroom and dressed separately. They headed toward the kitchen, following the smells of bacon and coffee and muted sounds of conversation. Morgan and Sarah were cooking breakfast. They stopped talking when the kids entered. Sam hoped whatever was being said about them wasn't something to worry about.

Breakfast was excellent. It included a bacon-like meat that Sarah explained was genetically engineered in a lab near hers. Sam had wondered if all the meat came from bugs and bacteria—he knew vegetables came from the hydroponic gardens, but he hadn't seen any evidence of farm animals. His mind conjured up a brief, bizarre glimpse of a cow riding down a two-mile-high glass elevator. *Not likely*, he thought. He actually preferred the idea of meat made in labs. He ate meat because people served it to him, and it did taste good, but the thought of killing animals, even for food, made him cringe. He should become a vegetarian, he thought.

After breakfast, Sarah left for work. Sam and Jade were excited. Maybe now they would find out the mysteries of Area 51! But Morgan seemed disinclined to satisfy their curiosity about UFO sightings and alien bodies.

"Look, the Visitors want me to show you something down here, but I don't know what. I have to guess—or read their minds. With other people I've guided, I've had vibes from the Visitors, so I had at least some idea what to do. But not with you."

"They must have told you something," Jade said.

"You've told me how they operate with you," he said. "They never tell you what to do. They wait for you to figure it out. Maybe that's what's happening here."

"They expect us to figure out what we need to see? How can we do that? We don't even know what's here."

"I don't know. And there's something else." He looked worried—an unnerving change from his usual upbeat demeanor.

"What?" asked Sam.

"I need to warn you to be very careful when you go back."

"Careful about what?" Jade asked.

"That's just it—I don't know. Everything. I know the Visitors test people, especially people they're serious about, like you two, by causing, or allowing, dangerous or—awful—things to happen to them in the 'real world.'"

Jade and Sam looked at each other.

Morgan sighed. "I really want to go with you when you leave here and deliver you home to your parents and try to explain all this. But if the Visitors beam you out, I won't get the chance. I just want you to be careful and prepared. For the Visitors, as well as Jepson."

Having delivered his warning, Morgan pivoted to the day's plans. "Now it's time to crack the Visitors' secrets, or try to."

CHAPTER 35
DUMBS WITHIN DUMBS

THEY ENTERED THE CITY, trailed by their young guards. Sam wondered if he would ever learn to navigate the mazelike DUMB cities. But Morgan knew every twist and turn, and within minutes they were facing a long, narrow corridor with rows of side corridors extending at right angles along both sides.

"So, this *is* where the secret research happens," Sam said. "I figured."

Morgan looked surprised. "You've seen these before?"

Sam nodded. "I found one in every city I visited. But I haven't tried to get in them since the first one, in Colorado Springs."

Morgan grinned. "Let me guess. You tried an optical scanner. And got caught."

Sam nodded again. "The cop called me a kid and told me to go home to my parents. I ran straight for the maglev station and took the first pod out of there. I figured that was safest, since I'd given him a fake name. But it was frustrating. I knew all the interesting stuff was happening in these places, and I couldn't see any of it."

"I can tell you two hate being treated like kids. But in this case, you'd have been in a world of trouble if you'd looked more adult." He eyed Sam, still grinning. "A fake name, huh? Getting a head start on your criminal career?"

Sam shrugged and grinned back, looking guilty.

"Well, you're in luck today. My security clearance can get you in most places."

It even got them into places their guards couldn't go. When the guards arrived at the entrance to the corridors, Morgan said, "Thanks. I've got it from here. I'll text when we're ready to leave."

Both guards said, "Yes, sir." When Sam looked back, the guards were watching their progress down the main corridor.

Morgan obviously had a specific destination in mind, but he didn't share it. As they walked, he filled them in—finally—on what lay above them. Groom Lake, he said, was a twenty-five-square-mile area of restricted airspace. Its dry lake bed was a salt flat, perfect for runways and a natural location for a secret air force facility. Area 51 was a smaller square inside Groom Lake. Security was extremely tight around the whole area.

"Much of what goes on up top," Morgan said, "has to do with building and testing new, secret aircraft. A lot of times, people think they've seen UFOs around Groom Lake. But usually, they've seen test flights of secret aircraft, like the SR-71 Blackbird or the F-117 Nighthawk."

"Usually?" Sam asked.

Morgan grinned at him. "Yes, usually. Who knows what the others are?" And that was all he would say.

By this time, they were almost at the end of the main corridor. At the last side corridor, they turned left and walked to the very end, toward a glass elevator like the one in Cassidy Base. Morgan fitted an eye to the elevator's retinal scanner and stood quietly for several seconds. The elevator opened, and he gestured for them to enter. He pressed the Down button, and the elevator began its descent.

"Where are we? Where are we going?" asked Jade.

"DUMBs within DUMBs," Morgan said. "The level we live on is about 1.5 miles deep. It's where most of the standard secret research goes on. Sarah's lab is there. They do genetic engineering research. Others do projects on high-energy physics, quantum mechanics, artificial intelligence, spookier stuff—teleportation, time travel."

Sam and Jade looked at him in disbelief. "People really study that stuff?" Sam asked.

Morgan nodded. "They do. Teleportation, at least, shouldn't surprise you. Think about how you got here."

They looked at each other. "Oh," Sam said.

"So, it was the military, not the Visitors, who brought us here?" asked Jade.

"No. It was the Visitors," said Morgan. "Most of the military don't know you're here. And not all who know are happy about it. But the Visitors don't ask permission."

Sam was trying to work it out in his mind. "So, the Visitors used teleportation to get us here. And the humans here are studying teleportation. Why don't they just use the Visitors' technology?"

"Because the Visitors don't just give us their technology. They make us work it out for ourselves. It's called reverse engineering. People take alien technology apart and try to figure out how it works so they can recreate it. That way, we understand it—it's not just a mysterious black box. Think of the DUMBs—part of them, anyway—as schools for human scientists, run by the Visitors.

"But most of the research stays down here," Morgan continued. "They don't want this technology loose in the aboveground population. Not sure why."

The elevator was fast, but it still took a long time to descend.

"We're going down another half mile past the main level, where the really secret stuff happens. I'm not sure this is what the Visitors want you to see, but I'm guessing it is. If I'm wrong, we won't get very far."

He noted their alarmed looks and reassured them. "Don't worry. Nothing bad will happen. We just won't be able to get into some places. If that happens, we'll go back upstairs and visit regular secret areas instead of supersecret ones."

The elevator moved down into a bright open space, slowed, and stopped. Sam and Jade exited the elevator and looked around in wonder. Banks of computer screens lined the walls, and probably fifty people worked busily at computer stations. A short hallway near the back led to a huge room containing rows of rectangular structures. *A supercomputer?* Sam wondered. Most people ignored the arrival of the elevator; a few looked up and said, "Hey, Morgan." Morgan acknowledged them with a slight wave. Some gave Sam and Jade curious glances but asked no questions. Morgan did not introduce them.

"This way," he said, turning right. Another corridor, and at the end, another door with a scanner. He stopped before the door. "There's one favor I have to ask. You have to keep everything starting with this elevator secret from everyone—parents, teachers, friends, military, *everyone*. Okay?"

They nodded.

"You can talk about the DUMBs, even the secret research area upstairs," he continued. "But not this area. You're children—sorry, but you are," he said when they both glared at him, "so you can't get clearance, and almost no one else knows about this place. You're now part of a privileged few. But by bringing you here, I'm obeying the Visitors, not my human superiors, so if you say anything, I'm pretty much toast."

Sam was shocked. "Morgan, we would *never*—"

"I know. I trust you. I just had to say it." He clasped their shoulders, and turned to the retinal scanner. "Okay, let's give this a try."

Sam and Jade looked at each other. Morgan's request had brought home to them the seriousness of the situation. What was behind the door? Would it open?

It opened. Morgan looked pleased—and relieved, Sam thought. Inside the supersecret lab, the atmosphere was different. Or the mood. It was gloomy, deep. Jade grasped his hand; Sam could tell she was feeling it, too. His heart rate increased; his breathing became heavier. The air tingled. The lighting was dim; everything felt grayish, muted, and the lab areas around them seemed to lack distinct edges and corners. Sam took a deep breath; it felt like an abduction. *There are Visitors here*, he realized. Morgan was watching them, and he nodded at Sam. He had picked up Sam's thought—he was mind-reading again. Jade was trembling. Sam remembered that she recalled little of her direct interaction with the Visitors. He put an arm around her shoulders and whispered, "It's okay. Morgan's here."

She nodded, also whispering, "I know. But they're still scary."

"This is an alien genetics lab," Morgan said. "But I don't think that's what they want you to see."

He led them past the lab to an enclosed area with a broad, curved window along one wall. It was murky; Sam squinted but he couldn't see what was behind the glass. There was a tight feeling behind his forehead, a very slight electrical surge. Jade was rubbing her forehead as though her head ached. Suddenly, he knew what to do.

"Reach out," Sam said. "Reach out with your mind to the

Visitor we know."

He closed his eyes and called out to her, to his NP. *Please, show us what we need to know. We want to learn.* Jade leaned against him, breathing heavily, and he hugged her close. His NP appeared in his mind, her strange, pointed face bright. Her huge eyes looked straight into his mind. *Look now*, she said. He opened his eyes and looked through the window. It was clear, and within were Visitors, lots of them, working with people he somehow knew were abductees. Among the Visitors were humans in military uniforms. He had been here before—inside.

For a few seconds, there was an overwhelming rush of information into his mind. They were working to understand the human mind and meld it somehow with the Visitor mind. *Mind-meld*, he thought dreamily. Like Spock, only more so. A new type of mind that could produce solutions to help humans survive and flourish on a rapidly changing Earth.

He saw quick, intense, close-up flashes of environmental devastation, like the earlier hologram. A fracking operation, a series of earthquakes. Fires, droughts, floods, hurricanes, deserts, stripped and dying rainforests, melting ice caps, dead coral reefs. It seemed clear they expected him and Jade to hold back that devastation; surely, they couldn't be expected to do such a thing, certainly not alone—if, indeed, anything could stop it. Then, for an instant, everything became crystal clear, and he nodded. *Of course.*

He opened his eyes and looked at Jade. Her eyes were still closed; she was nodding slowly and saying, *yes, I understand.* The information dump was gone, but the memory remained, along with the memory of his Visitor's approving face. When Jade opened her eyes, he watched the impression of vast all-knowingness fade and disappear, and she was Jade again.

Morgan stood very still. He had watched them throughout the experience, first with confusion and then with dawning comprehension. Now, as they returned to themselves, he was studying their faces with an expression close to awe.

"You were communicating with them," he said softly. It wasn't a question.

Sam nodded, feeling a little dazed. He looked at Jade. She was nodding, too. They all looked at the concave window. For Morgan, it had never changed. For Sam and Jade, it was murky again.

"Time to go," Morgan said. "I think it's safe to say this was a successful visit."

As they took the elevator back up to the 1.5-mile level, Morgan asked them to describe their experience. They did their best; however, as usual, while impressions remained, the information itself was gone—except they both felt an even more intense urge to stop Earth's devastation.

Morgan smiled. "I think you got just what they intended you to get. The information is inside your brains, ready to be released when the time is right."

Sam shook his head. "I still don't understand. They seem to want us to do it all—to save Earth. But that's crazy! How can we? Why us?"

"Not sure any human can answer that question. You both have something they need, some trait or traits that make you capable of doing great things. I don't know what yet. Neither do you. But you'll figure it out, or they'll reveal it to you. Just be patient and open."

"I want to do it," Jade said, "but they're asking the impossible."

"You pleased your Visitor by asking for information and opening your minds to her. You're eager to learn, you want to understand, you try to communicate, and you experiment until you get it right. It's a surprisingly rare combination of behavioral traits. That alone is enough to make you special. And there are two of you! So don't worry."

CHAPTER 36
AREA 51

AS THE ELEVATOR STOPPED, Morgan paused, a pensive frown creasing his forehead.

"I think we'll go up to the surface," he said. He entered a code, and the elevator shot upward, splaying their bodies against the walls. Sam and Jade both gave him questioning looks. He shrugged and smiled. The ride was long, fast, and terrifying. Sam felt like an astronaut riding a rocket.

Finally, the elevator slowed and stopped. When it opened, they were surrounded by light—natural, blinding, desert sunlight. The spacious entryway was filled with comfortable sofas and chairs, all facing outward. The room was like a really high-class teachers' lounge, Sam thought. Its walls were all windows. In a corner kitchen area, a couple of people were fixing snacks. Half-a-dozen others relaxed on the couches, one reading a document, the rest staring out the windows. They looked up and smiled as Morgan, Sam, and Jade entered.

"Welcome to Area 51," said Morgan. He swept his arm around, encompassing the entire area, inside and out.

Sam drank in his surroundings. Outside were the pale sands of the Nevada desert, dotted in the immediate vicinity with low, modern white buildings and several towers that presumably supplied electricity, internet, and phone service. Farther out were several much larger buildings. Hangars, thought Sam. Jet planes, sleek and silvery, faced away from the hangars. Short runways led from each hangar toward two long, straight runways, one wide and one narrow, which faded into the glimmering desert. Rugged mountains surrounded the entire area. People dressed in desert camouflage strode among the buildings, their actions filled with purpose.

Morgan held the door open, and they stepped out. The October air was still, dry, and warm, in the low seventies. A perfect day. Sam breathed deeply—it had been five days since he had seen real sun and breathed fresh air.

"Are you going to show us something secret?" asked Jade. She was practically bouncing with excitement and her eyes were wide.

Morgan looked pensive again. "Not me," he said. "You know I told you I get vibes about what to show recruits? Well, I had one back there—that's why I brought you up here. Whatever you see, if anything, won't be up to me."

"So, what are we doing?" asked Sam. His excitement wasn't as obvious as Jade's, but it was just as real. This was Area 51! He wasn't sure why the prospect of seeing a UFO seemed more exciting than communicating with real live aliens—as they had just done—but it did. Maybe they seemed more—real—because they had vehicles?

"Let's just hang out for a few minutes," suggested Morgan. "If there's something you're supposed to see, it'll probably become obvious. Just be alert, and look everywhere —including up," he added, his eyes searching the skies.

Sam was impatient but did his best to contain himself. He knew patience was a necessity—the Visitors did things on their own time and in their own way.

Jade was turning around and around, scanning the skies above them. Suddenly, she pointed straight up and cried out, "What's that?"

It was a UFO, Sam realized—a real, honest-to-god UFO! It was high in the sky, and looked metallic and vaguely cigar shaped, but as he watched, it changed angles, and became a genuine flying saucer. He couldn't see the top, but the bottom was three-dimensional, with a wide outer circle and a slightly smaller inner circle adding depth. The center was lighter in color. He wondered if it would appear transparent if the craft were closer. Along one side of the inner circle were half-a-dozen darker, vertical ovals, like windows. The entire craft was circular—no rectangles or triangles, no points or squared-off edges. Odd. Were people—Visitors—looking down on them from inside those oval windows?

A memory slid through his mind—a brilliant light surrounding a gigantic circular craft, hovering close above him on a dark highway. And a briefer sense of floating upward, through the light, into an opening in the bottom of that craft. He gasped.

Suddenly, an ear-splitting klaxon sounded from one of the towers, scattering his memories. It was followed by a shout over an intercom turned up full blast: "Scramble, scramble, scramble!"

Sam tore his eyes from the UFO. He watched as three flight-suited men—no, two men and a woman—sprinted from nearby buildings and raced for the nearest jet.

"What are they doing?" demanded Jade.

"Forget them. Watch the UAP," Morgan told her, pointing toward the saucer.

"The what?"

"UAP—unidentified aerial phenomenon. It's what the military call UFOs these days, so they're not tainted by all the nutcases out there."

"You're kidding," Sam said. "Changing the name doesn't change what they are."

Morgan grinned at him. "Not my call. If UAP makes them happy, that's what I say."

Sam had no doubt most people would consider him one of the "nutcases." Still—proof of his sanity was here, right above him.

High in the sky, the UAP was putting on a show. Several times, it accelerated to an unbelievable speed and disappeared, returning seconds later in a new position. It made a sharp right turn, heading straight toward them, and then another, zipping across just in front of them—still at its incredibly high altitude. At one point, it literally stopped in midair, rotated on its axis, and zipped off again. Jets can't *do* those things, thought Sam.

Jade's eyes were round with wonder. Sam was sure his were too. He looked at Morgan.

"What *is* that thing?" he demanded.

"Not a clue," said Morgan. "But enjoy it! This show is definitely for you two."

Sam and Jade stared at him in disbelief.

"What are you talking about?" Sam asked.

Morgan shrugged. "This is an incredible UAP display. Very rare, maybe unique. And who's here that usually isn't? Just you."

"But . . ." Sam continued to stare at Morgan.

"Worry about it later. Right now, watch!"

Behind them, the jets had roared to life and were zooming down the narrow runway, taking off one by one.

"Are those stealth jets?" Sam asked.

Morgan nodded. "Similar. They're F-35 Lightning IIs."

"What are they doing?" asked Jade.

"They're going to chase it—try to intercept it and make it respond to them."

"They can't catch it," Jade protested. "It's way too fast!"

"If they do catch it, it'll be a first," agreed Morgan. "But they keep trying."

They watched the chase for about twenty minutes. The Lightning II pilots definitely kept trying. They closed in on the UFO—or UAP—from three directions, trying to surround it. They looked like bees buzzing around a gigantic flower. It let them get close, then darted straight up at an incredible speed, disappearing for a moment and reappearing behind one of the Lightning IIs.

Morgan snorted. "Whoever's flying that thing is having fun," he said. "Playing with them. Pretty amazing, considering it's so much bigger than they are."

Suddenly, six small balls of light—two red, two yellow, two green—darted out of one side of the UAP. They zipped through the sky, up and down and up again, as though tossed over and over by an invisible juggler. Several times, they formed triangular patterns—two sets of three. The triangles sat absolutely still for several seconds, before the invisible juggler took over again. Sam found himself laughing as he watched—it was so fantastic. He was torn between wanting the jets to intercept the UAP so they could find out exactly what it was and wanting the UAP to win, because the whole show was so much fun!

Finally, the lit balls stopped bouncing and began to drop gently, twirling like falling leaves, until one by one, they shot up and back inside the larger UAP. Sam sighed with satisfaction and looked across at Jade. She was grinning like a fool.

During the whole display, the three jets had flown around the UAP, bobbing and weaving, helpless. Now, the UAP let them surround it again, but when they got close, it shot straight up, high above them, did its dead-stop thing, and then streaked farther up and out of sight. This time it didn't return. *Faster than a speeding bullet*, Sam thought, watching the sky where it had disappeared. Maybe Superman was real after all!

Then, just because he was feeling buoyant and delighted with life and wanted to share his joy, he spoke in his head to the Visitors: *I don't know why you showed us that, but thank you!* To his amazement, his own familiar Visitor appeared in his head. Just a brief glimpse, her huge black eyes radiating her own feelings of satisfaction. The Visitors couldn't smile, but she might as well have. He gasped. He glanced at Jade, who looked as astonished as he felt.

"Why did they do that?" she asked. "Was it really for us?"

Sam gazed at Morgan, and then around Area 51, and realized that everyone was looking up, grinning and laughing and talking excitedly. They had all enjoyed the Visitors' show, and they were all basking in what had suddenly become a glorious day.

He answered Jade, "Maybe a reward because we communicated with them. But maybe they're also saying, 'We're real —and lots of humans know about us.'"

In his mind, he spoke to his Visitor again: *Okay, you're real. But what do you want from us?* No answer. Well, the environmental information was a clue. And building a new kind of mind was another. And he was patient.

———

After the UAP experience, Morgan took them home. The day's events had opened the floodgates. They talked for the rest of the day. Morgan advised them on how to stay safe, what to tell Mr. Macklin about Jepson, and how to help Jade's mom and Mr. Macklin accept the Visitors. He had talked with his CO and now had guidelines on the secrecy issues.

"Half of Americans already think aliens are visiting us, and the government is lying about it," he said. "And of course, they're right. So, telling them about aliens or UAPs will just confirm those. They're not really secret anymore," he added, shrugging.

"Can we tell them about the DUMBs?" Sam asked.

Morgan nodded. "Yes. You'll have to explain where you were, and the truth is best. Just do *not* talk about the research going on down here. And," he added wryly, "don't go blabbing about this stuff to everyone. Be selective."

He went into more detail about what they could and couldn't say. Sam hoped he could remember it all.

"We've never had kids this involved," Morgan admitted. "Usually, people don't remember anything. But it's clear the Visitors have some plan for you, so you and your parents need to be read in."

"Not my parents," Sam said.

"Why not?" asked Morgan.

"It's not a good idea," he said. He answered all of Morgan's questions, wondering why he wasn't embarrassed. They agreed to confide in only Jade's mom and Mr. Macklin.

Then, Sam and Jade described their Visitor experiences, trying to convey the creepiness, and their fear and confusion about what the Visitors wanted. Sam asked Morgan about his role with the Visitors. Morgan said he simply helped the Visitors understand them and treat them well. Sam thought it was probably much more, but he didn't press the point.

Finally, he asked about Morgan's mind reading. This answer was more satisfying. Morgan thought all humans had psychic powers—things like telepathy and psychokinesis—that were usually not genetically turned on. Like other talents, such as music or sports, they were more pronounced in some people than in others. And—he thought, but wasn't sure—the Visitors sometimes turned on, or enhanced, these talents. Like telepathy, or mind reading, in his case.

"Why don't we have psychic powers?" asked Jade. "If they think we're so special?"

"You do," Morgan said, smiling at her. "You both communicate with the Visitors using telepathy. No different than what I do, except I do it mostly with people. Besides, you're still young. Who knows what will happen in the future? Be patient."

Finally, Jade gave in, exhausted, and went to bed. Sarah followed soon after. But Sam was wired. He quizzed Morgan on everything he could think of about the DUMBs, the Visitors, and the UAPs. Long after midnight, he finally wound down enough to sleep. When they said goodnight, Morgan hugged him tightly. The hug made him feel joyous, like the UAP had. Like he was cocooned in love.

CHAPTER 37
FACING THE MUSIC

THE FOLLOWING MORNING, the Visitors beamed Sam and Jade back to Jade's bedroom. They had just met to go to breakfast, so they were dressed, but they had no chance to say goodbye to Morgan and Sarah. They came to, dizzy and tingling, side by side on Jade's bed. As the world came back into focus, Sam heard muted voices from downstairs. He guessed Jade's mom had called Mr. Macklin. Had he been here the whole time? What had they done to find Jade? Or had they just trusted her and waited? He doubted that.

Then, realizing where he was, he quickly stood up. They were already in deep trouble, without someone finding him in Jade's bed. He looked down at her. She was smiling at him, very slightly. She knew exactly what he was thinking. He reached out a hand to pull her up.

"You okay?" he asked softly.

She nodded. "I'm fine. This was convenient," she added, looking around the room. They could have ended up anywhere. Then, with a sigh, "I guess we'd better go face the music." She stopped and put a hand on his arm. "Sam, it really will be okay, even if they don't believe us."

"I hope you're right."

They held hands, this time for courage. They crept down the stairs and into the living room. Jade's mom and Mr. Macklin were bent over Jade's laptop, looking confused and stressed. Ravi stood behind them. He looked up, and his eyes widened. Jade put a finger to her lips.

"Mom?" she said. Sam continued to hold her hand but said nothing.

"Jade!" Mel shrieked. Then her mom was hugging her and crying and bombarding her with questions. "Where have you *been*? Why did you run away like that? Why didn't you tell me where you were going?"

An instant later, Sam was engulfed in Mr. Macklin's arms, being hugged so hard he could barely breathe. He hadn't realized how strong the man was. Mr. Macklin didn't say anything. His breathing was ragged, as though he was gulping back sobs, and he had laid his cheek against the top of Sam's head. It felt wonderful. Sam could never remember being hugged like that. Or being hugged at all except by Jade and Morgan in the last couple of days. But Mr. Macklin was his *teacher*. Had Jade been right? After a moment, he felt Dr. Mathieson pulling his sleeve, and then all four of them were hugging, adults embracing teens as though terrified they might blink out of sight—again.

Finally, Mr. Macklin pulled away, furtively dashing tears from his eyes. Across the room, Ravi watched them, looking uncomfortable—the outsider at a family reunion.

"Well, I'd better be going," he said. "I'm glad you're both okay."

Mr. Macklin crossed the room and put a hand on his shoulder. "No, Ravi, please stay. You've helped us all week, and you deserve to know what's going on. We all do."

He turned to Sam and Jade, and they knew the time for hugging was over. He glared at them and spoke in a harsh, angry voice.

"You two," he said, "are going to give us some answers right now. You're going to tell us exactly where you've been and why *you*"—he focused his glare on Sam— "thought it was okay to disappear for a week and why *you*"—he turned to Jade— "thought it was okay to terrify your mother by going after him."

Mr. Macklin had been stern before, but Sam had never seen him really angry. He trembled and felt Jade trembling beside him. He grasped her hand. Would Mr. Macklin get crazy and violent, like his dad? *No, get real, Sam. They're opposites.* Mr. Macklin would never hurt them. Still, he was furious, and he would never believe them, either. Morgan's advice didn't mean much at the moment.

Mr. Macklin was studying them, looking from one to the other. It must be clear that Sam and Jade were friends again. But Sam felt like *all* his secrets had been laid bare.

Mr. Macklin pointed to the couch. "Sit," he said. They sat.

"We should all get comfortable," Jade's mom said. "This will probably take a while."

She sounded much calmer—and kinder—than Mr. Macklin. Sam was grateful.

And she was right—it did take a while. Hours, in fact. Mr. Macklin was relentless. At first, he bombarded them with questions, demanding to know where they went, who took them, what they were doing. Of course, he assumed there was a logical, rational explanation for everything. And—given they had returned on their own—he assumed they had left on their own and could have returned anytime.

He was almost shouting, and he barely stopped to listen. Sam was used to adults either hitting or shouting at him, not expecting him to respond, and although he had answers, he didn't offer them. What was the point? They wouldn't believe him. Finally, Jade—obviously more comfortable dealing with adults than Sam—started shouting herself.

"Just let us explain, and stop yelling at us. If we could tell it in our own way, maybe it would make more sense!"

Mr. Macklin stopped and seemed to remember himself. He clenched his fists, closed his eyes, and took several long, deep breaths. Sam remembered that day in his office when Macklin had volunteered to teach him techniques for controlling his anger. He appeared to be using some of those techniques now—finally. After a few moments, he looked up, much calmer.

He looked at Jade, then Sam. "I'm sorry. Please explain."

So, they did. They explained everything that seemed necessary, trying to remember Morgan's secrecy rules. After a quick whispered consultation, they decided it was reasonable to include Ravi in their revelations—he had proven himself a trusted friend. As they talked, Dr. Mathieson's eyes grew wider. Mr. Macklin's eyes narrowed—either in deep thought or in disbelief. Sam figured he was trying to make scientific sense of their story. They glossed over exactly how they had entered the DUMBs. Sam knew Mr. Macklin was itching to ask but restraining himself. After they stopped talking, Sam's fear returned. He reached out and grasped Jade's hand.

Finally, Mr. Macklin sighed. "Why didn't you tell us any of this before when we asked?"

"Because you wouldn't have believed us," Jade said flatly.

"You could have given us a chance," Mr. Macklin said.

Jade looked him in the eye. She seemed more confident, more in control. "We just gave you a chance," she pointed out. "And everything we said, you refused to believe and condescended to us. And yelled at us. That's exactly why we didn't tell you before."

Mr. Macklin stared at her. She was not being disrespectful. She was simply stating the facts, and she had put him in his place quite neatly. Finally, he said, "Point taken. I'm sorry."

Sam covered his mouth to hide his grin. Score one for Jade!

Jade turned to her mother. "Mom, I tried to warn you I was leaving. I left a note so you'd know it was planned, not a kidnapping or something."

Sam wondered if the Visitors had been watching this conversation and helping. *If you are*, he thought, *thank you*. Suddenly, in his mind, there was a brief glimpse of their Visitor's face, her huge eyes radiating—approval? Wow, he really was seeing them in his mind. He sucked in his breath and looked at Jade. "Did you see...?" She smiled and nodded.

"See what?" asked Mr. Macklin. Sam and Jade shared another glance, and Sam shook his head slightly. Mr. Macklin's brow creased as he looked between them.

They had almost forgotten Ravi. Now, Mr. Macklin looked toward him. "You've been awfully quiet, Ravi. What's your take on this story?"

Ravi looked from his friends in the hot seat to the judgmental adults. Sam wondered if he was trying to choose sides. Finally, he looked at Sam and Jade and said, "Your guys' lives sound *way* more interesting than mine. So, if you ever need a third musketeer, count me in."

"Yes!" Jade exclaimed. She rushed across the room to hug him. Ravi looked over her shoulder at Sam, who nodded and grinned at him. Suddenly, they realized Mr. Macklin was laughing. He seemed almost out of control. Sam shared an amazed look with Jade. Mr. Macklin smiled and joked with students, but he rarely, if ever, laughed. Besides, he had been furious with them earlier. He leaned toward Jade's mom and grasped her shoulder, like he needed the support. Her mom looked surprised and a bit flustered.

They all watched as he got himself under control and sat up, shaking his head. "Sorry," he said to Jade's mom, "I just lost it for a minute. I kept thinking of all we went through this past week, and there were only two of them. And now they're adding a third. I'm not sure I can take the stress!"

Jade's mom started to laugh, too. "Me either," she said. "But right now, they need to finish this story. And Sam needs to call his parents."

She paused, looking guilty. "We should have done that first thing."

Sam knew what she was thinking. His parents hadn't missed him; they wouldn't care if he was back. She was right. Sam felt an ache at the thought but buried it quickly. Jade's mom had worried about him. And Mr. Macklin. He had been angry—not like Sam's father, but because he, too, was worried.

Jade's mom continued. "And sometime today, we have to tell the police they're back and explain where they've been."

CHAPTER 38
PRACTICING TRUST

THEY HAD TAKEN a short break while Jade's mom fixed snacks and drinks for everyone. But now they were back, sitting in the living room again—*in the hot seat for sure*, Sam thought. He knew Mr. Macklin would not like this part.

"Jade," he said, "I know I should explain this, but I just—can't."

She nodded. "Fine. But I'll need to talk about your past, at least a little. Is that okay?"

He winced. "Not really, but it's not like we have a choice. Thanks to the NP."

Jade hugged him and said, "It'll be fine, I promise."

Although their voices were quiet, it was clear the others had heard them.

"Okay," Mr. Macklin said. He had regained his composure; he was calm and no longer confrontational. "I'm guessing we're finally about to learn what it means to be dropped into a DUMB? How you got in and out?"

"Yes," Jade said, "but you're not going to like it. This is what Sam has been so afraid to tell anyone. The part that will make you think we're crazy."

Mr. Macklin nodded and looked directly at Sam. "Okay,

we're listening. And I promise I'll do my best to just listen and not judge."

"Thank you," Sam said.

Jade backtracked, reviewing the missing time after their first trip to the secret base.

"We got home two hours late that day, but we didn't realize it until Mom told us. Remember, Mom?" Dr. Mathieson nodded, her eyes wide.

"Sam told me that the lost time thing happened to him a lot when he was little. He never knew what happened then, either, and his mom used to get mad at him when he was late. I did some research on missing time and a lot of it had to do with—alien abductions."

Mr. Macklin made an involuntary sound, and Jade fixed him with a steely eye. "Just listen, don't judge, remember?" He pursed his lips and nodded once, looking mutinous but saying nothing.

Ravi said, "We found your research and notes on your computer. We were just starting to read them when you arrived. I'm sorry we snooped, Jade, but—you were missing, and your parents were really worried."

Sam and Jade glanced toward the adults, who both looked startled. Mr. Macklin's face was flushed. He had certainly been acting parental today. Jade smirked at him. Sam hid his smile.

"It's fine, Ravi."

Jade explained "beaming" and what it was like. She explained how they remembered only the two underground episodes—Cassidy Base and the DUMBs—and their suspicion that the kidnappers wanted them to know about the underground bases. Sam noticed that she glossed over how she had arrived in the DUMBs. As Jade talked, Sam carefully avoided everyone's eyes. Baring his deepest secrets was terrifying, even when he wasn't doing the telling.

After Jade stopped talking, everyone was quiet. Ravi looked amazed and excited. Sam was surprised—he had assumed Ravi would dismiss the concept of aliens, let alone abductions. Jade's mother looked stunned. Sam thought she would likely believe their story eventually if she didn't already. Mr. Macklin wouldn't, but maybe he would at least discuss it. He had been silent since Jade had challenged him earlier. As she talked, he had stared thoughtfully at Sam. Now he stared at the floor, frowning slightly.

"Mr. Macklin," Jade asked, "do you have questions?"

He looked up and gave her a slight smile. "I'm just thinking. Sam, I would like some information from you, if that's okay?"

Unlike earlier, Mr. Macklin spoke quietly to Sam and seemed considerate of his feelings. Sam wasn't sure why his attitude had changed, but he was relieved. He nodded.

"Earlier, when Jade asked if it was okay to discuss your childhood, you said it had to be done 'thanks to the NP.' I just wondered if the NP are the little people Jade talked about? The ones that transport you?"

Sam closed his eyes. Jade said he should learn to trust. Here was his chance. Mr. Macklin still seemed interested and accepting, rather than scornful.

"I saw them for the first time when I was five. They surrounded my bed, and one of them was touching my face. It had skinny, cold fingers." Sam shivered.

"I started screaming and they disappeared—just faded away. By the time my mother got there, they were gone. When I tried to explain what I had seen, I called them Night People, and later I shortened that to NP. Now, I know they don't just come at night. They transport us and . . . do things to us. They've kind of controlled my life. Sometimes I've thought they had to be real, but other times I just felt crazy. Morgan says most people call them

Visitors, capital V, so I'm trying to remember to call them that."

Mr. Macklin nodded. He was staring at the floor again, his brow furrowed. *What's he thinking?*

Finally, he said, "Thank you for sharing that, Sam. I have one last question, if it's okay. When you told your mother what you saw, how did she react?"

Sam hesitated for a long time. He did not want to answer that. *Trust*, he reminded himself. He grasped Jade's hand again and finally spoke. "She screamed at me and told me it was a nightmare, and under no circumstances could I ever tell anyone I had seen little people. I never mentioned them to her after that, or to anyone else until Jade, and now you."

Jade's mom made a small, choked sound; Mr. Macklin reached over and squeezed her hand. As they both stared into Sam's eyes, he felt five years old again—only this time, someone cared.

Everyone sat quietly for a few moments. Jade held Sam's hand tightly. Finally, her mom stood up and said, "We need a break. I'm going to make lunch."

She stopped beside Sam and Jade and bent down to kiss Sam's cheek. "You are a very brave young man," she said. Then she whispered, "I think you're both off the hook now. He's been so worried, he kind of overreacted. He thinks of you as his own kids."

She smiled at them and left. Mr. Macklin regarded Sam and Jade somberly.

"Ravi, come join us," he said. He motioned toward the couch, and Ravi came to sit beside Sam. Mr. Macklin pulled his chair closer and looked around at each of them.

"Ravi, if you're willing, we could use your help deciding what to tell the police. Because I'm pretty sure the story you two just told is not going to fly with them," he added, giving Sam and Jade a slight smile.

"You're going to help us lie to the police?" asked Jade.

"Does that mean you believe us?" asked Sam simultaneously.

"No—and maybe," Mr. Macklin said. "No, we're not going to *lie* to the police, but do you really want to tell them that aliens abducted you and took you into a secret underground military cabal and kept you for days?" They were silent.

"I didn't think so. Besides, if this is as top secret as you say, we can't tell them everything."

Oh. That hadn't occurred to Sam.

"And, Sam, I don't *not* believe you. I know how honest you both are, and your story has the ring of truth, and nobody fakes. . .. Well. It's clear you've had some frightening experiences. But I'm sorry, I'm just not ready to believe in your aliens. Frankly, I don't know *what* to believe, although I'm guessing the military could answer a lot of my questions. Now, I'd like to concentrate on getting past the police interview, and when they're satisfied, we can discuss all of this in a *lot* more detail."

"I'd like that, too, if you're willing to include me," said Ravi. "I have a million questions."

"Of course," Sam said. "You're one of us now."

"And," Mr. Macklin continued, "I hope you'll both forgive me if I research some of your claims, like the DUMBs and beaming. My old CO is already looking into how the army, and Major Jepson, might be involved in your disappearances."

"You're a scientist—we expect you to investigate," Jade said. "We know it all sounds crazy. It sounds crazy to us, and we've been living it."

He nodded. "Anyway, he'll be calling soon. I'd like to compare your story with his, if that's okay."

Sam nodded too. He'd already lost control of the story. Jade was right; neither adult had called him a lunatic or threatened him with a shrink. Even Ravi seemed okay with it. But other people would not be, he thought. He wondered about Mr. Macklin's CO.

He sighed. "Um, Mr. Macklin? I hate to cause any more problems, but . . ."

"But there's a complication you haven't told us about. Of course, there is. Spill it, Sam."

"You remember I said I was running from people while I was down there alone? One of the people who saw me was Major Jepson. And," he added, "Morgan said to tell you Jepson is dangerous. He told us a lot about Jepson that you need to know."

Mr. Macklin gave a short laugh and put his head in his hands. "Why should anything be simple?" he said. "Where's the fun in that?"

CHAPTER 39
MORE CONFESSIONS

RAVI HAD BEEN SILENT, just listening. Suddenly, he spoke up. "This may be a dumb question, but if all of this stuff is top secret, why are you telling us?"

"Good point, Ravi," said Mr. Macklin. "That was actually my next question."

"Well." Sam hesitated, looking at his teacher. "Morgan says aliens are part of the culture, and it's okay to talk about them, at least to people we trust. About the DUMBs and other stuff—he knows you and says you can be trusted with top secret information."

Mr. Macklin looked floored. "How can he know me? I've never heard of him."

"He recognized your name when I told him about you and Mom looking for Sam," said Jade.

"From where?" Mr. Macklin had a hand over his mouth, like he was dreading the answer.

"From something you did in the army. He checked you out. Don't worry, he didn't tell us anything. He just said you understood secrecy and would know what to do."

Mr. Macklin blew out a breath. "Well, thank heaven for

small favors, I guess." He thought for a moment. "What's Morgan's military rank, do you know?"

"Colonel, I think," Sam said. "He never told us, but one of the other army guys called him 'Colonel.'"

Mr. Macklin's eyes widened. "Really? Well, if he's checking on me, I'll return the favor. The general can get his file."

Mr. Macklin was a little touchy after he learned that Morgan had checked up on him. But after lunch and a lengthy telephone conversation with his ex-CO, he calmed down. He informed Sam and Jade that General Greenwald wanted a Zoom call so he could meet them. Meeting a general sounded intimidating, but Mr. Macklin reassured them. "He's a nice guy, and he wants to help. Be your usual polite selves and talk to him like you would anyone."

It was Sunday afternoon, and the general was at home in front of his computer, wearing an Army sweatshirt and looking relaxed. But he had a penetrating gaze, and both Sam and Jade squirmed a little as he looked them over. Finally, he smiled.

"So, you're the two that have had Mack terrified for the past week. Sam and Jade, is it?" They nodded.

Mack? thought Sam. "Yes, sir. We're really sorry about that. We didn't have much control over it. And thank you for helping Mr. Macklin find us."

Jade nodded. "Yes, sir, thank you very much."

The general shook his head. "I wasn't much help—it sounds like you got yourselves home. Now, how about the two of you tell me about this underground trip you took?"

Mr. Macklin was standing behind them, and they both looked up at him, uncertain. He squeezed their shoulders gently. "It's okay. I gave him the highlights, but he wants to hear it from you. Just be honest—he's on your side."

"How about if I start you off with a couple of questions?" the general suggested.

The kids nodded.

For almost an hour, they answered his questions. They described the DUMBs and what they had done there. They described their Visitor experiences. They told him everything they knew about Jepson. The general asked precise and detailed questions and accepted their responses without comment. Finally, he seemed satisfied. He thanked them and called them excellent witnesses. He had talked with them as equals and did not assume they were imagining the Visitors. That alone made him a friend. By the end of their discussion, Jade was her usual bubbly self, chatting and looking forward to their next visit. As always, Sam was much more reserved, but he, too, was relaxed and enjoying the conversation.

Mr. Macklin sent Sam and Jade to rest while he and the general talked. Sam was relieved that he could nap in the Mathieson's spare bedroom instead of going home. Before lunch, at the insistence of Jade's mom, he had called his mother. He was vague about where he had been, and apologized for worrying her. She hadn't been worried, she said, just embarrassed. Sam sighed. He wished she would decide—one day she was furious because he was late, the next she didn't notice, or care, if he was gone.

Sam felt another brief pang of envy for Jade: What was it like to have a mother who cared? But at least, his mom wasn't constantly checking up on him. He asked the question that worried him most: How was his dad taking his disappearance? The hidden question was: *Is it safe to come home?* The answer was no. He gave the phone to Dr. Mathieson, and she made arrangements for Sam to spend the next few days with either her or Mr. Macklin.

The next day, the four of them went to the police station. Sam's mother did not go—her attitude was "you got yourself into this mess; you can get yourself out." Sam was relieved. Mr. Macklin made him feel much safer than his mother would have.

The police seemed skeptical of their story. After about five tense minutes, Mr. Macklin insisted the detectives call General Greenwald. Sam wasn't sure what the general told them, but after the call, they were much friendlier. They told Sam and Jade to go home and stay out of trouble, but they were smiling.

With the police problem settled, the four of them went to lunch to celebrate. They drove all the way to Pittsburg to a Thai restaurant Mr. Macklin liked. While they ate, Sam and Jade described the weird food Morgan had introduced them to in the DUMBs. Both adults were fascinated.

"I wonder why it isn't available aboveground," said Mr. Macklin. "Surely the food isn't top secret."

Their meal was long, relaxed, and full of laughter. Tomorrow, life would be normal again—Sam, Jade, and Mr. Macklin would return to school, and Jade's mom to the ER. But as they finished eating, Mr. Macklin kept glancing between Sam and Jade; it was clear he wanted to speak but was hesitant.

Finally, Jade asked, "Is something wrong, Mr. Macklin?"

He lowered his head, avoiding their eyes. After a moment, he looked up, embarrassed. "Sorry. I'm just . . . so relieved to have both of you back. I was terrified I might never see you again, and now, I kind of . . . never want to let either of you out of my sight."

Both Sam and Jade watched him, silent.

His face was flushed, and his mouth twitched nervously, but he held their eyes. "I've always been . . . protective. I took care of my little brother. Younger guys in the army. And now, my students. I just feel—responsible." He hesitated, shaking his head.

"But this has never happened to me before. I don't just want to protect you two. I feel—compelled to take care of you. Keep you safe. I can't let it go. I'm—sorry."

Jade's mom watched him with a faint smile. "You don't have to apologize for caring about them, Greg."

He flushed but continued. "Last week when you were gone, Sam, it was torture. We had no idea where you were, and we imagined the worst possible things. And, Jade, I was so furious when I found out you'd left on purpose. I still don't understand how you did it."

He shook his head. "But I was also relieved. The fact that you *could* do it meant Sam might be safe, somewhere you both knew about. So, there was hope for the first time since he disappeared."

Sam and Jade stared at him. Sam was overcome with guilt. Jade said, "Mr. Macklin, we're so sorry we put you through that. But we're home safe now. You can stop worrying."

"Can you promise me the same thing or something worse won't happen tomorrow?"

They looked at each other. Of course, they couldn't promise. The Visitors were in control. But that didn't seem like the sort of thing they should say. They remained silent.

"I thought so. But it's not just the, um, Visitors. Jade, I don't worry so much about you, because you have a loving mother." He touched Mel's hand, and she smiled at him.

"Sam, I know you're private, and you don't like to talk about your personal life." He smiled briefly. "I get it—I'm the same. But we all dealt with your parents last week. I'm . . . afraid for you, for your safety. And I want you to know you can call me anytime, for any reason, and I'll come. Do you understand?"

Sam was shaken. Mr. Macklin was his teacher: strong, confident, in charge. But these—confessions—made him feel, again, like more than a teacher. Made him seem vulnerable. And he, Sam, was the cause. He said the only thing that seemed appropriate.

"I understand. Thank you."

Jade's mom added, "Sam, we all want to make sure you're safe. You can call *me* anytime you need help, too. And come to our house every day after school if you want. Okay?"

Sam was having trouble believing this. Jade was smiling at him, wearing an "I told you so" expression. Finally, he said, "Thank you, Dr. Mathieson."

"We could probably be a little less formal than that. Why not call me Dr. Mel?"

Sam nodded, smiling back. "Okay."

She turned to Mr. Macklin. "And Greg, since you and I bonded over our lost kids last week, you're already like part of our family. So, I want you to feel free to drop by anytime, too. Check on Sam and Jade, stay for dinner, just hang out. In fact, why don't we consider our house the official hangout for all four of us?"

Mr. Macklin stared at her in amazement. She shrugged and smiled at him.

"After last week, there's no way you can go back to being just their teacher. And Jade and I have been lonely for a long time now. You and Sam will be doing us a favor."

Jade was hugging Sam, who was too overwhelmed to speak. Suddenly Mr. Macklin was hugging Jade's mom, too, and whispering in her ear, "Thank you!" It was a buoyant, laughing group who finished their lunch quickly and returned to their new hangout to spend their last free afternoon together.

PART FOUR

The bond that links your true family is not one of blood, but of respect and joy in each other.
--Richard Bach, author

CHAPTER 40
EXTRAORDINARY EVIDENCE

SAM AND JADE quickly settled back into the school routine. Several people smiled at them in the halls, welcomed them back, even seemed glad they were okay. Much of the friendliness was likely simple curiosity: Where had they been? Why was their story so secret? But curiosity was a definite improvement over bullying. The bullies hadn't disappeared, but they were subdued, even a little nervous.

The teachers were nervous, too, although they acted matter-of-fact, giving Sam his missed assignments without comment. Sam wondered what they had been told. Jade had only been gone two days, but Sam had missed a week, and everyone knew he had disappeared. Mr. Macklin told them not to give any explanations, so, when asked, Sam just said, "Sorry, can't talk about it." It was strange being back in the classroom with Mr. Macklin. Sam and Jade were careful not to act too familiar around him, and he remained strictly professional, except for an occasional tiny smile or wink.

The major downside to returning was that Ms. Mott was eager to begin their counseling sessions. Besides Sam's "uncontrolled anger," Mott was laser-focused on the alien rumors, his disappearance, and whether he had inherited his

Aunt Lucy's "loony" tendencies. Her questions during Sam's first session were similar to Major Jepson's and suggested considerable knowledge of Cassidy Base. As he was arriving for his second session, he heard Ms. Mott on the phone. He stopped outside her door and listened.

". . . said anything yet, but I have another session right now. Don't worry, I'll get him to talk. Okay, later." She was talking to Jepson. He knew it.

That afternoon, he told Mr. Macklin everything Mott had said on the phone and in the session. Mr. Macklin called General Greenwald. Within hours, the general discovered that Mott had served under Jepson in the army. That, plus the phone conversation, seemed to confirm it—Mott and Jepson were working together.

The general had also located Jepson's file. Much of it was redacted, but thanks to Morgan, Sam and Jade knew he had been demoted for trying to sabotage the Visitor project. He had then been reassigned from a large base in the Southwest to tiny Cassidy Base in southeast Kansas. Until recently, he had been doing his job. Now, he had apparently gone rogue.

Outside of class, Mr. Macklin checked on Sam and Jade daily, and ate several meals a week with them at Jade's house. He began bringing groceries, and they had dinner ready when Dr. Mel came home. He suggested that Sam and Jade call him Mack in private. It was his army nickname, the name his buddies had called him. After checking with Dr. Mel, Mack even began bringing his dog, Barker, when he visited.

"Barker is a border collie," Mack explained, "one of the smartest dogs on the planet. If they don't keep learning, they go crazy, so I'm always teaching Barker new things."

Soon Sam and Jade were teaching him, too. And Barker loved the Mathieson's huge backyard, which was perfect for Frisbee, his favorite game. He even made friends with Sadie.

During these times, Mack was more relaxed than Sam had

ever seen him. At school, he'd always been friendly but formal and serious. Now, he teased them and joked around and even laughed sometimes. He felt like a father. To Sam, these afternoons were like visiting an oasis, a peaceful, sheltered world where he could finally be himself. Still, he did his best to maintain some distance from Mack. What if it was all ripped away? In Sam's world, people who cared, if they existed at all, didn't stay. Like his abuela. Like Grandpa Joe.

Jade, in contrast, grew closer to Mack. One day, returning after retrieving Barker's Frisbee from a tree, Sam saw them together. Jade was crying and Mack was holding her, stroking her hair, and talking softly to her. After a few minutes, she pulled herself together, giving him a tremulous smile. Sam wasn't sure he should intrude, but Jade came to him. Her eyes were red-rimmed but she was calm.

"You okay?" Sam asked.

"Better." She paused. "I . . . heard a song earlier, something my dad and I used to play together. I kind of fell apart. Mack asked me what was wrong, so I told him. He said he'd lost someone musical, too, and has a hard time listening to music at all. It helped to hear that."

"He's good at making people feel better." Sam paused. "I wonder who he lost."

"I think it was someone close. He didn't say much, but he was really sad. I'd never seen him that way."

"He does act sad sometimes. I never noticed until recently." Sam smiled slightly. "Until him, I'd never thought of teachers as real people, with lives."

"I'm . . . drawn to him. He's not my dad, but he's so much like him."

Maybe Mack could ease some of Jade's sadness and uncertainty. Sam always felt so helpless when she was like that. He might have the same type of mind as her dad, but Mack gave her more emotional support. Maybe he understood her feelings because he had the same ones. Mack was a natural dad, Sam thought. He was so kind and caring. And handsome. Sam couldn't understand why he wasn't married, with his own kids. Jade was convinced he was attracted to her mom and vice versa. She said she felt "sparks" whenever they were together. Sam hoped she was right. Mack did touch Dr. Mel sometimes. Light touches, like he wanted to but wasn't sure he should. Like he felt about touching Jade. Mack was far too private—they could never ask him. But no reason they couldn't spy a little!

Besides being their substitute dad, Mack used their times together to tackle the Visitor mystery, often with Ravi joining them. He was serious about deciphering the Visitors, but he didn't push. He was respectful, never condescending. (Jade had cured him of that, Sam thought with amusement.) They couldn't convince him that the Visitors were aliens, or that they even existed, but he honestly seemed to want the truth. He couldn't explain what Morgan had said about the Visitors. He couldn't explain how first Sam, then Jade, had disappeared and reappeared days later. Or how they had entered and left the DUMBs. He accepted the DUMBs, now that he had evidence—Jade had finally remembered the photos she had taken inside Cassidy Base. Mack shared these with the general, who was also satisfied, although the military wouldn't officially confirm them.

Sam knew Mack and General Greenwald were trying to link his and Jade's information to military projects. He overheard them arguing about it on a Zoom call. Mack thought the U.S. black budget was far too small to support the extensive DUMB infrastructure Sam and Jade had described. The general thought the black budget was far larger than the usually estimated fifty billion per year. He thought private sources were secretly funneling in billions of dollars more. They also argued about whether the underground residents lived there permanently or alternated above- and below-ground. Sam told Mack everything Morgan had said. He was personally convinced that the Visitors helped keep the DUMBs secret and said so. Mack frowned but didn't argue.

One day, after another inconclusive discussion about the Visitors, Mack—ever the science teacher—asked, "Do you two know the concept of Occam's razor?"

He explained the essentials: In any situation, the simplest explanation is most likely true. Assuming the Visitors are extraterrestrials or extradimensional requires too many assumptions. The true explanation is most likely earthly and ordinary. "Extraordinary claims require extraordinary evidence," he insisted.

In other words, if you claim aliens are transporting you, you need much stronger evidence than if you assume humans are responsible.

"What would you consider extraordinary evidence?" Sam asked. "Alien bodies? Crashed spaceships?"

Mack smiled. "Well, as long as they're *real* alien bodies or crashed spaceships—not just people claiming they saw them. That's stronger evidence than remembering strange people in dreams. When you're taken into the DUMBs, or somewhere else, you never see who takes you. Why would you assume they're not human?"

Sam sighed. He had experienced them, and seen them, when he was five and many times since. He *knew* they weren't human. But there was no way to explain it so Mack would understand. How could he convey what it was like to have a Visitor appear in his head, those huge eyes staring into his, calming him? Or radiating approval?

Jade, however, was looking at Mack as though a light had turned on.

"What about an actual experience? Would you consider *that* extraordinary evidence?"

"What do you mean?"

"What if you came face to face with them? Saw them for yourself, instead of just hearing us talk about them or reading descriptions?"

"Of course. If I see something for myself, I know it's real."

Maybe there was a way to convince Mack, after all.

Later that day, Sam and Jade hatched their plan. Jade had begged the Visitors to reunite her with Sam when he was in the DUMBs, and when she finally asked in the way they preferred, they complied. So, why not ask them to show themselves to Mack?

Both of them tried asking. They explained how important Mack was to them, how smart he was, how much he had to offer. They asked the Visitors to please show themselves or abduct him so he would know they were real. Nothing happened. Maybe their pleas weren't precise enough, or the Visitors didn't think they were serious. Maybe they just weren't interested. Then, Jade had another idea. They knew the Visitors had a plan for their lives, and although Mack didn't believe in the Visitors, he feared anything that threatened Sam and Jade. He would try to protect them from all threats—including the Visitors. Perhaps the Visitors should know this.

Sam looked at her in awe. "You really get them," he said.

"Maybe. We don't know if it'll work."

But finally, it did. On a Sunday afternoon, they were in the Mathieson's backyard, after a barbecue. Dr. Mel, Sam, and Jade sat in the sun, talking. Sadie snuggled between Sam and Jade, purring as Sam tickled her belly, and Barker dozed near Sam. Mack was lying back with his hands behind his head, staring up at the clouds.

Without warning, Mack's whole body began to crackle with static electricity, and he was surrounded by twinkling lights. Both animals shot upright and streaked toward the house, their eyes wild and their fur standing on end. Mack sat up. For a second, he stared, astonished, straight into Sam's eyes, and then he disappeared. Sam and Jade shared a delighted glance, followed by a high five.

"Finally!" Sam said, laughing. "Now he'll *have* to believe us!"

"What happened? Where did he go?" gasped Dr. Mel. Her face had lost all color.

"Mom, he'll be fine. I'm sorry—I forgot you've never seen someone beam out before."

"*That's* what's been happening to you two?"

"Yes—and we're fine! See?" Jade held out her arms, smiling at her mother.

Jade had been snippy with her mom earlier, but now she sounded reassuring. Sam was relieved.

"Why did they just take Greg? Why not me too?" Dr. Mel sounded almost envious.

Jade looked at her with suspicion. "Mom! Are you jealous?"

Her mother looked flustered. "Well, maybe a little. I believe you; I really do. But it's hard, the thought of you disappearing. Going somewhere I can't follow, can't protect you."

"I'm sorry, Dr. Mel," Sam said. "It's my fault. I wanted them to take him because he doesn't believe they're real. He tries, but he just can't. It has to happen to him. So, we asked them to make it happen. We weren't sure it would work."

"It's my fault, too," added Jade. "I knew you already believed us, so I didn't think you needed proof. But Mack needs to believe it, too."

Sam stared at the empty space in front of them. "I wonder how long they'll keep him. And what they're doing to him. I hope he's not too freaked out."

They kept him forty-five minutes. Sam, Jade, and Dr. Mel

were there, waiting, when he beamed back amid crackling electricity and flickering lights. He sat up, looking shocked and very pale. He rubbed his arms and looked around, disoriented. Finally, his gaze moved to Sam, who was grinning at him.

"Hi, Mack!" Sam said. "Have a nice trip?"

Jade giggled.

Mack closed his eyes for a moment, trembling and breathing heavily. Then he looked at them, a slight smile playing around his lips. "You two are really enjoying this, aren't you?"

"Oh yeah!" said Sam, still grinning. "So, do you believe us now?"

"You know I do. I'm so sorry I didn't before." He seemed embarrassed, and it was a moment before he spoke again. "We all have our blind spots. You have trouble trusting people. I have trouble accepting things I haven't experienced."

Dr. Mel was still shocked. She insisted that Mack and Sam spend the night. She took Mack into the house and gave him a quick exam. His heart rate was accelerated, but gradually slowed back to normal. His trembling continued, but Sam convinced her this was expected after seeing the Visitors face-to-face. He knew all too clearly what that felt like.

Mack seemed either reluctant or unable to describe much of his experience. At least, he remembered seeing the Visitors. But hours later, he was still trembling and staring off into space for moments at a time, unaware of those around him. That's all they needed, Sam thought—for Mack to finally accept the Visitors but to be too traumatized to deal with the knowledge. Jade was less worried.

"Give him time, Sam. He's just had his whole world turned upside down. He was so sure the Visitors weren't real."

"It's just weird and scary to see him like this," Sam said. "He's always so . . . in charge of things. What if he stays this way?"

"He won't. He just needs time to process it."

Jade was usually right about such things—she seemed to have a natural understanding of people. A gift from her dad, the shrink, she'd said once, with a bittersweet smile. He wondered if the gift was genetic or taught; either way, it gave him hope.

Besides the possible trauma, Sam was afraid Mack had undergone an information exchange. Something about his halting descriptions reminded Sam of his own dreamy encounters in the woods, where the Visitors both downloaded information into his mind and uploaded his mind into theirs. *What have we done?*

"We practically forced the Visitors to take him," Sam told Jade. "What if they turn him into one of us—someone with no control over his life, who's terrified most of the time, and who has to lie to everyone?"

"Oh, Sam, that was before. Now, we have people we don't have to lie to. We talk to the Visitors, even control their actions sometimes. They took Mack when we asked them to. And if they take him again, we'll be here to help him. He won't be alone, like you were."

―――

At school the next day, Mack still wasn't quite back to normal. The whole biology class noticed. On lab days, Mack was constantly busy. He circulated through the room, observing students' progress, helping them, asking questions, making suggestions. Today, he was quiet, a bit aimless. A few times, he seemed to forget what he was doing.

"Hey, Mr. Macklin," one guy called, after holding up his hand, waving it around, and getting no response.

Mack jumped and hurried over, saying, "Sorry, Juan, what do you need?"

Juan grinned at him and looked around to make sure others noticed. "You're actin' awful dreamy today, Mr. Macklin. You maybe got a new girlfriend?"

There were snorts of laughter from the guys and giggles from several girls. Sam could see Mack's neck coloring, but he grinned back and said, "No, but if I get one, I promise you'll be the first to know."

Then he clapped his hands together and said, "Everyone, get your photosynthesis results ready. I want to see your data tables and hear exactly what you did and what your results mean."

Crisis averted, Sam thought with relief. He wondered if this had been happening all day. And how long Mack's "dreaminess" would last.

CHAPTER 41
WORST FEARS

THE NEXT DAY, Sam's counseling session with Ms. Mott felt weird. As always, Sam gave terse answers to her questions, remaining barely polite. But she acted more self-satisfied than usual, as though she knew something he didn't. It made him uneasy.

After school, Jade texted him:

Mott wants to see me??
Meet you at the picnic table soon

What was that about? Jade didn't have a counseling session today. Whatever—he would find out soon enough. As he rode his bike toward the park, he noticed the black SUV following him. *Damn!* He thought Jepson had finally given up. At the park entrance, the SUV pulled up beside him, and a voice called out—his mother's voice!

"Sam!"

Sam spun around. His mother was leaning out the back window of the SUV, beckoning to him. What was his mom doing with Jepson? This couldn't be good. His skin prickled with fear, and he approached her warily.

"Mom? What are you doing with these people?"

A quick glance at the front passenger seat confirmed his fears—Jepson. Jimenez was driving. As usual, he stared straight ahead and did not acknowledge Sam. His mother opened her door, and Sam quickly backed up.

"Get in the car, Sam. These people can help you. They can give you what you need."

This was just wrong. Since when did his mother know—or care—what he needed? And what did she think Jepson could give him? Had Jepson brainwashed her? She sounded nice—too nice. Usually, she just snapped at him.

"*What?* I don't know what they've told you, Mom, but these are *not* good people. I don't need anything from them. Neither do you."

"Sam! This man is an army officer. The army knows about the things that are happening to you. They can get rid of your delusions. Make you normal. Don't you want that?"

"This man is a *demoted* army officer. A *disgraced* army officer. The army is trying to stop him. He's dangerous, and I'm not going anywhere with him—or with you. And I am *not* having delusions. You know better."

Sam turned to get on his bike, but in an instant, Jepson had left the car and grasped his arm.

"You're going with us. You don't have a choice. Your mother has given her consent for you to be treated in our facility."

As he spoke, Jepson pushed Sam toward the SUV, shoved him into the back, and got in after him. Sam kicked and fought, but it was no use; Jepson was much stronger.

"Stop this!" Sam shouted. "You're kidnapping me. What facility? What kind of treatment? I don't need treatment!"

"Calm down, Sam," his mom said. Now that he was safely in the SUV, she reverted to her usual snappish, angry voice.

"This is best for everyone. Lucy fought, too, but everything was better once they took her to the mental hospital."

"It wasn't better for Lucy!" Sam shouted.

Oh god. His worst nightmare was coming true. His own mother thought he was crazy. He couldn't believe she was having him committed! Just like his Aunt Lucy—and not just any mental hospital, but one run by Jepson. What on Earth had Jepson told her? Of course, his father would be thrilled to see the back of him. That might be the only good thing about this, Sam thought grimly—locked up, he would be away from his father.

Sam fought down his panic and tried to think. Keeping his hand hidden, he checked his pocket. Yes, he had his cell phone. But wherever he was going, it would be confiscated. He had to text Jade before that happened. She would tell her mom and Mack, although getting him sprung from an army mental hospital would not be easy. Mack was still acting dreamy after his Visitor encounter, and Sam felt guilty—and worried. Mack said he preferred to know the truth, no matter how frightening. He assured Sam that he would adapt to the Visitors. But could either he or Mel help Sam out of this latest predicament? Despite his fear, he felt a quick surge of wonder. A couple of months ago, he would never have asked *anyone* for help.

Sam turned to Jepson, who wore his usual arrogant smirk.

"You can't get away with this!" Sam hissed. "You can't hide from the whole army. They're looking for you."

Jepson raised an eyebrow. "You'd be surprised what I can do. Right now, I'm in charge, so you might as well accept it. You heard your mother—we know what's best for you."

"You're the crazy one, not me. You're afraid of them because they're smarter than you."

Jepson frowned. "You know, I don't think I want to listen

to your ranting for the whole drive. Let's do something about that."

He pulled a loaded syringe from his pocket, and before Sam could react, injected the contents into his arm. Sam stared down at the syringe in horror. His mother gasped, "Was that really necessary?"

But it was too late. Almost immediately, Sam began to feel faint. Within seconds, his head lolled to one side, and a minute later, he was out cold.

Sam's return to consciousness was slow. His brain writhed like a seething nest of maggots. He felt nauseous, and a murky fog obscured his thoughts. He lay quietly, eyes closed. Memories came rushing back, and a bolt of fear shot through his body. Mott's weird behavior, the SUV, his mom, Jepson. The syringe. Jepson had drugged him! That probably explained the writhing in his head. Mott must have delayed Jade so Jepson could get him alone. Where was he? The quiet was ominous. There was no warmth, no sunlight. He forced himself to breathe deeply and not open his eyes, but once again, he was barely controlling his panic.

He'd been drugged before he could text Jade, and he knew his phone would be gone. Jade, Dr. Mel, and Mack would have no idea who had taken him or where. Jade would find his bicycle, but that wouldn't help. They might even think he was with the Visitors, not Jepson. He must be somewhere in the Cassidy underground base. Jepson knew the place. He'd probably found deep, hidden warrens where he could set up whatever kind of torture chamber he wanted. Sam shivered. *Don't go there!* He couldn't count on the others finding him or wait for them. He was on his own. Again.

He needed a plan before his captors realized he was

awake. He couldn't sneak out—too many people. And locks. The only thing that occurred to him was contacting the Visitors. They had spoken to him. They had brought Jade to him. They had taken Mack when he and Jade asked. Now, they might be the only thing standing between him and permanent confinement in an army mental facility. He lay still and talked to them in his head, begging for their help.

Nothing happened—no Visitor's voice or face appeared. But he would keep trying. Now, time to suck it up. He balled his hands into fists, willing himself to stop trembling. He opened his eyes and looked around. He was in a narrow bed, crammed into a corner. Across the tiny room, a small desk sat in one corner, a toilet and small sink in the other near a floor drain. One door. No windows. He couldn't see out, but they could see in. One obvious camera pointed toward the bed. Other tiny ones, in the corners of the ceiling, pointed toward the desk, the foot of the bed, the toilet. It was disgusting that they wanted to watch him use the toilet. It was best to assume he could be seen from anywhere in the room. And heard—there must be audio, too. He had no experience with hospital or mental ward rooms, but surely, they weren't like this. This was a jail cell. Whatever "mental health" facility Jepson had brought him to, it had to be fake.

Sam got out of bed. The drug must have mostly worn off —physically, he felt okay. Even the weird squirming in his head had eased. He was wearing flimsy pajamas. His clothes, shoes, and underwear were gone. And his phone, of course. He checked the door. Locked. He used the toilet, glaring into the camera and making a rude gesture as he did so. He did some calisthenics, trying to remember Mack's routines. Mack wanted him and Jade to be more fit to prepare them for attacks like this one. *Should've worked harder.* As he exercised, he wondered about his mom: What had made her willing to hand him over to Jepson? He hadn't done anything—well, except get abducted and taken to the DUMBs. Like when he was five, the Visitors had done it. Both times, she had blamed him. He sighed. She hated him, no question.

"Don't know. Don't *know!*" Sam could hear himself saying the words, and he knew he sounded whiny, even weepy, but he couldn't help himself. He was blindfolded, seated in a chair with his arms and legs immobilized. Jepson and another guy were questioning him—back and forth, questions from one, then the other. Jepson was in charge. He kept asking about the Visitors—who they were, what they wanted, why they were interested in Sam. The other man was a doctor, he thought. He was in charge of drugs. They asked mental health questions, but mostly they asked about the Visitors. Sometimes Mott questioned him, too, but it was usually Jepson and the doctor.

Sam didn't want to answer their questions, but he couldn't stop himself. He heard his voice saying "No! Won't answer!" and then answering anyway. *Truth serum*, he thought. He'd read about drugs that made you tell the truth, even when you didn't want to. That was Jepson's style. Sam knew nothing about who the Visitors were and almost nothing about what they wanted, so he couldn't tell Jepson much. Jepson should know this stuff anyway; he had already questioned Sam and Jade. And bugged them. But truth serum was new. How long would he put up with Sam's incomplete answers? And what would happen when he got fed up?

Sam had no idea how long he had been here—wherever "here" was. It seemed like forever. The shot they gave him every morning lasted most of the day. It was different from the first drug, the one that knocked him out. This one left him feeling sluggish and disoriented, not quite in touch with reality. And it made him tell the truth. He did his best to fight it, but willpower was no match for body chemistry.

When the drug wore off near evening, he seized those rare moments of clarity, trying to give his handlers no clue that he was now, however briefly, in control. The hardest thing was stopping himself from shaking with fear. They gave him sleeping pills as the shot was wearing off, timing them to keep him woozy most of the time. Pills were better than shots, though—he had a chance of not swallowing them. The second night, he slid the pill deep under the back of his tongue and took a gulp of water. He was in luck. His handler wasn't a nurse, just one of Jepson's grunts. He didn't even check.

So now, every night he pretended to sleep, while trying to plan his escape. At first, he was so overwhelmed that he couldn't think clearly; his mind just wandered randomly through a landscape of disconnected thoughts and worries. How could he signal Mack or Dr. Mel or Jade? The Visitors? Each day, his moments of clarity lasted slightly longer.

At least Jepson's motivations were clear—basically, he *hated* aliens. Morgan had said this, but the verification was bone-chilling. Late one day, during his questioning, Sam heard part of a conversation. He listened closely and tried to memorize everything. It was hard; Jepson and the doctor were off to one side, talking in low voices. Jepson was furious about Sam and aliens, the military and aliens, aliens in general.

"Dammit!" Jepson raged. "I *know* that kid knows more than he's saying. I've *seen* him in places he couldn't be without their help. Why can't we get it out of him with the drug?"

"Maybe he doesn't know what he's doing. Or *how* he's doing it," the doctor suggested.

"Nah—he's covering for them somehow. He fawns over those revolting creatures just like everyone down here."

Down here, Sam thought. He was definitely in the DUMBs. That probably meant the Visitors were his only hope of getting out.

"Well, you got one new thing out of him—that human-alien mind thing. You didn't know that, did you? I sure didn't."

"No, I didn't." Sam could practically feel Jepson's shudder.

"Sickening, ugly alien monstrosities," Jepson said. "I can't believe the military didn't wipe them out as soon as they started showing up. Worst mistake they ever made. The only sane response is to exterminate them like the vermin they are. But these idiots are treating them like *people*! Trying to *learn* from them."

"They may be ugly, but they have good technology."

"And first chance they get, they'll use it to take over. We can't let that happen."

"But Major, we need to be careful. You know what happened before."

Jepson snorted in disgust. "Well, now we know a little more about what the creatures are planning. But what are they doing with those kids? Maybe we'd get more if we doubled the kid's dose?"

"No, we can't do that!" The doctor sounded panicked. "It's a barbiturate. He's already getting a high dose. Doubling it would kill him."

Jepson grunted. "Wouldn't care if it did. But I suppose we'd better not."

Sam's heart nearly stopped as he listened to this exchange. At least, the doctor had a conscience. Thank goodness.

"But we need to get the information out of him!" Jepson

continued. "That damned ex-ranger is still poking around, and when he sets his mind on something, he gets it. So, we'll probably have to disappear soon."

The two men moved away and Sam couldn't hear anymore. But this information was new—and frightening. He wondered who the ex-ranger was and why he was poking around. He fixed the conversation in his mind. He would tell Mack and the general; maybe they could figure it out. But first, he had to get out of here. Things were getting dangerous.

Back in his room, his handler gone and his sleeping pill *not* taken, he reached out to the Visitors again. He closed his eyes and concentrated on drawing his own Visitor into his mind. He begged for her help. He told her Jepson was out of control, that he feared for his life. He told her he would do what they wanted—he would even *enjoy* working on environmental problems, although the human-alien mind thing freaked him out. Did he have a right to ask for their help? *Yes!* He had given them plenty in the past, willing or not, and now he was offering more—his whole life, maybe. It seemed more than fair. But would they think so? Would they help? And when? Exhausted, he fell into a heavy sleep.

CHAPTER 42
BREAKOUT

SAM AWOKE STARTLED, feeling as though he'd been dropped from a height. It took him a second to register that he was no longer in his bed in the cell. He was outdoors, in the dark. In the cold. The Visitors had come through!

Slowly, he sat up, trying to get his bearings, and realized he was outside Cassidy Base—but inside the twelve-foot fence. If he didn't get himself on the other side of that fence, and soon, he would be captured again and this time, they would probably chain him to his bed. For a second, he was angry at the Visitors: Why couldn't they just drop him at home, like they had so many times before?

But anger didn't help. They had put him outside. To be fair, he hadn't been specific about *where* outside, and the Visitors didn't see walls or fences as barriers. They had done what he asked! He remembered how that had shocked Morgan. Feeling ashamed, he used telepathy to thank his Visitor. The only response was a brief sensation of euphoria.

Okay, the Visitors had done their part—now it was his turn. Sam felt groggy, still half-drugged. He was shivering. Plus, he was exhausted—it was the middle of the night. But he had to hide! He moved away from the gate and cameras and toward the back fence, walking carefully, trying to disappear behind the warehouses. Moving rapidly was out of the question; he was barefoot, it was too dark to run, and if he fell, he might accidentally cry out. He couldn't afford to make a sound. He wanted to reach the far end of the fenced-in area —the farther the better—but it made more sense to climb the fence while he was still hidden by the warehouses. They could still catch him if he was on the other side, but it would be harder.

Sam stopped behind the last warehouse and began to climb. *Oh, this is going to be hard.* He could get good fingerholds on the chain-link fence, but toeholds were harder. His feet weren't that tough—they were used to shoes. He clenched his teeth and tried to ignore the pain as he climbed. Halfway up, he heard shouts near the gate. They had discovered he was gone! He had minutes, at most, before they found him.

He climbed faster. In his haste, he reached up without looking and grabbed a handful of razor wire with his right hand. *Ahh, that hurts!* He bit back his cry of pain and wiped the blood on his pajamas. The cuts felt deep. Risking a glance upward, he quickly adjusted his hand and fingers, trying to avoid the spikes. It wasn't easy. Three straight rows of barbed wire were surrounded by a spiral of razor wire. And it was so dark—the spotlight over the buildings barely reached here, and the moonlight was dim. One more step and then over. He was pretty sure there was no way he could manage this without serious cuts. But the alternative was capture.

Steeling himself, Sam balanced on the very top of the fence with his left fingers and toes, and heaved himself partway over the razor wire, grabbing onto the other side with his right hand and foot. He grabbed downward, below the wire, and managed to hold on, but just as he released his left hand and foot, there was a shout—much nearer. He panicked and wrenched the rest of his body over. Razor-sharp spikes cut into his left hand, arm, torso, and leg as he slid rapidly to the ground, leaving blood on the fence. He looked around wildly. What now? He had never been on this side of the fence. Ahead were more chat piles and, eventually, the highway. Sam could see bobbing lights near the buildings; no doubt there would be brighter lights soon. If they found the blood, they would know where he was headed.

A huge chat pile loomed in front of him. He hurried right, toward its far side and away from his pursuers. His cuts were smarting and bleeding, and he limped as gravel cut into his bare feet. He was probably leaving an obvious trail, but there was no help for it. Maybe he could reach the highway and flag down a passing motorist before they found him. Sam had no idea how many confederates Jepson had in his fake mental hospital and therefore no idea how many pursuers he had. He wondered what Jepson had told the others—those who didn't know he was kidnapping and drugging teenagers to get information about aliens. He gritted his teeth and stumbled toward the highway, trying to ignore his aching feet and stinging cuts.

Hidden within the chat piles, Sam could no longer see the bobbing lights, and he heard no signs of pursuit. Maybe they'd given up? *Not likely*. He desperately hoped the highway was close. He struggled on, clenching his fists to stop his palms from bleeding. His arm, chest, and thigh were quietly oozing blood, and the ground was a carpet of sharp rocks, torturing his bruised feet. His shivering was getting worse. Finally, there were no more chat piles. Just three or four hundred yards of open ground between the last pile and the highway. He would be exposed the whole way. Well, at least it was grass, not gravel. Groaning, he started across.

It must have been very late—there was almost no traffic. As he reached the circle of light under the nearest pole, headlights appeared to his right. Not ideal—they were coming from the direction of town—but maybe he could at least use their phone. He waved madly, and the car stopped. Too late, his mind registered that the lights had not come from town. The car had just turned off the county road from the direction of Cassidy Base. How could he have been so stupid! He had just flagged down Major Jepson. *Damn! Where did he get the car?*

Jepson leapt out of the car, his gloating expression visible even before he darted across the highway. Sam turned and began to run back toward the chat piles, but it was too late. Jepson was not hampered by sore, cold, bare feet. Sam tripped after only a few steps, and Jepson was on him like a starving tiger. He grabbed both of Sam's wrists and twisted.

"Aagh!" Sam cried out in pain.

"Got you now, you slimy little bastard. You're not getting away this time!"

Sam writhed from side to side, trying to loosen Jepson's hold, but the man was strong. If he could turn over, maybe he could get in a good kick. But Jepson's knee was in the middle of his back. Sam kicked his legs over and over, trying to contact some part of Jepson's body. Nothing was within reach, but at least he was making Jepson's life more difficult. He gave a vigorous lunge, and Jepson's knee slipped sideways. At that moment, he saw headlights coming toward town. There was a screech of brakes and the sound of a car door opening. Distracted, Jepson loosened his hold enough for Sam to pull free and jump to his feet.

"Hey, what's going on over there?" someone shouted.

"Help!" Sam screamed. "Call 911. He's trying to kidnap me!"

Jepson grabbed Sam's shoulder with one hand and tried to clamp the other hand over his mouth. Sam bit down hard, and Jepson screamed, but kept pushing him toward the chat piles. Sam resisted, trying to force them both backward toward the light. Footsteps jumped the ditch, and hands grabbed him away from Jepson.

"Hey! What're you doing?" The guy from the car glared at Jepson. "This is a kid—and he's covered in blood! What the hell did you do to him?"

"He didn't do that," Sam said hastily. "That's my fault. I—climbed a fence."

"What *kind* of fence?"

"Razor wire. Doesn't matter. Please, could you call the cops? He's—"

"Butt out of this, you goddamned black bastard!" Jepson roared.

Sam gasped in horror. Jepson had grabbed Sam's arm again, trying to pull him away, and his voice dripped with venom.

Sam looked up at his rescuer, who was tall and young and looked tired, like he'd been driving all night. He was returning Jepson's glare with considerable venom of his own. And yes, he was Black. Sam realized he wasn't surprised by Jepson's racism—disgusted but not surprised. The unease he felt around Jepson suddenly made sense. Jepson hated anyone who looked different from him, like Black and Brown people. Like Sam, like his rescuer. No wonder he despised the Visitors—they were too different from him to fathom. That, plus he's a bully and a coward, Sam thought. *Just like my dad.*

"Please, sir, call 911," he begged his rescuer. "He kidnapped me. I thought I'd got away, but—"

"What's your name, kid?"

"Sam."

The young man nodded. "I'm Chris."

Chris had his eyes on Jepson and an arm around Sam's shoulder. With his other hand, he pulled his phone from his pocket and handed it to Sam.

"You call. You know what's going on. Tell them to hurry."

When Chris turned toward Sam, Jepson lunged toward him, fists raised. He caught Chris in the shoulder, knocking him off-balance. Sam dropped the phone—Jepson was attacking the guy who was helping him? No way! He slammed into Jepson's chest with his head and both fists. Jepson staggered, and within seconds, Chris had recovered and subdued him in an armlock that pinned both of his elbows back and prevented him from moving.

Breathing heavily, Chris looked at Sam. "Thanks! Call them, quickly!"

"You bastard, get your hands off me!" Jepson spat. "You have no right to touch me!"

"You make one more move toward this kid, and I'll do a lot more than touch you."

Jepson was furious, but he couldn't move, and he remained quiet.

Sam was impressed by the young man's handling of Jepson—the guy obviously knew karate or something. He found the phone and made the 911 call. When the operator answered, he tried to be concise and give just the facts, but he was shaking from his recent ordeal, and from the cold, and he stumbled through his explanation.

Finally, he said, "I know it's late, but could you maybe call Detective Pierce? He knows me. Tell him it's Sam Costas, and Major Jepson took me. He'll understand. Okay, thanks."

He looked up at the stranger. "They're coming. Is it okay if I make another call?"

Chris nodded. "Of course."

Sam called Mack and nearly collapsed with relief when he answered on the first ring. Their conversation was brief. Mack was out the door the instant he heard Sam's voice. He was five minutes away. Sam finally began to relax. Mack was coming, and police sirens were approaching. He had escaped

Jepson. Well, with help from the Visitors. And now Chris and the police and Mack. He closed his eyes. Maybe Mack and Dr. Mel and Jade were right—sometimes you need help. You don't have to do everything alone. You can trust people. At least some people.

Within minutes, two police officers arrived. After a couple of terse sentences from the young man, whose name was Chris Johnson, and Sam's identification of Jepson, whose name they recognized, they cuffed Jepson's hands and feet. Then, Mack was running toward Sam and engulfing him in a bear hug. Sam grunted in pain and Mack stepped back. Holding Sam at arm's length, he surveyed his blood-encrusted pajamas and filthy bare feet with shock.

"What *happened* to you?"

"I, um, climbed the razor-wire fence and ran through the chat piles."

Mack quickly wrapped his jacket around Sam's shoulders, wincing as he surveyed his bloody hands. His lips twitched, then he sighed. "Of course, you did."

He turned to the police officers. "I need to get him to the ER. Can you take his statement there?"

"Sure," said Officer Harris. He grinned at Sam. "I'm sure it'll be a good story."

Harris had obviously heard about Sam and Jade's earlier escapade. Did he know about the DUMBs?

"Make sure you lock *him* up tight," Mack said grimly, nodding his head at Jepson, who glowered but remained silent. "I'll call General Greenwald. He'll be in touch."

"Don't worry, we've got him."

CHAPTER 43
CONSEQUENCES

AS HEAD OF THE ER, Dr. Mel put herself on duty so she could tend Sam's injuries personally. Jade came with her. She wouldn't leave Sam's side once she arrived, nor would Mack. They distracted Sam while Dr. Mel and a nurse cleaned, disinfected, and stitched his wounds. The police came while she was working. Mack was calm at first, but became agitated as Sam recounted his story. Sam was relieved—Mack was clearly in the moment, no longer dreamy. He was as normal as he could be, with the Visitors in his life.

Chris Johnson, Sam's rescuer, came with the police. He wanted to make sure Sam was okay—and, he admitted, he wanted to hear Sam's story. Sam gave them all the sanitized version—true except without Visitors or DUMBs. Afterward, Mack shook Chris's hand and thanked him over and over for helping Sam. He brought coffee and they chatted as Dr. Mel bandaged Sam's wounds.

"Why did you stop?" Mack asked.

"I saw the fight—it looked really unequal. I thought the smaller person needed help." Chris shrugged, grinning wryly. "Guess I just can't mind my own business."

"Or you're just a really decent person," Mack said. "And

we're all very grateful." He paused. "What do you do for a living, Chris?"

Chris gave him a diffident smile. "I'm an entrepreneur, or trying to be. It's early days yet, but I build websites. When I can find clients."

Mack raised his eyebrows and smiled at Sam. Sam could almost see the wheels turning in his brain as Mack connected two of their earlier conversations. One conversation had involved serendipity in science, the "happy accidents" that had led to discoveries like penicillin, pulsars, and X-rays. The other dealt with how the teens could fulfill their intense need to do something to save the environment—a need instilled by the Visitors.

So far, their best idea was starting an online environmental school, which in turn would require building a website. Mack, with his environmental science degree, could help with the school. But none of them, even Ravi, had ever built a website. Looking across at Chris, Sam decided there might be something to this serendipity idea, after all.

He grinned at Chris. "We need to get to know you. Before long we might need someone who can build websites. And we have a good friend you might want to meet. He's only sixteen, but he's a great IT guy."

Before he left, Chris had become a friend. He promised to check on Sam's recovery. He was intrigued by the online school—although he didn't yet know it was inspired by the Visitors. And he was anxious to meet Ravi. As Chris had said, it was still "early days," but Sam was sure their small Visitors group had a new member.

———

Later that day, Sam finally met General Greenwald in person. He was gruff but friendly, just as he was on Zoom, and he hugged like Mack. Sam liked him immediately. The general filled Sam in on events that occurred while he was gone. When told of Sam's second disappearance, he had come to Cassidy to help. He and Mack had led the search, concentrating first on Ms. Mott and then, after her hostile and suspicious comments, on Sam's mother. They had assumed Jepson was hiding in Cassidy Base, but they had not been allowed in. That had led the general to contact Morgan, and with Morgan's help, he was now a full member of the Visitor team.

The general also relayed a message from Morgan to Sam and Jade.

"First," he said, "Colonel Grant wants you to know that Jepson is no longer a problem. He's disgraced himself and the army. He'll be court-martialed, and Colonel Grant says he'll be lucky to get out of prison before he's ninety."

"Good!" the kids chorused in unison.

"What about the people helping him?" Sam asked. "His—gang? Won't they still be out there?"

The general frowned. "Part of my new job includes hunting down and stopping his cohorts. The local police will deal with Mott—she's left the army. But we're looking into Sergeant Jimenez and the doctor who drugged you. And several others."

Sam was relieved, but he wasn't convinced the alien haters had disappeared.

The general continued, "Colonel Grant apologizes for not visiting you in person, but he's setting up a new project and can't leave the DUMBs. He says to keep listening to the Visitors, and prepare yourselves. It might be months, but he will see you. That's a promise."

The message was disappointing—they really missed Morgan—but also intriguing. *Just what we need*, Sam thought, *mystery from Morgan as well as the Visitors.*

After Sam's return and Jepson's arrest, Ms. Mott was arrested for aiding and abetting in Sam's kidnapping and was fired. Sam and Jade were relieved—at least, she could no longer harm students. The police also questioned Sam's mother, who insisted that both Mott and Jepson had assured her that Sam needed psychiatric treatment. They still found her motives highly suspicious and reported her to Child Protective Services. Both Mack and Dr. Mel also filed complaints against her with CPS. Mack was apologetic, but firm, when he told Sam.

"I'm sorry, Sam. I know she's your mother, but what she did is—not normal. You deserve so much better."

Although Sam was furious with his mother, he felt obligated to defend her. "She didn't really mean any harm. They convinced her there was something wrong with me."

"She's your mother, Sam. If she spent any time with you, she would know what's going on in your life. She would know you do not have mental problems. She would protect and defend you. Yet, she did almost nothing when you disappeared into the DUMBs for a week. And when Jepson kidnapped you, she sided with him, despite knowing the army considered him a criminal. She refused to give us any information to find you—that's obstructing justice. Think about it, Sam: Are those the actions of a fit mother? A loving mother?"

Sam was quiet. Mack was right. Sam understood his and Dr. Mel's reasons for filing the complaints, but he hated it. He hid his mother's actions away deep in his brain, and tried not to think about them.

———

But everything that happened during and after his kidnapping took second place to one event that Sam hoped would change his life forever. Jade had stayed close since he returned—she admitted being afraid she would never see him again. Before, Sam had been far too shy to show how he really felt about her—except for that first spontaneous hug in the DUMBs, and a few furtive touches. He assumed she couldn't possibly feel the same way. Since returning, they had been preoccupied with helping Mack understand the Visitors and getting the Visitors to take him. They had spared little time for personal things. Like . . . feelings. And then—Jepson. But now, the way she looked at him made him think maybe . . .

Shortly after he returned, they were at Jade's house, discussing how to prepare for the Visitors. Suddenly, Jade stopped talking and looked at him in *that* way. He met her eyes, hesitated, and after a moment placed his hand gently over hers. He felt her indrawn breath, but she didn't move. *Show some guts, Sam!*

"Jade, there's something I . . . really want to do."

"What's that?" Her voice was low and, he thought, hopeful.

"Would you . . . let me kiss you?" He held his breath. He didn't want to think what he would do if she said no.

But she whispered, "Yes, please."

He took her face in both hands and leaned toward her. Her mouth was soft, inviting. Their kiss was short and slightly awkward. Sam kept his eyes closed for a moment. The world swayed and seemed brighter through his closed eyelids. His heart was beating hard.

Finally, he pulled back and looked into her eyes, her beautiful, warm, green-speckled eyes. "Thank you," he whispered. Then, "The Visitors brought us together. Do you think that matters?"

She touched his face, smiling. "No. They brought us together, but they didn't make us care about each other. We did that."

"Do you think . . . we could do that again?" Sam asked. He was looking down at his hands, and he knew he sounded shy. It was just so new.

"I'd like that," she said softly. This time, the kiss was longer and Jade participated fully. *This gets better with practice*, Sam thought. *We'll have to practice a lot.*

CHAPTER 44
SAM ENDURES

ONCE MORE, Sam was readjusting to school after a week's absence. His teachers gave him his missed assignments without comment—they knew he would catch up. He was staying at Jade's house. Dr. Mel said she wanted to keep him close so she could check on his injuries. Jade said her mom just wanted to mother him and was using his injuries as an excuse.

Sam worried that Jade might feel neglected, but she just laughed. "Hey, when she's mothering you, she's not hassling me," she said. "I can do what I want."

Dr. Mel was gentle and caring, and Sam thoroughly enjoyed being mothered. But sometimes, like today, he had to return home to get clothes. He was optimistic as he biked home after school. He and Jade had worried about Morgan's warnings that something awful might happen to them, but surely, since the kidnapping and Jepson's arrest, they could put that fear aside. And he and Jade had kissed, something he'd thought might never happen. He smiled, remembering her sweet face and the feel of her lips on his.

Lost in his daydream, Sam didn't notice his father's truck, nearly hidden on the far side of the house, or the angry face at the window. As he walked through the door, he didn't see the belt swinging toward him until it was too late. Before he could react, he was face down over the back of the sofa, his hair held in an iron grip by a huge, calloused hand. There was no way to fight back. His father was roaring with rage as he swung the belt from his other hand. Sam screamed in agony as his back, from shoulders to thighs, was quickly covered in angry red stripes and deep bruises. The beating went on and on, the lashes ripping through his shirt and flaying his bare back.

Through his screams and the haze of pain, he heard his father shouting, cursing Sam's connections to the loony bin, the military, his lunatic aunt, high-and-mighty teachers, and smartass know-it-all floozies. Each accusation was punctuated by a blow—or several. Dimly, Sam recognized that his father was very drunk, and would eventually stumble or loosen his grip.

Finally, he lurched sideways, and Sam jerked free, lunging away from the still-swinging belt. He made for the kitchen door but tripped and fell flat. His father flung the belt aside and kicked him. Sam groaned as a steel-toe work boot connected with something deep inside him. Desperately, he crawled across the doorsill and rolled, forcing himself to his feet. Sobbing and shaking, he ran toward the woods, praying his father would not follow.

As Sam pushed deeper into the trees, his adrenaline rush began to fade; he became faint and stumbled. He reached out, steadying himself on trees as he ran. Finally, he fell, landing heavily on the path and crying out as a fresh wave of pain ripped across his back and shoulders. Now, he lay still, on his stomach, his half-healed razor-wire cuts pressed into the ground. He waited for time and the chilling air to ease his torment. The pain was knives and hammers and searing heat all bombarding him at once. But the humiliation was worse.

All year, he had tried to act grown-up, to prove he could deal with anything, but it was just an act—he was a child, a weakling, a worthless coward. Was this the Visitors' way of telling him he had failed their tests?

Sam shored up his resolve. Whatever the Visitors thought, he would hide his cowardice from the world. He would cover the welts and wounds with clothes, and go to school as usual, and no one would *ever* know about this. Dr. Mel would expect him back tonight. If he called, she would come and get him; she would take care of him. But Jade would find out. And Mack. *No!* He would not admit his shame and humiliation to the only people who thought he was worth something. Painfully, he dragged his cell phone from his pocket and texted Jade and her mom:

Staying home tonight. See you tomorrow.

Sam lay on the path for hours, taking shallow breaths and finally dozing, until the darkness was deep, and the penetrating chill of the November night forced him to move. Standing and walking were agony; his wounds had dried and each movement broke open newly forming scabs, triggering fresh waves of pain. Quietly, wincing with each step, he crept slowly toward the house. No lights. He stopped outside the kitchen door and listened. No sound. And he would leave early in the morning, before they woke up.

First, a shower. Maybe warm water would ease the pain enough to let him sleep. He tiptoed into the kitchen and listened again. Nothing. In the shadows of the living room, he saw the belt, discarded in a heap on the floor. He shuddered and gave it a wide berth. He crept up the stairs and past his parents' room. His father was snoring. So far, so good.

Removing his jeans and briefs was difficult, but he

managed. Showering, usually relaxing and enjoyable, was a painful ordeal. Dried blood had plastered his ripped T-shirt to his back. As warm water poured over him, he worked the shirt loose and peeled it off inch by inch. He had trouble lifting his arms. What would it be like tomorrow, getting dressed and going to school like nothing had happened? He shuddered, but he had no choice.

He found a bottle of Tylenol and took two tablets, keeping the bottle. Naked, he eased himself into bed on his stomach, lying with his head turned sideways. As he tried to relax, the tears started again. He did his best to cry quietly. The night was miserable. His back throbbed and burned, and sleep was out of the question. Every time he dozed off, he moved, and another shard of pain cut through his body, jolting him awake.

Around five, he got up and took more Tylenol. He would go to school early. The simplest task was excruciating and took ten times longer than usual. Dressing—oh, so slowly—in his loosest T-shirt and softest pair of jeans. Trudging to school, carrying his backpack, because there was no way he could ride his bike. Sitting carefully in the back row at school, and leaving the room last to avoid the hallway crush. He skipped both morning classes with Jade.

The morning passed in a slow, aching blur, but he managed until lunch hour. Then, an impatient football player clapped him hard on the back, shoving him sideways against the wall, shouting, "Move it, alien boy!" Sam gasped in agony. He was disoriented and dizzy; everything faded out for several seconds, but he was leaning against the wall so he remained upright. *This must be what fainting feels like*, he thought. Eventually, the world returned, the hallway cleared, and he made his way toward the front doors. Outside, he walked slowly to the edge of the steps and sat down carefully, resting his head against the railing.

Jade found him a few minutes later.

"Sam, why didn't you come home last night? Or answer my texts? And why did you miss class this morning? I was worried. Don't you want lunch?"

He shook his head. "I'm not hungry," he said.

"What's wrong? Are you sick?"

She sat beside him and put a hand on his back. Even her light touch was painful, and he couldn't help his quick intake of breath. She drew back, giving a small gasp.

"Sam, your back is bleeding. What happened? How did you get hurt?"

"It's nothing—I'm fine."

He felt her studying his face but didn't meet her eyes. She was quiet for a moment. Then she said, "Hey, I forgot something, but I'll come right back and keep you company, okay?"

He nodded. She left, almost running. He closed his eyes and sat still. Moving took too much effort. When Jade returned, she was not alone. He felt vaguely annoyed at being disturbed, but he was too tired to react.

Someone sat beside him on the steps. Long legs, army boots. Mack. Dimly, he realized that if Jade had brought Mack, she was really worried.

"Hey," Mack said quietly. "Having a bad day?"

"Kind of. Just . . . not feeling so good."

"What's wrong? Something to do with the blood on your back?"

Sam glanced toward him and shook his head. "No, I'm fine, really."

"Sam, can you stand up?" Mack asked. Sam closed his eyes. He shook his head again.

Mack stood. "I'll help. Give me your hands."

"No, please. I'm fine."

"Sam, I'm not asking." Mack's voice was still gentle but fractionally sterner. His no-nonsense voice. But so quiet, not like his angry voice after they returned from the DUMBs.

He took Sam's hands, and slowly pulled him to his feet. Sam clenched his jaw, his face contorting. He gave a short, involuntary cry as he came upright. Mack looked him in the eyes.

"I'm going to pull up your shirt and look at your back. Just for a second, to see what we're dealing with."

"No, please, it's fine."

"It's not a request, Sam. I'm sorry."

Mack moved to prevent Jade from seeing and pulled Sam's T-shirt up partway. He gave a quick indrawn breath. The shirt dropped and Mack placed a gentle hand on Sam's shoulder. "Your father did this?"

Sam did not want to answer, but Mack continued to look at him, and finally, he nodded once.

"When?"

Sam did not respond.

"Sam, when did this happen? It's important."

Sam closed his eyes. Finally, he whispered, "Yesterday. About f-four."

Mack pulled out his phone. Sam heard a one-sided conversation.

"Mel, we need your help . . . No, Jade's fine. It's Sam. He's been badly beaten. He's in shock and needs medical attention . . . Yes, him. Twenty hours ago. We have to do this right, make sure he pays. You know the protocols; I'll let you call the police and Child Services. Give them my name and tell them I'll talk to them there. We'll be there in fifteen minutes."

Jade helped Sam to Mack's car while Mack checked them out of school. During the drive, Sam kept his eyes closed, drifting. The car stopped outside the emergency room, and hands helped him out. He was horrified when he saw a stretcher. He shook his head and begged Dr. Mel, "No, please. I don't need this."

She whispered in his ear, "Sam, honey, it's okay. No one will see you; it's more private this way." She smoothed his hair back and put a soothing hand on his forehead.

Sam closed his eyes. He cried out once as two nurses lifted him onto the stretcher, laying him carefully on his stomach. They placed a sheet over him and wheeled him through the ER and into a curtained space. He felt the sting of a needle in his arm. A nurse began to cut off his T-shirt; another removed his jeans. He was embarrassed, but he was too weak to object.

Vaguely, he was aware that Jade's mom had left the cubicle. He could hear her, just outside, talking to Mack.

"The police and Child Protective Services are on their way," she said. "I'll take photos and send them to you, and you can talk to them. He's in no condition . . ."

Sam drifted off to sleep. Mack and Dr. Mel were in charge. He could give in. He could trust them.

CHAPTER 45
ACCEPTING SAFETY

SAM AWOKE TO A COLD, wet nose nuzzling his cheek. He opened his eyes. A furry black-and-white face was inches away, and warm brown eyes looked intently into his. Barker! Mack's house. They had talked in the hospital. Mack had asked if he could bring Sam home and take care of him. He remembered feeling relieved, so he must have said yes. He had spent last night in the hospital, and today they had given him tests. But mostly, he had slept. A drugged, restful sleep.

Sam patted Barker, who whined happily. He tried to sit up, then winced and lay back. The pain triggered a vision of the belt coming at him and his father's enraged face. He shuddered. Now, he was lying on his side on a comfortable couch, covered by a soft blue blanket. A small gas fire burned in the fireplace across the room. Bookshelves flanked the fireplace. Through the window, he saw soft, blurry twilight. He was wondering what to do when Mack came in.

"You're awake. How are you feeling?"

"Okay, I guess." Sam still felt a bit groggy.

He tried to sit up again. Mack helped him. Barker stayed as close as possible. When Sam was upright, he looked at

Mack and away again. "This is really nice of you, but I should go home. I shouldn't bother you."

"No, this is the best place for you. Your mom knows you're here. She's still dealing with a criminal charge. Why did you go back? I thought you were staying with Mel and Jade—I thought you were safe."

"I went to get clothes. And afterward . . . I didn't want anyone to know."

Mack closed his eyes. "Oh, Sam. Why can't you trust us?"

Sam hid his face. He did not reply.

"Sam," Mack said gently, "you are *not* going back there. If your father gets out of jail, you won't be safe. Your mother can't protect you. I can, and will."

"But—"

"No buts. You're badly injured. While you recuperate, I'm taking care of you, along with Dr. Mel and a certain young lady who was desperately anxious to stay with you today."

Sam looked up hopefully, but Mack shook his head.

"She's not here. You'll see her tomorrow morning. You both need to sleep tonight."

"And," he continued, "we need to get something clear from the beginning. You will do what I say and what Dr. Mel says. You will not try to do things on your own, unless we say it's okay. You *definitely* do not try to go anywhere on your own. I mean that. Do you understand?"

Mack was looking down at him. His look was stern—not angry, just no-nonsense. But beneath the sternness, there was so much kindness and caring. His mom hadn't looked at him like that since he was five. His father never had. His lips quivered, and his eyes filled with tears. He felt like a little kid. Again.

In a small voice, he said, "Yes, sir. I understand."

"Hey." Mack knelt, cupped Sam's chin in one hand, and looked into his eyes. All his sternness was gone. "I don't want to be a drill sergeant. I just want to keep you safe. I know you're used to taking care of yourself, and I respect that. But everyone needs to be taken care of sometimes. That doesn't make you weak or childish, it makes you human. So, let us take care of you, okay?"

Sam nodded. He didn't trust himself to speak.

"Now," Mack said. "I'm betting you're pretty hungry. Shall I bring you something here, or do you think you can walk to the kitchen?"

Sam wasn't sure how well he could move, but he wanted to. "Kitchen," he said.

He watched while Mack prepared a simple supper. He couldn't believe Mack was doing all this for him. Could he really care about Sam the way Jade and Dr. Mel said? It seemed impossible. But Mack had looked for him when he was lost in the DUMBs. He had fought to save him from Jepson and Mott. And the hug Mack had given him when he returned from the DUMBs—it had felt like a dad hug. It had made him feel—cherished.

As they ate, Sam asked, "Mack? How long am I going to be here?"

"A while, I think. We'll talk about it later."

―――――

Back in the living room, Mack made him comfortable on the couch and sat facing him. Sam was nervous. It was humiliating enough that Mack knew what had happened to him. How could he possibly discuss it? But Mack was practical, even clinical, as he told Sam about the pain meds and the antibiotic shot Dr. Mel had given him. He'd already had a tetanus shot because of his encounter with the razor-wire fence. Because he'd been in shock, Dr. Mel had also given him medication to return his blood pressure to normal. And he'd undergone a CT scan to check for broken bones and internal injuries. This revealed a badly bruised kidney, which Dr. Mel said would require at least two weeks to heal. *The kick*, Sam thought.

"Tomorrow," Mack continued, "you'll start a week-long course of antibiotics—two pills a day. And pain pills for as long as you need them. Dr. Mel will help you decide that."

"Now, I'm taking the rest of the week off school, as are you and Jade. But I have some business in town. Every morning before work, Dr. Mel will check you over and change your bandages. During the day, you'll stay at their house, with Jade."

Sam's face lit up, and Mack smiled.

"I thought that would please you. But you have to stay in bed most of the time. And you have to obey Jade, too. Dr. Mel will give her instructions." He paused. "I might ask if Barker can stay with you. Would you like that?"

Sam nodded. He liked Barker. "Yes, that would be great."

"Okay, next item: what's going to happen to you after you've recovered. Sam, Child Protective Services is planning to remove your father's parental rights because of his abuse."

Sam was both shocked and relieved. But he just said, "Okay."

Mack frowned. "How do you feel about that?"

Sam shrugged. "I hope I never see him again." He paused. "I hate him."

"Can't say I blame you." Mack's mouth was pressed into a thin line. "I hope by the time he's out of prison, you'll be an adult. And you won't need to be afraid of him."

"Why not?"

"Because I'm going to teach you to fight," Mack said flatly.

"What about . . . my mom?" Sam asked.

"What do you want to happen with your mom?" Mack asked.

"She didn't really do anything wrong. She kind of—lets me go my own way, but she never hurts me." He knew it wasn't really an answer. He wasn't sure what to say.

Mack sighed. "Sam, I've told you why I think she's a bad mother. And now—she's admitted knowing your father has beaten you many times, and she told no one, just let it happen. To me, that's criminal. But CPS makes the decision. With your help, probably."

"What do you mean?"

"You're old enough, I think they'll ask what *you* want to do. You have options."

"I do?"

He nodded. "You could continue living with your mother. Or you could ask to go into foster care. Or you could live with another family, just informally. Teenagers do that sometimes, if their home life is bad. And there are two families more than willing to take you."

Sam looked up, puzzled. "There are?"

Mack smiled at him. "Of course. Dr. Mel—and me."

"You would take me? Why would you do that?"

"Is it so hard to believe I care about you and want to take care of you? I told you how I felt when you came back from the DUMBs."

"But I'm nobody special." Mack was kind, but surely, he didn't really mean he would take Sam in—like a son.

"I disagree. I think you're very special. I've wanted to take care of you since the first day I saw you in seventh grade. You were so small and quiet and sad. But I discovered I could make your eyes light up if I talked about the right things."

Sam looked up. "You gave me a book about spaceships."

"I remember," Mack said. "Spaceships made your eyes light up."

Mack was smiling at him, but his eyes were serious.

"Sam, you're incredibly smart and brave and honest and independent—too damned independent, sometimes," he added. But it didn't sound like a criticism.

"And," Mack continued, "you're kind and thoughtful and responsible, even polite—which, believe me, is a rare thing for a teenager! You're very special. And I want to take care of you. If it were possible, I'd like to be your dad."

Sam was amazed that Mack had noticed him since seventh grade, and he couldn't help feeling a surge of hope at the thought of living with him, dad or not. He'd loved spending time at Dr. Mel's house after he and Jade returned from the DUMBs and having Mack drop by most days to check on them. With Mack, he felt safe for the first time ever.

He looked up at Mack. "But—the Visitors."

"What about them?"

"You hate them. And they're—with me. They won't just go away."

"Sam, I don't hate them. I'm afraid of them. So, I'm going to learn about them, and I'll be less afraid. And whatever they do, I'll try my best to protect you. Always. Okay?"

Sam stared at Mack. He couldn't speak.

Mack watched him closely. "This is a lot to take in, I know. Why don't you sleep on it, and we'll talk again tomorrow?"

Sam nodded. Suddenly, he felt like crying. Again. He seemed to be crying all the time. Mack was so nice, but he was making a huge mistake. When he understood what a coward Sam was, he wouldn't want to take care of him. *I have to tell him*, he thought. He looked up.

"What's wrong, Sam?"

The tears were threatening to spill over. It was easier to hold them in if he didn't look at Mack, so he stared down at the floor. "It's more than the Visitors. You wouldn't want me if you really knew me."

"What don't I know?"

"You called me brave. But I'm not. I'm a complete coward."

"Sam. I've seen the things you've gone through—the Visitor experiences, the bullying, escaping Jepson, dealing with your father. *How* can you think you're not brave?"

He didn't want to talk about it, but he had to. Mack was right about one of those qualities—he was honest. He kept his eyes on the floor. "He whipped me like I was a little kid. And I was screaming and crying like a little kid. And I ran away the first chance I got. I just ran away and hid."

Mack stared at him in disbelief. "Oh, Sam, how can you think that makes you a coward? Don't you realize anyone would have run away? You took a savage beating that would have killed a little kid. It could have killed you. That bruised kidney—it could have ruptured. You are here tonight, in relatively good shape, only because you're strong and healthy, and because you got away. You did what you needed to survive. You are brave, Sam."

He lifted Sam's chin. "Sam, look at me. Do you understand what I'm saying?"

Sam could not speak. He was choking on his tears. He shook his head. Mack just didn't understand. After a few moments, Mack seemed to come to a decision.

"Sam, I'm going to show you how brave you are. I'm going to show you some awful photos. I never planned to let you see these, but I think you need to. I'll stay right beside you."

He moved closer. "I'm staying close because, when Jade saw these, she ended up crying in my arms. And you know how brave Jade is."

Sam knew what the photos were. He dreaded seeing them. And he was horrified that Jade had seen them.

"Are you ready?"

He had no choice. He nodded. Mack pulled out his phone, opened the photos, and handed the phone to Sam. "There are six of them," he said. When Sam saw the first photo, he began to tremble. By the sixth, he was shuddering all over. He dropped the phone and buried his face in Mack's chest. Mack held him gently, careful not to hug him and cause more pain.

"That's what your back looked like at noon yesterday," he said. "It's not much better now. Anyone who sees these photos will know what excruciating pain you've been in, but you were trying to carry on as if nothing had happened. You think that's cowardice? I think it's incredible bravery."

Sam gave no response; he just lay against Mack's chest, trembling. Mack turned his head and looked into his eyes. "Do you hear me?"

Sam nodded. He was still doing his best not to cry. Mack smiled at him. He caressed Sam's head, smoothing his hair back from his face. He continued talking, very quietly.

"I think you've been very brave, but I don't think you were smart. Smart would have been calling me or Dr. Mel as soon as you could get to your phone. We both told you to call us if you needed help. Either of us would have taken you to the hospital immediately and saved you a great deal of suffering. But you chose to do everything on your own. Brave, but not smart. Sometimes, being smart means asking for help."

His soft voice was calming, and Sam heard a steady heartbeat where his head rested against Mack's chest. It felt soothing and safe. Eventually, his breathing slowed and his trembling ceased. He looked up. "Jade . . . saw those?"

Mack nodded. "My fault. I wasn't fast enough. She grabbed the phone out of my hand."

Despite his misery, Sam managed a tiny smile. "Sounds like Jade."

Mack smiled back. "Yeah. The photos horrified her, but she said she needed to know what you'd been through so she could help you. And she cried because you were in pain, and she couldn't fix it. She's a treasure, Sam."

Sam hid his face again. "I know. I don't deserve her."

"Of course, you do! You're both wonderful, and you deserve each other. You are an incredibly strong, brave young man, and I'm incredibly proud of you."

Sam looked up at him. "You really mean that?"

"I really do. And I would be honored to be your dad, if you'll have me."

Sam wanted so much to be strong and grown-up, but his lips trembled, and tears began to flow down his face.

"It's okay to cry, you know," said Mack gently. "It doesn't mean you're weak or cowardly or a child. It means you have a lot of strong emotions that need to come out, so you can feel better. And you're in a safe place now. You can cry as much as you need to."

And finally, Sam gave in. Mack held him until he cried himself out and then led him to bed, supporting him carefully with an arm around his shoulders. Barker jumped up and lay beside him, his nose burrowed in Sam's neck. Soon after, his Visitor faded in and gently touched his temples. A familiar phrase drifted through his mind: *You are together*.

The Visitor faded out.

CHAPTER 46
LETTING GO

JADE WAS WAITING outside the next morning when Sam, Mack, and Barker arrived. She ran to the car, looking anxious, and seemed greatly relieved to find Sam much like his normal self. Mack opened Sam's door and helped him out. Sam had dreaded appearing weak and helpless in front of her, but she had seen the photos; she knew what he was dealing with. He suddenly realized he was okay with her knowing; in fact, he felt grateful that all of them—Mack, Jade, her mom—knew. Not long ago, he had been completely alone; he'd thought he couldn't have friends.

Jade looked like she was about to hug Sam, but Mack intervened.

"He's better, but he's still very stiff and sore, Jade, so give him some space," he cautioned. "It's probably best if you swear off hugging for the next few days."

As soon as Mack and Dr. Mel left, Sam settled on the living room couch, having persuaded them that "couch rest" was equal to "bed rest." Barker and Sadie stayed close, and Jade fussed around him, taking her nursing duties seriously.

Sam was feeling different. Yesterday, he had been weak, helpless, completely dependent on others. Mack had cared for him as if he were a small child, but this morning he hadn't made Sam feel ashamed of his weakness. He had just seemed relieved to find him back to normal. And Mack himself was behaving differently. He seemed really serious about wanting to be Sam's dad. But the strangest thing wasn't what he said.

In the night, Sam had awakened and lay quietly, his eyes closed. Mack had come to check on him and obviously thought he was asleep. He had sat on the bed and begun to sing softly. First, a lullaby in a foreign language. Then, "Bring Him Home" from *Les Mis*. His voice was . . . magical. Sam was afraid to open his eyes—Mack might stop singing. He remembered the afternoon when Jade had been crying. Mack had said listening to music made him sad because he had lost someone. He hadn't mentioned that he also made music. But only in secret, it seemed. Sam had never heard him sing or even hum.

Sam felt much better today, partly because of Mack's singing. He closed his eyes, hearing the song in his head. He was sure Mack had sung it for him, about him. It made him feel loved. It made him want to let go and trust. His Visitor's face flashed briefly inside his head. *Okay*, he thought. *You win. I'll try*. Her huge eyes radiated approval. Or what Sam interpreted as approval, though others insisted the Visitors don't have emotions. And then he heard again, quite clearly, *you are together*.

He jumped slightly, startled. Jade was sitting beside him, holding his hand.

"What's wrong?" she asked. He wanted to tell her about Mack's singing, but that wasn't his secret to tell. He did tell her about hearing the Visitor's voice. She nodded.

"I think they've been watching you since you were hurt. I felt them around you in the hospital."

"When she said 'you are together,' I don't think she

meant us," Sam said. "She knows we're together. I think she meant Mack. That I should trust him like I trust you."

"And you should," Jade said. "He really does love you. How can you not trust him?"

Sam sighed. "You're right. I'm working on it."

Jade described how angry both her mom and Mack had been in the ER and how determined they were to make Sam's father pay for attacking him.

"And I found out something about Mack. He's been an army ranger."

Sam's eyes widened. "Really?"

She nodded. "I don't think he meant to tell us. It just—slipped out."

Sam remembered Jepson's comment at Cassidy Base: "That damned ex-ranger is still poking around." He was talking about Mack! He told Jade what Jepson had said.

Jade smiled with satisfaction. "Well, he was right. Mack got what he wanted—Jepson."

Sam had never known any rangers, but he'd heard they were smart and tough. Like Mack. That probably explained how he took charge of any situation so easily. How he made you obey him without question, with just a look or a few words. Maybe even how his tall, lean body felt like steel when he hugged you.

"But," he said, "I guess I wouldn't expect a ranger to be like Mack—teasing and joking, or being so gentle, like he was last night." *Or singing*.

She looked surprised. "Why not? He'd be all serious and tough when he was working, being a ranger. But off duty, he'd have his own personality. Like anyone."

Sam nodded. "Now that I know him better, he just seems so—complicated."

Jade gave him a slight grin. "Yeah. And we definitely need to stay on his good side. He was scary that day. He said it was a good thing he wasn't the one arresting your father. His fists were clenched, and his face . . ." She shook her head.

"There's more," she said after a moment. "I heard them talking later—they didn't know I could hear. He really wants to take care of you. He said, if you're willing, he might be able to use being a ranger to help him become your guardian or even your dad."

Sam was startled. Mack really was serious about this.

"He mentioned being my dad last night. How would being a ranger help?"

"He's a war hero. He said he hates that term, and he never talks about it. But he has medals from the army. And his CO called him that in his recommendation letter. The Child Services people think it makes him a great role model for a teenage boy. So, he's willing to use it if it gets him approved faster. But it depends on what you want and what happens with your mother."

"Wow." Sam felt a thrill of excitement. He wasn't surprised that Mack was a war hero—and he loved Mack for his quiet humility. And Mack must really care about him, love him even.

Suddenly, he wanted to share his newfound joy with Jade. He held out his arms, but she said, "I'm not supposed to hug you, remember?"

"But kissing is okay, right?" His voice was hopeful.

Laughing, she moved closer. And this time he knew what to do.

In the afternoon, he watched Jade play Frisbee with Barker. Because he couldn't participate, his mind tumbled haphazardly through the possible turns his future might take. When Jade and Barker finally finished their game, Jade settled with him on the pillow-covered porch swing. They relaxed, soaking in the autumn sun, and talked about where Sam would end up living.

"You'll stay here, won't you? Preferably with Mack? You won't move away?"

"I want to stay. Mack says I can stay with him informally, even if my mother still has custody. CPS has the final say, though."

Jade sighed. "I'll be so glad when we're finally old enough to make our own decisions, and they stop treating us like children. I *hate* that."

"Me, too," Sam said. "At least, Mack always listens and asks what we think."

"But I hate that look he uses when he doesn't like what you've done. It makes me feel about six years old."

"He's really good at stopping you with a look or a few words. I feel like a little kid when he does it, too. He did it last night. I wasn't trying to be difficult; I guess he thought I wasn't taking things seriously enough. But I didn't really resent it because . . ." He stopped.

"Because why?"

"Because . . . he makes me look into his eyes. And when I do, I don't just see the sternness. Behind that, there's this incredible caring and concern. Like he wants you to know he's being stern because he's trying to protect you. I feel so . . . *safe* with him, even when he's scolding me. Does that make sense?"

Jade's eyes filled with tears. "Yeah, it does. Here I'm getting upset with him, and he's just—being a good dad. I'm so glad he makes you feel safe."

She paused. "But, Sam, he can't protect us from the Visitors. When you were gone, I was so afraid they had taken you again and left me. Being separated from you scares me so much."

"Don't worry. It's driving me crazy, too, not knowing exactly what they want, but we always end up together. They need us both."

"We know more since the DUMBs. There's the whole 'fix the environment' thing."

Sam nodded. "And apparently, they like the way we think. I guess that's a good thing. Morgan thinks they've already told us what they want, and we'll remember it gradually."

Jade agreed. "I just wish we had more control," she said.

CHAPTER 47
WHAT THE VISITORS WANT

BARKER HAD BEEN DOZING on the porch beside Sam. Suddenly, he whined, leapt up, and fled. Before Sam and Jade could react or feel the flickering lights and electrical charges, they were whisked away.

Sam came to, dizzy and shaky. The Visitors. Again. At least Jade was here, too. They were lying side by side on polished metal tables. He looked around. This was where Jepson had brought him, deep under Cassidy Base. The space was large and curved. Shiny white walls. A sterile, medical feel. The unpleasant smells and creepy vibe that heralded the Visitors. But they were alone. Suddenly, he realized he was not in pain. His back felt normal, like he'd never been hurt. How was that possible?

He spoke softly to Jade. "Let's be tough this time—not freak out, not give in, demand answers. And remember everything. Okay?"

"I . . . I'll try," Jade said. "But they're so scary."

"I know. But we're stronger together," Sam insisted. "We can use that. When you start to lose it, think of me. And I'll think of you. Okay?"

Jade took a deep breath. "Okay," she said. "But there's no one here. And you're hurt."

"No. Nothing hurts right now." She gave him an incredulous stare, and he shrugged. He couldn't explain it. Why try?

Then, their Visitor appeared. She didn't walk in; she just appeared. And Sam realized he could no longer move—he was powerless, lying on the table. It made him furious. He was grateful to be pain-free, but why were they doing this? This time he would not be intimidated. He wanted answers!

But the Visitor was forcing his attention toward her. As always, she didn't ask, she just made him obey. Today, he felt more resentment than fear. And somehow, she had moved—she was now *between* the metal tables, between him and Jade. *How do they do that?* She waved one hand, with its skinny fingers, between them, and he heard her thought clearly: *You are together*. He glanced at Jade. Her eyes were wide—she'd heard it, too.

"Yes, we are together," Sam replied, staring straight into her eyes. He said it aloud. He'd never done that before, and he could swear the Visitor looked surprised. He said it telepathically, too. He looked at Jade and spoke softly. "Tell her. Voice and telepathy."

Jade looked straight at the Visitor and said, "Yes, we are together." Her voice was tremulous but clear. Her mental assent was just as clear. Sam gave her a slight smile.

He turned back to the Visitor. "Why does that matter? What do you want from us?"

He decided that, from now on, he would still use telepathy, which—for some reason—he was getting better at. But he would also speak aloud. It was a small thing, but it would show the Visitors they were not completely in charge. And he would ask questions.

The Visitor moved her huge eyes back and forth several

times between Sam and Jade, lying immobile on their metal tables. She spoke again, in both their heads. *You are ready*.

Sam's eyes widened. "Ready for what?"

Her telepathic voice was clear, and, Sam thought, matter-of-fact. *You are together. You will fix the planet.*

His mouth dropped open and he shot a glance at Jade. She looked as blown away as he felt. He thought: *This is the first real conversation we've had with a Visitor. And we get their resident nutcase.* He couldn't help himself; he laughed. Another first—laughter, instead of abject terror. Again, she looked surprised. Was he the first abductee who had laughed?

"Seriously?" Sam said. "We're in high school. You're forcing us to lie on these tables like—lab rats. And you expect us to fix the planet? How?"

For a second, the Visitor looked confused. Then, she placed a finger on each of their foreheads. And the world changed. They were no longer in the DUMBs, lying paralyzed on tables in a sterile room with a Visitor. They were alone, hovering high over a vast pine forest. The forest was a blazing, roaring inferno of wildfire. Sam felt like he was falling into the sun. And then, a surge of power flowed through him. Below, the immolation stopped, and new pine trees grew and spread, restoring the forest. Beside him, Jade's eyes were closed; her face glowed. Resonant, joyful music surrounded them, growing in volume as the forest regenerated.

Minutes? Hours? Sam had no idea how long they remained above the forest. Then, they were somewhere else. And again, and again. High in the air, hovering over agricultural fields, coral reefs, rainforests, Arctic tundra, coastal cities. The places varied wildly, but in every place, Sam felt the surge of power, heard the music, and watched nature heal and rejuvenate beneath them. Magical. Impossible. Insane.

Then, in an instant, they were back on the metal tables,

immobile and staring at their Visitor. She looked from Sam to Jade. *Fix the planet*, she said. *Use your gifts.* Her telepathic voice echoed within them. She sounded intense, firm.

They stared at each other and then back at her. *What gifts?* Sam asked. He didn't bother to speak aloud. Telepathy works better anyway, he thought.

The Visitor placed a cool finger on Sam's forehead, just between his eyes. He felt a tiny surge of electricity; warmth briefly suffused his brain. When she removed her finger, he felt different. He shook his head, wondering what had changed. The Visitor took his hand and moved it toward Jade. She guided his index finger until it almost touched Jade's forehead. *Touch. Listen.*

Sam stared into Jade's eyes. She looked nervous but not frightened. "Are you okay with this?" Sam asked. "I don't know what will happen."

She took a deep breath and nodded. "They need us. She won't hurt us," she said.

Sam closed his eyes, preparing himself—for what, he had no idea. He touched Jade's forehead. And fell back, gasping and jerking his finger away as an overpowering flood of information surged through him. Sights, sounds, thoughts, memories, emotions—especially emotions. The Visitor grasped his finger and returned it to Jade's forehead. *Listen.* Her voice was still telepathic, but it sounded angry, almost a hiss. He dared not disobey. Tentatively, he touched Jade's forehead again. He was more prepared, but he still felt inundated. He'd kind of assumed a mind would be an orderly place—maybe like a library, with facts and thoughts and feelings neatly arranged on shelves, with labels. But Jade's was a seething mass. A boiling cauldron. This was worse than a Visitor download—because it wasn't just one topic, it was *everything*. How did she make sense of this? Was his mind like this?

He looked up at Jade. "Did you feel that? Could you tell I was in your mind?"

She nodded.

You. The Visitor was still stern and insistent. She touched Jade's forehead, then grabbed her hand and placed her finger between Sam's eyes. *Touch. Listen.* Jade followed her instructions, giving Sam a worried look. Sam stayed very still, trying to calm his mind, hoping his thoughts and emotions would shock Jade less than hers had shocked him. Apparently not. She jerked her hand away and cried out. The Visitor returned her hand. *Touch. Listen.* And Jade did, closing her eyes and breathing hard.

Finally, the Visitor was satisfied. She didn't relax—Visitors never relaxed—but she stood back, releasing them from her control. They could move again.

You are ready, she said. *Practice. Learn. Touch. Fix the planet.*

Sam rolled his eyes at Jade. *Yeah, right,* he thought at the Visitor. Did they get sarcasm? Probably not. *Why us?*

She looked confused again. *You are chosen. You understand.*

Sam looked at Jade again, his brow creased. She gave a helpless shrug.

Okay, Sam said. *Can we please remember all this? We can't practice or learn or do anything if we don't remember.*

You will remember. Practice. Learn. Touch. Fix.

And then, they were home on the back deck. Sam cried out as he landed on the swing. His back hurt again, a lot.

"Should have made sure she healed it permanently," he said to Jade, his teeth clenched.

Jade helped him sit up and arranged his pillows. She looked thoughtful. "Maybe it's—secrecy."

"What do you mean?"

"If she'd healed you, we'd have to explain it. Maybe she's telling us to keep—the abilities—secret. But we *have* to tell Mack and Mom."

Sam nodded. It was time to start trusting adults. "Wish we could talk to Morgan."

"I think that answers one question, though," Jade said. "I think the Visitors are good, not evil—or maybe like humans, a bit of both."

"Agreed," Sam said. "Not evil, just weird. And this was a breakthrough. We weren't completely terrified. We had a real conversation. And we remember everything!"

"Yeah," agreed Jade. "Of course, it makes no sense. What do we do? Why mind-reading? And what was that power surge when we were—fixing the planet?"

"No clue. And did any of that really happen?"

"Probably not."

"But we keep coming back to certain things—fixing the planet, mind-reading, emotions. And music," he added, shaking his head in confusion. The music was weird. Mack singing. Music when they fixed the planet.

"And 'you are together,'" added Jade.

CHAPTER 48
A NEW DAD

THEY SHARED their Visitor experience with Mack, Dr. Mel, and Ravi. Sam felt an urgent need to figure out what the Visitors wanted. And when they mentioned the music, Mack went totally quiet. Yet another Mack mystery to unravel.

The next day, "real life" intruded. Sam completed a difficult interview with the police, answering questions about his father's abuse. Detective Pierce was now kind and protective. He questioned Sam about his father's history of violence and beatings and Sam's attempts to avoid him. He grilled Sam about his mother—how she treated him, how he felt about her, what rules she set. He hated discussing this, but Mack was adamant: answer all questions honestly.

Then, he met with his mother in a police interrogation room. She wasn't under arrest, but the police were considering obstruction of justice charges. Their conversation was awkward and too long. Sam wasn't sure what to say—they never talked. He asked how she was; she shrugged. They stared at each other for a while. This was his best chance to get answers, but would she give them? He had to try.

"Why did you sic Jepson on me?" he asked.

She looked startled. "Sic him on you? He's an army

psychologist. He knows how to treat people with your problem."

"My *problem*?" He wanted to jump up and scream at her but instead clenched his fists hard and counted to ten before answering.

"So, you're still ignoring what's happening. You'll sacrifice me rather than admit the truth. You know Jepson is no psychologist. He's a fraud and a rogue and a kidnapper, and even after they told you that, you helped him keep me prisoner."

She hung her head and didn't reply. Sam put his head in his hands. *Mack was right about her*, he thought again. But she was his mother—even if she couldn't deal with the Visitors. Or Jepson.

"You and Aunt Lucy saw them when you were kids, didn't you?"

She hesitated, then nodded without looking up.

"I thought so. You could have told me, instead of treating me like I was crazy."

She bit her lip, looking ashamed. "I'm sorry," she whispered. "You changed after they came. There was always electricity around you. And I never knew when they would show up. I was scared."

He glared at her. "So was I. And I was five." She didn't respond.

He tried to get her to describe what she and Lucy had seen, but she said nothing useful. After a while, he gave up.

"Has Dad seen them?"

She looked up, surprised. "I don't know. He'd never admit it."

She was right about that. Finally, he asked, "Did you know he'd beaten me?"

She hung her head again. "Not until that teacher called from the hospital."

"Did it bother you? Did you care?" He tried to keep the bitterness out of his voice.

"Of course, I cared. I never wanted him to hurt you."

"But you never stopped it." Definitely bitter now. Mack's criticisms were falling out of his mouth, without his realizing he'd absorbed them.

"Why does it matter? You don't want to live with me anyway." She actually sounded hurt.

"It's not up to me, it's up to Child Services."

"But you're okay with it?"

"Not living with you?" He sighed. Talking with her was helping him make up his mind. "Yeah, I am. You've never loved me. You've always acted like you were stuck with me. Mr. Macklin actually wants me. I never realized how much that matters, until I spent time with him. And he makes me feel safe."

"You'd be safe with me, with your father in jail." Was she actually trying to persuade him? *Too little, too late.*

"I suppose. Unless they let him out."

"And I do love you."

Sam stared at her in disbelief. "You've always treated me like I was—garbage. And you just tried to put me in a mental hospital. Doesn't scream 'love' to me."

He asked more questions, but she kept giving non-answers. He sighed and stood up.

Both Mack and Detective Pierce witnessed the interview. He wondered what the detective knew about the Visitors. Not that he cared anymore.

Afterward, his arm around Sam's shoulders, Mack asked, "Do you feel better now?"

He shrugged. "I guess." Mostly he felt angry and hurt. His mother had acted guilty but not loving.

"You need time to process everything. You can talk to her again later."

Confronting his mother was uncomfortable. But his father—Sam preferred never to see Mike Costas again. How had his sweet, loving abuela produced a son so mired in hate and violence and fear? He hadn't really known his abuelo. He had died when Sam was very young, before his abuela returned to Mexico. What had happened to their son? Sam knew he resented Sam's birth and felt frustration over his own ruined plans. And he would bet his dad was frightened of the Visitors. Sam was almost sure he had seen them.

Anyway, Mack insisted he needed closure, which meant, "Talk to your father." Mack offered to sit with him during the interview. *No.* Sam had berated himself often enough for being a coward; here was his chance to show some actual courage.

"Be honest and open," Mack said. "Tell him what you want him to know."

They were in the jail; his father's hands were cuffed behind him and he had a guard. Sam was safer than he'd ever been at home. Costas glared at Sam as he walked in.

"What the hell do *you* want? You've got some nerve showing your face—you're the reason I'm in here."

Sam had promised himself he would be calm and collected. Not defensive. He sat across from his father and raised his eyebrows.

"Yeah? How do you figure that?"

"You told these bastards my personal business. If I want to give my kid a beatdown, that's my right."

"I didn't tell anyone. People found out because I ended up in the hospital."

"It's nobody's business."

"Did anyone show you what you did to me? I brought pictures, in case they didn't."

Mack had sent his photos to Sam's phone. Sam pulled out the phone and held it in front of his father, scrolling slowly through the photos. He tried to stay impassive but felt a grim satisfaction when he saw his dad flinch at each photo. It was the first actual human reaction he could remember—the first sign his dad had a conscience.

"Get that away from me. I don't need to see that crap!" Costas turned his head away.

Hmm, Sam thought, *maybe there is a real person in there*.

"Okay. No reason to look at photos when I've got your actual handiwork right here. It probably looks better than the photos, now that I've had several days to recover. Here you go."

Sam stood up and carefully removed his T-shirt. He was far from healed and moving still hurt. He turned around, showing his back to his father—and to the guard, who smothered a gasp. Sam wasn't sure what it looked like now, but he knew it was a mess. The welts were still red and swollen, plus there were colorful bruises, scabs, and unhealed puncture wounds. Dr. Mel had not bandaged anything this morning. She wanted air to reach the wounds to speed healing.

"That's enough!" his father said. His voice sounded choked. *Good*, thought Sam. He felt slight shame at being vindictive, but not much.

He put his T-shirt back on and faced his father. "I just want to make it clear—*you* did that, not me. That's why you're here. And I did nothing to deserve it. Nothing. I just walked into the house after school, and you laid into me. My fault in a way, I guess, for getting careless and not avoiding you. But why should any kid have to avoid his father? Can you tell me that?"

"You're a miserable little bastard. And a weirdo. Unnatural."

"Ah, that's it, isn't it? I'm a weirdo. I see things that

aren't real, like Mom and Aunt Lucy do. But *you* never see anything weird. Right, Dad?"

Costas gave his son a vicious look. He started to lunge forward, but was stopped by the guard and the handcuffs. Sam backed up a step, but he saw the fear in his dad's eyes.

"You think if you beat me to death, the craziness will disappear from your life? And everything will be normal?"

Costas stared down at the table, scowling. The guard looked from Sam to his dad, obviously wondering what Sam was talking about.

"I should be so lucky," Costas muttered.

Sam sighed. "I came here hating you, like you've always hated me. But there's no point in that. I feel sorry for you. I hope you'll get some help while you're in jail. And I'm learning self-defense. I won't be helpless if you come after me again. Goodbye, Dad."

Mack was waiting just outside the room. He squeezed Sam's shoulder but said nothing. Back on the street, he stopped and turned, smiling broadly.

"You were incredible, Sam! I worry about you constantly, but you handled yourself like a pro. I'm so proud of you —again!"

Sam relaxed. "Okay, I've talked to both of them. Am I done now? Please?"

―――

Sam stayed at Mack's house while he recuperated and while Child Protective Services decided what to do with him. The delay frustrated him, and it was scary that a group of people he didn't even know—and who didn't know him—were deciding his fate. CPS had found Grandpa Joe and Aunt Lucy living together on the Osage Reservation in Oklahoma. This was good news, but what if CPS made him live with them?

He wanted to see them, but he didn't want to live with people he didn't even know. Or leave Jade and Dr. Mel. Or especially Mack.

He felt slightly better after CPS interviewed him. The interview was private—they didn't want Mack's presence to influence him. Still, when they asked him point-blank who he wanted to live with, he chose Mack. When they asked why, he said Mack was the first person who had ever made him feel safe and loved. He didn't think his mother loved him or cared what happened to him. And he didn't even know his grandfather or aunt.

Mack had fixed up a bedroom for Sam and already treated him like a son. They still spent most afternoons with Jade and Dr. Mel. It was like having two homes, and he hoped it never changed. Mack was applying to be a foster parent, and he wanted to start the adoption process to make Sam his "forever son." Of course, this depended on CPS's decision. Mack told him the adoption decree didn't matter—that he considered Sam his son even without it. But Sam knew it was important to him. Still, adoption terrified him. Deep down, he was afraid Mack would disappear. That the Visitors might scare him off.

Jade and Dr. Mel couldn't understand his fear.

"Sam," Dr. Mel said, "he adores you. Can't you see the love in his eyes? And the Visitors make him all the more determined to protect you."

Sam felt ashamed to doubt Mack, but trusting was still . . . hard.

"Sam." He looked up at her. "Has Mack *ever* given you any reason to think he doesn't love you? Or that he would leave?"

He shook his head.

"Then trust him. He needs you, too. You belong together."

It was late afternoon a few days later. Sam felt almost recovered. Mack arrived at Mel's house, carrying a canvas bag of groceries and looking preoccupied. As he strode up the sidewalk, slanted sunlight caught his tousled blond hair, streaking it with gold highlights. Watching him, Sam thought, *He feels like my dad.* He smiled at Mack's longer, messed-up hair. It fit their messy lives. Plus, Mack was always so neat—maybe not noticing his messy hair meant he was starting to relax a bit and would be less nervous about the Visitors. *So maybe I should relax, too.*

Mack's smile encompassed them all, but his gaze lingered on Mel. Jade was right about them. The thought made Sam happy.

"Why are you all waiting out here? Am I late? Or has something happened?"

"Greg," Dr. Mel said, "Sam has something to tell you."

Mack stilled. His gaze returned to Sam, and he seemed to be holding his breath. "Okay. What is it?"

Sam took a deep breath and looked directly at Mack. "If you're really sure you want me, and CPS agrees, I'd like to be adopted. And be your son."

Joy illuminated Mack's whole face, and any lingering doubts Sam had about his decision evaporated like dew in sunlight. That smile was his proof, whether the adoption happened or not. Mack set down the grocery bag and gathered him in a hug, laying his cheek against Sam's hair.

"Oh, Sam, thank you," he whispered.

They stood quietly together, their arms wrapped around each other. Finally, Mack stepped back, his hands on Sam's shoulders, and turned his blinding smile on Mel and Jade.

Their smiles matched his. Jade was dancing up and down.

Mel looked ready to hug Mack, too. Instead, she picked up the grocery bag.

"How about dinner to celebrate?" she said. "We'll cook."

For the first time since he could remember, Sam felt totally happy. He knew he could trust this man with his deepest secrets. With his life. Until a few months ago, he had trusted no one, had no one. Now, he had a girl who loved him. A woman who mothered him. And a man who wanted to be his forever dad. All because he had finally let go and learned to trust. He felt strong and confident. Whatever the Visitors wanted from him, he could handle it.

His attention was briefly distracted by a face inside his mind. And a voice saying *you are together*. When his gaze returned, Mack's eyes were wide.

"What was that?" he whispered. Mack had seen her, too!

Sam smiled at his forever dad. "That was our Visitor, congratulating us," he said.

THANK YOU

Hi, I'm Jade. I hope you've been enjoying Sam's and my adventures.

Sam should really be asking you this, but you know how shy he is. (We're working on that.) I'm not that shy, so I'm just going to ask. If you liked the book, would you please leave a review on Amazon? We would *really* appreciate it.

And if you want to keep up and learn more about all of us while you're waiting for our next book, we hope you'll sign up for our newsletter, *Sam and Jade Updates*, at:

http://tinyletter.com/C_S_Hand

When you sign up for our newsletter, you'll get a **FREE GIFT** – two extra chapters: "Sam Meets the Night People" and "Sixth Grade Meltdown," describing two of Sam's earlier adventures with the Night People.

You can also visit our Facebook Author page at:

https://www.facebook.com/CS-Hand-110469511506801

ACKNOWLEDGMENTS

My sincerest thanks to everyone who has provided help and support to make this book possible, including:

Content editors Bethany Bryan and Kristen Susienka, for believing in my story and showing me (with kindness and tact) how to do it better.

A sterling beta reader, Lena Vorobets, for pointing out inconsistencies of plot and character that completely eluded me.

Tech friend Shelby Mansker, for assistance on internet and phone service both above- and belowground. (Any remaining tech errors are mine, not his!)

Cover artist Rafael Andres, for an *amazing* and evocative cover!

Copy editor/proofreader Michael Jarnebro, for catching everything I missed, removing my unnecessary commas, and appreciating my characters!

Formatter Nola Li Barr, for making the inside look so good.

The Self-Publishing.com community, for help, advice, support, and positive examples. Special thanks to my excellent SPS coach, Barbara Hartzler, and my wonderful launch team.

Finally, thanks to friends who have provided support and encouragement over the years, who said "You can do it" and "Don't give up." A special friend, always there to cheer me on even while working on her own books, is Dale Marie Bryan. Thanks, Dale!

If you enjoyed the book, much of the credit goes to these people.

EXCERPT

Song of Earth
(SAM AND JADE'S ALIEN ADVENTURES, Book 2)

Chapter 1
Save the People!

A haunting voice was singing, clear and sad. Sam's eyes opened wider and his heart beat faster. He couldn't see the singer, but the voice was unmistakable. It was Mack—his new dad! The words were in English, but their meaning slid past his understanding, leaving him with a feeling of deep melancholy. He had never heard music during an abduction. Why now? Why his dad?

The round room was chill and eerie, shrouding him in fear. Sometimes it felt huge, other times small and cramped. Today it felt—crowded. He was seated, uncomfortable but able to move. He took deep breaths, trying to control his shaking. Small figures, maybe four feet tall, blurred past him at triple speed. Skinny, grayish skin, big heads, huge black eyes.

Why were they in such a hurry? They had come before he

went to bed. He'd been in the kitchen; he'd made a sandwich and was just about to eat it. And suddenly, he was here.

Where was Jade? He reached out and clasped her hand. He relaxed. As long as they were together, things would be okay.

Behind the little people—the Visitors—were taller figures wearing muted greens and browns. Military camouflage. The tallest, broadest one was familiar: Morgan! Staring straight into Sam's eyes. They hadn't seen Morgan since last fall when the Visitors had spirited first Sam, then Jade into the DUMBs. Sam slumped in relief. The Visitors never hurt them, but Morgan worked with them; his presence was comforting. Morgan smiled and touched his temple, his eyes penetrating Sam's mind. *Concentrate.* Sam fixed his eyes on Morgan's. *Remember everything.* His voice echoed inside Sam's head.

As Morgan's eyes shifted, Sam's followed. The golden ball appeared in the middle of the room and the Visitors faded backward, slowing down, forming a semicircle in front of the military guys. Like last time, the golden ball morphed into a rotating Earth, beautiful at first, then speeding up and darkening with disasters and tragedies. Like last time, Sam watched helplessly.

The rotating Earth disappeared, merging back into the golden ball. Scene after scene appeared inside it, cast in glowing detail. He saw himself, Jade, Ravi, strangers working urgently. Fixing the environment. Trying hard but making little progress. Like thousands of hamsters on thousands of wheels, all their frantic energy going nowhere. Watching the activity, Sam ached with fatigue. He felt limp, exhausted, hopeless.

Inside the golden ball, visions hurtled past at a pace too great to comprehend. Earth, beautiful then devastated;

people loving, then outraged; people working together, then fighting and killing. Destruction. Beauty. Death. Life.

And through it all, his dad's voice singing the same melancholy song over and over, tying the visions together in a desolate, grief-stricken soundtrack. The song was unfamiliar, hauntingly beautiful. He could decipher only one word: "Gaia." Was his dad really here? Or were the Visitors somehow generating his voice? And why? No question the music made all this more . . . emotional. He really wanted to cry. Was emotion the point?

From the blurry mass of small figures around him, Sam's own Visitor emerged. She looked no different from the others, but he recognized her vibe, her essence. It wasn't friendly, exactly, but it was familiar. Her intense black eyes stared straight into his and as usual, he couldn't look away. She slowly brought her index fingers up and placed them on his temples.

An electrical charge seared his brain, and his eyes rolled back in his head. Information poured from her mind into his, a message—an order, a demand—terrifying, unbelievable. He couldn't stop her from storing it in his mind, but she couldn't make him accept it. *It could not be true!*

The next morning, Sam recognized the signs of a Visitor encounter. He was chilled through; his skin and brain prickled with electricity. Flashes of terror and wisps of a haunting melody floated through his mind. He felt uneasy, desperate—but as usual, most of his memories were gone.

He and Jade had been expecting the abductions to start again. Over the past months, they had seen glimpses of their Visitor in their heads, waiting, watching. This morning, Sam felt different—like a long-buried piece of his mind was awakening, reaching out to . . . something.

The Visitors had first come to Sam when he was five. His birth parents had hated and feared them and blamed Sam for their appearance. Now, they were both out of his life, his birth father in prison for abuse. Mack was his new dad, and his everyday life was happy. Mack was many things: his former science teacher, the man who saved him from his abusive father. But mostly, he was love and comfort and safety.

But the Visitors were still with him, and now with Jade too, and he felt as though he lived in two different worlds: the ordinary "real" world of humans and the creepy, crazy Visitors' world. The Visitors drew him in whenever they wanted—like last night—and little tentacles of their world, where the people were alien and everything was fuzzy and nothing quite made sense, kept invading his real world. Morgan had said he and Jade needed to accept that it was all one world. He hadn't succeeded. And now, those alien tentacles were burrowing into his mind and, he feared, depositing secrets he did *not* want to know.

At sixteen (well, almost), he was far too old to be this frightened. He had to get it together! People who hadn't experienced the Visitors just didn't understand. His friend Ravi didn't see why Sam thought the Visitors were scary, compared to his abusive birth father. Sam couldn't explain how Visitors were different from humans. They were just— alien. It wasn't that they looked different; he could handle that. It was the creepy, shivery feeling that kept him from thinking straight, from functioning normally. He was sure they did something to protect themselves around humans— but he had no idea what.

Last night, his Visitor had given him and Jade a command —a command he knew was terrifying, if only he could remember what it meant. He remembered his new dad singing. And a single phrase: *Save the people!* What did that phrase mean?

Sam left for Jade's house an hour earlier than usual. It was early April, and this had been their new school since January. They had left Cassidy High and enrolled in a free online school, planning to complete high school early. They had convinced Mack, and Mack had convinced Jade's mom that this approach was preferable to the glacial pace and bullying students at Cassidy. His dad had even convinced Ravi's parents, so now the three of them studied together.

Today, Sam was trying to unravel last night's encounter with his Visitor. The Visitor's vagueness coupled with his own inability to remember frustrated him. He knew something life-changing had happened, but what? Jade usually remembered even less about their Visitor abductions than he did. Maybe today would be an exception.

Still, anxious as he was, there were times when he was at the mercy of his teenage hormones. As Jade stood in the doorway, golden streaks of morning sunlight touched her face and long brown hair—she hadn't even braided it yet—and the green flecks in her hazel eyes sparkled like gems as she smiled at him. She looked so beautiful that for a moment, nothing else mattered. Even his alarm about the Visitors' warnings flew out of his head as he stared at her.

"Hi!" she said, giving him a searching look. "You're early. Everything okay?"

Sam started. "Fine. I just woke up early and thought I'd get a head start. You don't mind, do you?" He tried to sound matter-of-fact, hoping she hadn't noticed him staring.

"Of course not! Mom's still asleep, so I can welcome you properly."

She put her arms around his neck and kissed him on the lips. Sam groaned and gave in to his hormones, pulling her close, wrapping his arms around her, and melting into her kiss. He loved that he was so much taller now—five-ten to her still-petite five-four. He breathed in her sweet scent, reveling in how lucky he was. Holding and kissing Jade made him feel at home, where he was meant to be. It was a huge change from last November when he had been so shy, he could barely ask her permission for their first kiss.

When they came up for air, Jade rested her head on his shoulder and asked, "Do you think they know we kiss? Mack and my mom?"

"I'm sure they do. They know we're a couple. In fact," he added with a slight grin, "I think Dad's a little worried about what else we do. He's just afraid to ask."

Jade giggled. "Don't volunteer anything. Let's keep them guessing." Then she frowned. "Although—maybe if we were more open it would give *them* some ideas."

Sam shook his head. "We can't force them together, Jade."

"I know. But it blows my mind how a guy as gorgeous as Mack, who's so kind and loving and funny and smart, could be almost forty and still single. What's *wrong* with him?"

"No clue," Sam admitted. "You're right, you can feel the sparks when he's with your mom, and you know she wouldn't turn him down."

"He does touch her sometimes, when he thinks no one's looking. But he always backs off," Jade said. "And I've seen their expressions when they look at each other. They're both infatuated. They just never look at the same time! So, I'm not giving up. But right now, you're worried about something else. Spill."

"How do you always know?" he asked, frowning. He hesitated. "I have some . . . memories from last night. I wondered if you did, too."

"Visitor memories?" He nodded.

"They abducted you?" He nodded again. She studied his face, and he met her eyes somberly.

"I woke up early this morning, too," she said. "I've been jittery, like there's some calamity waiting just around the corner. I know something happened; I just can't remember what."

Sam sighed. *Why* wouldn't the Visitors let them remember? There had been that time last fall, when their Visitor said they were supposed to "fix the planet." Sam had hoped it was a turning point, and they would remember everything from then on. Obviously not. And apparently, she wasn't going to answer their other burning question: Why us? She hadn't answered it last fall or last night. Two ordinary teenagers out of what: eight billion people on Earth? What could they possibly do? Why not pick someone—competent?

They headed for the remodeled bedroom that was now their online classroom. As Sam sat at the study table, he forced his mind back to the Visitors, and the tension and fear of last night's vision came rushing back. He told Jade about Morgan urging him to remember. As he talked, he relived it: a rapidly turning Earth torn by disasters, a golden ball with desperate people working and fighting. He did his best to convey the visions and their urgency, but most of it was just —gone.

Jade closed her eyes, thinking. "Can you remember anything specific?"

"Two things, besides what I just told you. Music—a really sad song that kept repeating the word 'Gaia.' And Dad was singing it."

Her eyes widened. "Mack?"

He nodded. "He has a beautiful voice. And the word 'Gaia' must mean the song was about Earth or the environment. It was really sad."

"Well, most things about the environment are sad these

days," she said. "And that fits what the Visitor told us last fall about fixing Earth. What was the second thing? Besides music?"

"A phrase. *Save the people!* I have no idea what it means. Save what people? Save them from what? But it's stuck in my mind."

"Okay. *Fix the planet. Save the people.* Something related to the environment. Talk about vague. Maybe discussing it with Ravi will help?"

Sam and Jade depended on Ravi to provide a different perspective. He didn't interact with the Visitors, so he was more objective, and he always got right to the heart of the matter.

When he arrived, Sam and Jade told him what little they could remember. Ravi listened quietly, his eyes closed and his brow creased. When they finished, he gave them a wry smile.

"Do you know how jealous I am that you two get to experience all these cool things?"

Sam stared at him. "*What* cool things? We don't even know what we experienced!"

"But you know they took you, and you'll eventually remember or figure it out. And you're always safe, you know? No matter what weird things they say or what situations you get into, you're always fine."

Sam and Jade looked at each other. "He's right, you know," Jade said.

"He's right so far," said Sam. "But my feelings this time are way different. I'm sure what she told us is much more serious than anything before. Scary serious."

"Okay, let's try to figure out how the environment fits in," suggested Ravi.

"Last fall, when she let us remember that whole abduction," Jade said, "she told us we were ready. She said: *Practice. Learn. Touch. Fix the planet.* We thought that referred to learning telepathy because she gave us telepathy that day. So, we've been practicing. But because she said 'fix the planet,' we've been researching the environment, too."

"And last night she added *Save the people*," added Sam. "Whatever that means. Also, there's never been music before, and it feels important."

They looked at each other. Nothing fit together. They needed more information.

Printed in Great Britain
by Amazon